DOROTHY GARLOCK

Sweetwater

WARNER BOOKS

A Time Warner Company

WARNER BOOKS EDITION

Cover design by Diane Luger
Cover illustration by Michael Racz

Warner Books, Inc.
1271 Avenue of the Americas
New York, NY 10020

Visit our Web site at
http://warnerbooks.com

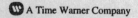 A Time Warner Company

Printed in the United States of America

First Printing: March, 1998

10 9 8 7 6 5 4 3 2 1

"I WISH I DIDN'T HAVE TO GO."

"I . . . wish it too."

She looked at him with wide, clear eyes. As if vaporized, Virginia's thoughts fled, and emotion took over. Feeling more daring than ever before in her life, she lifted her face to his. Their breaths mingled for an instant before he covered her mouth with his. Although his lips were soft and gentle, they entrapped hers with a fiery heat. There was such a sweet taste to his mouth!

With a leap of joy, Trell realized he had actually kissed this angel of a woman. He could not speak above the sound of his thundering heart. Silently, he held her close.

His voice came finally in a husky whisper. "I'll watch until you're back in the house. I'll be back . . . "

Books by Dorothy Garlock

Published by
WARNER BOOKS

≈≈≈

A KEEPSAKE GIFT FROM DOROTHY GARLOCK TO YOU

≈≈≈

TASTES FROM THE FRONTIER

Recipes from the Past used by characters in Dorothy Garlock's books of early America

≈≈≈

In my books of the Old West, I have tried to show you the world in which our ancestors lived and in which my characters made their way: to let you smell the wilderness, feel the rockiness of the road as metal-bound wagon wheels jolted you along the trail, experience the loneliness of the endless prairie and shiver in the icy mountain streams. This booklet is intended to bring you the flavor of the food. Here are thirty recipes, just as they were passed among the settlers—imprecise and improvised—not especially for *your* kitchen or table, but food for your imagination.

If you have enjoyed this addition to Sweetwater, I would like to hear from you—and if you have a recipe from the past you would like to share, I will add it to my collection. Who knows, the collection may result in a book . . . someday.

To my readers—your letters are precious treasures. Thank you.

Dorothy Garlock

c/o Warner Books
    1271 Avenue of the Americas
    Time Life Building
    New York, N.Y. 10020

Love and Cherish
(Warner Books—1995)

1779 Kentucky

Running frantically into the Kentucky wilderness after being sold to a pair of despicable trappers, Cherish Riley met a tall, lean, buckskin-clad man with a large brown dog who offered her his protection. Within hours he had proposed marriage. He needed a woman to care for his motherless child. Cherish agreed because she had nowhere else to go. There were miles to travel, angry pursuers, hostile Indians and frigid winter weather to face before they reached the safety of his cabin on the Ohio River, but plenty of time for Cherish to fall in love with the mysterious, silent man.

INDIAN PUDDING

Mix a scant cup of molasses and one of corn meal. Add one egg, a heaping spoonful of butter or fat, dash of salt, ginger or cinnamon to taste. Beat this, then stir it into a quart of sweet milk that has almost come to a boil. Remove from the fire and add a cup of cold milk, Pour into a pan and bake one hour.

BLACKBERRY MUSH

| 1 quart wild blackberries | 1 teacup sugar |
| water | enough flour for thickening |

Add small amount of water to washed and picked-over berries. Cook until berries are soft. Mash through a sieve. Mix sugar and large spoonful of flour. Add to berries and return to cook until thick, stirring constantly. Cool. Good with milk.

Wild Sweet Wilderness

(Warner Books—1985)

1803 Missouri

Berry Rose Warfield was eighteen years old when she arrived at the village of St. Louis on the Mississippi River. With only her gentle stepmother beside her she left the wagon train to search for her father's claim and brave an unforgiving frontier. Trappers, rivermen, riffraff and savages stood between her and her land. Spunky and mouthy, Berry was fast with a musket and slow to believe in a man. She was determined to prove that she was a match for the hardworking cynical trader who fell in love with her, temper and all.

~

TO DRY APPLES

Slice apples into thin slivers or core and slice into rings. If in rings, string on a cane pole and set out in the sun until the slices are brown and rubbery. This usually takes three days to a week.

FRIED APPLE PIE

Cook apples in a little water. Add sugar and cinnamon or nutmeg. Roll pie crust out on a floured board. Cut in circles by tracing around a saucer or small bowl. Place a large spoonful of apple mixture on one side of the circle. Fold over and pinch tightly to seal. Cut three or four small gashes in the top to let out steam. Fry in a small amount of grease in a shallow skillet until brown on both sides. Sprinkle with sugar and cinnamon.

Annie Lash
(Warner Books—1985)

1806 Missouri

When her parents died, Annie Lash Jester was left alone in old St. Louis. Since a single, healthy woman was a prize, suitors, young and old, lined up at her door. The willful lass would have none of them, for she yearned for a man who would love her completely and whom she could love in return. A young frontiersman named Jefferson Merrick offered her a chance to escape the town and live in a distant settlement on the Missouri River. She accepted, never realizing that she would have to deal with river bandits and Jefferson's political enemies. Even harder to cope with were the problems of her heart.

CATFISH CHOWDER

Cut a large skinned and boned catfish into small pieces. Simmer in a covered pot for a while in a small amount of salted water. Add diced salt pork, chopped onion and potatoes (amounts according to size of family) to the fish broth. Cook until potatoes are done and water almost gone. Add milk, pepper and butter.

CORNMEAL MUSH

Bring a scant quart of water to boil in heavy pan. Add dash of salt. Slowly pour in a heaping cup of cornmeal, stirring constantly. Simmer for ten minutes. Eat with butter and molasses, or pour in greased pan and let set. When solid, cut in slices and fry slowly in hot meat fat until brown.

River of Tomorrow
(Warner Books—1988)

1830 Illinois and Kentucky

Blond Mercy Quill grew up to be as sassy a spitfire as she had been as a child. An orphan raised by Liberty and Farr Quill along with her foster brother Daniel, she often needed his loving protection. When two Kentucky brothers arrived, bringing a stunning secret, one that could separate Mercy from Daniel forever, she knew that he would stand by her and fight against her enemies. If she dared to confess her love, would he respond with his dependable brotherly kindness and break her heart? *River of Tomorrow* is the third book of the Wabash Trilogy, which began with *Lonesome River* and its sequel, *Dream River*.

PUMPKIN

Slice the pumpkin into circles. Remove peel and seeds. Thread the circles along a pole and hang crosswise of the joist of the house for several weeks until dry. Store in a bag. Soak overnight, then cook for several hours. Season with hog meat for table use or add sugar, eggs and cinnamon to make pie filling.

FRIED HAM AND REDEYE GRAVY

Slice smoked ham ½-inch thick. Cook in heavy skillet until ham is brown on both sides. Remove from pan and keep warm. To the drippings in the skillet add ½ cup of hot water. Cook until gravy turns red. Serve the ham and gravy with hot biscuits.

This Loving Land
(Warner Books—1996)

1852 Texas

Summer went home to the vast Texas range, hoping to find Sam McLean, the man who had cared for her family long ago. Instead she rode into a future filled with renegade Apaches, a scheming enemy, and Sam's son, Slater. Hard and handsome, Slater lived and worked for one thing: to find the outlaw who had killed his father. Summer was a sweet memory from his boyhood; he had told her, *Go get all growed up, Summertime girl.* Now she had arrived—a beautiful woman. She could bring joy into his life, but a secret long hidden, long feared, imperiled their love.

~

COLLARD GREENS

(Collard greens are best in autumn after they've been through a frost.) In a large pot cook chopped ham or a hock. Wash greens in cold water, throw away stems and yellow leaves. Tear in bite-size pieces. Add to ham with enough water to cover greens. Put in a small dab of sugar, salt and pepper. Simmer about an hour.

BAKED ONIONS

Peel and slice enough onions for the meal. Cook in salted water for about 10 minutes. Drain and cover with milk. Place on stove until milk is scalded. Dip out onions, arrange alternate layers of bread (biscuits can be used, but not cornbread) and onions. Dot with butter, pepper and salt. Pour the scalded milk over and bake until brown.

Yesteryear
(Warner Books—1989)

1865 Arkansas

Addie Hyde spent four years waiting for the husband she had married in haste to come back from the War. He never returned to her, her young son and the two foster children she cherished. Deserters and drifters were making Addie's isolated farmhouse a dangerous place for a pretty woman without a man. John Tallman, a freighter, arrived in town asking about a Mrs. Hyde. Soon he was protecting her from a self-serving preacher and a despicable hill family. Addie's heart told her not to fear traveling with him across Indian Territory to his ranch in New Mexico.

&

CHRISTMAS COOKIES

To a pint of sugar add four eggs, beating after each one. Add one pint of flour and a pint of chopped nuts (hickory or walnuts) and a handful of raisins. Work well into eggs, sugar and flour. Add cinnamon and a grated nutmeg. Drop by spoonfuls in baking pan. With only eggs to make them rise, the cookies bake quickly and spread out to the right size. Sprinkle with sugar.

HARDTACK

(Hardtack was the staff of life for a soldier when he was out in the field.) Mix plain flour, salt and water to the rolling stage. Roll out 3/16" thick. Cut in squares. Place on baking sheet and punch holes in dough with a fork. The dough will rise to a fourth of an inch and brown on top. (Hardtack is much like our crackers today, except much tougher.)

Midnight Blue
(Warner Books—1989)

1866 Wyoming Territory

Leaving a girls' school in Denver, Mara Shannon McCall traveled to the lawless country near Laramie to reclaim the ranch that was her father's legacy. Her heart beating wildly in her breast, she rode toward the home she scarcely remembered. She stopped short when she saw a wounded man lying across the rugged trail. Pack Gallagher was beaten and bloody. She took the handsome Irish brawler with the midnight blue eyes along with her. Maybe he could help her take back her ranch from her drunken uncle who was in cahoots with criminals who used her ranch for a hideaway.

MOLASSES CANDY

Mix equal amounts of molasses and water in a heavy pan. Add a dash of salt and boil without stirring until a drop forms a hard ball when dropped into a dipper of water. Remove from the fire and let stand until cool enough to hold in greased hands. Press one end on a chair spindle and pull the other until the color of the taffy changes to a light tan. Twist into a rope and cut into pieces.

YEAST

Place one pint of hops in a cloth bag and boil for a couple of hours in a gallon of water. Peel and slice a gallon of potatoes and boil with the hops for another hour. Pour the liquid over a pint of flour. Add mashed potatoes, a cup of salt, one of sugar and three large spoonfuls of ginger. The yeast should be kept covered and in a cool place.

Restless Wind
(Warner Books—1986)

1868 Colorado

On a cold rainy night Logan Horn came to the door of the isolated cabin where Rosalee lived with her blind father, her brother and small sister. The woman the stranger carried in his arms was an Indian, his dying mother. When Rosalee gave him a place to rest and his mother a peaceful place to die, she unleashed the anger of neighboring rancher, Adam Clayhill. He had Logan beaten, Rosalee's cabin burnt and harassed her friend, Mary. Were Logan's pride and Rosalee's devotion strong enough to win against Clayhill's power? *Restless Wind* is the first book of the Rocky Mountain Trilogy. *Wayward Wind* is the second. *Wind of Promise*, the third.

VINEGAR PIE

Melt butter, size of an egg. Beat 2 eggs, add 3 spoonfuls of vinegar, the butter and a cup of water. Mix together a scant ½ cup of flour, a cup of sugar and a grated nutmeg. Add to the egg mixture and pour into an unbaked pie shell. Bake 30 minutes. Cool until the filling is firm enough to cut.

FRIED CABBAGE

Shred a firm head of cabbage very fine, sprinkle with salt and let stand 5 minutes. Melt large spoonful lard in a hot kettle, add cabbage, stirring briskly until the cabbage is quite tender. Add a cup of milk, remove from heat and stir in 3 spoonfuls of cider vinegar.

Forever Victoria
(Warner Books—1993)

1870 Wyoming Territory

Victoria McKenna was a *Western* woman—tough when she had to be, but soft inside where she kept her secrets and dreams. Her cattle ranch on Wyoming's notorious Outlaw Trail was the only home she had ever known. But her cheating half brother, Robert, had sold it to a stranger named Mason Mahaffey, who turned out to be a rangy, handsome cowboy with five orphaned brothers and sisters. Victoria had to choose whether to fight him for her land or listen to the instincts that told her he was a man who could love a woman with a lonely heart.

CABBAGE AND APPLE SALAD

(Amounts are according to family size.) Shred cabbage, chop apples and raisins or nuts. Mix equal amounts of cream and honey. Dribble over the mixture. Mix lightly. Let stand a while before serving.

POTATO CAKES

Cook and mash 8 medium-sized potatoes. Add two beaten eggs, a grated onion, pinch or two of baking powder, dash of salt and just enough flour to hold mixture together. Shape into patties and drop in hot fat. Fry until brown on both sides.

FRIED VENISON STEAK

Rub slabs of meat with salt, pepper, then coat with flour. Fry in hot fat until brown on both sides. Remove. Add a chopped onion and several spoonfuls of flour to fat. Let brown. Add hot water and stir. Add steaks to gravy and let simmer until tender.

Nightrose
(Warner Books—1990)

1873 Montana Territory

Katy Burns, her sister, Mary, and her tiny niece were the only people left in a desolate Montana ghost town. Without a horse, they hadn't a chance of crossing a wilderness crawling with outlaws, Indians, and grizzlies. All Katy had was a firm will to survive and a derringer in her pocket. Then a stranger named Garrick Rowe rode down the empty main street. He wasn't a desperado; he was a rugged, frontier-smart man with a daring scheme to bring this town back to life. After he met Katy, he also had personal plans for her. All she wanted from Garrick Rowe was a way out of this miserable town.

❧

COTTAGE CHEESE

Do not throw out a pan of milk that is turning sour. Cover it and set it in a warm place until it becomes a curd. Pour off liquid. Tie curd in a clean bag with a small hole so it can drain. Hang it up. Do not squeeze the bag. After 10 or 12 hours put the curd in a bowl and add rich cream and a dab of fresh butter. Press and chop with large spoon until it is a soft mass.

FRUIT COBBLER

Soak dried fruit or berries overnight. Sweeten and cook, leaving a large amount of juice. To regular biscuit dough add a half cup sugar, nutmeg and cinnamon to taste. Pour hot fruit and juice in a shallow pan and cover with dabs of biscuit dough. Bake until top is brown.

A Gentle Giving
(Warner Books—1993)

1880 Bighorn Mountains

Willa Hammer had narrowly escaped the lynch mob that unjustly hanged her foster father. She had nothing left but her dog and her faith in herself. Forced by circumstance to join a strange, secretive family heading west, Willa ended up on a run-down, intrigue-ridden ranch in the Bighorn Mountains. There she had to depend on the protection of a hardened cowboy with a haunted past who wanted nothing to do with her. He could infuriate her, hurt her, and . . . love her, if both dared to take the risk.

∾

STEW

Stew was a staple in the Old West. There was no set recipe for it. It was made with squirrel, rabbit, pheasant, beef or venison. It included potatoes, onions, peppers, cabbage, corn, turnips, beans and carrots. At times it was made in a 20-gallon black iron pot hung over an outdoor fire to feed a roundup crew or a platoon of soldiers.

Coat meat in flour and brown in hot fat. Remove meat and place in large kettle. Add several spoonfuls of flour to the fat, brown, then add water to make a thin gravy. Pour this over the meat in the kettle, add more water, salt and pepper. Cook until meat is almost tender. Add whatever vegetables are available and cook for several hours. On the second day, you can reheat, adding several hot peppers to give the stew a different taste.

Glorious Dawn
(Warner Books—1992)

1880 New Mexico

Johanna Doan is a golden-haired, slender woman whose tragic beauty hides her bold, determined spirit. She has lived through her parents' murder, her sister's rape and pregnancy; now she must survive the intrigues at Macklin Ranch. Hired as a housekeeper, she discovers that her cruel employer expects her to marry his son. Her racist boss reasons that because his son Burr is blond and blue-eyed as Johanna is, the children they would produce would be too. Burr Macklin arouses her anger as well as her passion; he needs to learn that a woman's heart can never be taken by force . . . only given with love.

∽

FLOUR TORTILLAS

Three cups flour, spoonful salt, lard the size of a lemon, baking powder to cover your palm. Mix flour, salt and baking powder. Cut in lard. Add warm water to make a stiff dough. Form dough in balls the size of a lemon. Roll out on floured board to 6- or 8-inch diameter. Bake on ungreased iron griddle until brown and spots appear on both sides. When cool, wrap in a cloth and store in a cool place.

BURRITOS

Cook pinto beans until tender. Drain. Season with garlic and chili powder. Mix in cooked ground beef. Place by spoonfuls down the center of flour tortillas and roll up. Can be eaten as is, or covered with chili and heated in the oven.

The Listening Sky
(Warner Books—1996)

1882 Wyoming Territory

When Jane Love answers an advertisement for people to re-build the town of Timbertown, she has high hopes of escap-ing a haunting past and a mysterious tormentor. Her hopes are dashed when she meets handsome T.C. Kilkenny. He is deter-mined to rebuild the town, and what better way to find wives for his lumberjacks. T.C. delights in teasing Jane until she be-comes furious. She is ready to leave town, especially since someone here knows her secret. When she suffers a humilia-tion that is almost too much to bear, it is T.C. with his strength and love who shows her that she need not be ashamed.

SQUASH PIE

Cook, drain and mash a yellow squash. Add a cup of sugar, a cup of milk, half a grated nutmeg, cinnamon, and a spoonful of vanilla. Salt to taste. Pour in prepared pie shell and bake one hour. Tastes a lot like pumpkin pie.

GRIDDLE CAKES

Three or 4 eggs (depending on size), 1 quart flour, 1 quart but-termilk, small handful of sugar, melted lard (size of 2 eggs), 4 pinches baking powder mixed with flour, 4 pinches of soda mixed with a little hot water.

Beat all this together for several minutes. Pour onto hot griddle from a pitcher. About a half a cup makes a good-sized flapjack, easy to turn over.

Larkspur

(*Warner Books—1997*)

1883 Montana Territory

Kristin Anderson arrived in Big Timber to take possession of Larkspur, a ranch she inherited. She was a twenty-three-year-old Swedish *spinster* with silvery blond braids wrapped primly around her head. She didn't know that she'd have to outsmart a land-grabber, and she never dreamed that Buck Lenning, the *old* ranch foreman she expected to meet was a young, lanky, secretive cowboy taking care of his elderly father on *her* ranch. Soon Kristin and Buck were butting heads, hunkering down to protect Larkspur from hired henchmen, and discovering that they both wanted the same thing—a home and a love worth fighting for.

∾

POTATO BREAD

Boil and mash potatoes. Rub them with flour in the proportion of ⅓ potatoes to ⅔ part flour. Add yeast softened in half cup of lukewarm water. Knead in enough flour to make stiff. Put in pan and keep warm until it rises. Bake at once.

BISCUITS

Melt large spoonful lard in heavy skillet. Make a *well* in large bowl of flour. Add lard, size of an egg, two pinches of baking soda, salt, and a cup of buttermilk. Stir with spoon until enough flour is worked in to make the dough. With your hands, fold dough until well floured. Pinch off dough the size you want your biscuits, pat in both hands, dip top in hot grease before putting in the skillet. They will brown nicely.

Homeplace
(Warner Books—1991)

1885 Iowa

Ana Fairfax was a stranger in the lonely farmhouse. She had come there at the urging of her stepdaughter, Harriet, and stayed to raise her child when she died. The farmhouse was filled with danger for Ana and the child. Esther, the child's crazed aunt, didn't want her there. Owen, the child's father was a silent, brooding Norwegian, hiding dark family secrets from her. Ana had married the first time without love in order to survive. Would she be forced to do so again in order to raise the child and protect him from the strange Jamison family?

❧

WATERMELON PICKLES

Peel and remove pink pulp from 4 pounds watermelon rind. Cut rind in one-inch cubes. Soak in cold water with a large spoonful of lime for an hour. Drain. Cover with fresh water and simmer until tender. (about 1½ hr.) Combine 1 quart cider vinegar with 4 pounds sugar. Heat until sugar dissolves. Tie 2 large spoonfuls whole allspice and 10 sticks of cinnamon in a cloth and add along with rind to hot vinegar mixture. Simmer two hours. Pack rind in clean hot jars. Fill jars with boiling syrup. Seal. Makes about 6 quarts.

GINGER BEER

Put a pint of molasses and two large spoonfuls of ginger in a 2-gallon pail. Fill half full with boiling water. When well stirred, fill with cold water, leaving room for a pint of liquid yeast which is added when mixture is lukewarm. Place pail on warm hearth for the night. It will be in good condition to drink the next morning.

Dear Reader,

    I hope you enjoyed reading SWEETWATER.

    In it, as in so many of my previous books, the hero and heroine triumph over the hardships of a westward-expanding America. I've enjoyed writing my Western romances, hope you've enjoyed reading them, and still intend to write more of them.

    Yet lately I've been longing to tell a story from a more recent time in our history, the period between World Wars I and II, years when young lovers faced a different kind of hardship: the Great Depression. Drama and romance flowered then as well. Gangsters, every bit as nefarious as western outlaws, made violent headlines while young people danced to new jazz rhythms that shocked their elders. As always, strong family ties were the keys to survival.

    With Hope is the first of at least three novels I'm writing set in the 1930s. It tells the story of a woman trying to keep her farm and misfit siblings together after her parents' deaths, and of the strong, kind-hearted man who helps her but can't offer her the one thing he wants to give her the most.

    On the pages that follow you'll find a chapter from this new book. I hope you'll enjoy it and enjoy reading all of *With Hope* when it comes your way in the fall of 1998.

                With thanks to all my loyal readers,

                Dorothy Garlock

                Dorothy Garlock

ALLENTOWN, PENNSYLVANIA 1884

Prologue

Her throat tightened, and her mouth filled with the metallic taste of anxiety.

The frenzied hammering of her heart was so loud that she thought Uncle Noah must hear it as he stood beside her concealed in the hedge of bridal-wreath bushes that edged the lane. She peered through the inky darkness toward the unlighted house that had been her childhood home.

"Something has happened or they'd be here."

"Patience, ducks! It's only an hour past midnight." Noah flavored his speech with expressions he had picked up during his travels abroad. "Tululla said Cass got the message."

"What if they were locked in their rooms?"

"Then I'll get on my trusty steed, jump the moat, and rescue the fair damsels."

"Be serious, Uncle Noah."

"I am, love. I'm just so sure that Cassandra can pull it off."

The one reassuring fact that penetrated the whirl of Jenny's thoughts was that her nine-year-old sister was far smarter than their half sister, Margaret, or that disgusting religious fanatic she had married. The child had had two days to plan on how to get herself and four-year-old Beatrice out of the house to meet them at this place.

Jenny peered into the inkiness toward the house. *May the Lord forgive me for not coming back home sooner to see how my little sisters were faring.*

Two weeks ago, after receiving a letter from Tululla, the cook, Jenny had taken leave from the academy in Baltimore where she was teaching and returned to her childhood home for the first time since her father's death a year ago.

She had not been welcomed.

On their father's dying bed he had made his oldest daughter, Margaret, and her husband, Charles Ransome, guardians of his two youngest daughters and executors of their sizable inheritance. Poor sweet Papa would have been heartsick if he had known what would happen to the business he had worked so hard to create and the treatment his young children would receive.

Charles ruled the house with an iron fist. The girls were severely and cruelly punished for the slightest infraction of his rules. The day after Jenny arrived, Charles had slapped Beatrice so hard for dropping food on the tablecloth that he knocked her from her chair.

More angry than she had ever been in her life, Jenny had loudly and furiously rebuked her brother-in-law for his actions. When Charles had stood over Beatrice, refusing to allow Jenny to comfort the sobbing child, and ordered Jenny from the house, Margaret had stood by her husband.

According to Tululla, it was Cassandra who had borne the brunt of Charles's cruelest discipline. She was allowed

CHAPTER 1

1920
Busbee, Oklahoma

"How'er ya gonna keep 'em down on the farm after they've seen Pa-ree? How'er ya gonna keep 'em away from Broadway? Paintin' the town—da-da-da-da—de-de-de-de—"

Dorene gazed into the mirror as she sang, adjusted the neckline of the thin sleeveless dress she wore, then licked her fingers and flattened the spit curl on her forehead.

"Are you leaving . . . again?" The small girl who stood in the doorway watched her young, pretty mother preen in front of the mirror.

"Uh-huh."

"Why'd you come?"

"To pay you a visit." Dorene turned from one side to the other so that the long fringe at the bottom of her dress would swirl around her knees.

"Daddy said you came 'cause you needed money."

"That's right. Your daddy owes me. I'm still his wife and he has a legal obligation to support me. But I wanted to see you, too."

"But mostly you came for the money," the child said. "Will you be back?"

Dorene turned from the mirror. "Maybe. Do you care, Henry Ann?"

The child shrugged indifferently. "I guess so. Will you?"

"I don't know. Maybe, maybe not. Depends on my luck." Dorene gave the girl a casual pat on the head and closed the packed suitcase that lay on the bed. "You won't miss me. You've got your . . . *precious* daddy and your . . . *precious* horse, and this . . . *precious* dirt farm."

"Daddy'll get you a horse . . . if you stay."

"Good Lord!" Dorene rolled her eyes. "I want a lot of things, snookums, but a horse isn't one of them."

"Don't call me that. My name is Henry Ann."

Dorene rolled her eyes again. "How could I possibly forget? Where's your daddy now?"

"In the field. Are you goin' to tell him good-bye?"

"Why should I traipse way out there and get all hot and sweaty? He knows I'm going."

The deep felt hat Dorene put on her head fit like a cap. She was careful not to disturb the spit curls on her cheeks.

"You could thank him for the money."

"He had to give it to me. I'm his wife. Your daddy don't like me much or he'd not have made me live out here in the sticks where I was lucky if I saw a motor car go by once a week. Work is all he thinks about. *You* . . . and work, I should add."

"He likes you too. He just didn't want you to cut off your hair like a . . . like a flapper, rouge your cheeks and wear dresses that show your legs. Daddy says it's trashy."

"Oh, yeah, he likes me," Dorene said sarcastically. "He likes me so much he wants me to walk behind a plow, hoe cotton, slop hogs, and have younguns. I'm not doin' it. I'm goin' places and seein' thin's. And that's that."

"I like it here. I'm never going to leave," the child said defiantly.

"You may think so now. Wait until you grow up."

"I'll like it then, too."

"Stay then. Eat dirt, get freckled and wrinkled so no man will have you but another dirt farmer. It's city life for me."

"Are you goin' to the city in a motor car?"

"We're goin' to Ardmore in a motor car and take the train to Oklahoma City. I've . . . got things to do there." Dorene put her foot on the chair and straightened the bow on the vamp of her shoe. The child watched but her mind was elsewhere.

Yeah, I know. I heard you tell Daddy that you've got a little boy back in the city. You've got to go take care of him!

Dorene picked up her suitcase and went through the house to the porch. A touring car was parked in the road in front of the house. A portly man with a handlebar mustache got out and came to take her suitcase. He wore a black suit and a shirt with a high neck collar. His felt hat tilted at a jaunty angle on his head and he smelled strongly of Bay Rum. He looked from the barefoot child to Dorene.

"This one of yours?"

" 'Fraid so, lover. She's only six. I had her when I was sixteen, for Christ's sake."

"I'm seven. Almost eight."

Dorene glared at the child as if she'd like to slap her; but when she turned to the man, she was all smiles.

"This is Henry Henry. Ain't that the most godawful name you ever heard of, Poopsy? I named her Henry Henry after her daddy. It was all my doing."

"No doubt," he muttered.

"I pulled one over on old Ed and got it on the birth certificate before he knew what was what. He 'bout had a calf! Lordy! He run the doctor down before he could file it and got 'Ann' stuck in between the Henrys. Ain't that rich?"

The man frowned. He looked from the child to the mother thinking there was a resemblance and hoped for the child's sake it was only skin deep.

"I like my name. No one else has one like it."

The child spoke quietly and with such dignity that the man felt a spark of dislike for her mother. He'd dump her right now, he thought, if it were not for the favors promised when they reached Ardmore. The ride was little enough payment for a couple hours in the sack with this hot little number, especially when he was making the trip anyway.

"Let's get goin'."

"I'm ready, Poopsy." Dorene failed to notice her friend's reaction and gave him a bright smile.

He looked at the child again, then quickly away, picked up the suitcase and headed back to the car.

"Are you going to kiss me good-bye?" Dorene hesitated before stepping off the porch.

"Not this time."

"My God!" Her musical laugh rang out. "I can't believe I've got a seven-year-old kid who acts like an old woman. I hope to hell when you *do* grow up, you'll have sense enough to kick the dust from this dirt farm off your feet." She stooped and kissed the child's cheek, and then hurried across the yard to the car, the fringe on the bottom of her dress dancing around her knees.

Henry Ann stood on the porch and watched her

mother step up onto the running board and into the car. The man cranked the motor, detached the crank, threw it in the back, and slid behind the wheel. Dorene waved gaily as the motor car took off in a cloud of dust.

I'll not be like YOU! Henry Ann thought. *I'll never go off and leave my little girl no matter how much I hate her daddy. You won't be back this time . . . and you know what? I don't care!*

1932
Clay County, Oklahoma

The bus was an hour late but it didn't matter to the man who leaned against the side of Millie's Diner. He wasn't meeting anyone. When the bus finally arrived, the passengers poured out and hurried into the cafe to sit on the stools along the bar for the thirty-minute supper break. Converted from an old Union Pacific railroad car that had been moved to Main Street ten years ago, the cafe, one of two in town, had only two things on the menu this time of day: chili and hamburgers.

Last to leave the bus were a woman and a skinny teenage girl who slouched along behind her. The contagion of haste seemed not to have touched the woman as she patted the top of a ridiculously small flower-trimmed hat firmly down on her head and walked behind the bus to where the driver was unloading a straw suitcase and a box tied with a rope.

Cupping the bowl of his pipe in his hand, the man watched the free swing of her legs beneath the calf-length skirt, the grace of her slender body, the tilt of her head, her curly brown hair and heavy dark brows. He noticed the brows because most women had taken to plucking them to a pencil slim line that, to him, made them look *bald-faced*. He knew who she was. She wasn't a kid. He judged her to be at least five years younger than his own age of twenty-eight.

He shrugged her from his mind and headed for the lot behind the grocery store where he'd parked his ten-year-old Model T coupe. He kept the car in tip-top shape and when it was washed and polished, it looked as if it had just come out of the show room. He treasured it next to his two-year-old son.

Stopping, he knocked the ashes from his pipe on the sole of his boot, and put it in his pocket. Sooner or later he might have to sell the car. That would depend on whether or not he had a fairly good cotton crop and what price he could get for it. But for now he'd put off having to make the decision by offering to install a new motor in the grocer's truck.

Henry Ann Henry thanked the bus driver and picked up the straw suitcase. The girl reached for the box.

"We can leave the box at the store and come back for it later."

"I can carry it. How far do we go?"

"A mile after we leave town."

"That far? Well, I'm not leavin' my stuff. Somebody'd steal it."

"Mr. Anderson wouldn't let that happen. But never mind. Let's go. I want to be home before dark."

The few people passing them along the street nodded a greeting to Henry Ann Henry and curiously eyed the girl with her. Henrys had lived in the Busbee area since the town's beginning. Ed Henry, Henry Ann's father and the last male to carry the name, was a hard-working dependable man who had made the mistake of marrying Dorene Perry. According to the opinion of most folk here, the Perrys were trash then and the Perrys were trash now.

Ed Henry had adored his sixteen-year-old bride but had never been able to make her happy. She so despised being a wife and mother that she had bitterly named their baby girl Henry Henry. After all, it was *his* child; *she* hadn't wanted her. Dorene had left him and their child a few years later. Ed had not filed for divorce, and it had not seemed important to Dorene to make the break official.

Henry Ann was used to her name and liked it even though she'd had to endure a lot of good-natured teasing at school about it. She believed that her father was now secretly glad—

Her thoughts were interrupted by the sound of a motor car coming up behind them. She urged Isabel to the side of the road and kept walking. The auto slowed and inched up beside them. It was a Ford coupe with a box on the back. She had seen the car go by the house several times but had never met the neighbor who owned it.

"Do you want a ride?" The man was big, dark, and held a pipe clenched between his teeth. He was hatless. His midnight black hair was thick and unruly, his eyes dark, and his expression dour. "You're Ed Henry's girl. I'm Thomas Dolan. I live just beyond your place."

"I remember when you moved in. I met your wife."

"You can have a ride if you want. If not, I'll be getting on."

"We'd appreciate it."

"Put your suitcase in the back and climb up here.

Careful. I've got a glass lamp back there." *I'm hoping it'll last longer than the last one. Glass lamps aren't made to bounce off the wall.*

Isabel waited for Henry Ann to get in first so she'd not be next to the man. He started the car moving as soon as they were settled in the seat.

"How is Mrs. Dolan?" Henry Ann asked politely.

"All right."

"She's very pretty."

He grunted, but didn't reply. An uncomfortable silence followed.

"We have a quilting bee twice a month at the church. I'd be glad to take Mrs. Dolan if she would like to go."

"I doubt it." After a long pause, he added, "She don't go to church."

"Oh . . . well . . ."

The awkward silence that followed was broken when he stopped in the road in front of the Henry house and Isabel asked, "Is this it?"

"This is it. Thank you, Mr. Dolan. Tell your wife I'd be happy to have her pay a visit one day soon."

"Why? *You* didn't get much of a welcome when *you* called on *her*."

"How do you know?" Henry Ann replied testily. "As I recall, you weren't even there."

"I know my wife."

Black hair flopped down on Dolan's forehead and hung over his ears. The shadow of black whiskers on his face made him look somewhat sinister. His dark eyes soberly searched her face. If she could believe what she saw in his eyes it was loneliness . . . pain.

to read nothing but the Bible and forbidden to give her opinion on any subject. One of her duties was to empty the chamber pots each morning and scrub them. When religious friends came to call, she was commanded to recite long passages from the Bible; and if one word was wrong, she was whipped with a paddle or a willow switch. Sometimes she was banished to sleep alone in the barn at night.

Jenny had been so outraged that, after leaving the house, she had immediately begun to plan for the girls' escape. She had called on her Uncle Noah for help he had been glad to give.

"Missy—" The whisper came out of the darkness.

Jenny whirled around so fast she bumped into her uncle.

"Sandy, you scared me."

"The buggy is down da road by dem willow trees."

"Thank you, Sandy." She put her hand on the young man's arm. "Is your mother all right? I don't want either of you to get in trouble over this."

"Ma say, 'Do it for the girls.' Ma say this ain't a good place for Mister H's babes."

"I'll never be able to thank her enough for getting in touch with me. Sandy, if the girls don't manage to get out of the house tonight, we'll be here tomorrow night. Will you try to get the message to Cassandra?"

"Yes'm." The boy turned and disappeared in the darkness.

"Uncle Noah, what will Charles do if he finds out that Tululla and Sandy helped us?"

"He'll be madder than a wet hen, I'm sure. But Tululla's been running this house for a long time, and he knows that Margaret's incapable of doing it without her. The jackass is fond of eating, and Tululla is the best cook in the county.

She'd have no trouble getting another position. The girls are the reason she's been staying on.

"And he does get work out of Sandy. He treats him like a slave, but not in Tululla's presence. Sandy has always been kind of . . . dim-witted, but he's harmless and devoted to the girls. Uncle Noah, I wish I could be sure that Charles will not be able to use the law to come after us when he finds out the children are with me."

"We've been over that, ducks. You're going to a place where the bloody bastard can't reach you. Meanwhile, the lawyers will be working for you to be given legal custody."

A half hour passed. The sky cleared, and a few stars appeared. The night breeze turned cold. It seemed to Jenny that she had been standing here in the bushes forever, although it couldn't have been more than three or four hours. She backed against Uncle Noah for warmth.

"They're not going to get out tonight." She whispered the words sorrowfully. Then, at a rustle of leaves, she instantly became alert. "I heard something."

"Shhh . . . shhh—"

She turned her head to catch the sound and heard her name being called in a whisper.

"Vir . . . gin . . . ia—"

"Here I am, honey."

Out of the darkness emerged one small figure. Jenny's heart sank, but only for a moment.

Nine-year-old Cassandra, carrying her sister on her back, moved toward them. Jenny rushed to meet them, then stopped and gasped.

Both girls were stark naked.

"Oh, dear heaven!"

"Margaret takes our clothes away every night, 'cause she's 'fraid we'll run off."

"That's outrageous!"

"They locked Beatrice in the closet 'cause she wet her drawers. But I found the keys. I locked their door. I . . . locked all the doors. And I dropped the keys down the well. Oh, I hate them. I wish they were . . . dead!"

Jenny tried to lift Beatrice off Cassandra's back, but the little girl let out a choking cry and clung desperately to her sister.

"It's Jenny, Bea," Cassandra said gently. "Go to Jenny. We'll be all right now."

Jenny took the child and wrapped her in her cape. Uncle Noah, still sputtering obscenities in a foreign language, wrapped his coat around Cassandra, and they hurried to the waiting buggy.

Chapter One

Virginia Hepperly Gray, her stomach churning from the rocking, lurching movements of the stagecoach, sighed with relief when it came to a jerking halt. She patted her dark auburn hair in place, adjusted the hatpin in the crown of her hat, and pulled on her gloves.

The door opened. She took the hand offered by the driver, stepped down and surveyed the huddle of buildings that made up the town of Sweetwater. She had seen quite a few new towns on the way west, but none was as primitive as this. It was all very new to her—this raw, wild, sparsely settled country. But it was just the place for her and the two small girls who followed her from the coach with confused looks on their faces.

"I'm thirsty." The younger of the two whimpered as she had been doing for hours.

The woman controlled her irritation and reminded herself that she couldn't fault the little one for complaining. The children had been under a terrible strain for a year, and it had been only two weeks since they had escaped from their home in the middle of the night. So much had happened to them in such a short time.

"We'll get a drink of water at the hotel . . . if there is one."

Standing beside her trunks, which had been dumped onto the split-log porch of the unpainted building that served as the stage station, Virginia was aware of the stares of the crowd. Her stylish dark green blouse suit, trimmed with black satin strips around the lapels and the bottom of the skirt, marked her as different from the people lined up to watch the stage come in. Roughly dressed, whiskered men eyed her, but turned away when she sternly returned their inquisitive looks.

A sign on an unpainted building caught her eye. Well! At least this ramshackle town had a hotel.

The girls waited beside the baggage, the younger girl taking refuge behind the older one.

"Cass, you and Beatrice stay here by our trunks while I get someone to take them to the hotel."

"Please call me Cassandra, Virginia. I've told you that I don't like being called Cass. It's something you'd name a dog . . . or a horse. I'm surprised you allow yourself to be addressed as . . . Jenny."

"I don't mind in the least being called Jenny."

With a sigh, Cassandra wrinkled her brow and looked disgustedly around at the unpainted buildings, the rutted roadway littered with horse droppings and at the persons who stared at them rudely.

"This is a poor excuse for a town. It isn't at all what I expected."

"It isn't exactly what I expected either, but it's perfect

for us. We agreed on that before we set out on this journey. Remember?"

"I understand. They can't extradite us back to Allentown from a territory."

At times Jenny was in awe of this little half sister who at nine years of age had such an adult grasp of their situation. She looked down into the upturned freckled face, exposed to the sunlight by the new blue velvet bonnet with the brim turned back. Both girls had the blue eyes of their mother, who had been their father's third wife, and Beatrice had her blond hair. Cassandra had dark red hair, almost the same color as Jenny's, inherited from their father.

In the course of his three marriages George Hepperly had sired four daughters, all the while longing for a son to take over his shoe business and carry his name into the future. He had been wise with his investments but unwise in his choice of guardians for his children.

When George remarried a year after Jenny's mother died, Margaret had been ten years old and had resented Jenny from the day she was born. On the other hand, Jenny had loved the woman her father married next and had been delighted when her little sisters came along. She had not spent much time with them because she had been educated at a boarding school and had spent summer vacations with her mother's relatives in Baltimore. After finishing school, she had stayed on with an aging aunt and had been unaware of the situation that had developed back home after her father's death until Tululla, George Hepperly's cook for many years, had written to suggest a visit.

"I'm thirsty." Beatrice tugged on Jenny's hand.

"There'll be water at the hotel, sweetheart."

"These unwashed barbarians obviously do not intend to help us with the baggage." Cassandra's voice rang out.

"Shhh . . ."

"They have no manners," she continued, but this time more quietly.

"That's no reason for us not to use ours."

A man in a black serge suit emerged from the building. His coat was open, showing a gold watch chain stretched across a brocaded vest. His black boots were polished, but dust-covered. The men on the porch parted to make way for him. He eyed Jenny, and then the girls, with a frown before he carefully removed his hat. His hair was jet-black with wings of white at the temples. His mustache was sprinkled with gray and trimmed to slant down on each side of his mouth.

"Mrs. Gray?"

"I'm Virginia Gray." Jenny, annoyed at the irritation apparent in his voice, grew even more so when he so limply shook the hand she offered.

"Alvin Havelshell, ma'am." Steely blue eyes went to the girls standing beside the baggage. "I didn't know you were bringing your children."

"Is there a problem with that?"

"No. It's just that I expected a much older woman . . . ah . . . not a young married lady with children."

"Are you objecting to the children?"

"Not at all, Mrs. Gray—"

"*Miss* Gray. I've never been married." Jenny was a tall woman. Even though she and Havelshell were of equal height, she managed to look down her nose at him and watch his face redden and his lips flatten in reaction.

"It's just that you're not . . . not what I expected." The frown on his face drew his brows together.

"Where have I heard *that* before?" Cassandra murmured.

Mr. Havelshell's cold stare caused the child to move slightly behind Jenny.

"I have a copy of my contract with the Bureau of Indian Affairs. My attorney went over it carefully. It specifies nothing about age or marital status. Would you like to see it?"

"That won't be necessary." He spoke curtly and stepped out into the road to motion to the driver of the wagon to pull it up to the station porch. "I've arranged for your transportation out to Stoney Creek. This all yours?" He gestured toward the huge pile of baggage.

"It is. The driver can take it to the hotel. I plan to spend the night there. The children are tired and thirsty, and I'll need to buy supplies in the morning before we go out to Mr. Whitaker's ranch."

"The supplies have been taken care of. A full bill of goods, paid for out of Whitaker's estate as stipulated in the will, is in the wagon. Here, you fellows, help Frank load the lady's trunks." He stepped to the station door as the men came reluctantly forward. "Harvey, bring a bucket of water and a dipper. The ladies are thirsty."

Jenny seethed over the high-handed way he was overruling her wishes but decided not to make an issue of it now.

"How far is it to Stoney Creek?" she asked when she could get his attention.

"Not far. Not far a'tall."

"Considering that it's already afternoon and we're tired from the journey, I'd rather we spend the night in the hotel and have a full day tomorrow to get settled in."

Havelshell came so close to her that Jenny backed up a step. He lowered his voice and spoke in a confidential tone.

"Ma'am, the hotel has been taken over by . . . ah . . . ladies of the night. It's not a fit place for you and the young ones."

"He means whores, Virginia," Cassandra prompted in a loud whisper when a blank expression crossed Jenny's face.

"What's whores?" Beatrice's childish voice carried her question to the men loitering nearby. They snickered.

"I'll tell you later." Cassandra took the dipper of water offered and held it while the little girl drank.

"You'll do no such thing," Jenny admonished in a whisper, glancing at the man who stood at the end of the station porch holding on to the reins of his horse. He, like the others, had an amused smile on his face. She shot him a look of dismissal, then swept her flashing green eyes over the other men like a hand, wiping the grins from their faces.

While leading his horse to the water trough beside the station, a dark-haired, clean-shaven man paused, as had every other person on the street, to observe the scene on the station porch. He tilted his head and grinned. If the Indian agent had expected a docile maiden lady to take over Stoney Creek Ranch and Indian school, one he could either bend to his will or scare off, he was in for a surprise. This auburn-haired woman, although slender as a reed, was obviously no spineless creature. She hadn't come all this way to be sent packing because folks didn't want her here. He would bet his bottom dollar on that!

This morning Trell McCall had picked up enough information at the saloon to know that folks in town were pretty worked up about the Indian Bureau bringing in a teacher for the Indian children when they didn't have one for their own kids. It had something to do with old Whitaker's will and his arrangement with Indian Affairs back in Washington. The townsfolk didn't care about that and would be sure to give her the cold shoulder. Their attitude usually wouldn't bother Havelshell in the least. He must have another reason for wanting to get her out of town.

Trell seldom visited the town cradled in the bend of the Sweetwater River, but he was glad he had come this day. The lady was something to see. She was tall, proud, and as handsome as a thoroughbred filly. She reminded him of Mara Shannon, his brother Pack's wife, who had come out of a fancy school in Denver and had taken over the McCall ranch near Laramie. She had tamed the wild, bare-knuckle-fighting freighter and taken his young brothers, Trell and Travor, in hand as well.

Trell stifled a chuckle. From his position at the end of the porch he'd heard every word said. The lady had a mind of her own. She had refused to satisfy Havelshell's curiosity about the children. That was sure to set the busybodies to talking! Not that they needed much of an excuse. The fact that she was the long-awaited teacher for the Indian school was enough.

Havelshell was speaking in low tones to the wagon driver, who was tying his horse to the tailgate. He was stocky with longish hair and a short, curly beard. He peered at Jenny with large dark eyes and she looked boldly back, seeking to evaluate this man with whom she and the girls would be leaving town. It was impossible to judge his age. He could be twenty-five or fifty. She decided that he was nearer to twenty-five when he sprang up agilely into the wagonbed and rearranged the sacks and boxes to make room behind the wagon seat.

"Here you are, little ladies. You'll have a nice easy ride on the feed sacks."

Without asking permission, Havelshell lifted first Beatrice, who let out a frightened yelp, and then Cassandra into the wagon. Both girls were shocked when grabbed by the strange man. Beatrice climbed up onto the grain bags, but Cassandra continued to stand and glare at the man who had put her into the wagon.

"Just sit down, Cassandra." Jenny sympathized with her sister, but there wasn't anything she could do about it now.

"Figured you'd need feed." Havelshell ignored the young girl's obvious resentment and spoke to Jenny, then added, "That is if the chickens haven't been carried off by those thievin'—" He left his words hanging.

"Carried off by animals?"

"No, I mean stolen by the Indians. They'll steal you blind if you don't watch them. They have no sense of honesty, you know. Don't expect the little bastards, oh, sorry, excuse my language, to learn anything. They'll come to school, all right, to see what they can steal. They're a stupid lot. Don't seem to want to catch on to the way decent people live. Don't give them any slack, or they'll run you in the ground. If you find you can't manage them, let me know, and I'll deal with it. They don't understand anything but a strong hand."

Jenny decided then and there that Mr. Havelshell was an arrogant bigot. He continued, speaking in a confidential tone, as if they were the only two people in the world smart enough to understand what he was talking about.

"Just let them know who's boss right off, and watch

them like a hawk watches a chicken." He tilted his head toward the wagon. "Frank will see you out to the place. The team and wagon belong out there. I've taken the liberty to lay in what I think it will take to get you started. There's grub, lamp oil, and feed for the chickens. If there's anything you need—send word. We'll run a tab for you here at the store and take the money out of your pay when the Bureau sends it."

"I'll pay for whatever we need with a check drawn on a bank in Laramie. I insist that any communications that come to me from the Bureau remain unopened."

"I don't think you understand, Miss Gray. I'm in charge here." His face reddened angrily.

"I understand perfectly that you are the agent in charge of Indian affairs on the reservation. I am in charge of the school. My contract is with the Bureau in Washington, not with you. I will repeat what I said: any mail that comes to me, personal or from the Bureau, is to be sent out unopened."

She turned her back, dismissing him. She was so angry that she was afraid she would say something she would regret later on. If she had embarrassed him, it was his own fault for bringing up the subject. The idea that he had the gall to suggest he take payment out of her pay! Lordy mercy! She was going to have to work with this arrogant, jackass of a man!

Never in her life had Jenny climbed the wheel of a wagon to reach the seat. She had ridden in farm wagons to the field or on picnics, but always sitting on the tailgate. She gritted her teeth, lifted the hem of her skirt, and placed her foot on the spoke of the wheel. It was easier than she had expected once she grasped the hand of the driver and he pulled her up. She heard something in her skirt rip as she fell into the seat. The driver clicked the horses and the creaking wagon moved away from the station.

Jenny was sure that she had given the men who were lined up along the station wall a glimpse of her legs, but it was of no consequence to her. She had more important things on her mind.

Admitting to himself that he was as bad as the loafers who lingered in the road and in front of the station to gawk at the new arrivals, Trell McCall waited until the wagon left town before he tied his horse and went into the station. Harvey, the station manager was looking out the dirty windowpane trying to get another glimpse of the departing wagon.

"Ain't she somethin'?" He turned and shook his head.

"Who're you talking about?"

"Ah . . . ya know. The Indian teacher. Too bad, is all I can say."

"Too bad for what?"

"Too bad she come all this way for nothin'. She ain't goin' to last out there. She ain't stout enough fer one thin'. 'Nother thin', what's a city woman like her know 'bout the Shoshoni? Havelshell ort to aput her back in the coach and sent her back to where she come from." He shook his head again. "Folks ain't likin' it that the government sent a teacher to teach the Indian kids when they ain't got no teacher for theirs."

"They could hire one. If I understand it right, it's old Whitaker's money that's paying for this one."

"There's been three teachers here this past year. One even stuck it out for a month. One stayed three days. One kid let loose a jar of ants in his bed, another a hornets' nest in the schoolroom. One of the little devils put a frog in his coffeepot. But when the Perkins boy put a rattlesnake in his desk drawer, he took off like a scalded cat."

"It isn't Miss Gray's fault that folks can't make their younguns behave so a teacher will stay." Trell went to the door to see Havelshell walking back up the street with a group of men, talking and gesturing with his hands.

"Makes no never mind," Harvey was saying. "Folks'll give her a cold shoulder and no help a'tall. She could stay out there and starve, and nobody would lift a hand to help her."

"Not even you, Harvey?" Trell asked.

"Well . . . yes, but folks'd not like it. Say . . . a feller was in here askin' 'bout you when ya was here last. Asked if ya was a McCall from over near Laramie. I'd not thought much of it, but he was a stranger and wore two tied-down guns. Don't trust a man, somehow, with two tied-down guns."

"Could've been someone who had seen me over around Laramie."

"He asked where your place was."

"I suppose you obliged him."

"No reason not to."

"Any mail for me?"

"No. You expectin' some?"

Trell ignored the question and went to the door. "I got to be getting on. See you the next time I'm in town."

"I'd look out for that feller, McCall. He might be up to no good."

"I'll do that. Thanks."

Trell stopped at the mercantile on his way out of town. A group of people were gathered on the porch. Two women were among them, and one was commenting loud and long about the teacher for the Indian school.

"It's a cryin' shame that them heathens has got a teacher and our younguns ain't. Wait till I see that Havelshell. Seems like he could've done somethin'."

"We might'a had one if Otis Perkins had taken a board to the backside of that kid of his."

"Hell, the kid was bigger than that little pip-squeak of a teacher. I ain't blamin' the boy for not wantin' to be bossed around by a silk-shirted namby-pamby."

"Law! It ain't decent fer a woman to be out there all by her ownself. Ever' horny drifter in the country will be a makin' a path to Whitaker's place." The woman who spoke took the snuff stick from her mouth, dipped it in her snuff can and stuck it back in the corner of her mouth.

"Harrumph!" another snorted. "Maybe it's what she was lookin' for—coming all this way without a man."

Trell nodded to the men that he knew on the porch and went into the darkened store. He passed the clutter of harness, tools, and leather goods and made straight for the cracker barrel. He took out a handful, stuck one in his mouth and headed for the counter.

"Howdy, McCall. It's been a while since you've been in."

"Not so long. Needed to get my horse shod. Give me a couple cans of peaches, a bag of salt, one of cornmeal, and five pounds of coffee. Grind it in that fancy grinder you got there. New, isn't it?"

"You bet. Ain't it a dandy?" The near-bald clerk had a waxed mustache that twitched when he grinned. "It'll grind that five pounds all at one whack."

"You don't say? Well, load her up and let me see what she can do."

The clerk turned the giant red wheel and the aroma of freshly ground coffee beans wafted up.

"Did you see Whitaker's teacher?" the clerk asked as he poured the ground coffee into a cloth sack.

"Yeah. Nice-lookin' lady."

"That damn Whitaker had everyone fooled. The old son of a bitch had a whole pisspot full of money and gave it all to the damn Indians for a school. Don't that beat all?"

"It was his money. He could do with it what he wanted."

"They say he had three or four little bastards by a couple of Shoshoni squaws. It sure rankled old Havelshell to have the managin' of things taken out of his hands. He only gets to handle this end. He'll get rid of the woman as soon as he can. You can bank on it."

"Why would he want to do that?"

"Guess there's a lot goin' on 'round here you don't know about."

"Guess there is."

"He don't want no strangers nosin' around who could be gettin' word back to the Indian Bureau. He might lose his job." The clerk lowered his voice. "He's got him a good thin' goin'. Big herd of cattle come in every fall to feed the Indians over the winter. Not all them steers make it to the reservation, I'm told."

"That kind of talk is dangerous unless you've got something to back it up."

"I ain't tellin' it to just anybody what comes along."

"Good idea. Tally my bill. I'll pay and be on my way."

Trell picked up his purchases. The crowd on the porch had increased since he had come into the store, and he had to step into the street to pass. Havelshell had joined the group and was trying to soothe the feathers ruffled by the arrival of the teacher for the Indian school. Trell noticed that Havelshell was also enjoying the crowd's rapt attention to every word he said. Trell was tempted to stay and listen, but he wanted to get back home before dark.

The Sweetwater River was high because of the heavy rains in the mountains. Trell traversed it at one of the few rock crossings. His ranch was beyond and upriver from the Whitaker place. Old Whitaker had been dead some time before Trell's move onto the land that he and his brother had contracted to buy, but he had been by the old man's place a time or two. The house was a squat, solid affair. It had good outbuildings and set of corrals. It was right along the edge of the Indian reservation.

His own house was small and tight and set back from the Sweetwater River. Little by little he had added a few furnishings and had built it with plans to add on if the need ever arose. It suited him just fine.

Trell rode through tall grass toward the foothills. From somewhere across the meadow he heard a meadowlark. That song was a sound he had loved since he was a boy.

His thoughts suddenly turned to Virginia Gray. He'd bet that she was a lot like his sister-in-law Mara Shannon. He had caught only a glimpse of flashing green eyes, but he'd seen plainly the set of her stubborn chin and the squaring of her shoulders as she prepared to do battle with Havelshell. Her features, her statuesque figure, and her regal bearing were striking. Yet it was not so much her pretty face that lingered in his memory, but her spirit and her fearlessness. Only a brave woman or a fool would come into this wilderness alone. And he doubted that Miss Virginia Gray was a fool.

He wanted to see her again . . . close-up. Of course, an educated woman like her wouldn't want anything to do with a rancher who had only a handful of steers and several hundred head of wild horses to his name. Hell, he reasoned, he could still call on her, take her a haunch of deer meat. Be neighborly.

If just half of what he'd heard about Havelshell's dealings at the Agency were true, the lady was going to have a tough row to hoe. All the way home Trell mulled over reasons why he should call on Miss Gray at Stoney Creek, and why he should not.

Chapter Two

The land they were passing through was beautiful, but Jenny was too tired to enjoy it. To add to her tiredness, Beatrice's, *"Jenny, I'm hungry,"* had frayed her nerves to the breaking point.

"How much farther, Mr—?"

"Wilson. But call me Frank." He turned and stared at her for the hundredth time since they left town.

"How much farther?" she repeated the question.

"Ten miles . . . maybe."

"How far from town?" she asked tight-lipped.

"Twenty miles or more."

"We're only halfway? Mr. Havelshell said it wasn't far."

" 'Taint. Hell, some folks have to go a hundred miles to get to town."

"I'll thank you not to swear in front of the children."

"That ain't swearin'. Now if ya want to hear some pure-dee old hoedown swearin'—"

"I don't."

"What's a high-toned woman like you doin' out here?"

"That is none of your business, Mr. Wilson." The question wiped all traces of politeness from her expression and blunted her speech.

He grinned, showing a row of white teeth. "I'm a beggin' your pardon, ma'am."

"I'm sorry for being short with you. This has been a very trying day. I was hoping to have a conversation with Mr. Havelshell. He is the Indian agent, isn't he?"

"Yes, ma'am. Headquarters is on the reservation 'bout five miles from Stoney Creek. Got a store there for the Indians, but spends most of his time in town. He reads law, you know."

"I was told that. Why is it that I have to buy my supplies in town? Why can't I trade at his store on the reservation?"

"Don't know." Frank wrinkled his brow. "He don't care much for white folks goin' out there. Says it's for the Indians."

The road was really just a trail, probably used by horses more than wagons. The wagon bumped along. Jenny was tired, but there was excitement in her, too. She was going to a new place, and would be doing new things. It never once occurred to her that she would fail to do the job. What she did worry about was keeping the children safe.

Jenny kept her eyes on the land ahead of them, politely refraining from probing questions. She glanced back at the girls. Beatrice had fallen asleep. Cassandra's shoulders drooped, disappointment in every line of her young body. Circumstances back home had robbed her of much of her childish eagerness. She was so bright. She needed stimulation to learn. Jenny had brought material to teach her, but was it enough?

Jenny sighed deeply. This was the best she could do. She consoled herself with the thought.

"What do you do, Mr. Wilson?" she asked, brushing unhappy thoughts from her mind.

"Oh, this and that, I reckon."

"Do you have regular employment?" She stole a surreptitious glance at the holstered gun on his side.

"I work for a rancher over near Forest City."

"Doing cowboy work?"

"Yeah," he said, and grinned again.

The man had been respectful enough—considering his rough ways, but something about him irritated her. Behind the curly brown beard he tried to hide a smirk as if he had a secret he was itching to tell.

They traveled steadily westward through an emptiness of grass and sky; distance and openness were all around them. The country they were passing through was the most beautiful Jenny had ever seen. Birds rose from the tall grass along the trail as they approached. The mountains were a purple shadow in the distance. She normally would have been enthralled by the landscape, but fatigue and the pain in her back that came from sitting on the hard, low-backed wagon seat nagged at her.

They had passed one homestead shortly after they left town. For the past couple of hours the only sign of civilization she had seen was a herd of cattle and a deserted shack. Even the wagon track seemed seldom used.

"I was told the Whitaker land was next to the reservation, but I didn't realize it was so . . . isolated."

"Isolated? What's that mean?"

"Means set apart. Are there no homesteads nearby?"

"Couple."

When it became obvious he was not going to say more, Jenny prodded.

"Farmers?"

He laughed as if she had said something terribly funny.

"People don't farm out here, lady. Oh, some grow little patches of this and that. Mostly they run cattle or sheep. There's a horse ranch across the river and 'bout five miles up. Squatters has set up on Whitaker land four or five miles south. Havelshell just heard about 'em. He'll have 'em off afore they got time to spit."

"Why will he do that?"

"'Cause they ain't supposed to be there, that's why."

"Surely Mr. Havelshell doesn't have all the say about who squats on Whitaker land. I'd think that on six square miles of land there would be room for a dozen or more homesteaders."

Frank chuckled. "Tell him that."

"I will. Who owns that herd of cows we passed?"

Frank laughed so loud and so long, she wanted to kick him.

"Those cows belong to the Sweetwater Cattle Company."

"What so funny?" she asked irritably.

"They're steers, lady. Not cows."

"Why are they on Whitaker land?"

"Havelshell is the Sweetwater Cattle Company. Ask him."

"I will," she said again firmly. She turned to look at her sister, who sat uncomfortably on the feed sacks behind the wagon seat. "Are you all right, honey?"

"No, I'm not all right. I doubt if I'll ever be again."

Cassandra had removed her bonnet. The warm sun beat down on her small freckled face and dark auburn hair. Jenny understood the child's feelings.

Frank hauled on the reins and drew the sweating team to a halt.

"Why are we stopping?" Jenny asked.

"Deer yonder," he said, taking the rifle from beneath the seat. "I'll get you some fresh meat."

"You'll do nothing of the kind!" Jenny's voice was shrill. "You will not kill that animal in front of the children."

Wilson looked at her as if she had lost her mind. "Wh . . . at the hell?"

"Are you deaf?" She fired the words at him. "I would not allow you to kill that deer even if the children were not present. She has a young one. Can't you see it?"

"Hell, yes, I see it. What difference does that make?"

"The difference, Mr. Wilson, is that the fawn would starve or be brought down by wolves if you kill the mother. Any fool should be able to figure that out."

"Anyone that lets fresh meat go by is the fool!" For a long moment their eyes locked. "We'll see how ya feel about it come winter when ya ain't got none." He slid the rifle back under the seat, picked up the reins and slapped them unnecessarily hard against the team's back. The unexpected blow sent the horses lunging forward.

"Now are you convinced, Virginia," Cassandra said when the wagon was moving again.

"Convinced of what, honey?"

"That these are barbaric people and this a barbaric land."

"I wouldn't go that far. They just need some . . . enlightenment."

A snort came from Frank Wilson. He cracked the whip, urging the team to greater speed. The wheels of the wagon began lifting streamers of dust into the air as the horses trotted briskly along the narrow lane.

"Jenny, I'm thirsty." Beatrice had awakened and was leaning on Jenny's shoulder.

"I am, too," she said gently and looked at the driver, who was staring stoically ahead. "Excuse me, do we have any water?"

He reached under the seat, uncapped a canteen, took a swig, then handed it to her.

"Thank you." She passed it to the child.

"Where's the cup?"

"There isn't a cup. Just drink." Jenny wiped the opening with her handkerchief and spoke over Frank's loud snort.

Beatrice spilled water down the front of her dress when she drank, and began to cry. Both girls were proud of their new clothes.

"Don't worry about it, honey. It'll dry."

Jenny handed the canteen to Cassandra. She took a small sip, grimacing as if she were taking a dose of bad-tasting medicine. Jenny raised the canteen to her own mouth and drank several swallows of the stale water, even though it ran down her chin and into the handkerchief she held there. Reluctantly, she admitted to herself that being uncivilized might not be proper, but at certain times it was exquisitely expedient.

Jenny was suddenly aware of a change of scenery. They had entered a valley that flowed out of the grassland. Wildflowers and berry bushes flourished in abundance. Tall aspens dotted the area. A hawk rode the wind below billowing white clouds. A silent, brooding quality emanated from the surrounding hills. A small band of antelope stood at attention at the far end of the valley. The region, now, was no longer empty, but warm and comforting.

"This is beautiful!" Jenny exclaimed.

"Old Whitaker must have thought so. His place is just ahead."

"Where?"

"Yonder." Wilson pointed to a grove of cottonwood some distance away. "Ya can just see the top of the chimney." Jenny's enthusiasm had somehow caused him to lose his surliness. He grinned at her.

"What's this place called? Beside Stoney Creek Ranch?"

"Valley of the Sweetwater. River's a few miles from here."

"What a beautiful name. Where is the school?"

"Just a hoot and a holler from the ranch house. Ya walk across the yard into the schoolhouse. It's on the reservation 'cause the Indians can't leave it without permission from Havelshell."

"You mean they aren't allowed to come to the ranch house when it's right next to the school?"

"It's off the reservation. Havelshell has put 'em in jail for leaving the reservation. He's a stickler for rules. He says if they step one foot off, they is as guilty as if they go five miles."

They were pulling into the grove and Jenny got her first look at the ranch house. It was small, rather like the hunting lodge her uncle had in the mountains of upstate New York, and made of heavy logs. A rock chimney rose from one side. Glass panes in the front windows shone in the late-afternoon light. There was no porch. One stepped out of the house onto the doorstone. To the left and behind was an open shed attached to a building and two corrals with poles tiredly sagging. A couple of horses were in the corral; a big roan and a spotted pony, the only signs that the place was not abandoned.

"Who is that?" Cassandra stood behind Jenny.

"Where, honey?"

"Over there in the trees on that white horse."

Jenny's gaze followed Cassandra's pointed finger. An Indian boy sat on a brown-and-white-speckled pony. She lifted her hand and waved. The boy wheeled the pony and was out of sight in an instant.

"That's one of old Whitaker's half-breed bastards. He's got them little suckers all over the reservation. That'n slips in and out a here more times than ya can shake a stick at. If he's caught, Havelshell'll give him a few cuts across the back with a buggy whip."

Jenny gasped in outrage.

"Not while I'm here, he won't!" she said stoutly.

Frank drove around to the back of the house and pulled the team to a stop. A huge cottonwood stood between the house and the outbuildings. There were no windows on the back of the house and no porch. The back door stood open. Grass and weeds were a foot high next to the house. A dead tree had been pulled up into the yard, and it looked like whoever had been staying there had cut just enough wood to satisfy daily needs.

"Lord, help us," Cassandra muttered.

"It isn't bad, honey. Look! There's a pond." Jenny's eyes had caught the gleam of water tumbling over rocks into a wide pool. She backed off the wagon, her feet reaching for solid ground. For a moment she held on to the wheel until her legs were steady under her. "Come on, girls. Get down."

Jenny's excitement transmitted itself to Beatrice who giggled happily when Jenny swung her down. Cassandra refused her help and climbed down, backwards, over the wheel as Jenny had done.

"Has someone been taking care of the—" Jenny turned to speak to Frank, but he had untied his horse from the tailgate and was leading it toward the pool.

She stood in the yard and waited for him to return. Beatrice gripped her hand and Cassandra stared, unbelievingly, at their new home. After Frank had watered his horse, he mounted him and rode up to where Jenny and the girls stood beside the wagon. He sat looking down at them, a silly smile on his face.

"My job was to get ya here all in one piece. So long and good luck." He put his heels to the horse's flanks and headed back down the trail. Stunned, Jenny looked after him, then back to the sweating team hitched to the wagon. Her temper flared.

"Come back here, you . . . low-down, son—" She caught herself before she said something she shouldn't in front of the girls.

"What did you expect, Virginia?" Cassandra said dejectedly.

"Cass, don't whine! I've got enough to deal with."

"—And it seems we'll have to deal with it without any help from him. Well." Cassandra tossed her bonnet up into the wagon. "The first thing we should do is get the wagon over near the door so when we unload the trunks we don't have to carry them so far. Then we've got to get the team unharnessed and to water. If anything happened to the horses, we'd be stuck here."

"Oh, honey, you're right. Beatrice stay back out of the way."

Jenny prided herself on knowing good horseflesh. The two big sorrels hitched to the wagon were a sound, strong team. She climbed back up the wheel to the seat and unwound the reins from the break handle. She had driven her buggy to town many times, and driving a team couldn't be too much different. Besides, the team was tired, and there was no danger they would run away with her. The sorrels were obedient to her commands, and she stopped them when the wagonbed was near the door.

"It'll take a while to unload. We can do it later and let the wagon sit here. Now to unharness—"

"Don't unharness now, Virginia. Just unhook them from the doubletree and lead them to water. We can unharness them when we get them inside the corral."

Jenny looked at her little sister in amazement. "How do you know all this?"

"I watched the stableboy do it many times. Remember, occasionally I was so naughty that I was not allowed in the house and spent a lot of time in the barn . . . with the *other* animals." Cassandra began unhooking the chains on the tugs.

"Be careful going behind the horses," Jenny cautioned.

"Get the reins and move them out."

When the team was free of the wagon, they moved so quickly toward the water that Jenny almost had to run to keep up with them.

"Don't let them drink too much . . . at first," Cassandra called.

While the horses drank, Jenny looked around with a fear she didn't dare let the girls suspect. They were alone in this vast land. She had been told that she need not fear the Indians. She had come to teach their children, and they would not harm her. Mr. Havelshell was clearly hostile and for some reason did not want her here. She had thought about it off and on all the way from town. She and the girls were here and here they would stay . . . for at least five years. That was the deal Mr. Whitaker had made with the Bureau. There were many things more important than bodily comfort.

Jenny's fingers felt for the light little derringer she had in her pocket. She and the girls were not without protection. As soon as she could unpack her trunk, she would keep handy the other two guns—the Sharps rifle and the pistol. She was grateful now for the shooting lessons she had taken at her uncle's gun club.

Cassandra opened the gate for Jenny to lead the team inside the pole corral. The two horses in the other corral nickered a greeting. The sorrels stood impatiently while she and Jenny struggled to get them out of the heavy harnesses. Cassandra fell when one of the horses nudged her, and Jenny's hat was knocked askew by a bobbing head. Both were sweating and Jenny was swearing under her breath by the time they pulled the tackle off the horses. Once free, the pair went a distance and rolled in the dirt.

"Look at my dress!" Cassandra wailed, looking down at the dirt and the two-inch rip in her skirt. "It's ruined."

"It'll wash and I'll mend it. Where's Beatrice?" Jenny looked around. The child was not in sight. "Beatrice!" she yelled at the top of her lungs and began running toward the house.

"I'm in here." The child came to the door. "There's a little brown thing like a dog in here, but the man won't let me pet it."

"Man? Oh, dear heavens!" Jenny and Cassandra both tried to crowd through the doorway.

It took a few seconds for Jenny's eyes to become accustomed to the gloom. When they did, she saw a man lounging in one of the chairs at a large square table. A bottle and a glass were in front of him.

"Who are you?"

"Linus Bowles. Boss said ride over and stay till ya got here. It's what I done."

"Then why, for Christ's sake, were you sitting here while we were struggling with that harness?" Jenny was so angry she was completely unaware that she had sworn.

The chair legs made a screeching sound when Linus moved back from the table and stood. He was tall and thin. He wore a tall-crowned hat pulled down to the tops of his ears. Sparse whiskers covered his cheeks. Heavy eyebrows came together over the bridge of his nose. He was young, possibly in his middle or late teens. Nothing about him frightened Jenny, except his unexpected presence.

"Warn't my job to unharness no team."

"Then get out!" Jenny spoke through clenched teeth. "That is unless you've got enough manners left in you to help unload the wagon."

"What'll ya pay?" He grinned cockily, showing a wide space between big front teeth.

"To you? Not a cent," Jenny pulled the derringer from her pocket. "Now go before I shoot you."

The grin broadened. "With that?"

"With this! I know what it can do. Right now it's aimed at a spot six inches below your belt. Do you want to bet I can't hit what I'm aiming for?"

The grin turned nasty. He grabbed the bottle from the table.

"Gawddamn Indian-lovin' bitch!" he snarled as he passed her.

A small hairy animal scurried out the door after him.

"What in the world!" Jenny exclaimed.

"It's a . . . a rac . . . raccoon," Beatrice said, proud to be able to explain something to her older sisters. "Her name is Hot Tw— Oh, I know, Hot Twat, that's it. He said it's 'cause she goes out at night and gets with boy raccoons and makes babies. What's it mean, Jenny?"

"Lord, have mercy! What next?"

"Don't be so shocked, Virginia. It's perfectly natural for a female raccoon to mate with a male raccoon."

"That is all very well. But . . . it is not a decent conversation for a grown man to have with a child!"

"He wasn't a grown man. He was a boy trying to act grown."

Jenny put the derringer back in her pocket and went outside to watch the boy saddle his horse and wait for him to ride out. Before he mounted, he carefully placed the small animal in a bag that hung from his saddle horn. He rode toward them and pulled up on the reins so that the horse danced on his hind legs. Then he doffed his hat in a salute and took off on a dead run.

"That was childish," Cassandra said, more in the tone of a schoolteacher than a nine-year-old. "He was showing off. He probably thinks we were impressed."

"We haven't met a gentleman since we came here. I'm

beginning to think that all the men here are uncouth boors."

"I've never heard of anyone taming a raccoon, Virginia. Do you think we could try it."

Jenny nodded, but her thought was— *This is a day I'll remember for the rest of my life!*

There wasn't time to do more than glance through the house which consisted of one large room and two smaller ones. In the large room, the walls were covered with white birch bark and adorned with various trophies. Several beautiful fur pelts were stretched and nailed to the walls. The widespread antlers of a buck were nailed to the wall beside the door and there Jenny hung their bonnets and the jacket of her suit.

One glance was enough to tell her that the place was in need of a good cleaning. The wind had blown leaves in through the open door and swished down the chimney to scatter ashes over the floor. Mud tracked in on boots had dried and now crunched underfoot. Soot had collected in the cobwebs that hung in lacy strings over the black iron range. Jenny had no time to worry about any of that now. The trunks and boxes had to be brought in out of the wagon before dark.

"Margaret would be delighted to know that we're living in this place that's more of a pigsty than a house. She would say that it was fitting for the daughters of a whore." Cassandra wiped her hand across the table and grimaced at the dirt her fingers picked up.

"I wish you wouldn't repeat Margaret's words in front of Beatrice."

"It's nothing she hasn't heard before . . . a hundred or more times."

"My hope is that we can forget about Margaret and . . . *him*."

"*Him* is going to be hard to forget."

"Shall we try, sweetheart?" Jenny hugged her little sister. "You know this place won't be so bad once it's clean and we get our things in place."

"I like it, Jenny." Beatrice opened a cabinet to look at the heavy earthenware dishes. "It's like a playhouse."

An hour later, all their possessions and the supplies from the store in Sweetwater except for the grain sacks had been dragged into the house. As she looked at them, the thought came to Jenny that she had not seen or heard a chicken. Cassandra had found a flat plank in the shed and had leaned it against the back of the wagon. The heavy trunk was slid down the plank, then pushed up the plank into the house. By the time they had finished, Beatrice was crying for something to eat; it was growing dark, and Jenny's back felt as if it would break at any moment.

"We need some light in here and a way to bar the doors in case we have an unwelcome guest," Jenny said as she opened one of her trunks to take out a box of sulfur matches and light the glass lamp on the table. "We'll have to be careful with the lamp oil until we see how much of it there is. Now before dark, I'll take the bucket and get water. Cass, go through the foodstuffs and see what there is we can eat tonight. Tomorrow we'll cook a hot meal."

"It's cold, Virginia."

"Put on a shawl. It's too late to build a fire tonight. I'm not sure I know how anyway."

"I know how to build one in the cookstove. I did it for Tululla lots of times. She said I made a better fire than Myrtle, who helped her sometimes."

"I hope she taught you to cook on it, too."

"She let me help, when Margaret wasn't around." Cass wrinkled her nose when she said her half sister's name. "Oh, excuse me! She wants to be called Margo now. She said Margaret was so common."

Jenny wondered, as she made her way to the crystal-clear water tumbling down the mountains over the rocks into the pool, if Cassandra would ever fully recover from the physical and mental abuse she and Beatrice had suffered at the hands of Margaret and her husband all in the name of discipline. Thank heaven they had not completely destroyed the self-confidence her intelligence and resourcefulness had given her little sister; her cynicism might fade with time.

After filling the bucket, Jenny turned to go back to the house. It was then that she saw at the edge of the grove the shadow of a building that must be the school. She paused for only a moment before walking rapidly to the house. There would be plenty of time to look over the school tomorrow. Right now she had to get back to the girls.

Virginia Hepperly, what in the world are you and the girls doing in this isolated cabin miles from another human being?

Chapter Three

Jenny and the two girls washed in the lukewarm water from the cookstove reservoir and bedded down in the double bunk in one of the rooms after Jenny had made up the bed with linen from her trunk.

The girls went to sleep almost instantly, but Jenny lay awake, mentally checking the two doors she had barred and the window shutters she had closed and locked. The loaded rifle hung on the pegs over the fireplace, the Smith & Wesson rested on the chair she had pulled close to the bunk.

For the hundredth time since their arrival in Sweetwater she mulled over the wisdom of coming here. Back in Baltimore, the opportunity had seemed to be the answer to her prayers. With the help of people in high places in the Bureau, she had covered her tracks well. It would take some time for Charles Ransome to find her and the girls . . . if he ever did. And if he did, he would have to take her by force to get her back to Allentown to stand trial for kidnapping.

Beatrice whimpered in her sleep. Jenny turned and took

the small girl in her arms, as much to comfort herself as the child. She grimaced, recalling the bruises and cuts she'd found on the child's little body, and prayed that God would forgive her for not having gone back to Allentown sooner to visit her siblings.

In her mind she saw flashes of the events that led to her flight with the girls; the meeting with an officer of Indian Affairs who told her about Walt Whitaker's will, the transfer of money from her trust to the bank in Laramie. Thank heaven for Uncle Noah, her mother's younger brother. Without his help she would have never been able to spirit the girls away.

Every minute of the long flight she had suffered the cold fear they would be discovered. Jenny had chosen their destination carefully and had been assured by the best legal counsel that once within this territory, she and the girls would be comparatively safe. No extradition agreements had been made with other states, and here women had the legal right to own property, to raise their children, and even to vote!

As added insurance against the danger of their being found and the children taken against her will back to Allentown, she had changed all their names from Hepperly to Gray. Her rascal of an uncle had thought of that, and he knew the right people in the right places to get it done.

She had feared the homestead would be exactly what it was. But she hadn't anticipated Mr. Havelshell's antagonistic attitude nor the hostility from Frank Wilson and the young man with the raccoon. And she had expected to be provided help with both inside and outside chores.

Lordy mercy! How was she going to cut wood, carry water, care for the livestock, and the girls, and teach school? How was she going to store food, much less firewood for the long cold winters? They had been whisked out of town so fast that she hadn't been able to discuss with Havelshell the hiring of help. Obviously, the man didn't want her here. All the hardships were part of his plan to get rid of her. If the teacher who came didn't stay, and the conditions of the will were not met, the land would be sold at auction. She had been told that when she signed her contract.

Jenny had no idea of how she would use the thousands of acres of land if she got it. She would hire a land manager. Yes, that's what she would do. The money left to her by her mother and her mother's family would pay for his services.

Her tired body overcame her troubled mind and she slept soundly.

"Caw! Caw!"

She woke abruptly.

At first she was confused, conscious only of the pain in her back, shoulders and arms. Reality returned quickly. She threw off the bedclothes and got out of bed, her heart thumping.

"Caw! Caw!"

She knew the call of a crow, but hadn't she heard that Indians sometimes used birdcalls to signal one another?

She slipped on a robe, picked up the pistol and went to the back door. After unbarring it, she opened it a crack and looked out. The area was bathed in the soft glow of dawn. The eastern sky was rosy with light from the rising sun. Two big black crows were perched on the side rails of the wagon where they had left the bags of grain. When Jenny opened the door wider, the creaking of the rusty hinges alerted the birds and they took flight.

Stepping out into the quiet cool morning, Jenny breathed deeply of the fresh mountain air. She felt . . . free. There was so much to do here, and she had a lot to learn. A favorite teacher once told her that when faced with a difficult task to do, she should take it apart, look at it closely and learn all she could about it. Then proceed one step at a time. In order to survive here and provide a home for her sisters, that was what she would have to do.

One of the first steps was to find out if there was an outhouse on the ranch, or if she and the girls would continue to use the chamber pot she had brought in her trunk. She walked away from the house . . . in her robe, her hair hanging down her back. There was no one here to see or care how she looked. It was a glorious feeling. For too long she had been the prim and proper Miss Hepperly, role model for the daughters of those who could afford to send them to the academy. But out here she would not have to wear the hated boned corset! Hurrah!

Jenny walked toward the grove where a small ramshackle structure stood leaning precariously to one side. It was the only building in sight that could possibly be an outhouse. However, there wasn't a path leading to it. It sat in the middle of a grassy area. The door sagged on leather straps used as hinges. As she neared she could see that grass was high even at the door. Fresh wagon tracks and clods of sod dug up by horses' hooves surrounded it.

When she opened the door, she could see that the building had been brought there in a wagon . . . recently. There was no floor in the building, which was not surprising, and the grass was as green inside as it was out. A soiled plank extended from one wall to the other—a place to sit. But a hole had not been dug in the ground for the body waste. Jenny backed away and closed the door.

The Bureau had apparently sent word to Havelshell that a lady would be coming to Stoney Creek Ranch and for him to arrange for a necessary building. He had hauled one out and just set it there, intending to make living conditions here as inconvenient as possible, thinking she would give up and go back East.

The nasty, hateful man!

Jenny went back toward the house, her mind working on the problems that faced her. First was food and how to fix it. Then the house had to be cleaned and made livable. They had to have a supply of firewood for the cookstove and for winter—a big supply for winter. In a few days, they would hitch up the team and go to town. She would post a notice that she needed someone to come, tend the animals, hunt fresh meat and cut firewood. Thank goodness she had money to pay for the help she needed.

Nothing had been said about when the school term would start. It was her understanding that the Indian agent would send word to the chiefs and that they would either send for her or come to the school. Thoughts of the school were cut off sharply when she came to the corral and realized that the two sorrels and the pony were eating at a pile of freshly cut grass.

Someone had been here last night or early this morning.

Jenny stood very still. The thought of someone's being about and her not knowing it unnerved her. Her eyes slowly swept the area from the house to the border of trees that surrounded the ranch buildings. What she presumed to be the school sat in a small clearing hacked out of the forest. Built of logs, it blended so well with the woods surrounding it that she had not noticed it.

A boy sat on the ground, his back against the side of the building. He wore a light shirt and britches. A white band was tied about his forehead. He was too far away for Jenny to see his face, but it was turned in her direction. She wondered if he were the boy on the spotted pony they had seen the night before, the one Wilson said was an offspring of Walt Whitaker.

Jenny waved as she had done the night before, but there was no response.

"Thank you for cutting grass for the horses," she called.

Still no response.

Were it not for her uncomfortably full bladder, Jenny would have gone toward the school. She hurried instead, to the house, found the chamber pot under the double bunk and let nature take its course. When she finished, she quickly dressed, tied her hair at the nape of her neck and went back outside, not taking time to do more than throw a shawl over her shoulders to ward off the cool morning air.

The boy was gone.

She was disappointed, but decided to visit the school while the girls were still asleep. Judging by the grass and bushes that surrounded the building, it had been there for several years. It was built of heavy logs set upright, but the door and window frames were weathered plank.

Jenny stood at the door for a long moment, looking out over the surrounding area. There was no sign of the boy or his pony, but she had the feeling that he was near . . . watching her. The quiet was absolute. She wondered why she wasn't frightened.

Slowly she pushed open the door and stepped inside. When her eyes adjusted to the gloom, her breathing quickened. What had once been a schoolroom was a shambles. Planks had been ripped from the benches and tables; splintered pieces lay on the floor, others had been carried off. Pages of books littered the floor amid pieces of broken slate. Stick chalk had been smashed and ground into the floor under the heels of heavy boots. A large slate at the front of the room had been broken, and only the frame remained attached to the wall.

Anger rose within her. Words she had heard muttered on the docks of Long Island by the sweating stevedores came to her mind. Not for a moment, as she gazed at the destruction, did she assume that the Shoshonis had done this. The room had been vandalized by someone who didn't want the Indians to have a school and probably when it had been learned that a teacher was coming.

Thank goodness she had brought a trunk full of books and slates. On her first trip to town she would send an order for more. Someone was trying to deprive the Indian children of the education arranged for so carefully by a caring old man who had wanted to give back to the Shoshoni some of what they had given to him. Stoney Creek Ranch must be the prize, and Alvin Havelshell was a part of the conspiracy to get it. But why was the schoolroom destroyed and not Whitaker's cabin? Of course! Someone planned to live there after she was gone.

So angry was she, so deep in thought, so preoccupied with how she would confront Havelshell when she saw him again, that she was unaware of the boy standing in the doorway until she almost bumped into him.

"Oh!" She stopped short. Then, "Hello—"

He stepped outside and she quickly followed. He stood not ten feet away and looked at her with eyes so dark a blue she would have thought them black if the rising sun had not cast a beam of bright light upon him.

"Hello," Jenny said again. "Please don't run away. Oh, I don't know if you understand me. I hope you do."

"I do. Will you leave now?"

"No. Absolutely not! I came to teach and that's what I'll do, if I have any pupils."

He said nothing for a minute or two, but he never took his eyes off her face. Jenny returned his scrutiny. He was a tall boy with a slim, well-muscled body.

Finally he said, "What's pupils?"

"Students . . . children who want to learn."

The boy seemed to be about thirteen or fourteen. His face was beautiful with features sharply defined and framed by hair as black and shiny as a raven's wing. It hung in two braids over his shoulders. The white band around his forehead was tied in back and in the knot was a white feather. His shirt and britches were well worn but clean.

"I'm so glad you speak English. I was afraid I'd have to learn Shoshoni."

"Not all who come to your school will speak your language. If you stay," he added after a pause.

"Will you be here to translate?"

"Translate?"

"Will you help me teach them English?"

"You will not stay."

"Why do you say that?"

He shrugged. "They do not want you here. They do not want anyone here."

"Who are . . . they? And why don't they want me here?"

He shrugged again and turned to go.

"Please don't go. There's so much I need to know . . . if I'm to stay and carry out Mr. Whitaker's wishes."

He walked to a thick stand of sumac, stepped behind it, then reappeared leading the spotted pony.

"Will you come to the school?"

He shrugged and looked away from her. He seemed reluctant to leave.

"Thank you for cutting grass for the horses."

"They must eat."

"What are you called?"

"*Woksois.*"

"Your Shoshoni name? Do you have an English name?"

"My father called me . . . Little Whit. But I am no longer little."

"You're Walt Whitaker's son?"

"He was proud to call me son," the boy answered defiantly.

"I should think so. Any man should be proud to call you his son."

"Any man? Ha! Ha!" He spit contemptuously on the grass. Eyes that had been so clearly expressionless were now dark with resentment and suppressed rebellion.

Jenny didn't know what to say. She studied him closely. All her experience had been with girls. She was unsure how to handle a proud young boy.

"I am determined to stay. But there is much I need to know. Will you help me?"

His gaze left her face and he looked toward the house. When his eyes returned to her, they were hard, resentful.

"I am not to go there . . . to my father's house."

"Because it is not on the reservation. I was told that. I will write to the . . . Big Chief in Washington and tell him it is unfair that you should have to sneak onto your father's homestead."

"I am not considered real son by the whites."

"Was your mother not legal wife to Mr. Whitaker?"

"In the eyes of the Shoshoni. He had two Shoshoni wives. One old, one young. My mother was the young one."

"Will she come to the school so that I can meet her?"

"She is dead."

"Oh, I'm sorry."

He frowned. "Why sorry? You not know my mother."

"That's true, but I know *you* . . . now. And I'm sorry you have no mother."

"I have mother. My father's second wife my mother now. She is old. I take care of her till she find other husband." He leaped upon the pony and turned away.

"Whit," Jenny called. "It will take me a while to get the school ready for classes. Will you come?"

"I will not be far away," Whit called, and rode into the woods.

Jenny watched him leave, wishing she had asked him how far it was to his village and if the elders would come to see her about the school, or if she should go to them.

On the way back to the house her steps were eager, her petticoats swishing in the tall grass with each long, graceful stride. She stopped at the woodpile to gather an armful of small sticks and twigs.

"Use this bucket, Virginia. And you'd better wear gloves. I found this old pair in your trunk," Cassandra said as she came from the house, dressed, and with her hair brushed and tied back.

"Thank you." Jenny pulled on soft leather gloves, not at all suitable as work gloves but better than nothing. "I've already poked my finger with a splinter."

"Tululla brought kindling in each night so she'd have something to start the morning fire. She always used a bucket."

"Oh, honey. I didn't realize that I was so ill equipped to cope with life out here."

"We'll manage." Cassandra tossed her head. "We're as smart as that Frank Wilson and twice as smart as that dumb clod that was here yesterday. We may not be as strong physically, Virginia, but we're smarter. I'll bank on smartness over strength."

"You're right, Cassandra. We'll not let a few inconveniences discourage us."

"These are major inconveniences, Virginia. Some of them are life-threatening."

"I know, honey. I worry for you and Beatrice."

"That's as you should, for you are the adult in the family. But we'll be all right once we get organized." She picked up the bucket Jenny had filled. "Bring a couple of big pieces of wood. We've got to cook breakfast. Tululla said food is fuel for the body like wood is fuel for the stove. While we're cooking you can tell me about that Indian boy you were talking to."

The morning went quickly. Jenny was surprised at the amount of work four-year-old Beatrice could do willingly while working with Cassandra. The girls put the kitchen area in order, scrubbing the work counter and washing the dusty dishes beneath. Jenny swept the floor with a piece of broom she found propped in the corner behind the stove. After dragging her trunk into the room with the single bunk, she made up the bed and set her toilet articles out on a shelf.

Cassandra started a list of things they needed. Soap was the first item. They had washed the dishes using Jenny's perfumed hand soap. High on the list were a decent broom and a washtub that they could also use for bathing.

"Jenny, I wonder why Mr. Havelshell sent chicken feed when there are no chickens." Cassandra's pale blue eyes never missed anything that was important.

"He said they may have been stolen."

"There were never chickens here. Not for a long time anyway."

"How do you know that, honey?"

"Because there's not a feather or a dropping . . . anywhere. I looked yesterday and I looked again this morning. All I found were bird feathers and some splatters made by a blackbird or a bluejay who had been eating berries."

"Well, forevermore." Jenny brushed the hair from her forehead with the back of her hand. "Why in the world did he send two sacks of chicken feed when he knew there were no chickens?"

"Because he wants you to think the Indians steal . . . and heaven knows what else. It's part of the campaign to discourage and frighten us so we'll leave." Cassandra spoke as if she were explaining something to a child. Then she asked Beatrice, who had come running in the back door, "Did you fill the bucket with chips?"

Beatrice ignored the question. "Jen . . . ny—" she gasped. "Indians out . . . there."

Jenny went quickly out the door and looked toward the school.

"One of them is Whit, the boy I told you about. You needn't be afraid of them." She waved to the pair who sat on their ponies staring at the ranch house.

No response. Evidently waving was not one of their ways of communicating.

"Come along, girls. Let's go talk to them."

"Shouldn't we take the gun?" Cassandra asked.

"I have the little one in my pocket. I don't think we'll need it."

As they neared the two riders, Beatrice took shelter behind Jenny's skirt. The man who waited with the boy was thick in shoulders and chest and had streaks of gray in his hair.

"The sun is halfway across the sky and you have not watered the horses." Whit spoke in an accusing tone.

"Oh my goodness! I completely forgot the horses!" Jenny turned back to look at the corral where the three animals stood with their heads over the rail fence. "Will they come with me if I put a rope around their necks?"

"The pony will not."

"Who does the pony belong to?"

"To me!"

"Then why do you leave him here?"

"Because Havelshell says I have no claim. The pony was not listed on the paper my father left."

"For crying out loud! Couldn't you have told him—"

"You do not tell agent. Agent tell you," the boy said bitterly.

His dark eyes moved down to Cassandra, who stood

apart from Jenny, her hands on her hips, her face tilted up toward him.

"I wonder why Mr. Whitaker preferred to carry water rather than build his corral over by the pond."

Whit's dark eyes moved back up to Jenny's face.

"When he built the corral, water flowed in the ditch that runs through it. When he was gone, the *Wasicun* build dam like the beaver to stop water."

"*Wasicun?*"

"White man."

"Mr. Havelshell?" When the boy didn't answer, she said, "Why would he do that?"

"He had reason."

Jenny looked to the older man. He had not spoken. He was not as clean as Whit, nor did he have the boy's fine features; his skin was several shades darker and his face pockmarked.

"He is not right in head and does not speak," Whit exclaimed. "But his heart is good and his back is strong. If teacher say fix so water go to Whitaker land, we fix."

"Could you do that? Heavenly days! That would be a great help. But . . . is the dam on the reservation land?"

"It is. Water come out of rock and make a small stream that flow into corral. *Wasicun* make water go to river."

"If you take out the dam will it affect the pond?"

"That water come from mountain."

"Then take out the dam." She smiled to take off the edge as she spoke in a firm demanding tone. "I demand that you take out the dam and let the water fill the ditch so the horses can drink."

"You will say that to agent?"

"I will tell him that I ordered you to do it. How long will it take?"

"Not long. Horses can wait. Why you look at me?" His dark eyes had settled again on Cassandra.

"Because I thought Indians said only 'ugh' and 'how.' You speak pretty good . . . for an Indian."

"Ugh! How! Ugh! Ugh! How! How!" He spit the words. "I'm not stupid Indian. I know English. I read, too."

"If you're not a stupid Indian, why do you wear that silly feather in your hair?"

"So you know I savage who will come and take your scalp." He placed his hand on the hilt of the knife in his belt.

"You just try it and I'll . . . shoot your gizzard out!" Cassandra lifted her small pointed chin defiantly.

Jenny looked from one to the other in amazement. "That's about enough of that kind of talk. Whit, these are my sisters, Cassandra, and Beatrice."

"Cassandra. What that mean? Girl-Who-Squawk-Like-Jaybird?" Whit turned the pony and headed for the woods. The older man followed.

"It means prophetess," Cassandra yelled. "But I doubt you know what that means, Boy-With-Chicken-Feather-Growing-Out-Of-Head!"

"I like him and I was hoping you would, too." Jenny put her arm across Cassandra's shoulder as they walked back to the house.

"He's a smart-mouthed know-it-all. You'll not be able to teach him anything."

"I liked him." Beatrice piped up in her childish voice. "He's pretty. I wish I could ride on his pony."

"You noticed, did you?" Jenny laughed. "Did you think he was pretty, Cass?"

"Pretty? Some people would think the back end of a mule was pretty!"

"He's only a boy, but I feel better knowing he's out there keeping an eye on us."

"Will he come to school?"

"I don't know. I hope he does. He seems mature and bright for his age. His father may have set up this program with him in mind."

"Virginia," Cassandra tilted her head to look up at her sister. "There's something going on here that I don't understand. It doesn't make any sense that a boy can't cross an imaginary line to come onto a place where his father lived, even if he is a . . . a . . . bas—"

"Bastard. You can say it. It's a legitimate word that's in Mr. Webster's dictionary. Whit is one only in the eyes of some white people. Mr. Whitaker married Whit's mother according to the Shoshoni tradition."

"As I said"—Cassandra continued on toward the house—"there's a lot here that I don't understand."

Chapter Four

For three days after his trip to town Trell McCall worked from dawn to dark building a corral for the mares he wanted to breed to his best stallions. His hired hand, Joe Fiala, was in Forest City getting married. Trell and Joe had spent days making the room next to the bunkhouse into quarters for the newlyweds.

It would be nice, Trell mused as he wiped sweat from his forehead with his shirtsleeve, to have a woman on the place. Joe was young, but he was getting a woman who would be a helpmate. He had told Trell that she was the youngest of six children. After her parents died, she had been living first with one married sibling and then with another. A couple of her brothers' wives were not pleased to be losing their unpaid help.

And Joe and his girl were in love. Trell thought about that a lot. He wondered how it would be to have a wife love him with all her heart as Mara Shannon loved his brother, Pack. Trell sometimes cursed the shyness that had kept him from having a serious relationship with a woman.

While Joe was away, Trell found himself thinking more and more about the slender, determined woman and the two little girls who had come to take over the Whitaker school for Indians. The possibility that the woman and the children might be over at Whitaker's alone worried him. He had few qualms as far as the Shoshoni were concerned—they were peaceful enough. The drifters and outlaws who roamed the territory provided the danger to an unprotected woman on a homestead. Even though a man could get himself hanged for bothering a good woman more quickly than for killing a man or stealing a horse, the lure was too great for some to resist.

When Joe returned to the ranch, his bride sat beside him on the wagon seat. The new black serge suit he had bought for his wedding was dust-covered now. The freckle-faced, skinny, down-at-the-heels boy who had drifted in several years ago and asked for a job, now jumped down and reached for his bride. Amid squeals of laughter he swung her down. Once her feet were on the ground they held on to each other until they saw Trell watching them.

"Morning," Trell called as he went toward them. "Do I get to kiss the bride?"

"Wal, now, I ain't knowin' 'bout that." Happiness was spread all over the young cowboy's face. "Boss, this is Una May."

"Pleased to meet you, Mrs. Fiala."

Una May, a small, round-faced girl with a sweet smile and two deep dimples in her cheeks, looked down at the ground, her face aflame. Trell had seen her once or twice in town, although never with Joe because the two men did not usually leave the ranch at the same time.

"Ah . . . shucks. Might as well give the man a treat, honey." Joe put his arm around his bride, his broad grin showing his widely spaced front teeth. "Ya can stand it fer once. Won't last long."

Trell bent his tall frame and pecked the girl on the cheek.

"I don't know how you're going to put up with this old boy, ma'am. He's so ugly he'd put a mud fence to shame."

"I ain't seein' it that way, Mr. McCall." She smiled shyly and looked adoringly at the grinning cowboy.

"Didn't I tell ya she was smart, Trell? Didn't I tell ya?"

"Now that he's got a pretty wife, I'm wondering how I'll ever get the ornery critter away from the house long enough to do any work," Trell said with a teasing smile.

Una May looked stricken. Her cornflower blue eyes flew to her husband.

"He's teasin'," Joe said quickly, and put his arm across her shoulders. "Ya know what teasers them Irish is. He's glad yo're here, honey-pie. He's thinkin' 'bout fillin' his belly with them good biscuits ya make."

"I do make a pretty good biscuit, Mr. McCall."

"They'll be a sight better than Joe's, I'm sure of that. It'll be pure pleasure to come in and have a hot meal without having to cook it. I'm glad you're here, Una May. And call me Trell. You two go on and get settled in. There's nothing pressing that has to be done right now except maybe strengthen that pole corral. In another week, Joe, we'll go out and drive the mares in."

Trell went back to the house and hung his hat on the peg beside the door. He poured himself a cup of lukewarm coffee from the blackened pot on the cookstove and stood with his back to the stove while he surveyed his home. It was a tight, neat two-room cabin. The furnishings—sturdy oak table and chairs, cupboards, desk and chests he had chosen were all of good quality. In the other room was an iron bedstead with wire springs and a thick cotton mattress, a wardrobe and a washstand.

Trell was proud of his home . . . but somehow, today, it seemed lonely. It needed a woman's touch. Una May was going to cook, clean and do the washing, but each evening she and Joe would go to their private quarters. Seeing the happiness on their faces had somehow reminded Trell how empty his life was without anyone to share it.

Trell plucked his battered hat off the peg and slammed it down on his head. On his way to saddle his horse, he stopped by the bunkhouse and knocked on the door. He was about to walk away when Joe came to the door shoving his shirttail down into the waistband of his old duck britches.

"I'll be gone most of the day, Joe. I'm going to stop and see the folks at the Whitaker place. I suppose you'll be sticking around here."

"Ya betcha." Joe's hair, sandy and thick, was in total disarray. He ran forked fingers through it and grinned sheepishly. "I'll keep a eye on thin's."

"Take Una May in and show her where things are. Don't wait supper for me. I'm not sure when I'll be back."

The door was closed again when Trell rode past the bunkhouse and headed toward the river. The horse and Trell were of similar mind. They took their time, just breathing the good air, keeping an eye out for trouble. Ten minutes later, far off and below, he saw a dot that had to be buffalo. Most of them had been killed off, but here and there groups of three or four had taken to the mountain valleys.

Crossing the river, he passed through a corner of the Shoshoni reservation and onto the Whitaker land near where, he had heard, a nester had built a shack. As long as he was near, he'd thought to drop by and let the man know that he was in a dangerous situation because Havelshell was dead set on getting him off the land.

From a distance the nester's newly built shack backed against a sheer rock bluff. It blended with the background. A thin line of smoke wafted from the rock chimney. A wash pot stood in front of the cabin and behind it a wagon. The only livestock were two mules staked out a distance from the house. The smoke and the mules were all that kept the place from looking deserted. Trell was within a dozen yards of the house when a man in overalls and a round-brimmed hat stepped out with a rifle.

"Stop right there!" The voice was gruff and strained.

Trell held up his hands. "I mean you no harm."

"Who are ya and what'a ya want?"

"Trell McCall. I have a ranch across the river. I'm just paying a neighborly visit."

"Yeah! Fine time to be payin' a neighborly visit!"

The voice had lost the gruffness and Trell realized the person holding a rifle on him was a boy. *No, by golly, it was a girl!*

"Look. I came by to warn you that you'll be getting some trouble from the Indian agent about squatting here."

"Kind of ya, mister. Why'er ya comin' 'round now for?"

"Because I just heard about it a few days ago."

"Yo're too late. Trouble's already been here."

"It seems you were prepared to handle it without any help from me. I'll just mosey on."

"We didn't get a chance to handle anythin'." Although still angry, the girl's voice was not quite so steady. "So?

What'er ya waitin' for? Get on down the trail to wherever ya was headin'.."

"Good day to you." Trell turned his horse.

"Wait!" A small white-haired lady came out the door.

"Stay inside, Granny. We don't know about this sidewinder. He could be one of 'em!"

"I don't think so, Colleen. And we need—"

"Where was he when we needed help?" The girl shouted angrily. "We don't need him now!"

"Maybe we do, child." The woman stepped out into the yard. She was stooped from years of hard work. Her gnarled hands clutched a Bible and her lined face was wet with tears.

"We'd be obliged if you'd help bury my boy. The girl can't dig the grave and get him in it all by herself."

"I can do it, Granny! I've got it started."

"I'll be glad to help." Trell stepped from his horse. "If it'll put your mind at ease, I'll leave my rifle and handgun with you."

"It's best you keep them." Tears rolled unchecked down the old woman's cheeks. "They give us two days to leave, but they got a look at Colleen when she flew at 'em, after they killed her pa. Bein' the kind a men they be, I'm a-fearin' they'll be back." Her nearly toothless mouth trembled.

"When they come, I'll be waitin' for 'em!" the girl declared.

"We was just a standin' here . . . listenin' to 'em tellin' us we got to get off the land. Miles said he was goin' to talk to a government man. One of 'em said, 'I ain't thinkin' ya are.' He just moved his horse up, pulled out his gun and shot him down."

"Pa had told us to leave the guns in the cabin so there'd not be no trouble. The dirty, low-down, belly-crawlin' snakes!"

"How many?"

"Three."

"Had they been here before?"

"Never laid eyes on 'em. I'll know 'em if I see 'em again. Ya can bet yore life on it."

Trell dropped the reins to ground-tie his horse. "If you show me where you want him buried, I'll get started."

"I started it up there . . . in the grove overlookin' the river. Pa liked the . . . view." The girl's voice broke.

"It's a pretty place."

"Pa thought this the prettiest place he ever did see. He heard it was gon' to be let out for biddin'. He wasn't going to stay if he couldn't get title to the land. Now he'll be here forever."

"Stay here with your grandma. I'll come back when it's ready."

"We're obliged . . . I guess."

The hand that held out the shovel was large and strong. Trell could see the girl's face plainly now. The skin that stretched tightly over her high cheekbones was smooth and sunbrowned. There was a bitter twist to her wide, full mouth. Stormy blue eyes were bright with unshed tears. She was not what he would consider a raving beauty, but she was far from plain-looking. The hair that escaped from under the old hat was as black as midnight, and there appeared to be plenty of it. She was tall and willow-thin, but he didn't doubt that she had a steel rod for a backbone.

When Trell returned from the grove an hour later, he went directly to the water bucket that sat on a bench behind the house. After drinking and washing the sweat from his face, he knocked on the door.

The girl, wearing a faded black skirt that came only to the tops of her black shoes, opened the door. A black shawl was wrapped around the upper part of her body to cover a white shirtwaist. She had tried to put her hair in order, but the unruly curls had broken away from the pins and were flattened against her tear-wet cheeks.

"If you want, I'll put together a box," Trell said. "I can use the side boards on the wagon."

"We don't have any nails. Pa traded them and the saw for sugar, flour and coffee."

"Well, in that case, I'll line the burial hole with cedar boughs . . . if it's what you want."

"Me and Granny would be obliged." She stepped back and closed the door.

The next time he came to the house, the old lady was waiting for him. Like her granddaughter she had dressed in black for the burial. She came across the yard to meet him.

"Mister, don't be put out 'cause Colleen's short with ya. Murphys has got a good bit a pride. It's been hard on the girl seein' her pa shot down like a cur dog and hard to have to take help from a stranger."

"I understand. She's got a right to be edgy. If you're ready, ma'am, I'll bring up the wagon."

When Trell saw the body of Miles Murphy, he wondered how the women had moved him into the house, much less up onto the bed. The man was huge, big-framed and heavily muscled. They had dressed him in a moth-eaten black suit; his hair and beard were combed. Trell stood back while the girl placed a tintype photograph in the hands folded on his chest. The two women gently wrapped him in a pieced quilt. When they finished, the girl looked at Trell with something like agony in her eyes and nodded.

Staggering under the weight of the corpse, Trell managed to get it in the wagon. Before leaving the cabin, he took his rifle from the scabbard on his saddle and placed it under the seat.

"You drive. Grandma and I will walk with Papa."

Trell walked the mules slowly out of the yard and toward the grove, knowing it would be hard for the elderly woman to keep up. He looked back one time to see her leaning heavily on her granddaughter's arm.

To Trell's way of thinking, anyone who would shoot down an unarmed man was as low-down as a human being could get. To do it in front of the man's womenfolk made him unfit even to be called a human being. The Indian agent who wanted Whitaker's land had sent cold-blooded killers to do his dirty work.

The grove was cathedral-quiet. Even the team stood noiselessly while Trell lifted the body out of the wagon and placed it in the hole where Miles Murphy would spend eternity. Trell stepped back to leave the women alone with their loved one before he filled the grave. The girl began to speak to her father.

"You were a good papa and did your best to take care of us." With her arm across her grandmother's shoulder, Colleen spoke in a clear and controlled voice. "Ya loved Mama and grieved when we lost her. I hope yo're with her now. Yo're not to worry. Granny and I will be all right. I want ya to know, Papa, that if ever I set eyes on that low-down, dirty, son of a bitch that shot ya, I'm goin' to walk right up and put a bullet in his head. Thank ya for what all ya taught me 'bout right and wrong. Good-bye, Papa."

After a moment of silence the girl began to sing in a sur-
prisingly clear voice. It wasn't a song Trell expected to
hear, but somehow it seemed appropriate.

> "As the blackbird in the spring,
> 'Neath the willow tree, sat and piped, I heard him sing—
> Au-ra Lee, Au-ra Lee, maid with golden hair—
> Sunshine came along with thee, and swallows filled the air."

When she finished singing, the girl took the shovel and
began to fill the grave while her grandmother watched her
son's body disappear beneath the rich dark soil. When Trell
took the shovel from her hand, Colleen gave it to him willingly.

"I suppose you think I should have sang 'Rock of Ages'
or something like that. 'Aura Lee' was Papa's favorite
song. Mama's name was Laura Lee—" Her voice broke.
She turned quickly and went to the end of the wagon.

Trell felt that nothing he would say would ease their
grief, so he remained quiet. Back at the cabin, he unhitched
the team and watered them. He was reluctant to leave the
women alone and told them so.

"You don't owe us anythin', mister. Me and Granny
thank ya for what ya done."

"Can I help you load up?"

"We ain't sure what we're goin' to do or if we're even
goin' to leave. If them fellers come back, I'll shoot 'em out
of their saddles."

"If you try it, there's bound to be shootin' on both sides.
Do you want your granny left to bury you?" Trell knew the
words were harsh, but he wanted to shock her into being
sensible.

"You think I should let it go? Let them get away with murderin' Pa? He wouldn't've if they'd a killed me."

"I think you should report it to the Territorial marshal."

"Ha! Havelshell's got ever'thin' and ever'body in the territory eatin' out of his hand."

"You're wrong about that. The teacher for the Indian school won't be kowtowing to him."

"If he don't, he'll be the first man I've met since we come to Sweetwater that don't lick his boots."

"Teacher isn't a man. She's a woman. I'm on my way over there to make a neighborly visit."

"Yo're right neighborly, ain't ya?"

"You could say so."

"Then ya'd better get on yore horse and get goin'. Granny and I got some thinkin' to do."

"Mister, I'll hold ya in my prayers for what ya done." Granny Murphy held out her hand. Trell took it gently.

"I'm glad I happened by. I'll stop again on my way back. If you like, I'll take you to my place until you decide what you want to do." He looked at the tall girl, then back to the little woman. "You can't stay here. You must know that."

"It 'pears to be so. We be thankin' ya for the offer."

Trell mounted his horse. Colleen stood beside the door and never lifted a hand to wave when he rode away. He hoped the girl would come to her senses and not go looking for trouble. When he stopped on his way back, he would invite them again to go to his place until they decided what they wanted to do.

He put his horse into a fast trot. The sun showed an hour or so past noon. He certainly hadn't planned on burying a man when he left home this morning. He wished he'd thought to bring the Murphys and the teacher a couple of smoked turkeys or a haunch of deer meat. It would have been better than paying a call empty-handed.

It was less than an hour's ride to the Stoney Creek Ranch. Trell figured to pay his respects and return to the Murphy's. He had an uneasy feeling that the men that killed the father might return for the daughter.

"You stupid son of a bitch! You want the Territorial marshal down on us?"

The man who spoke swiveled around in his chair. Cold blue eyes beneath bushy white brows glared at the Indian agent.

"I never told them to kill him. I said scare him and if he didn't move, burn him out." Havelshell leaned against the doorjamb. He had not been invited to sit down.

"I don't like bringing in uncontrollable gunmen."

"Hartog said the man drew on him. What was he to do?"

"It doesn't stand to reason that a lone man would draw on three armed men unless he had no choice."

"I wasn't there. I only know what they told me," Havelshell replied.

"I hear that Hartog is pretty mean with women. Tell him not to try any of that rough stuff around here. I don't want to get people riled up. There is nothing that draws people closer together than to be against someone. It's already known that Hartog's your man. What he does is reflected on you."

"I've already talked to him about that." *Not that it'll do any good. The horny bastard will do as he pleases.*

"If that land comes up for auction, the squatters on it will be given compensation for the improvements they've made. I went to considerable trouble to get you appointed Indian agent as soon as we learned of Walt's will. I want those squatters off without any trouble that will draw attention. What about the teacher? Anyone been out to see how she's doing?"

"I plan to let her stew out there for a week or two. I want to give her time to be good and sick of it. I've put out the word that no one's to give her a hand, no matter what she offers to pay. She'll be gone by the first of the year. She'll not stay when the weather gets to below zero and she doesn't have help."

"I'm depending on you to see to it." The man rocked back in his chair and studied the agent. "Who is with Arvella out at the reservation store now?"

"Linus is still there and a Shoshoni girl. Two, sometimes three, hands to take care of the stock. Old Ike Klein comes and goes. 'Course, old Ike is more Indian than white. I heard that he and Whitaker came west together. Ike hunted meat for a freight line, and Walt went to the gold mines and made a fortune. Shows you how smart old Ike was."

"He's a gutsy old buzzard, from what I hear. I'm not sure it's a good idea for him to be nosing around."

"He's harmless. No one pays any attention to what he says. They figure he's got mountain fever. It happens to a lot of men who spend time alone in the mountains."

"How about old Chief Washakie? Is he still up north in the Wind River country?"

"As far as I know."

"I'll expect to hear from you as soon as you call on Miss Gray. Don't let her hoity-toity manner put you off. She's a gentlewoman from the East; one of them suffrage women come to help the *poor* Indians. She'll put on a show of having a stiff backbone, but you can bet she's shaking in her shoes."

"She's got a right to be. If she's got any brains at all, she'll realize she and those girls will starve or freeze to death this winter when snow is about six feet deep."

"Is Walt's Indian kid still hanging around?"

"He knows better than to go off the reservation. I'll take a whip to him if he does."

"That will be all, Havelshell. Report back after you've been out to Whitaker's."

Alvin Havelshell seethed as he left the house and got into his buggy. Damned old fool sitting in his fancy house treated him like he was one of his hired hands. *A hired stud.*

He wished that he'd never brought Walt Whitaker's will to the man. But, hell, after that first cattle drive, when he saw how easy it was to cut out half the herd that went to the reservation, he had needed the man's help getting the steers to market.

They had been partners . . . he thought. He wished to hell he'd not agreed to the old man's conditions. He hadn't realized that it would be so difficult.

The old fool better watch himself when he gave orders to Alvin Havelshell, or he might be tempted to turn Hartog loose on *him*!

Chapter Five

Trell saw the cloud of smoke as he neared the Whitaker ranch. Borne on a light breeze, the acrid scent stung his nostrils. It was far too much smoke to be coming from a chimney. He put his heels to the roan, and the horse's long stride ate up the distance to a rise where he could see the flames. The fire was in an open area north of the house and was so far confined to grass and the brush edging it.

He saw little flames lick across another expanse of grass and into the brush, then run up a small tree like hungry red tongues. The fire was out of hand and racing toward the ranch house. At his urging, the roan jumped a small stream, sped along a pole corral, and skidded to a stop behind a woman beating at the flames with a blanket. A small girl staggered from the stream carrying a bucket of water.

Trell leaped from his horse and grabbed the blanket from the woman's hand.

"Use your feet on the small patches," he shouted. "Keep upwind from the flames. Watch out for the girl and stay away from the heavy smoke."

Jenny beat at the larger flames with the grain sack Cassandra had dropped when she rushed to fetch the water. Jenny held up her skirts and stamped out the small ones with her feet. Like red-and-gold dancers the flames raced back and forth, edging closer and closer to the house. With a swish of the sack she beat them back.

No! You will not get to my house!

Tears streamed down her face from the smoke and blurred her vision. The heat seared her throat. She did not know who the man was who had come to her aid, nor did she care. She was exceedingly grateful he was there. When the flames engulfed a bush, she circled behind it, flailing the grass with the sack to keep the fire from spreading. Jenny worked strictly on instinct while the sweat rolled down her face and her hands became locked onto the end of the sack. It was an exhausting effort.

Cassandra carried bucket after bucket of water from the stream. Jenny dropped the sack in the water to wet it and poured the rest on the flames. She had no time to think of her parched throat, or her heat-flushed face. Her arms felt as if they weighed a hundred pounds each. As fast as one patch was stamped out, another seemed to flare into being. She worked as if her life depended on it, and gradually they began to win against the flames.

When it was over, they stood smoke-grimed and red-eyed in the blackened section.

"Well, we did it." Trell grinned at Jenny. His face was smudged by smoke and his head wet with sweat.

"I'm Jenny Gray. I'm so glad you came." Jenny dropped the sack and extended her hand.

"Trellis McCall. Glad to know you." He shook her hand firmly.

"I could use a drink of water. How about you? Oh, this is my sister, Cassandra. Honey, I'm so proud of you!" She hugged the girl. "Are you all right?"

"I expect so. I haven't decided yet. I'm sorry, Virginia. I didn't realize that there were embers in the ashes when I dumped them."

"It's all right. We're learning, aren't we? It was a lesson we won't forget. One that turned out all right thanks to Mr. McCall. Where's Beatrice?"

"In the house. I threatened to give her a good whipping if she came out."

"You did . . . what?"

"I merely threatened. I wouldn't have, but she didn't know that. It kept her out of the way." Cassandra tilted her head and looked up at Trell. "Do you have a job, Mr. McCall? If not, we have need of a man to work here."

Trell's amused eyes went from the child, who spoke like a grown-up, to her sister.

"You'll discover, if you get to know Cassandra, that she comes right out with what's on her mind."

"I thank you for the offer, miss, but I have a horse ranch across the river that demands more time than I have to give it."

"Well." Cassandra's shoulders slumped. "It did no harm to ask."

"Will your horse wander off?" Jenny asked as they walked toward the house.

"No, ma'am. He's ground-tied when I drop the reins."

"How remarkable. Back home we tie the reins to a weight on the ground." At the door Jenny stopped. "Won't you come in? The least I can do for what you've done for us is to offer you a meal."

"Flitter!" Cassandra snorted. "You'd better know before you accept that it'll be burnt beans and rock-hard biscuits."

Laughing green eyes met Trell's.

"Now you know. Cooking is a skill of which I know very little. But I'm learning . . . from my little sister. We haven't yet discovered how to control the darn cookstove, but we will."

"Even if she could *control* the stove, she couldn't cook."

"Cass," Jenny chided. "Why do you always have to be so frank?"

"I'm being honest. And don't call me Cass."

"I'm sorry. I forgot."

"You don't like the name?" Trell asked. "I've always liked it."

"Why? Did you have a horse named *Cass*?"

"No. I knew a woman who was the prettiest little thing I ever did see. She was sweet as sugar and . . . smart. Lordy, she was smart! And she could sing like a bird. Her name was Cass. The name's been a favorite of mine because of her."

"Really? Did you love her?"

"Like a sister."

"Well. In that case, *you* can call me Cass. But no one else can." With the air of a queen, Cassandra walked into the house.

Jenny watched her with a proud smile. She lifted her brows in question when she turned back to Trell.

"It's true."

He couldn't stop looking at her. She didn't seem to care at all that her face was smudged with black smoke and her hair hung in strands down her back. A sudden burst of happiness sent his heart galloping like a runaway horse.

"I've met Irishmen before, Mr. McCall. You're full of blarney, But I forgive you. You made Cassandra happy."

Trell took the water bucket and went to the pond. His observant eyes had spotted a well without a rope and a pulley. Had it been deliberately put out of use in order to make things here difficult for the teacher? He washed at the pond and ran his fingers through his hair before he put his hat back on his head. On the way back to the house he passed the woodpile where an axe lay on the ground. He picked it up, wiped it off and sank the blade in a stump.

"I can bring over a rope and pulley so you can use the well," he said when he returned to the house with a full bucket of water.

"I would appreciate it. It would be easier than carrying it from the pond."

Jenny had washed and pinned up her hair. She introduced her younger sister, who was so bashful that she hid behind Jenny's skirt.

"You are our first visitor. Whit, Mr. Whitaker's son, comes at night and brings grass for the horses. He's Shoshoni and isn't allowed off the reservation."

"Not even to come here and help with chores?"

"I was told by the man who drove us out here that the agent would take a whip to him if he caught him. He'd better not touch that boy while I'm here! It is the silliest rule I ever heard. I intend to write to the Indian Bureau in Washington about it." Jenny motioned for Trell to sit down. Cassandra and Beatrice took their places.

"Jenny!" Beatrice whined. "I want bread and jam."

"We don't have bread and jam, honey. Eat a cookie." Then to Trell, "Cassandra made the cookies. They are really good."

"Too bad Tululla didn't teach me to make biscuits."

"Help yourself to the beans. I'll pour you a cup of tea. I do make a decent cup of tea."

"A person can't live on tea, Virginia." Cassandra passed Trell the plate of cookies. "I think you'll find that these will go down much easier than Virginia's biscuits. Tululla, our cook back home, said that the route to a man's heart was through his stomach. I'm afraid Virginia will never get a man."

"I'm not looking for one, Cassandra." For the first time Trell heard impatience in Jenny's tone. "I admit that cooking isn't something I know a lot about. Thank goodness you spent time in the kitchen at home, or we'd starve."

"You need some hired help if you're going to stay here."

"We're staying. That disgusting man hopes to run us off, but we're staying," she said again. "As soon as I can get to town, I'll hire a cook. The children need better meals than I'm capable of making."

"What makes you think Havelshell doesn't want you here?"

"It's obvious. Oh, I don't think it's me . . . personally. For some reason, he doesn't want a teacher to occupy this ranch. Why else would the school be torn up, the books and slates destroyed? Why else would he dam up the stream so the horses can't get to water, or take the rope and pulley from the well? Why else would he tell us there were chickens when there never have been chickens here? He wanted us to think the Indians had stolen them." Her eyes flared with indignation. "It's clear to me that he's trying to discourage and frighten me so I'll back out of my contract with the Bureau."

"Has he succeeded?"

"He's only made me angry and more determined than ever to stay here." Jenny's face relaxed and she laughed. It was the loveliest sound Trell had ever heard. "I realize that I'm ill equipped for this life, but I will learn. The girls and I are going to stay and claim Stoney Creek Ranch when the terms of the will are met."

"You'll need help."

"Yes, I know. Will you be our friend?" she asked on a sudden impulse.

"You can bank on it."

"Jen . . . ny. I don't like these old beans." Beatrice put her spoon down hard on the table.

"Are you married, Mr. McCall?" Cassandra moved the plate of cookies to within Beatrice's reach. "Take one," she ordered. The younger girl swallowed her mouthful of cookie and stuck her tongue out at her sister. Cassandra ignored her, and said to Trell, "Well, are you?"

"No, Cass. I've not found a woman who'd have me."

"Well. Virginia isn't married either and, of course, I'm too young. She may get desperate enough to take you."

"Cassandra! If you're not the limit!"

Trell observed Jenny's rosy cheeks. His dark eyes sparkled with amusement, and he thought for a brief moment of how soft those cheeks would be if he stroked them.

"I'd not be that lucky, Cass."

Jenny and Cass cleared the table. Trell watched. His mind was filled with impressions filed away to bring out and think about later. The past hour had been the most pleasant he could remember. He'd not even minded that he'd had to swallow a couple of times after every bite he took. He liked the way Jenny admitted her shortcomings. He admired her spunk for refusing to let Havelshell frighten her and for taking up for Whit Whitaker, the Indian boy. He liked the way she treated her sisters.

With that reddish brown hair and green eyes, she was a sight to see. When she got off the stage, she had been all dressed up in fancy clothes and he'd thought her a beautiful haughty woman. She was prettier now with her face reddened by the heat from the fire, her dress dirty and wetly clinging to her slender, young figure. Uncomfortable at his observation, Trell averted his eyes.

He was not sure that she realized how dangerous it was for her and the girls to be here alone. He fully intended, before he left, to bring up an idea that had begun floating around in his mind.

With the dishes in the big pan, Jenny poured cups of tea for herself and Trell, then spoke to Cassandra.

"Honey, would you take Beatrice outside while I talk with Mr. McCall?"

"I'll let her look at my picture book. Whatever you have to say to Mr. McCall will affect me and Beatrice, and I want to hear it."

Trell was surprised to hear Jenny say, "Very well. Would you like a cup of tea?"

"No, thank you."

After getting Beatrice settled, Cassandra sat down at the table and waited for the conversation to begin.

"Mr. McCall, we've been here four days—almost five now. I would be a fool not to know that I'm fighting an uphill battle. Frankly, I've never had to cook, clean, wash or care for animals. It is not something I'm proud to admit, but I'm not ashamed either. Our father provided for us very well. He never believed his daughters would be required to do those things. He is gone now, and it is up to me to provide for my sisters.

"I can teach. I came here to teach the Indian children. I know that I must have more wood than I can scrounge from that pile out there. I need it for the cookstove as well as for this place and the schoolroom when winter comes. I can go to town and lay in a supply of food, but we need fresh meat and the children need milk . . . and—" Jenny's voice trailed and Cassandra's voice filled the void.

"After meeting that disgusting boy with the raccoon and the man who drove us out here, we have come to the conclusion that we are not going to get help from anyone in that miserable town of Sweetwater." The little girl spoke with her hands clasped on the table. Her serious blue eyes were focused on Trell's face.

"Very well put, honey." Jenny reached out and squeezed her sister's hand then looked back and met Trell's eyes squarely. "We welcome any suggestions, Mr. McCall."

"I have one you may want to consider."

Trell told about stopping at the Murphys and learning about Miles Murphy's being killed. He explained that the girl and her grandmother had been warned to leave within two days' time or the men who killed Murphy would be back to burn them out.

"That's terrible!" Jenny exclaimed. "Frank Wilson, the man who drove us out here said something about squatters on Whitaker land. The Indian agent doesn't *own* this land. How can he do this?"

"It's a matter of who is in possession at the moment. The girl had started digging her father's grave when I got there. She can use a rifle. At least she was dead set on using one on me when I first rode up to their shack. But she can't stand up to Havelshell's men. I think she and her grandmother would be of help here."

"Are they . . . ah . . . decent women? You understand I couldn't have someone here with the girls who was . . . loose."

"I'd stake my life on it. The grandma is elderly and I'd say the girl is nineteen or twenty." He grinned to Cassandra. "I'm sure they know all about a cookstove." Then to Jenny, "If they could come here, it would give them time to decide what to do, and who knows, it may work out that you'd want them to stay."

"Is the girl pretty?" Cassandra asked.

"Well . . ." Trell frowned as he studied the question. "She isn't ugly."

"I do need help with Beatrice, Virginia. Maybe the granny could keep her amused while the girl cooked. It would be heavenly to have a decent meal."

"They could sleep in the little room. I'd have to sleep with you and Bea."

"I can stand it if you can."

"It wouldn't take much to put in another bunk, if you need one," Trell said.

"Does that mean you'll come back?" Cassandra asked.

"Do I have an invite?"

"As far as I'm concerned you can move in and stay."

"I swear, Cassandra," Jenny exclaimed. "You never cease to amaze me." She dismissed her sister with a frown, then spoke to Trell. "Do you think the Murphys will be agreeable to coming and staying on a trial basis?"

"I can ask them. It might not sit well with Havelshell if they come here."

"He has nothing to say about who lives with us. We will still need a man to do chores."

"You may find that the girl will do that. I'll see about getting a crew to come out and cut a supply of wood." He stood and reached for his hat. "I've got to be going. It'll be almost dark by the time I get back to the Murphys."

Jenny and the two girls walked out into the yard and watched as he mounted his horse.

"Thank you for helping to put out the fire."

"You're very welcome. Thanks for the meal."

"Ha!" A snort came from Cassandra. "You could hardly choke it down."

"If the Murphys are willing to consider your offer, I'll bring them over in the morning. Is that rifle I saw in there loaded?"

"It is and I know how to use it."

"Glad to hear it. It eases my mind some. 'Bye, girls. 'Bye . . . Miss Gray." He tipped his hat and put his heels to his horse.

"Call her Jenny," Cassandra yelled.

He turned in the saddle and waved.

"Do you like him, Virginia?"

"I do," Beatrice said. "He's not fat like Charles."

"Whit's over by the schoolhouse." Jenny saw the boy squatting beside the building, holding the reins of his pony. She waved. As usual, no response. "Let's walk over and talk to him." Holding Beatrice's hand, she headed for the school. Cassandra lagged behind.

"Hello, Whit," she called as they neared. "We've had a lot of excitement today. First a grass fire, then a neighbor came to help us put it out."

"Girl-Who-Squawk is stupid to make fire in the grass."

"I am not stupid, *Boy-With-Chicken-Feather-Growing-Out-Of-Head!*" Cassandra's voice was shrill. "How was I to know there were hot coals in the ashes? And how come you didn't come help?"

"You want me to feel the lash?" he spit. "Three *Wasicun* watch. But I would have come if McCall had not."

"You know Mr. McCall?" Jenny asked.

"Have heard talk of him. He is not one of *them*."

"Men were watching us and didn't come help? Did you know them?"

"They come to store with agent."

"Did they stay after Mr. McCall arrived?"

"They go first to see where dam was broke. Then go toward river. I have grass for the horses. I'll bring when dark comes."

"Where is it? We can carry it over."

"I bring when dark comes," he said stubbornly. His beautiful face was expressionless, but his dark eyes darted back and forth along the edge of the forest that surrounded the ranch buildings.

On the way back to the house, Cassandra walked ahead. Once she looked back at the boy still squatting beside the building.

"I could like him if he wasn't so smarty. I know how he must feel not being allowed on his own father's land. It was almost like that back home. I wonder what he'll do when he grows up. I sure know what I'm going to do."

"You do? What's that?"

"Well. I'm going to hire some men, the meanest men I can find. I'll have a fine carriage and the men will ride alongside as I go up the drive to the house. Margaret and Charles will think they're getting a fine visitor, but it'll be little old Cass. I'll walk right in and slap Margaret so hard and so many times her eyes will cross. Then I'll take over the house and demand that she clean and do the washing . . . naked. The men will laugh and pinch her butt when she walks by. She'll sleep on the floor without a blanket and Charles will spend his nights sleeping in the barn with the rats. I'll put my fingers in his eyes and pull on his *thing*!" Cassandra's voice became almost a whisper. "I'll whip him with the razor strop like he whipped us and make him say the Lord's Prayer a million times. I'll tell him how ugly he is and that his mother was a whore. Then . . . I will kill him!"

Jenny had put her hand to her mouth to keep back the sobs while her sister was speaking. With tears running down her cheeks she put her arm around the little girl.

"I'm sorry, darling. Oh, I'm so sorry."

Trell felt an urgency about getting back to the girl and her grandma. He hadn't mentioned it to Jenny, but he had seen three riders on the reservation land while they were fighting the fire, and they were not Indians. He rode the roan hard and arrived at the Murphy's just as it was getting dark. He pulled up and shouted his name. There was not a light and no answer to his call.

He rode around to the back of the house to see if the wagon was there. There was no sign of it or the mules. He bent low from the saddle to see if he could tell from the tracks if the wagon was loaded when he left the cabin.

"Yo're mighty careless a-ridin' in like that. Ya could'a got yore head blowd off."

Trell recognized Colleen's voice and turned to see a dim form emerge from a clump of bushes.

"I called out."

"I heard ya, or I'd'a been twitchin' my finger on this here trigger. I had ya in my sights."

"Where's your grandma and the wagon?"

"Hid. I come back to see if them skunks was out tonight."

"Do you have everything out of the house that you want?"

"Ever'thin' but the cookstove Pa bought. There was no way Granny and I could get it on the wagon."

"I'll help you get it out if you want. We can hide it in the bushes and come back for it."

"Pa worked hard for the money to buy that stove."

Trell stepped off his horse. "Let's get it out."

The stove was not large and the girl was strong. Fifteen minutes later they had carried it a hundred yards from the house and covered it with brush.

"Now," Trell said, wiping the sweat from his forehead. "What do you think about firing the house? It could be that when they discover you're gone, they'll decide to use it."

"I'd thought of it."

"We'd better do it if we're going to. If they plan on coming back tonight, they'll be here soon."

"I've got a can of lamp oil in the wagon."

"Take my horse. We've got no time to waste."

It took only a few minutes to splash the cabin with the oil. Trell lit a swatch of dry grass with a match, threw it in the door and backed away as the cabin burst into flames. He took his rifle from the saddle scabbard and urged Colleen back out of the light made by the fire.

"Go back to your granny. I'll wait and see if the flames bring out the skunks."

"It's not yore fight. I'll wait."

Trell knew that it would be a waste of time to argue and hunkered down beside her in the bushes.

While they waited Colleen told him that after her mother died, her father couldn't bear to stay in the house where they had lived when they first married and where she was born. Miles Murphy sought to build a new life for himself, his daughter, and his mother in the territory. He had been told the land was in an estate that would soon be auctioned off. With his meager savings, he'd hoped to buy a bit of it and eke out a living. First the Indian agent had come and told them to leave, then the men had come who had gunned her father down.

"Where did you live before coming here?"

"Missouri. Then we went to Timbertown, but Papa would rather farm or raise cattle than work in the sawmills."

"Did you know T.C. Kilkenny and Colin Tallman?"

"You couldn't live long in Timbertown and not know them."

"T.C. and Colin have a big ranch north of here. T.C. helped build the town for Rowe Lumber."

They talked on in low voices. Trell was comfortable with the girl; and as he sized her up, he was more convinced than ever that Jenny Gray would like her. They were a lot alike. Both had an overdose of spunk.

A half hour later, just as the flames of the burning cabin were beginning to die down, they heard the sound of horses' hooves, then three riders came across the grassland to stop just inside the circle of light.

"Mother-a-Christ! That little twister-tail done burnt the shack. Reckon she knowed we wanted it?"

"Told ya she was a corker, Hartog. Bet she's wilder than a turpentined cat."

"I know how to take the starch outta her."

"That's the one," Colleen whispered and raised the barrel of her rifle at the same time.

Before Trell could stop her she had fired off a shot. The bullet grazed the horse the man was on. The frightened animal reared throwing the man off-balance. Nonetheless, he pulled his gun and fired off several rapid shots in their direction. Colleen continued to shoot and miss the moving targets. Trell fired and hit a man who had moved his horse toward them.

"I'm hit! Goddammit! I'm hit!" The wounded man spurred his horse out of the light of the fire. The other two followed.

Colleen shot at the fleeing men and heard one of them cry out when her bullet found its mark.

"I hit one," she said, reloading rapidly.

"With two of them hurt, they'll not be back tonight."

"I better go see about Granny. She'll have heard the shots and be worried."

"Take me to her. I've got something to talk over with the both of you."

Chapter Six

With Colleen behind him, Trell guided the horse down the dark trail to where she had left the wagon and mules. It was well concealed, but would be easily tracked in the daytime. Mrs. Murphy was not with the wagon.

"She's on a ledge above the creek. I was 'fraid to leave her with the wagon, case they tracked it." Colleen slid from the rump of the horse. "I'll get her."

Trell built a small fire behind a boulder well back from the wagon. He was squatting beside it when Colleen and Mrs. Murphy came down from the ledge.

"Evenin', Mr. McCall."

"Evening, ma'am."

"I'll get a bench for ya to sit on, Granny. And a blanket. Yo're shiverin'."

When Colleen returned with the small seat, she brought the blanket and a cloth bag. From it she took a blackened coffeepot.

"A spot of coffee would go down good."

Trell watched as Colleen filled the pot at the creek and

set it on a rock she kicked into the fire. Obviously she had done so many times before. After the coffee boiled, she took the first cup to her grandmother, making sure a rag was wrapped about the tin cup so that the elderly woman wouldn't burn her hands. He decided that he liked Colleen Murphy and believed that Jenny Gray would like her, too.

"Did ya see the teacher over at Whitaker's?" Colleen sat on the ground beside her grandmother.

"Got there in time to help her put out a grass fire."

"Thought I smelled smoke on you when you rode up."

"You got a keen nose."

"Yeah. I can smell a skunk a mile away."

Trell drained his cup. "The teacher is having a pretty rough time."

"That's too bad," Colleen said sarcastically. "So are we."

"She's got her two little sisters with her," Trell continued. "Havelshell is trying to run her off. He's using different tactics than those he used on you. He's got to make her back out of her contract with the Indian Bureau back in Washington."

"What's that got to do with us?"

"I'm about to tell you. She wants you to come, stay there and help her out. The woman doesn't know how to *control* the cookstove, as she put it. I ate a meal there that would choke a horse—burnt beans and biscuits hard as bullets. They're city people and know nothing about living in this county, much less alone on a homestead."

"Why is the agent trying to run her off?"

"It's got to do with Walt Whitaker's will. If a teacher comes, stays a certain length of time and teaches a certain number of Indian children, she or he, can have the ranch.

If not, the agent can then auction off the land. You can guess who will buy it . . . cheap."

"The agent's took himself a lot of say-so, if ya was to ask me," Colleen put her tin cup back in the cloth bag.

"Whitaker was smart enough to make his arrangements with the Indian Bureau back East. Havelshell is just in charge on this end."

"What is it yo're wantin' me and Granny to do?"

"Go meet with the teacher. It could be that you'd have a place to live and she'd have someone to help her out."

"What about the agent?"

"Miss Gray said it's not his business who stays with her at the ranch. If the two of you team up, you just might put a kink in his plans to get it."

"What'a ya think, Granny?"

"We'd have a roof over our heads, child. The way Mr. McCall puts it, we'd not be takin' a handout. We'd be workin' for our keep."

"She needs you more than you need her," Trell said after a small silence.

"She's got a roof over her head. It's more than we've got."

"She won't have it long if she's left there by herself. There's not a stick of stove wood on the place."

"Any fool can go out and get firewood."

"Not if you've never done it."

"I'm not sure I'd cotton to a uppity city woman. We just might get into a hair-pullin'."

"I doubt that. She's got book learning. But she's not high-toned. Well, I've said my piece. If you want to go there, I'll take you. If you want to go to my place for a day or so until you can decide what to do, I'll take you there."

"Colleen, we could give it a try."

"Ya think we ort to, Granny?"

"It won't hurt to go see how the wind blows. Leastways it'd be better'n worryin' them killers would foller after us 'cause we know which one killed yore pa."

"Maybe they'll foller us there. Maybe we'll be bringin' our trouble down on the teacher."

"I don't think so," Trell said. "Havelshell will keep his men away from the school. He's got to make her leave on her own. He'll not harm her. If he did, the Bureau would have Federal marshals here quicker than he could spit. He wouldn't like that."

"All right. Me and Granny will go and give it a try. I ain't promisin' to stay."

"Good enough." Trell went to his horse who was cropping grass beside the creek. "I'll bed down where I'll know if anyone comes this way. I'll take you to Whitaker's in the morning."

"Ya got a blanket?" Colleen asked.

"Always carry one behind my saddle. Never know when I'll get caught away from home."

Three men rode into Sweetwater, turned down a side street and stopped behind one of the buildings. The town was closed down except for the two saloons. Light spilled out of the doorways as well as the sound of drunken laughter and clinking glasses.

"I ain't knowin' if I can climb them stairs."

"Ya better or ya'll sit there till ya bleed to death." Hartog slowly slipped from the saddle. He held himself stiffly and started up the steps to the doctor's office. "Get

Havelshell," he said to the third man, who was helping the other rider dismount.

Ignoring the order, the man continued to help his friend until they were at the top landing where the doctor, after first lighting a lamp, had opened the door.

"Get to doctorin'." Hartog was angry and hurting. "A sonofabitch shot me in the back."

The doctor helped him remove his sleeveless vest and then his shirt.

"Bullet was almost spent. You can thank that cowhide vest you're wearing for slowing it down. It's there under the skin."

"Get it out, damn you. I got thin's to do."

"Looks to me like your friend is in worse shape than you," the doctor said calmly.

"Let him wait. I was here first." Hartog glared at the rider, who lingered after easing the wounded man down in a chair. "Thought I told ya to get Havelshell."

The man looked at the doctor, then back at Hartog.

"The doc'll fix ya up and we can go over there. Don't think the agent will want to come."

"Goddamn it, Armstrong. I don't care what *he* wants. When I tell ya to do somethin', do it."

The man shrugged. "I'll tell him what ya said."

Several minutes after Armstrong knocked, Alvin Havelshell finally came to the door. When he saw who it was, he stepped out onto the porch.

"What is it?" he asked impatiently.

Armstrong gave him Hartog's message, and Havelshell responded with a string of obscenities.

"Damn brainless sonofabitch! He's not giving the orders. Does he think I want the whole town to know what happened out at Murphy's?"

"Hartog ain't hurt much. He's mad and swears he'll go back and get the one who shot him. Eastman got it pretty bad."

"Why did you ride out there again tonight? I told Hartog to give them a couple of days to pack and get out."

"He had his mind on the gal. She's somethin'. She flew at him when he shot her pa and pert near pulled him off his horse. He had to shove her off with his foot. He said nothin' got him up like a fightin' woman."

"I warned him about being mean with women. Folks here won't stand for it."

"This'n got him stirred up. She's somethin', all right. Got plenty a guts. She buried her pa, moved the old lady out, and set fire to the place. We saw it a long way off. When we got there, two of 'em started shootin'. If one of 'em was the old woman, she sure can do some fancy shootin'."

"It wasn't the old woman. Linus rode in and said Trell McCall from across the river was at Whitaker's helping the teacher put out a grass fire. When he left he was heading toward the nester's place."

"I don't reckon that bird knows which way the wind blows here."

"Somebody's going to have to wise him up."

"I'll tell ya somethin', Mr. Havelshell. When it comes to followin' orders accordin' to law, I'm your man. Hell! I'll even shave the law a mite, if need be. But when it comes to shootin' down an unarmed man, in front of his ma and his kid, I got no stomach fer it."

"You're saying that's what Hartog did?"

"I ain't sayin' nothin'. I keep my skin wrapped around my bones that way." Armstrong was a washed-out, mustached, frame-shrunk man whose rheumy eyes appeared to seek but never quite meet the pair staring back at him. "I'm thinkin' it's time I pulled foot outta this country, Mr. Havelshell."

"I'd appreciate it if you'd stay, Armstrong. I need a man with a head on his shoulders to keep an eye on Hartog."

"I only seen McCall a time or two, but he ain't goin' to push easy."

"He keeps to himself. I don't know much about him. Haven't needed to until now."

Havelshell stood on spread legs, his thumbs hooked in his belt, and rocked back and forth on his heels. Someone was waiting for him upstairs, but he knew he'd have to deal with Hartog before he could get back to her.

McCall was another matter. It could be that the reason he was at Whitaker's was that he had smelled smoke and come onto the fire. Anyone with any brains at all would have helped put it out. That fire could have spread and taken everything in its path for miles and miles. Linus said that Hartog and the others just sat there and watched. The damn fools!

It was smart to keep Linus out at the reservation store. He was a good snoop. He had also reported that Whitaker's bastard and another Shoshoni had taken out the dam Havelshell had had thrown up to divert water from the ranch buildings. He would take care of the Indian kid and he would also set Miss Gray straight about giving orders for something to be done on reservation land.

"I'll get my coat, Armstrong," Havelshell said after his

long thoughtful silence. "I'll wait for Hartog behind Doc's. I don't want him coming here."

Havelshell went back into the house and up the stairs to the bedroom. He bent over the woman on the bed, kissed her and fondled her naked breast for a long moment.

"I'll be gone for a while. Go to sleep so you'll be all rested when I get back."

"How long will you be gone?"

"Not long."

"I hope not, Alvie. Our nights together are short as it is."

"I know. Someday—" He left the promise hanging.

"Hurry back."

"With you waiting for me, how could I not hurry back." He kissed her again and left her. The minute she was out of his sight, his thoughts turned to the problems at hand.

Damn that trigger-happy Hartog. Damn that rancher, McCall, for sticking his bill in. Hartog could be taken care of; he'd just hire another killer to kill him. McCall was another story. If he insisted on dealing in, he would have to have an accident. It wouldn't do to kill him openly or to burn him out. Folks would start pushing for a Federal marshal to come in.

Havelshell left the house. Just the thought of something going wrong with his scheme made cold prickles dig into his belly.

Armstrong waited with Havelshell until Hartog came down the stairs from the surgery. A thickset man, the gunman was almost as deep from chest to spine as from shoulder to shoulder. He was not fat, and was considered tough in a fight. He was also a man who liked to play on the winning side. Yet when he felt slighted about almost anything, he would kill a man as quickly as he would step on an ant and give it as little thought.

"That bitch not only shot me, she burnt the place down! She ain't gettin' away with it."

"I've told you that we don't want trouble here that would bring in the Federal marshals. If you bother that woman and folks get wind of it, there will be hell to pay."

"Ya think I'm a fool? Folks won't get wind of it. I'll beat her ass and screw'er in the ground. When I get through with'er, she'll hightail it out of the country."

"Leave the woman alone," Havelshell said firmly.

"Ya tellin' me what to do?" Hartog shoved his face close to the agent, and Havelshell took a step back.

"I'm paying you. I have the right to tell you what to do."

"Not 'bout her, you don't."

"She didn't shoot you."

"How you know that?"

"Linus saw McCall, the rancher from across the river, headed that way about sundown. Armstrong said two were shooting. It's not likely one of them was the old woman."

"I'll kill the sonofabitch! I'll kill 'im for shootin' me and I'll kill 'im for messin' with that woman."

"Make it look like an accident. If you gun him down, there'll be talk. I've put out the word that you went to notify Murphy to get off the land and he opened fire. Isn't that what happened?"

"It's what I said. Is somebody callin' me a liar?"

"Not that I've heard. Stay away from the reservation for a week or two and let things quiet down."

"Yore sour-mouthed old woman'll be glad of it. Ain't no wonder to me ya keep her out there."

"My private life is no concern of yours."

"Yeah? Might be if I decided I'd like a go at that woman what runs the hotel."

Havelshell knew that Hartog was shrewd, cunning. But how had he found out about Melva?

"Stay away from her and keep your mouth shut about my business. Hear?" There was a limit to the agent's patience, and it showed in the angry tone of his voice.

"Don't be gettin' in a sweat. I ain't sayin' anythin' . . . yet." Hartog laughed and walked away.

Havelshell watched him go up the walk toward the saloons. The man was dangerous. He wished to hell he'd never set eyes on him.

In the ranch house north of Cheyenne the name McCall was also being raised. Silas Ashley drew deeply on the Havana cigar and questioned the man who stood across from him in his study.

"You say you found him?"

"Sure did. I'd know that bastard anywhere. Never talked to him, but I saw him plenty of times that last month. Cocky as ever. Struttin' 'round like he owned the world."

"Where is he?"

"Over west. Near a town called Sweetwater. I asked the feller in the stage station if it was McCall, just to be sure. He said it was and he either *had* a horse ranch or was workin' on one 'cross river and 'bout five miles up."

"He got a woman over there?"

"Not that I heard of."

"Did he see you?"

"If he did, he'd not connect me with this place. It's been a while."

"How did you happen to run onto him?"

"Told folks I was a horse buyer and learned a feller named McCall had horses over on the Sweetwater."

"It took you long enough," Ashley growled and drew deep on the cigar.

"It's a big country," the man said irritably; but when he saw the hard look in the rancher's eyes, he finished lamely, "Lots a places a cowboy can hide."

"If I thought she'd get over the—"

"Papa, did I hear you say . . . they'd found . . . ?" The whiny voice trailed away.

Ashley rose quickly to his feet and went to the girl in the doorway. Hope lighted her small pinched features and enormous light blue eyes. Thin yellow curls covered her head and hung over her shoulders. She was wrapped in a fancy robe trimmed with pink feathers.

"Baby! What'er you doin' up this time of night?" The big rancher towered over her protectively.

"I saw him ride in, Papa. I had to know." She leaned her head against his chest. "You said he'd bring him back. He didn't come, did he? What if he won't come? What if he don't want me?" She caught her breath as if the thought was unbearable.

"He'll come. A man'd be out of his mind not to want *you,* baby girl. Ain't that right?" The grizzled rancher looked over the girl's head at the man in the long, dirty white duster who stood beside the chair he had not been invited to take.

"It's the gospel truth, Miss Clara. Ain't a man alive what wouldn't charge hell with a bucket of water to get to ya, if he thought he had a chance in a million of havin' ya."

Hell! He'd say whatever the old bastard wanted him to say to his weasel-faced spoiled brat. She looked at him from the safe haven of her father's arms, her eyes tear-bright, but with a smile that showed her small white teeth. The man in the duster couldn't help but think that he didn't blame McCall for skipping out rather than staying and being devoured by this spiderlike woman. Still he'd find McCall . . . it was a job and the old man paid well.

"Ah . . . you're just sayin' that," the girl said and hid her face against her father's chest.

"It's the pure-dee truth, miss."

"Go on back to bed, baby. We'll get him back. You're not to worry, now. Hear?"

"Yes, Papa." Clara put her arms around her father's neck and kissed him beneath his chin, the only place she could reach. "You're the sweetest papa in the whole world."

"That's 'cause you're getting your way." His scowl was replaced by a pleased smile.

"Isn't either." She skipped to the door. "Dear, sweet, wonderful Papa! I'm so happy. Oh, I've so much to do. When will he be here?"

"It'll take at least a month."

"Oh, no!" Her face puckered in a frown.

"Honey, it's a long way over there. But I promise he'll be here as soon as possible. Go on, now. Your papa's got plans to make."

"All right. 'Night, Papa. 'Night, mister. And . . . thanks."

Ashley stood in the doorway and watched his daughter run lightly up the stairs. Clara Ashley was the only thing in the world he cared about. She was the moon and the stars as far as he was concerned. He didn't notice her whiny voice, her small pinched features or the fine, limp hair. To him she was a golden goddess; and from the day she was born, he had spoiled her shamelessly.

He waited until he heard the door to her room close before he shut the study door and went to his desk. Opening a lower drawer with a key he took from his pocket, he lifted out a stack of bills and placed half of them on the desk. He didn't speak until the drawer was locked again and the key in his pocket.

"Find that son of a bitch and kill him." He looked with hard flat eyes at the man standing before him and pushed the stack of money across the desk. "Bring his body back. I don't care if it's rotten when you get it here. Bring it, so she can see it and bury it. The other half of the money will be yours."

The man moved forward and reached for the bills.

"What'll you tell Miss Clara?"

"I'll think of somethin'. When she sees him dead, she'll get over him. The dirty, lyin' bastard!" Ashley growled angrily. "He made calf eyes at her, let her think he was courtin' her, then took off. He broke her heart is what he done. He'll pay for it. No man treats my baby that way and lives to tell it."

At the door, the man turned and looked at the gray-haired rancher. He understood the vanity of men like Silas Ashley. A deep fire of hatred for anything or anybody who slighted him or his smoldered in him until he was avenged. That McCall did not want his spoiled daughter Ashley took as a personal affront, enough reason to want him dead.

The hired gunman left the ranch house. Why Ashley wanted McCall dead mattered not to him.

Killing was his business.

Chapter Seven

Jenny came from the bedroom at the same time a figure appeared in the kitchen door. Her heart stopped with fright until she realized it was Whit. Without a word he ran to the cookstove, grabbed the poker and slammed shut the vents in the firebox. He reached to turn the damper handle and uttered what Jenny assumed to be an Indian obscenity.

"You crazy woman! You burn down house!"

"What did I do wrong?"

"You leave vents all way open." He banged on the iron door of the firebox. "Damper all way open. Wind come in door"—he gestured toward the doorway—"and sparks go up chimney to roof. Start fire."

"Oh, my goodness! I thought I had done exactly as Cass told me."

Whit snorted at the mention of her sister. "What she know."

"Apparently more than I do. Whit," she said when the boy moved toward the door. "Stay a while."

"I stay. Agent's weasel too lazy to come so early."

He looked around the room, and an expression of longing came over his usually stoical features as if he were remembering times he had been here with his father.

"Were you allowed to come here when your father was alive?"

"No Havelshell. I live here. After father die I no can come."

"Your father knew that they would not let you keep the ranch. He made provisions in his will for you to get an education so that you can fight for your rights and those of your people. I wish I had known him."

"He had books. Havelshell take them."

"Maybe someday we can get them back. Whit, what do you know about the people named Murphy who lived over on the edge of Stoney Creek?"

"Three *Wasicun* at store have bad talk, then go kill Murphy. McCall help woman bury him. McCall and woman burn house last night and shoot at *Wasicun* when they come."

"How do you know all this?"

"I keep eyes and ears open."

"What kind of people are the Murphys?"

He frowned. "Old woman and young woman."

"I know that, but are they"—she strove to find the right word—"clean?"

"Why you want to know that?"

"Mr. McCall is bringing them here today to help me."

"That is good. Old lady cook and not burn house down. Young lady chop wood, hunt, and cut grass for horses. You teach then?"

"After I clean out the schoolhouse. When I'm ready will

you take me to your chief so that I can tell him about the school?"

"His tongue not good with English."

"You could translate," she argued.

"He know about school, think it foolish."

"I'm sorry to hear it. Will he let the children come?"

"No honored son will come. Only those who do not belong to someone important and those who do not have parents to care for will come."

"I don't understand that at all."

"There is much you do not understand. I have not had my dream. I am not a man. I am not needed and will come."

"You said you took care of your father's second wife."

"She will go be second wife to brave and help his young wife. She no longer need me."

"I need you," Jenny declared quickly. "Whit, if you no longer have a home with your father's second wife, where will you live?"

"With my people. They will not turn me out. I go now."

"You could stay in the schoolhouse. It's on the reservation . . . and your father built it . . . mainly for you."

Whit turned. "He do it for all Shoshoni."

"I think he loved you . . . very much."

"Then why he die . . . and leave me?"

Jenny was taken aback, not only by the words, but by the anguish in the boy's voice. She had never seen him anything but sullen and angry. The words made him seem younger and more vulnerable. From the doorway she watched him run toward the school and disappear behind the dense hedge of mountain lilac.

* * *

"Jenny! Jenny! Somebody comin'."

Beatrice's shout came from the doorway. The child had been disturbed about the possibility of someone coming to stay with them. *Will they be nice? Will they hit me?* The questions her little sister asked tore at Jenny's heart.

In the smaller of the two sleeping rooms, Jenny looked around to be sure she had transferred all her possessions to the room she would share with the girls. Of course she wasn't sure the Murphys would come, or if they would stay, or if she would want them to stay. After the near disaster this morning, she realized more than before that she had to have help, and that would mean sharing the cabin with strangers.

Jenny and the two girls stood in the yard and watched the wagon and the rider approach. Trellis McCall came on ahead, stopped and dismounted beside the corral.

"Morning." Trell put his fingers to his hat brim.

"Good morning."

"Hello, girls."

"We weren't sure if you'd be back," Cassandra said with her usual frankness. "Jenny's been on edge. She almost burned the house down this morning. Whit came to our rescue this time."

"Sparks going up the chimney doesn't necessarily mean the house would burn," Jenny countered.

Her eyes shifted to the two women on the wagon seat. The older one wore a sunbonnet with a tunnel-like brim that shaded her face. A dark shawl covered her shoulders. The only way Jenny could tell that the one driving the team was a woman was because her long black curly hair swirled about her head in the light breeze. She was dressed in men's overalls and a faded checked shirt.

Trell walked out and held the cheek-strap on the harness to still the team when the wagon stopped. The driver wrapped the reins around the brake handle and jumped to the ground. Without as much as a glance toward those who waited, she turned her back and guided her grandmother's feet as the older woman backed off the wagon. When both women stood on the ground, they faced Jenny and the girls who waited beside Trell.

Trell made the introductions, adding, "These young ladies are Cassandra and Beatrice."

"How do, ma'am?"

"How do you do?" Jenny started to hold out her hand, then pulled it back and laughed nervously. "I don't usually wear gloves. I smeared salve on my palms and the gloves are . . . sort of a bandage."

Colleen said not a word.

"Come in. I'll make tea. Cassandra,—" Jenny smiled down at her little sister—"made cookies."

"They ain't good." Beatrice blurted the information while looking up at Trell.

"Well, what do you expect without eggs or butter or milk." Cassandra's tone was defensive. "They're strips of piecrust with sugar and cinnamon. I called them cookies so Beatrice would eat them."

"But they ain't good!" Beatrice insisted.

"Honey, don't make a fuss about it now. Let's go have tea."

"Wait a minute." Colleen put her hand on her grandmother's arm when the older woman made to follow Jenny into the house. "We don't need *tea* to decide if we're goin' to stay."

"You're absolutely right." Jenny smiled, although she was afraid her face would crack from the blistering it had taken the day before. "Whether you go or stay, a cup of tea would be refreshing; and we would be more comfortable sitting down while we talk about it."

Trell had thought that Colleen would have made some effort to make herself presentable. Instead, the overalls she wore appeared to be even larger and more worn than the ones she had on the day before. He had heard Granny Murphy chide her gently. Her whispered reply had not reached him because they had moved away.

"Let's water the horses, girls." Trell reached for Beatrice's hand. "You coming, Cass?"

The girl tilted her serious little face to look up at him.

"'Fraid not, Trell. You'll have to make do with Beatrice. This is a very important interview, and I've got to be sure Virginia doesn't put her foot in her mouth and mess things up."

"I'll help, Mr. McCall."

"All right, pretty little girl." Trell swung the child up in his arms and set her on the wagon seat. "We'll drive the team to the pond."

At the door Jenny stepped aside so that her guest could enter. After they were seated at the table, she poured tea in the thick mugs she had found in the cupboard.

"I'm sorry to hear about Mr. Murphy," she said quietly. "I know what it means to lose a loved one."

"Was yore pa gunned down right before your eyes by a cold-eyed, no-good warthog?" There was hurt and bitterness in Colleen's voice.

"No. Both of my parents were sick for a while."

"Then ya . . . don't know."

"You're right again. It must have been terrible."

"I've never seen a warthog," Cassandra said quietly. "Someday will you tell me about them?"

Colleen's eyes flashed to the small girl, then back to Jenny.

"McCall said you needed someone to stay here, keep the house, tend to the younguns while you teach the Indian kids."

"You don't have to tend me, Colleen," Cassandra said. "I'm old enough to tend myself. Beatrice is four and, well, she needs tending."

Both women looked at the youngster, who sat with her elbows on the table. Jenny started to correct her sister for calling Miss Murphy by her first name but changed her mind. If they stayed, they might as well get used to Cass.

Jenny's eyes moved over Colleen and away. She didn't want to make her uncomfortable. Trell had said that she wasn't *ugly*. She was really very pretty. Her flawless skin, tanned by the sun, would not be considered pretty back East where milk white skin was what most women desired, but the soft tan complemented her light blue eyes and dark lashes. Her hair, black as Whit's, was thick and curly and hung down her back without benefit of clasp or ribbon.

"I think you should know something about my situation here. It will help you decide whether or not to accept my offer."

"Don't tell them too much, Virginia. They might leave and, frankly, I don't think my stomach can endure another one of your meals."

Her complaint brought a small smile to Colleen's lips, but she wiped it from her face quickly as if it were disrespectful so soon after her father's death.

Jenny spoke of learning of Walt Whitaker's will and that being a teacher, she decided to come here. She told them she was unaware that Stoney Creek Ranch was so isolated and that so much, other than teaching, would be required.

"McCall said the agent was tryin' to run ya off. Why'er ya stayin'?" Colleen's clear eyes looked directly into Jenny's.

"Because I want something for myself and my sisters that I have earned with my own two hands."

"And mine," Cassandra added and rolled her eyes toward the ceiling.

"And yours." Jenny smiled proudly down at her sister. "Thank goodness Cassandra soaked up information back home about how to unhitch the team or they would have been standing there yet."

"What you're sayin' is that you want me'n Granny to stay here and work for eats and a roof over our heads. The agent that sent the men out to kill Pa won't want us here."

"I was employed by the Bureau of Indian Affairs in Washington. The agent has nothing to say about who stays with me here on the ranch. As soon as I can get a letter to the Bureau, he will have less say about anything here. The man is a crook!"

"Seems not many folks 'round here know that." At Jenny's forthrightness, Colleen's resistance softened a bit. "Granny was the best cook in the county back in Missouri when she had the fixin's to work with. What did ya have in mind for me to do?"

"Help me do whatever has to be done. Mr. McCall said he would bring a rope and pulley and fix the well, so that'll be taken care of. I've got the schoolhouse to clean out and get ready for classes. We need a cow and chickens, and . . .

I suppose it's too late to put in a garden. There's a root cellar out there that I'm afraid to go into—"

"Suppose ya get tired of me and Granny. Would ya send us off in the dead of winter?"

"Suppose you get tired of us. Would you pull out, desert us, leave us here alone without a hope of finding someone else to stay with us?"

Cassandra made a face, waving her hand in front of it like a fan.

"You're being dramatic, Virginia. If you say something that makes them leave, I'll never forgive you." She moved around the table to be closer to Mrs. Murphy. "I always wanted a granny. If you stay, can I call you Granny like Colleen does?"

"Of course, child." Granny's work-worn hand cupped Cassandra's cheek, and a pleased smile brightened her weathered face.

"I can offer you a small salary in addition to your room and board." Jenny continued the conversation as if her sister hadn't spoken.

"We're not fancy folk, ma'am," Mrs. Murphy put her arm around Cassandra who leaned against her knee. "But we always had our own place. We ain't never lived in the house with other folks."

"I'll tell ya right up front, I won't have my granny bossed around and treated like a slave." Colleen's eyes were hard as they looked into Jenny's.

"She'll never be treated as such. We will share the work. Cass and Beatrice will do what they can. You can have one room, the girls and I the other. Mr. McCall said he would come and build in a bunk—"

"Colleen, do you like Trell?" Cassandra asked from

close beside Granny Murphy. "His name is Trellis, but he said that I could call him Trell."

"Honey, must you ask such personal questions?" Jenny's voice was calm, but her face showed her exasperation with her sister.

"Why not? I asked him if she was pretty, and he said she wasn't ugly. I couldn't tell if he was sweet on her or not. I want to know if she's sweet on him."

Jenny looked quickly at Colleen to see if she was offended. She wasn't smiling, but there was an amused gleam in her eyes.

"Ya think I'm goin' to take him away from ya?"

"I'm too young for Trell. If I was older I'd set my cap for him."

"Ya'd probably land him, too."

"I don't know about that. Men don't like me much."

"They will when yo're older."

Cassandra shrugged. "I can wait. Well . . . are you setting your cap for him?"

"I've not give it any thought."

"If you decide to, I can help you spruce up. I'm not sure a man like Trell would go for a woman in overalls."

"Cassandra! Enough of that talk!" Jenny's face was flushed with embarrassment. "At times you try my patience."

"Don't fault her, ma'am." Colleen pushed back her chair and stood. Jenny noticed that her eyes changed easily; warm one second, cold as a blizzard the next. "I like folks that come right out and say what they think. Right now I'm thinkin' we'll stay a while. But, mind you, me and Granny can go on down the road if we start to get in each other's hair."

Jenny got to her feet. "I accept your terms. And, please don't call me ma'am. Call me Virginia or Jenny, whichever you prefer."

"We got to tend the mules and find a place out of the weather to put the things in our wagon." Colleen went to the door and out into the yard.

The next thing Jenny heard was the ring of an axe. Trell, hatless, sleeves rolled up, was working at the woodpile. He had pulled a deadfall up using the Murphys' mules and was chopping off branches to cut into lengths for the stove or fireplace. Beatrice sat a safe distance away watching something on the ground.

"Jenny! Cass! Looky what Trell finded for me." She scooped something up, placed it in the palm of her hand. "It's a baby frog!"

"Oh! Ugh!" Cassandra, curious at first, turned away in disgust.

Jenny bent over the small extended hand and with a gentle finger stroked the little creature's head.

"Ah, it's a baby! It's scared, honey. Its little heart is beating fast. You must let it go soon so it can find its mama."

Trell had stopped chopping the branches and watched Jenny come toward him. How gracefully her body moved under the soft linsey dress! A row of pearl buttons from neck to waist accented her high, firm breasts. Her smile, her nearness brought a funny tightening to his chest. Trell took a shallow breath and hoped to God she didn't know the effect her magnificent eyes had on him.

"They're going to stay. Thank you, Trell. Oh, thank you!"

Trell nodded and cursed himself for being so tongue-tied when he was near the woman. He sank the blade of the axe into the chopping block.

"I sharpened the blade on Murphy's grindstone. It's best to keep it up off the ground."

He walked beside Jenny to the wagon, where Colleen was handing down bundles to her grandmother.

"Is the room by the shed a good place for the things they don't want to take into the house?" Jenny asked.

"It's the only place." Trell propped open the door, and he and Colleen carried the heavy stove inside.

Cassandra was more than willing to help Granny Murphy. She danced alongside her, chattering, as they made trips from the wagon to the house.

The wagon was almost empty when Jenny's eye caught movement. A buggy and a rider were approaching. She began to get a sinking feeling in the pit of her stomach. Colleen took her rifle out from under the wagon seat and leaned it against the wheel.

"Is it Mr. Havelshell?" Jenny asked Trell.

"I can't tell from this distance." He squinted and stared. "But I don't think so—"

The buggy, pulled by a handsome high-stepping dapple gray came quickly into the yard. The escort riders stayed a distance away. After winding the reins about the brake handle, a pudgy little man with silvery white hair stepped down. Jenny went forward to greet him.

"Good morning."

"Morning, my dear. I'm the Reverend Henry Longfellow."

"How do you do? Virginia Gray."

"And before you ask, yes, I am distantly related to the poet Henry W. Longfellow."

"You must be very proud of your famous ancestor."

"I am. Although it's an honor to carry his name, at times

it becomes a burden. Some folk expect me to quote long narratives from his *Evangeline* or *The Song of Hiawatha*." When the little man laughed, his stomach jiggled. His eyes were a bright blue and merry, his clean-shaven cheeks rosy. "Frankly I can't remember but a verse or two of each."

Jenny introduced him to the others and then invited him into the house.

"Some other time, my dear. I'm expected at the agency. I could not come this close and not stop by to welcome you to our community and to invite you to attend church. We are exceedingly proud of our church in Sweetwater."

"Thank you for the invitation."

The preacher looked at Colleen and Mrs. Murphy. "The invitation includes you ladies. I'm sure you understood that. Are you staying on here, Mr. McCall?"

"No. My place is across the river, but I plan to come back from time to time."

"I can't blame you. Two lovely ladies on one ranch. Ah . . . to be young again." The Reverend Longfellow climbed back into the buggy. "I must go. It was nice meeting you . . . all of you. Come to church. It's good for the soul."

The escort rider fell in behind the buggy as it left the ranch house.

"At least there's one friendly person in Sweetwater," Jenny remarked.

"Granny and I are cooking dinner," Cassandra announced. "Are you staying, Trell?"

"You betcha. You couldn't pull me away with a team of mules."

Trell grinned; and when he did, Jenny realized that not only was he one of the nicest men she'd ever met, but that he really was quite handsome.

Since he had met Jenny Gray, she had not been far from Trell's mind. He admitted that he was rather pleased with himself for bringing the women together. It had worked out better and more quickly than he thought it would. After dinner of grouse and dumplings, cooked by Granny Murphy, (the grouse having been caught early that morning by Colleen), the women seemed to be more comfortable with one another.

Jenny, very much a lady in her dress and clean apron, her hair pinned to the top of her head, took Colleen, in her pa's overalls, hair hanging down her back, over to show her the destruction in the schoolroom. Colleen had been quiet, almost suspicious, at first. Trell could almost read her thoughts. *Why is she doing this—giving us a place to stay, feeding us? How can we repay?* Then she must have realized that a city woman like Jenny, alone on a ranch, was like a lamb in a pen with a coyote.

What worried Trell was the gunmen who worked for Havelshell. He was reasonably sure the agent would see that they didn't openly terrorize Jenny and the girls. He wouldn't allow it for fear of the reaction of the Indian Bureau. However, this would not prevent his arranging a very clever accident that would rid him of the teacher. Havelshell valued his job. Trell suspected that he had more at stake and that it was tied to his job as agent.

Colleen was another matter.

Trell felt that as long as he was responsible for Colleen and her grandmother's being here, it was only fair that he alert Jenny to the possible danger. He got his chance in the middle of the afternoon when she came to the woods that edged the homestead where he was tying a chain around a deadfall in preparation for dragging it to the woodpile.

"Mr. McCall, may I ask you something?"

"Only if you call me Trell." He straightened up and grinned at her. "Folks out here don't pay much mind to what's proper."

She laughed at that, her eyes sparkling like a fresh green meadow covered with morning dew. He was so fascinated that he couldn't look away.

"Then you must call me Jenny."

Jenny! Jenny! I've been doing that in my mind since the day I saw you in Sweetwater.

"Trell, do you know if the agent has the authority to whip a boy for stepping off the reservation?"

"I'm not familiar with *all* the duties of an agent, but it doesn't sound likely to me that he'd have that power."

"Whit's in danger of suffering Havelshell's wrath for taking out the dam his men had put in to divert the water from the ranch buildings. I'm writing a letter to the Indian Bureau in Washington; but I'm afraid that if I post it in Sweetwater, Mr. Havelshell will intercept it."

"I'll post it for you in Forest City."

"Will you?" Her shoulders relaxed in relief. "Thank you."

"And I'll pick up your mail there if you want me to. Now, there's something I want to tell you. Havelshell's gunman may come after Colleen. He'll try and get her away from the homestead and eliminate her as a witness to Murphy's killing—" His voice trailed. Jenny glanced at him and saw that he was staring at something beyond her. "Stand still, Jenny," he warned in a low voice. "Stand very still."

Jenny froze in place, moving nothing but her eyes. She watched Trell's hand slide down to the scabbard that held his knife. He grasped the handle and brought it up slowly. Behind her she heard the rustle of dead leaves, then in a lightning move, Trell sent the knife flying past her. She gasped as he shoved her out of the way and grabbed a thick stake he'd been using on the deadfall.

Jenny turned to see a large snake pinned to the ground by the knife. Its flat head and six inches of its body reared and swayed. Trell struck quickly, pinned the head to the ground with the club, pulled out his knife and cut the head from the body. The serpent in its dying throes tried to wrap itself about Trell's arm. Jenny shuddered and turned away.

After Trell had picked up the snake by the tail and thrown it into the bushes, he came to Jenny and put his hands on her shoulders. She was trembling.

"Are you all right?"

To his surprise she turned and wrapped her arms about his waist.

"Oh, oh, oh—"

"It might have crawled on off. I didn't want to chance it." He lied to comfort her. The snake had been coiling to strike.

Jenny was a tall woman. Her head lay nicely on his shoulder and her face fitted into the curve of his neck. Her body, from shoulders to knees fitted tightly to his. Suddenly she realized that she was holding on to him and that his arms were locked about her. Although she had no memory of rushing into his embrace, she had an overwhelming sense of belonging there. She felt him in every nerve, every bone.

Trell felt that heaven had been handed to him. His body heated and his blood surged. Here in his arms was the woman of his dreams. He closed his eyes and let his lips caress the wisps of her hair that blew across his face. *Just a little longer! A little more to remember—*

"Are you all right . . . now?" His breath was warm on her forehead.

Jenny moved back and looked at him. Her auburn hair framed her white face. Her eyes were large and bleak.

"Will I ever get used to . . . this country?" She gripped his upper arms.

"Of course, you will. You've done fine so far."

"I don't know, Trell. I may have bitten off more than I can chew."

"You're not thinking about giving up?" His gut tightened.

"No. I can't give up. I just wish I were as strong as Colleen."

"You're stronger in some ways than she is. You'll do fine." He smiled down at her, and both of them were suddenly embarrassed. He dropped his arms from around her and stepped back.

"Trell? You *will* come back?"

"You can count on it. You're not alone here, Jenny," he said, his promise steadier than his voice.

Chapter Eight

"Sure ya can handle this team?"

Colleen stood beside the wagon. She had hitched the two big sorrels to the wagon so that Jenny could ride to the reservation store. Whit was going along to show her the way.

"I'm sure I can, although I've never driven a team. Whit will be nearby should I get in trouble."

"Ya ort to take my six-gun. That little peashooter ya got ain't worth doodle-dee-squat."

Jenny laughed. "Not against a grizzly. Uncle Noah told me where to aim to cripple a man as effectively as if I shot him with a cannon."

"What if ya can't get a line on their dicky-doo?"

"Well . . . I'll think of something. Oh, Colleen, I'm so glad you and Granny are here. I feel like I've known you forever."

"Reckon that store's got dress goods?"

"Whit says they don't have much the Indians can trade their pelts for except knives and blankets. Are you want-ing—"

"—Not for me," Colleen was quick to reply. "For Granny."

The girls and the Murphys stood in the yard and waved as Jenny put the team in motion and crossed over onto the reservation where Whit waited. She had dressed to intimidate if it became necessary. She chose to wear a dark green suit-dress with a white blouse, ruffled to her chin, and a matching brimmed hat with a dark red plume.

Cassandra had approved when she saw her. "Playing the princess and the peasant? Good thinking, Virginia."

Not much could be put over on her sister. Jenny was sure that when she was gone, Cassandra would explain to the Murphys that by dressing in her finest, she would be viewed as someone of importance and would likely be treated as such.

The wagon track was a narrow, deeply rutted swath cut through the dense, dark, cool forest. It was quiet and eerie. At intervals there were breaks in the interlapping branches overhead that allowed scattered patches of sunlight to shine through. Jenny would have been frightened if not for the presence of Whit on his pony. The team behaved beautifully. Whether it was due to Whit riding ahead or her hands on the reins, Jenny was not sure, but her confidence grew because of it.

When Whit turned and held up his hand, Jenny pulled up on the reins to stop the team.

"I leave you. Store not far."

"I was hoping you would go with me."

"I come, but not with you." He gigged his horse and trotted back down the trail before she could reply.

The agency headquarters was a group of unpainted plank buildings set in a clearing. A large heavy-pole corral held fifty or more head of cattle. A group of Indians on ponies waited outside the corral. At a hitching rail in front of the main building, a saddled horse stood patiently, head down, only occasionally stamping its feet to rid its legs of pesky flies.

A man came out and leaned against a porch post to watch Jenny approach. As she neared, she recognized the boy, Linus, who had been at the Stoney Creek ranch house the day she and the girls arrived. She pulled the team to a halt in front of the store and backed down over the wheel to the ground. Linus stood chewing on a stick, not offering to assist, *as a man would do if he had an ounce of manners.*

Jenny hooked a lead rope to the harness as Colleen had showed her how to do and tied the end to the hitching rail. Completely ignoring Linus, she tilted her nose and walked past him into the agency store. The interior was smaller than she had anticipated—cramped, dark and terribly dirty. Even at a glance, Jenny could tell that the sparse merchandise on the shelves was of poor quality.

"What'a ya want?" Linus had followed her into the store.

"Are you in charge?" Jenny gave him a haughty stare.

"Nah."

"Get the person in charge, please." She spoke crisply, turned her back and began to remove her gloves.

A door opened at the back of the room. A short, immensely obese woman waddled in. A loose calico garment hung from her shoulders to the tops of beaded moccasins. Her light hair was pulled back into a knot at the back of her head. She didn't speak, so Jenny did.

"Hello. I'm Virginia Gray, the teacher at the school."

"I know who you are." The small mouth above the triple chins seemed scarcely to move when she spoke.

"And you are—?"

"Mrs. Havelshell."

"How do you do? I'd like a word with Mr. Havelshell."

"He's in Sweetwater." Linus said from behind her.

Jenny gave him an icy stare. "I was not speaking to you."

"La . . . dee . . . dah!" He grinned, showing wide-spaced teeth that appeared to be green near the gums.

Mrs. Havelshell wedged herself behind the counter as if seeking protection. She made no move to offer assistance or extend any courtesy. She merely watched as Jenny looked around the store.

When she returned to the counter, she opened her draw-string purse and took out the list prepared by Cassandra and Granny Murphy.

"This is what I need." She handed the paper to Mrs. Havelshell, who, without a word, held it out to Linus. The boy took the paper and scowled.

"Ya know I can't read this kinda writin'."

"What kind of writing do you read?" Jenny asked sweetly. "Shall I print it on a slate for you?"

"Just say what ya want."

"So you can't read. The school will be open in a few weeks. Come and I will teach you."

"I ain't sunk so low I'd go to school with a bunch of red-ass Indians!" he bellowed.

Jenny raised her brows. "No? Well. Remain ignorant; it's your choice." She turned and began to read her order to Mrs. Havelshell. "I would like a jug of vinegar, a can of baking powder and one of soda. Oh, by the way, do you know where I can purchase a milch cow?"

"No."

"Chickens? I'd like a dozen laying hens."

"No." The fat lady set two cans on the counter. "Linus, get the vinegar."

"While you're at it, Linus," Jenny said in a commanding tone. "Put a barrel of lamp oil in my wagon."

"A barrel?"

"You heard me. Are you deaf as well as dirty?"

"High-toned bitch—" he muttered as he stomped out.

Jenny continued reading her list, aware that many of the items on it were probably not in the store. When she came to any such item, Mrs. Havelshell would shake her head.

As she watched the woman waddle from one end of the small store to the other, Jenny had a hard time imagining her married to the well-dressed Indian agent she had met in Sweetwater.

Mrs. Havelshell's neck was enlarged by rolls of fat. She had been pretty . . . once. Now her cornflower eyes were made small by her fat cheeks. Jenny could not help but feel a twinge of compassion for the woman and tried to lighten the mood and make pleasant conversation.

"My, what lovely beadwork on your moccasins—"

"What else you want?"

"Well. Flour and coffee."

"Linus," she called to the boy on the porch. "Get her a sack of flour and one of coffee."

Jenny felt more than saw someone come into the store. She turned expecting to see Linus, but it was Whit with an armful of animal skins. He came to the counter.

"Trade."

"I'm not trading today."

"Today is trade day."

"I said I wasn't trading."

"What beautiful skins," Jenny exclaimed. "What are they?"

"They're only rabbit," Mrs. Havelshell said with disgust in her voice.

"Just the thing for warm hats and mittens and . . . oh, for trim on the girls' coats. What were you wishing to trade for?"

"Two blankets."

"They certainly should be worth that."

"One blanket." Mrs. Havelshell's mouth snapped shut. She would not show weakness in front of this woman.

"Two blankets," Whit insisted.

"One blanket. Take it or leave it."

"I would like to buy two blankets," Jenny said firmly. "I want these skins. I'll trade for them if you won't."

Mrs. Havelshell turned her back. "Suit yourself."

"Pick out your blankets," Jenny said to Whit. Then to the woman, "Tally up my bill. That's all I need today."

After a few minutes, Mrs. Havelshell muttered, "Twenty-five dollars."

Jenny was astounded, but refused to let her expression change on hearing the outrageous price for the goods.

"Are you sure you included everything? The blankets? The lamp oil?" she asked sarcastically, then realized her sarcasm had not registered with the woman.

"Twenty-five dollars."

"What are ya doin' in here, ya goddam little red-ass bastard?" Linus demanded as he came in. "Get the hell out!"

In two quick strides he reached Whit and kicked him in the backside.

Jenny's reason was suddenly blotted out by a heavy cloud of rage.

"Stop that! You stupid . . . insensible jackass." She reached Linus in time to prevent another kick.

"Tend to yore own business," Linus snarled.

"And you tend to yours. You've no authority to order anyone out of this place."

"What'a ya know about it?"

"I know you're an overgrown, uncouth, unwashed bully."

"Ya'd better watch who yo're talkin' to."

"I'll tell you again. Keep your hands off that boy."

"What'll ya do if I don't?" he jeered and pulled his fist back as if to hit her.

"What I told you I'd do the first time I saw you." Jenny's hand came out of her pocket. She pressed the barrel of the little derringer tightly against the soft flesh of his groin. "I can ruin you from ten feet away with this little thing. From this close it would kill you."

"He . . . ain't supposed to be here." Linus tried to back away. Jenny followed.

"Why not? This is the Indian store. He's an Indian. I'd say he has more rights here than you do."

"Ya ain't knowin' what yo're up agin."

"I know very well. Take your blankets and go," she said to Whit.

After the boy was gone, Jenny returned the derringer to her pocket.

"Mrs. Havelshell, does Mr. Havelshell know about the

ignorant, lowlife bullies hanging round the reservation store?"

For an answer the woman pushed the flour sack filled with Jenny's purchases across the counter. It was a gesture of dismissal, but Jenny was determined to leave when *she* was ready to go. She took out a lacy handkerchief and wiped her brow.

"May I have a drink of cool water before I go?"

At first Jenny thought the woman would refuse, then she opened the door to the living quarters.

"Moonrock!" she called.

Almost instantly a young Indian girl appeared. She was neatly dressed in calico, and a clean white apron was tied about her waist. Jenny guessed her to be near Whit's age.

"Get the woman a drink." Mrs. Havelshell issued the order kindly.

The girl disappeared from the doorway, giving Jenny a view of a heavy oak table surrounded by chairs, a sideboard containing lovely blue china and what appeared to be an expensive tapestry rug on the floor. The girl was back almost instantly, carrying a dipper of water. She approached Jenny shyly. She was quite pretty with large dark eyes and even features.

"Thank you." Jenny drank the water and handed the cup back to the girl. "The school will be opening soon. I hope you will come."

"She ain't comin' to yore stinkin' school no more'n I am," Linus muttered from a dark corner of the store.

"It was a pleasure meeting you, Mrs. Havelshell." Jenny smiled sweetly while putting on her gloves. "Tell your boy he can carry my purchases to the wagon." She picked up the bundle of furs and walked unhurriedly to the door.

She sat on the wagon seat for a moment or two, listening to the sound of Linus's angry voice and the firm tone of Mrs. Havelshell's. Finally the boy came charging out the door, sprang off the porch and dumped the flour sack of purchases in the back of the wagon.

"Ya'd better watch out, *teacher*," he said menacingly, and fled back to the porch.

"Thank you," Jenny called, and slapped the reins against the backs of the team.

As she made a circle to go back through the forest to the school, she saw that the Indians still sat on their ponies outside the corral where the cattle were penned. Why were they just sitting there? She would have to ask Whit. She glanced over her shoulder to see Linus leaning against a post on the porch, as he had been doing when she arrived. She had made an enemy.

Well, so that's the Agency headquarters. It certainly was not what she had been told an Agency headquarters would be. It was supposed to be there to serve the Indians on the reservation and see to their welfare. She wondered if Whit, being a very smart boy, had deliberately come to the store to trade his pelts while she was there. Was it his way of letting her see how the Indians were treated? She would have some very important information to add to the report she was compiling to send to the Bureau back East.

Trell had promised to come back in a few days to build the bunk and to pick up her letters to mail. She had lived over and over the short time she had been in his arms. His shirt had been wet with sweat, his dark hair damp and unruly, and his eyes looked into hers with a quiet, seriousness that made her pulse quicken. His eyes, when *not* looking at her, were searching the edge of the forest, ever watchful.

Jenny had not considered a man in a romantic way for a long time, but when she thought about the rugged rancher, her heart thumped alarmingly. She was being foolish, she admonished herself. He had been kind and helpful. *Nothing more.* Trell McCall would not be attracted to a woman like her who didn't know one end of a cow from the other. He'd want a helpmate. *A woman like Colleen Murphy.*

Unrest settled around the region of Jenny's heart.

All the way back to the ranch house she expected to see Whit come out of the trees on his pony. He didn't appear, but she felt that he was nearby. The trail was flat and wound between giant oak and ash trees with short sweeps of meadow in between. At one time Jenny thrilled to see, high above, two hawks circling in amorous pursuit of each other. In the forest squirrels scampered in the underbrush and raced for a tree trunk to scold the intruder from their lofty perch.

This was real. This was basic. This was how the world was supposed to be, Jenny mused. No streets paved with brick, no tall buildings or fast rail cars, no people clambering over each other to reach wealth and position. Well, perhaps *some* of the people here might be just as power-hungry . . .

The team, knowing they were headed back home, wanted to go faster than Jenny found comfortable. By the time she drove into the yard, her arms ached from gripping the reins. The pain was forgotten, however, when she saw the girls and Colleen talking to a small ragged-looking man holding the reins of a long-eared mule.

"Jenny! Jenny! Jenny's home!" With loose blond hair streaming out behind her, Beatrice came running toward the wagon.

Colleen darted after the child and scooped her up with one arm before she could reach the team.

"Ya'll scare the daylights outta them horses, ya little scamp." She turned the child, and Beatrice wrapped her arms about Colleen's neck, showing how completely she had accepted the dark-haired girl into the family.

When Jenny had her feet on the ground, the child reached for her. Jenny held her for a moment and kissed her cheek.

"We got company," Beatrice said when Jenny set her on her feet.

"I see we have."

"Jenny," Cassandra called. "Come meet Mr. Reginald Klein. He's a real bona fide mountain man."

"Bona what, gal? I ain't no bona nothin'. Howdy, ma'am. This youngun can spout more highfalutin words than a preacher."

"She's a talker." Jenny held out her hand. "Virginia Gray. Glad to meet you, Mr. Klein."

"Likewise. Stopped and et with the Murphys a few times. Shore sorry 'bout what happened to Miles. 'Tis a shame, that's what 'tis."

"It was a terrible thing. The men who did it should be brought to justice."

"Ma'am, there ain't no justice out here less'n ya take the bull by the horns and make it yoreself."

"Did you fix the well?" Jenny asked, seeing a crosspiece over the well with a rope dangling over it.

"Colleen and Ike did it. They wouldn't let me watch." Beatrice was holding Colleen's hand.

"'Cause we was 'fraid ya'd fall in, sugar pie."

"I know it. I'm not mad."

Colleen smiled down at the child, then spoke to Jenny.

"It'll do till Trell comes with a pulley. I had the rope in the wagon and Ike helped me put up the crossbar."

"How did you make out at the store?" Cassandra asked. "Ike says they don't have much."

"Ike? Who is Ike?"

"Mr. Klein. He said his name was Reginald, but folks call him Ike."

Jenny smiled at the little man with shoulder-length gray-streaked hair, bushy brows and chin whiskers. His dark eyes gleamed with mischief.

"Yo're wantin' to know why I'm called Ike. Well, it's like this—I come to this country in '52. Green as grass, I was. Met up with a couple fellers what had been to the gold fields. Fellers saved my hide more'n once. They knowed all the verses to 'Sweet Betsy from Ike,' and learned 'em to me. I'd never heard me no story like it and ain't to this day. I got to singin' that tune. Sung it in the mornin'. Sung it at night. Sung it till them fellers got tired a hearin' 'Sweet Betsy from Ike.' Ever time I'd start they'd holler here comes Ike. The name stuck. I been Ike ever since."

Cassandra's and Jenny's eyes caught in understanding.

"Mr. Klein, the title of the song is 'Sweet Betsy from PIKE,'" Cassandra said kindly.

"I know, youngun. It's what I said, 'Sweet Betsy from Ike.'"

"It's a wonderful story," Jenny cut in before her sister pursued the matter further.

"Why don't ya go on in and get outta that corset. It must be killin' ya. Ma and Cass'll unload the wagon," Colleen said.

Jenny looked at her sister to see if she was going to

protest the shortening of her name, but Cassandra had gone to the wagon with Colleen and was being lifted up into the wagonbed. Jenny shook her head. They had all changed since coming here. And most of it was for the good. She had not even been embarrassed when Colleen mentioned her corset in front of Mr. Klein . . . or Ike . . . or Pike!

"Put your mule in the corral, Ike, and come in. Granny will have something good for din . . . for supper."

"I'll do that, ma'am, after I help Colleen unharness the team."

Chapter Nine

Whit was hunkered down amid the lilac bushes.

He watched as the teacher arrived. He had kept pace with her, keeping out of sight, not willing yet to face her after his humiliation at the Agency. He watched her meet the man the Indians called Crazy Swallow. They called him that because he was constantly on the move, darting here and there. The old man traveled between two worlds and knew many things about the Indian and the whites at the Agency. It was good for the teacher to know him.

The embarrassment Whit had experienced at the store had been great, yet he had known how he would be treated when he took the rabbit skins to trade. How else could he make the teacher understand the abuse he and others of his tribe endured at the hands of the agent, his woman and Sneaking Weasel, as he called the boy who lived at the Agency. Although Whit had not seen him, he believed it had been Sneaking Weasel who had gone into the school and destroyed the learning books. Someday, he vowed, he would kill him.

Whit had been angry at the sad sight of his Shoshoni brothers waiting at the corral to get the allotment of cattle to feed the camp. The cattle were meant for *them*, but they had to wait for one of the *Wasicun* drovers to open the gate so they could drive the animals to the feeding ground.

Whit remembered the stories his father had told him of the old days. When the first whites crossed their land, on their way to dig for the white man's gold, the Shoshoni had been their friends. They had traded them meat and corn for gunpowder. They helped them to ford streams, to gather livestock that strayed, and had protected them from the Crow and the Blackfoot who hated all whites.

His father had told him the story of Sacajawea, called Bird Woman by her people. She was a Shoshoni maiden who had been a guide for the men called Mr. Lewis and Mr. Clark. It was said that she returned with them to a place called St. Louis, lived and died there, but that was not true. The tribe elders said she had come home to the northern Wind River range to live with her people. Whit had not seen her, but he had mourned with the rest of the tribe at her death early this year at the age of one hundred summers.

It was getting dark, and Crazy Swallow was still at the house with the teacher. Lamplight shone from the windows. Whit imagined they were sitting at the big table—his father's table, eating a meal cooked by Granny Murphy. In the white world the women and the men ate together. He remembered the day when the table, chairs and several other pieces of furniture had arrived on a big high-wheeled wagon. His father had laughed and teased his mother because she thought the table was another bed to sleep on.

Whit's stomach growled, reminding him that it had been empty most of the day, but he was not hungry enough to go back to the camp where there would be no one to greet him. Only a few would note his absence—only the boys near his age who had no parents or uncles would notice his sleeping spot was empty. He would stay here. He would take his blankets inside the school. It was as near to the home his father had built as he could get.

"I doubt if the floor had been swept this year, and dust covered everything. Mrs. Havelshell seemed uninterested in the store." Jenny was telling about her trip to the Agency. "That boy, Linus, is rude. He treated me as if I were his enemy. It got my back up and I'm afraid that I didn't help matters. When he kicked Whit, it was the last straw."

"Miz. Havelshell lets him do 'bout what he wants." Ike lolled in the kitchen as if he had been there many times. "The boy's mad at the world. Onlyest thin' he cares fer is that dad-blasted raccoon."

"He came to our place a time or two," Colleen said. "He got sassy with Pa and uncorked some pretty nasty words. Pa told him to shut his mouth or he'd give him a thrashin'. The kid left a-thumbin' his nose."

"Why did he kick Whit?" Cassandra asked.

"Whit came to trade his rabbit pelts. He said it was trade day."

"He was right. Tradin' day is first day of ever' week," Ike said.

"Mrs. Havelshell said it was not, but offered him one blanket."

Ike snorted in disgust. "Kid's skins was worth two blankets and a couple of good skinnin' knives if not more."

Jenny was liking Ike more and more although she was not yet sure how he fit in with Havelshell and the men who had killed Mr. Murphy. Granny and Colleen liked him; it was enough for now.

"I bought two blankets and traded him for the furs. I was afraid his stiff-necked pride would make him refuse my offer, and I really did want the pelts. We'll make mittens and hats for winter."

"But why did that pimply-faced saphead kick Whit?" When Cass wanted to know something, she was like a fox after a chicken.

"He told him to leave and Whit did not move fast enough to suit him . . . so he kicked him."

"If I had been there, I'd have kicked him back." Cassandra's face flushed and her blue eyes snapped angrily.

"Hee . . . hee . . . hee!" Ike's gleeful laugh was high-pitched. "Betcha ya would've, sister. Betcha ya would've."

"Didn't you do anything, Virginia?"

"Oh, yes. I told him to stop and when he got sassy, I got out my little gun and . . . poked him in a place where he didn't want to be poked." Remembering the startled look on the boy's face, Jenny burst out laughing.

"Good!" Cassandra exclaimed then, "Where did you poke him?"

The question brought a giggle from Colleen and a snort of laughter from Ike. Mrs. Murphy rolled her eyes to the ceiling.

Jenny hesitated and Cassandra's little, freckled face lightened as understanding dawned. She grinned and nodded her approval.

"Of course! That was quick thinking, Virginia." She looked at Colleen and explained. "She poked him in the region of his genitals. Men and boys are very protective of their . . . tender parts."

While Jenny was thinking of something to say to fill in the quiet that followed, Beatrice asked:

"Do I have . . . them things, Jenny?"

"What things, honey?"

"Them things boys has got."

"No, sweetheart. Not the parts we're talking about." Outwardly Jenny was calm as if men's and boys' *parts* were an everyday topic of conversation, but she dared not look at the others. "Finish what you have on your plate and we'll have some of Granny's cobbler. I was surprised and pleased to find canned peaches on the store shelves. I wouldn't think they would be something the Indians would trade for."

"'Twas a larrapin' supper, Granny." Ike finished his dish of peach cobbler and leaned back in his chair.

"Mrs. Murphy to you, Ike Klein. Yo're older'n me, or I miss my guess." Granny's tone was sharp, but there was a twinkle in her eye.

"If'n ya wish to think such, ma'am, it be yer right. Don't know as I ever et a finer mess a vittles cooked by sich a sightly young woman."

"That be hogwash and ya be knowin' it." Granny got up from the table. "It ain't gettin' ya a second helpin' of that cobbler if'n that's what yo're anglin' for."

"We thank you for the deer meat," Jenny said.

"Yore smokehouse needs fixin'. Ya'll be needin' to lay in a store a meat. Won't take much fixin' if ya got nails."

"I found a sack of steel nails on a high ledge in the shed." Colleen spoke while helping Granny carry dishes from the table. She almost choked up remembering that they'd had no nails to build a burying box for her father. "Screen doors are up there, too."

"Screen doors?"

"Two of 'em."

"Goodness sake! Why would he take off the screen doors?"

"Same reason he took the rope and pulley off the well and dammed up the creek."

"The . . . the scalawag!" Jenny looked at Beatrice, then back at Colleen and mouthed another word.

The lamplight shone on the faces of her new friends. Jenny and the girls were becoming increasingly fond of the Murphys. Granny not only knew the mysteries of the cookstove, but she was wonderfully patient with Beatrice's small demands for attention and Cassandra's never-ending questions.

Being partially freed from the job of looking after her younger sister, Cassandra trailed Colleen when she wasn't scanning one of the books from Jenny's trunk. They staked the horses out to feed, and did other chores.

Colleen cleared away weeds and debris near the cabin that a snake could take refuge in. She hated snakes, the harmless ones as well as rattlers, and was constantly warning the girls to be on the lookout for them. She was not put off by Cassandra's superior knowledge of almost any subject nor her direct way of saying whatever was on her mind. In fact, she seemed to welcome and enjoy the younger girl's company. To be accepted by an older person she admired was a boost to Cassandra's self-esteem.

"Let's take Whit some food. He's at the school."

"How do ya know that, Cass?" Trell and now Colleen

were the only people Cassandra allowed to shorten her name.

"Because the pony in the corral kept running to the fence and looking that way. He's nickering now. He does it every time Whit is around."

Jenny got to her feet. "If I'd known that, I would have insisted he come over—"

"Don't, ma'am. It'd only cause the boy hurt."

"You're right, Ike. I'll fix something and walk over."

As Jenny was wrapping a large piece of meat and several biscuits in a cloth, Cassandra lighted the lantern.

"I'll take it."

"Not by yoreself, ya won't." Colleen picked up her rifle. "Me and Cass'll take it to the boy, Jenny. Yo're wantin' to put down all that writin' for Trell to mail. Boy might not even be there."

"He's there. Don't you believe me?"

"Shore, sugarfoot. I believed ya, too, when ya told me that folks hundreds a miles apart was talkin' to each other over a wire. Didn't bat a eye when ya told me."

"It's true. The telephone lines are strung from Chicago to New York and people talk to each other."

"We ain't got no wires strung 'tween here and the schoolhouse. If'n we want to talk to Whit, we got to start puttin' one foot 'fore the other." Colleen opened the door.

Cassandra started out the door then turned back and hurried into the room she shared with her sisters. She returned with a book under her arm and scurried out the door.

"It's darker than I thought it was."

"Carry the lantern and don't look into the light." Colleen cradled the rifle in her arms. She had seldom been without the weapon since her father was killed.

"When I grow up, I want to live on a mountain where there are no people. I've got to learn all the practical things you know, Colleen."

"Live on a mountain and not talk to folks a hundred miles away on a wire? Betcha ya change yore mind."

"Betcha I don't."

As they neared the school, Colleen became more vigilant, walking slower, keeping the rifle at ready.

"Whit!" Cassandra called. "Whit! I know you're around here someplace."

"Have you got no brains? You make noise like a herd of buffer." The boy's voice came out of the darkness behind them.

"You knew who we were. Why didn't you call out? I hate people sneaking up behind me," Cassandra said sharply.

Whit took the lantern and doused the flame.

"How did you know I was here? It could a been bad white man."

"Yore pony told us. We brought you some food."

Cassandra held out the cloth-wrapped bundle. Whit refused it.

"I no take food from women." He crossed his arms over his chest.

"Stubborn, stiff-necked, clabberhead!" Cassandra sputtered.

"The meat is from Ike. He said the deer was on Indian land and part of it ort to go to a Shoshoni." Colleen hoped that for once Cassandra would not contradict her.

"Crazy Swallow got deer on Shoshoni land?"

"Yes." Colleen insisted.

Whit snatched the bundle from Cassandra's hand. "Then it is my right to have it."

"Are you going to sleep here?"

"Why you want to know that, Girl-Who-Squawk-Like-Jaybird?"

"Because, Boy-With-Feather-Growing-Out-Of-Head, I just naturally want to know things. Here." She thrust the book in his hands. "You *said* you could read. While you're reclining under the bushes watching the house you may as well be improving your mind."

"What's this?"

"A book, you dolt. A book about a brave Indian named Uncas, the last of the Mohican tribe, and an evil Huron Indian, named Magua. If you can't read it, I'll take it back."

"I not heard of Mohican or Huron. Where their camps?"

"The story took place a long time ago and a long way from here." She reached to snatch the book back. Whit held it out of her reach.

"You think I don't read. You think I lie."

"What I think is that you're rude and ungrateful. Be careful of that book, it was very expensive."

"What's expensive?"

"It cost a lot of money."

"Then take it." He thrust the book out.

"Keep it, Whit," Colleen said. "Prove to her that you can read. I don't read much myself 'cept for verses in the Bible. Someday I'm goin' to read a story."

"Do you want to? Jenny's got a book by Helen Hunt called *Ramona*. It's about a white woman and her Indian lover, Alessandro."

"You've read it?"

"Oh, yes."

"Oh, yes." Whit echoed sarcastically. The child/woman, with her superior knowledge, irritated him. It wasn't natural for a child, a girl, to know so much. "You go. It is not wise to go from the house at night. Or far into the woods in the light of day. Bad men talk of fire and being shot by two guns. Ask about man named McCall."

"Where did you hear this?" Colleen asked.

"Sneaking Weasel like to talk. Sometime I listen at window."

"Who is—?"

"I knew you would ask." Whit glared at Cassandra. "It's name for skinny boy at Agency store."

"Very fitting. I like it."

"Go. It is foolish to wear light clothes at night. Even stupid Indian know that."

"He's right, Cass. I should have known better."

"Sneaking Weasel speak of you," Whit said to Colleen. "Say man plenty mad at you for shooting him in back."

"I hoped I'd killed the buzzard!"

"Only not bad wounded. He say he screw you into the ground. What that mean?"

"I'm . . . not sure. We'd better get back to the house, Cass."

Cassandra stood staring at Whit even after Colleen turned back.

"What are you waiting for?" Whit growled.

"I'm waiting for a *thank-you*," she replied with all the dignity her nine years would allow.

"For what?"

"The food and book, you dolt!"

"The food was from Crazy Swallow. The book is teacher's. Why say thank you to silly child?"

Cassandra stomped her foot. "You make me so mad!" She spun around and hurried to catch up with Colleen.

Whit watched until they were safely in the house. Then clutching the book and the food parcel, he vanished into the darkness.

"Mr. Havelshell is here!" Cassandra burst into the schoolroom, where Jenny and Colleen were cleaning. "He's getting out of his buggy."

Jenny's expression changed from surprise to one of determination. She placed the pieces of slate on one of the few upright benches and went to the door. Mr. Havelshell was standing beside his buggy talking to the rider who had accompanied him.

"Cassandra, go tell him to come over here." Jenny decided to summon the agent to her rather than go to him. "Be polite about it."

"Do ya want me to go?" Colleen picked up her rifle.

"Stay. I'm proud to have you with me."

Jenny and Colleen waited beside the schoolhouse door and watched the agent come up the path from the house. He was dressed in a black business suit, white shirt and string tie. His face was clean-shaven and his mustache trimmed. The picture of his grossly fat wife flashed into Jenny's mind as the agent carefully removed his bowler hat and smoothed the hair at his temples with his palm.

"Good morning," Jenny greeted him with as much civility as she could manage. "Have you met Miss Murphy? She's the daughter of the late Mr. Miles Murphy, who was killed on this property not long ago."

"I've not had the pleasure. How do you do, ma'am?"

"Not good since ya had my pa killed, ya lousy, shit-eatin' pissant."

Havelshell took a step back from the slender, dark-haired girl in the tattered overalls. Her voice was not loud but her tone was one of pure hatred; and if her eyes had been six-guns, he would be dead.

"You are mistaken, ma'am. I—"

"Cut the windies, mister. I ain't buying it. Ya can tell the one that done it, I've got *another* bullet in this rifle with his name on it. The first one got 'em in the back and didn't do much hurt. The next one'll send him straight to hell."

Havelshell's face turned red with anger. Even so, he was careful when he put his hat back on.

"A man's got a right to protect himself. Murphy shouldn't have drawn his gun."

"If that's your man's story, he's a gol-damned murderin' liar! We left the guns in the house a-purpose. He gunned down a unarmed man like I'm doin' him when I set eyes on him, packin' a gun or not."

"You'll get yourself killed."

"Oh, I bet ya'd cry 'bout that," Colleen sneered. "Then what'd ya do? Go after my granny?"

Havelshell refused to answer. He stood silent and tight-lipped. Finally he turned his back and ignored the angry girl.

Fearing that her anger would bring tears that would shame her, Colleen went stiffly down the path to the house, cursing the man with every step she took.

Havelshell turned to Jenny. His face creased in lines of distress.

"I'm sorry about Mr. Murphy. The girl is mistaken about the way he was killed. Three men came back to town with the same story about how Murphy drew his gun and they were forced to kill him."

"I don't doubt that for a moment. Why would they incriminate themselves in a murder? Come in, Mr. Havelshell. I think you will be pleased at how thoroughly the schoolroom has been wrecked."

He followed her into the schoolhouse and stood just inside the door. His eyes swept the room, noting the piles of broken slates, torn books and broken and splintered benches.

"Miss Gray, are you implying that I ordered this destruction? If so, I resent it. I am the agent here. It is my responsibility to help these people adjust to life on the reservation. It's clear to me the little heathens don't want an education. They want to chase rabbits, dig for roots and steal as they've always done."

"I didn't come out here completely ignorant of the Indian ways. After I accepted the assignment, I read everything I could find about the Shoshoni and other tribes in the area. This destruction is not the work of Indians. They may steal, but they do not vandalize. This was done by a white man . . . or boy . . . with the sole purpose of keeping the school closed."

"So . . . you claim to be an authority on Indian behavior after only a few weeks in the territory," he sneered.

"How long have you been in the territory, Mr. Havelshell?" Jenny countered.

"Long enough to become a valued member of this community."

"No doubt," she said drily. "Tell your boy, Linus, to stay away from this school. I may mistake him for a robber and . . . shoot him. Of course, he will be armed and will be threatening me."

Jenny stared the agent in the eye. She knew she was not building a foundation for the request she was going to make before he left, but he irritated her to the point of near-complete frustration.

"First, he is not *my* boy," Havelshell declared, but his red face made Jenny wonder if she had not stumbled onto a secret connection. "He works at the Agency store."

"Yes, I know. I met him there yesterday. I also met your wife and purchased a few things."

His face darkened even more, and his nostrils flared when she mentioned his wife.

"You should not forget that I am in complete charge of this reservation. I hired you and I can send you packing."

"That is where you are wrong. As I told you the day I arrived, my contract is with the Bureau of Indian Affairs. The only way you'll get me to leave here is to kill me. Should that happen, by accident or otherwise, the Federal marshals will swarm all over the place. Another thing I wish to make perfectly clear: the Murphys are in my employ and will be living here with me. Keep your gunmen away from here and away from them."

Havelshell walked around the room picking up ripped books, some of which Jenny and Colleen were going to salvage.

"How are you going to teach without books or slates?"

"Oh, that's no problem. I brought a trunk full of books and slates. I was unaware that Mr. Whitaker had already furnished them."

"You're a gentle-born lady." He spoke to her from across the room, noting the proud way she stood, head up, shoulders straight. Deep within him a spark of regret began to stir. Why couldn't he have met such a woman years ago? With someone like her by his side he could have become anything he wanted to be.

"I'm familiar with the term, sir, but I do not concur with the accepted meaning. We are all *gentle*-born. It's what we do after we get here that makes a difference in our lives."

"What I was going to say, ma'am, was that this is not the kind of life you were born into or educated for. It is summer now, and you can see how difficult it is to keep the water bucket full, the stock fed and the firewood cut. Those hardships will be multiplied by ten when winter comes. Winters out here are long and cold."

"Do you think I am so . . . dense that I didn't know from the first day that you didn't want me or any other teacher here? And that you intend to make being here as unpleasant as possible. You want me to give up before I start classes?"

"It would be the wise thing to do. I'm sure that you want what's best for your sisters. It's a hard thing to see a small child cold and hungry. Wolves are dangerous here in the winter as are other . . . animals when they are hungry."

"What will you do, sir, if I leave? Find another teacher or inform the Bureau that a teacher could not be found and that Mr. Whitaker's land must be put up for auction."

"I will look for another teacher." Havelshell was so angry that his mouth snapped shut after uttering the lie.

Jenny smiled. "I'll lift the burden of having to make that decision from you. I'm not leaving."

He looked at her openly for a long while and began mentally to undress her. She would have a tight neat body; the kind of body he liked to have beneath his. The fabric of her simple dress draped her high, softly rounded breasts in a way that made it hard to tear his gaze away. Melva's breasts had started to sag, her belly was beginning to pouch and her hips were spreading, yet compared to his wife—

The mental vision of his wife unclothed made him want to puke. The only time he'd seen her naked was a couple of years ago. Even then she was the most repulsive thing he'd ever seen, with large rolls of fat from her triple chins to her knees. He shuddered thinking of the difficulty he'd had consummating the marriage. It was easy to believe she had gained a hundred pounds since then. *How could that arrogant bastard think he could get a son out of that fat sow?*

"Mr. Havelshell, before you go—"

Damned high-toned bitch was dismissing him.

"—There is another matter I wish to discuss with you." He said nothing, so she continued. "Your orders that prevent Whit Whitaker from visiting his father's house are ridiculous. I'm serving notice that I plan to hire the boy to work about the place."

"You are serving notice that you are going to break the law?"

"What law? Yours?"

He smiled. "Territorial law. Indians are to be confined to the reservation. All those who disobey are to be punished."

"And you follow the law to the letter," Jenny said cuttingly.

"Absolutely."

"And punishment means flogging?"

"Absolutely."

"Hmm . . ." Jenny put her forefinger to her cheek.

"Hmm . . ." she murmured again. "There's one thing I can do."

"Ma'am, there's nothing you can do. The law has been approved by the Indian Bureau."

"In that case the Indian Bureau can give permission for the Shoshoni to leave the reservation under certain circumstances."

"Should that be the case, I, as agent, will decide on the certain *circumstances*."

"That may be, but if you prove to be unreasonable and a lawsuit becomes necessary, it would draw attention to the reservation. Which in my opinion would be a mighty good thing."

"You are treading on dangerous ground, Miss Gray." The agent was so angry that his voice shook.

"So are you, Mr. Havelshell. As you leave here, sir, keep two things in mind. First and foremost, keep your henchmen, including Linus, away from the school and the Stoney Creek ranch. Second, keep your hands and those of the thugs that work for you off Walt Whitaker's son, Whit."

"Are you threatening me?"

Jenny smiled coyly and spoke softly. "Little old me? A prissy teacher from back East threaten the powerful Indian agent? How you talk, Mr. Havelshell."

He strode to the door with long purposeful steps and turned. "You keep in mind, Miss Gray, that I will not allow you to order the Indians on my reservation to do your bidding. I'm sending men out to put back the dam you ordered taken out."

"Nature sent the water this way. That is why Mr. Whitaker called this place *Stoney Creek Ranch*. You diverted the water to the Sweetwater River in order to inconvenience me."

"Yes, I did." He smiled for the first time. It was more of a sneer than a smile. "I must be going."

"I'm glad to hear it." Jenny felt as if her stomach was full of beetles. "You've overstayed your welcome."

Havelshell wanted to strangle her and yet she excited him, too. He had not been bested by many men and never a woman. He was reasonably sure that given time he could disabuse Miss Gray of the notion of staying at Stoney Creek. That is, unless McCall horned in. Fortunately, there were ways of taking care of him.

The Murphy girl was another matter. His mind began to work rapidly. By the time they reached the buggy, two ideas had been born and both rejected. The third idea stuck and grew; he had an ace in the hole and its name was Hartog.

Chapter Ten

"Ike, tell me about Mr. Whitaker."

Jenny had found the whiskered old man helping Colleen get the screen doors off the rafters in the shed. He was a small, quick-moving man and, as Colleen described him, "pack-crammed with handiness and talk."

"Walt was as square a man as I ever knowed. Met up with 'em back in '51. Both of us green as grass. He was smart. Had him a whole parcel of book learnin'. He hit gold on a small claim, sold out and come here. This here place was all he wanted. He was mighty proud of it. Had him a big herd oncet. Sold 'em and sent the money to one of them fellers to in-vest. Got along good with the Indians, he did. Never heared him put a bad name to a one of 'em."

"Do you know if he married Whit's mother?"

"He wed her the Shoshoni way. Walt never had no woman or wanted one till he set eyes on Rose. Don't know what her Shoshoni name was. Walt called her his Rose. She never got strong after birthin' the boy. Walt took a sec-ond wife to come take care of her and the boy. 'Course, that one wasn't really a *wife*. It was a matter a her savin' face."

"Did Mr. Whitaker father other children?"

"Naw. Havelshell says he's got plenty of 'em, but he ain't. Whit's the only one."

They carried the screen doors out of the shed and into the sunlight.

"How old was Whit when his mother died?"

Ike scratched his head. "Must'a been five or somethin' like that. Near kilt Walt to lose his Rose. He carried her all the way back to her people for buryin'—it bein' what she'd wanted. Must'a been fifteen mile and him not trottin' like a colt no more."

"I'm trying to understand why Mr. Whitaker didn't leave money and his property to his son."

"Walt thought the world and all of that boy. All the book learnin' that boy knows, and it's plenty, Walt learnt him. Walt knowed that if he left it to the boy, the money and the land would'a been et up by lawyers and land-grabbers a'fore the boy was grown. He fixed it so the boy would get schoolin'. I'm thinkin' he fixed it with a college back East for the boy to go there when he's learnt what you can teach him. Some feller at the Indian Bureau knows about it."

"Do you know if he had any relatives . . . brothers or sisters?"

"Ain't thinkin' he did. Reckon they was wiped out in the War. Walt figured the onlyest way he could get a teacher to come and stay and give Whit the book learnin' he needed was to give 'em Stoney Creek. It ain't like the boy was hankerin' for the land. Shoshonis think different from white folks 'bout land. They think no one can *own* land,

not like a man owns a horse or a blanket or a gun. Land belongs to ever'body."

"What a beautiful thought!"

"Yessiree. Walt fixed up the schoolhouse. He'd set his
mind on his boy going to college. Got in a whole parcel a
books and put 'em in a thingamajig with glass in front."

"There wasn't a bookcase or a book in the house when
we arrived. Whit said Havelshell took them. I should have
asked him about it today."

"Ya shore done somethin' to rile him. He had his dander
up good. He come back here wagging his lip and lookin'
like a sore-back bull with a mouthful of larkspur. Hee . . .
hee . . . hee."

"He even admitted putting in the dam and drying up the
creek to make things difficult for me. I think it surprised
him that it had been taken out. He's sending men to put it
back in."

"He say that?"

"That and more. He'll do everything he can to get me
out of here."

"The elders didn't like him dammin' it in the first place.
They ain't wantin' white men changin' the way the water
goes. Beaver can do it, cause it's *Mother*'s wish. Mother is
what they call the earth. I just might have'ta put a bug in
their ear."

Colleen had been listening and saying nothing. "Now I
know why folks hire gunmen. If'n I was rich I'd hire me a
few to cut down that sidewinder." She picked up one of the
screens and carried it to the house.

"The gal's hurtin'. She ain't meanin' what she said."

"I'm not so sure." Jenny watched as Colleen leaned the
screen against the house and swung Beatrice up in her

arms when the child ran to her. "Where did you sleep last night, Ike?"

"I rolled up in my bedroll here in the bunkhouse."

"It isn't much of a bunkhouse."

"Was when Walt was here. I'm thinkin' Havelshell stripped it."

"Could you fix it so it would be livable. If so, I'd like to hire you. I'll pay monthly wages."

"I ain't knowin' 'bout that. I ain't much of a stayin' kind of feller. I'll be driftin' in and out, missy."

"Do you know of someone I can hire?"

"Not right offhand. Ya might ask McCall when he comes."

"I'll do that. He said he'd be back in about a week. The week will be up tomorrow."

"His word is good. Colleen thinks a heap of him fer helpin' bury her pa and bringin' her and her granny here. Might be he'll take to her. She'd make him a good woman."

"Yes, she would." Jenny felt a little lonely. Was it the thought of losing Colleen or something else? "Ike, I've got to make a trip into Sweetwater one day soon. We need things they didn't have at the Agency store. The man who brought us out here said it was twenty miles—"

"—Horse-hockey. T'aint no sich. More like ten or twelve."

"It seemed an awfully long way. How far is it to Forest City."

"That's a mite more. I ain't knowin' jist how much. McCall'll know." Ike took off his battered hat and scratched his head. "Ma'am, these fellers ain't to be fooled with.

They got a stake here. If'n ya warn't a women, ya'd already be starin' at the sky and seein' nothin'."

"You mean if I were a man they would kill me?"

"And blame it on the Shoshoni or a drifter and have a big to-do at the buryin'."

"Would they harm my sisters?"

"I ain't thinkin' so. Folks'd get pretty riled up. Ma'am, if ya got menfolk what could come—"

"I don't. You said *they*. Who besides Mr. Havelshell wants Stoney Creek?"

"I ain't a knowin' that. Havelshell heads the Sweetwater Cattle Company. That be all Stoney Creek is . . . a cattle ranch."

"If I don't stay, he'll buy the land at auction. Maybe someone would outbid him."

"Hee . . . hee . . . hee! Ain't likely anybody'd get a chance."

The conversation with Ike lingered in Jenny's mind for the rest of the afternoon as she worked in the schoolhouse.

The day had not started off well for Alvin Havelshell.

At daybreak a rider had arrived with a message. *Stop here on your way to visit Arvella.* The tone of the message irritated Alvin. It was a reminder that this was the day he was to do his duty by his wife.

He had arrived at the house early. The *man* was sitting at the breakfast table when Alvin was ushered in by the rider who had brought the message. He looked up from the plate of ham and eggs and spoke without as much as a greeting.

"I trust you've not spent yourself on that whore from the hotel and will have something left for your wife."

"The whore from the hotel helps me keep the juices flowing so I can do the . . . job." Havelshell was unable to suppress his irritation. "A man's got certain . . . needs. I'm sure *you* understand that." He said the last as a young Chinese girl padded noiselessly from the room.

"Don't get lippy, Alvin. I've got a lot at stake here. There's nothing wrong with Arvella except that she's fat. Even the fattest cow can calve. I need an offspring from her. I need for folks to know that she's pregnant. I need for her to deliver a *live* child."

"How could they tell if she's pregnant?" Alvin muttered, then asked belligerently. "Is that all?"

"No, it isn't all. Stay the night out there. Do it as many times as you can, that is if she hasn't missed her monthly flow."

Of course I'll stay the night. Do you think I could screw that fat sow in the light of day?

"Do you want to come along and oversee the job?" Alvin despised these conversations with his wife's father.

"I may find it necessary if she doesn't catch soon." The man spoke as if he was putting a stallion to a mare. "Oh, yes. Stop by and see the teacher. The womenfolk of that nester your man killed are staying with her. What have you done about McCall? I won't have him nosing in."

"He's made an enemy of Hartog. He'll be taken care of."

"Make it an accident. Killings are something folks talk about. Go on." He made a shooing motion with his hand. "Hold up your end of the bargain and we'll get along fine."

Havelshell went back to his buggy in a seething rage. The puffed-up sonofabitch! Ordering him around like he was a hired hand! *Go on. Screw my daughter as many times as you can.* Hell. If he didn't look at her he might be lucky and get it hard enough . . . once.

How had he put himself into this situation—required to service that fat cow? He knew the answer without even thinking about it. He was a man who wanted, needed, wealth and position. He had thought that this was a good short cut. Now he wasn't so sure.

Alvin left Stoney Creek in a state of frustration. Virginia Gray was a woman who aroused emotion in a man. Thinking about her on his way to the reservation, he experienced an increase in the beat of his heart. It was a pleasant feeling, reminding him of his youth and when he had had dreams of haughty girls who would swear undying love for him. He kept his mind focused on the slim auburn-haired woman, and enjoyed his reverie as the horse pulling his buggy trotted down the trail and into the clearing in front of the Indian store.

Pud Harris, the rider who accompanied him, dismounted, tied his mount to the hitching rail and stood waiting for Alvin to step down from the buggy. Pud was a short, long-bodied man with thick brown hair and a mustache that bracketed his wide lips. He didn't talk much. Alvin doubted he'd exchanged more than a dozen words with him. He was usually the one the old man sent to accompany him on these trips. Several times he had caught Harris looking at Arvella without the expression of revulsion she usually inspired in men. Maybe the cowboy wasn't as revolted by her grossly fat body as other men were.

It occurred to Alvin that he might get the cowboy to take his place in his wife's bed some dark night. What stopped him was that he wasn't sure how tight Pud was with the old man. He had about made up his mind to invite Harris in to supper when Linus came out of the store and leaned against a porch post.

"I told you the last time I was here to keep the horseshit picked up," he snarled at Linus. "It's a foot deep along the trail."

"It ain't that deep."

"It smells like it."

Alvin walked past him and into the store. It was gloomy; the only light coming in through the open door. For a moment he saw it through the eyes of Virginia Gray. It was dirty, sparsely stocked and smelled like sweaty feet. But hell, it was good enough for Indians.

As usual the rooms in the living quarters were spotlessly clean. The oak table gleamed; the lamp chimneys sparkled. The scents of a delicious meal being prepared came from the kitchen.

"Hello, Alvin." The voice reached him as he hung his hat on the hatrack. He waited as long as possible before he turned to greet his wife.

"Hello, Arvella."

She had prepared herself for his visit. The loose garment of soft, blue-sprigged fabric that covered her massive bulk hung from her shoulders to the floor. Her blond hair had been washed and puffed. Alvin's eyes swept over her and away.

"Dinner will be ready soon. If you want to wash up, there's warm water in the pitcher in the bedroom."

"I think I'll do that. It's a long trip out from Sweetwater." At the door, he turned back unable to hold back the question he asked. "Do you have news for me, Arvella?"

"Not the news you want."

Alvin turned into the bedroom and closed the door. He glanced once at the stout bed on his way to the washstand. No doubt it had been spread with fresh clean linen for his visit. He closed his eyes briefly before looking at his reflection in the mirror that hung over the china washbowl. He saw a man with a sprinkling of gray in his dark hair and mustache. Hell, he was almost forty years old! He hadn't much time left to make a big name for himself.

Alvin indulged himself in a moment of self-pity. Not only had he the *man* and Arvella to contend with, but that damn Linus was like a millstone about his neck. Why couldn't the goddamn kid clean himself up? If he weren't so valuable a snoop, he'd put him on a train and hope that he'd end up in South America in the middle of a revolution.

During dinner Alvin sat at one end of the table and Arvella at the other. Moonrock served a perfectly cooked meal of chicken with dumplings, green peas and raisin cream pie. The linen cloth on the table was edged with lace tatting. The gleaming silver service was correctly laid alongside the thin china plates. Alvin enjoyed the meal. It was far better than any he could get in Sweetwater. Cooking was one, possibly the only, talent Arvella possessed, and she had taught the Indian girl how to serve.

After making a few futile attempts at conversation Alvin lapsed into silence. The only diversion other than eating was watching the young Shoshoni girl move from table to kitchen as she served the meal. Had she sprouted breasts since he was here last, or was he just now noticing?

She was dressed in a neat, but faded dress, with a white apron tied about her slender waist. Her black hair was parted in the middle and hung over her shoulders in two braids. She kept her eyes down, never looking at Alvin or Arvella. She must be about fourteen now, Alvin mused. You couldn't tell about Indian girls; they never seemed to be very young or very old.

After the meal, Alvin sat at the desk and looked over the books. The entries were made in a neat hand: the number of cattle brought to the agency, the number turned over to the Indians, the number of pelts traded and for which goods. A note was made about the kind of fur and its condition. He paid special attention to what had been purchased by Miss Gray, and was startled at what Arvella charged her.

His wife, he admitted begrudgingly, kept a set of books that would pass the Indian Bureau inspection, should the occasion arise.

She sat in the large chair, her small, plump hands clasped over her belly, her small feet just touching the floor. Alvin could feel her eyes boring into the back of his head.

"You've met the teacher the Bureau sent out." Alvin spoke without turning around.

"Yes. I listed what she bought and what I charged her."

"I see that. It was plenty."

"She didn't complain."

"Did you invite her to have tea or coffee."

"No. She and Linus had a set-to."

"Yeah." He stared down at the closed ledger. "What about?"

"The Whitaker kid. He came in to trade."

"Was it trade day?"

"Yes, but I wasn't going to trade in front of . . . her."

"I suppose Linus stuck his bill in."

"He told the kid to get out. *She* pulled a gun on him."

"Linus backed down?"

"You would have, too. She had the gun stuck in his privates."

Linus's voice came from the kitchen. He was whining about something while he ate his meal. Why didn't Arvella insist the kid eat in the bunkhouse with the other men?

"Go to bed, Arvella. I'll be there soon." He turned off the lamp on the desk and stayed with his back turned until he heard the bedroom door close. Then he heaved a heavy sigh and got to his feet.

Linus sat on a chair with one foot propped up on the table. *The kid was like a boil on his butt.*

"Get your feet off the table!"

Linus's foot came down with a loud plop. He glanced at Moonrock, who was hanging wet cloths on the line over the cookstove.

"The next time I come out here and find horseshit a foot deep under the hitching rail and dirt and mud all over the store I'm going to kick your ass from here to yonder. Understand?"

"What's got you all het up? Ya ain't said nothin' before."

"I've said it. You just didn't hear it. Now get the hell out of here. Linus," he called as the boy started out the door. "I understand you had a set-to with the teacher. Stay away from her. Just let me know about every person that comes to Stoney Creek, and I want to know if that Whitaker kid crosses the line as much as a foot."

"She's a snooty bitch. She was goin' to blow my balls off."

"That would have been a great loss, I'm sure," Alvin

said dryly. Then, in a commanding tone. "Stay away from her."

"Old Ike's been there three days." Linus thought to throw in a little information to put Alvin in a better mood.

"What's he doing there?"

"Helpin'. Him and that Murphy bitch fixed the well. Been workin' on the smokehouse—"

Hmm . . . Ike stayed out of sight while I was there.

"Get on out. Moonrock's waiting to blow out the lamp."

Alvin stepped through the door and into the other room. After the boy left, the Indian girl put out the lamp. When she passed him to go to her bed in the back of the store, Alvin grabbed her arm.

"You've gotten to be a real pretty girl," he murmured. She tried to pull her arm free, but Alvin drew her close. "Don't make any noise," he warned. She twisted until her back was pressed to his chest and muted frightened sounds came from her throat. "Shhh . . . I'm not going to hurt you. I just want to see what you're hiding here." He wrapped his arms about the small struggling girl, nuzzled his face in the curve of her neck, and cupped a breast in each hand.

"Be still, honey. You feel and smell like a woman. Have you been broken into yet?"

His hands moved over her small firm breasts and squeezed, then one lowered, cupped her crotch, and pressed her hips against him. He worked his sex organ into the crack between her firm hips and it began to harden. He forced his hand into the front of her dress sending buttons flying. His fingers fondled her naked breast, stroked and pulled at her small nipple.

"Sweet little thing. Pretty little gal," he murmured. "Someday I'm going to suck these titties."

He found himself thinking about a slim auburn-haired woman with clear green eyes. His arousal grew. In the heat of his excitement, his mouth fastened onto Moonrock's neck and he sucked vigorously.

Finally, the sounds coming from her throat and the wetness of her tears caught his attention. He jabbed his rock-hard sex viciously against her several more times and whispered a string of vulgar words in her ear. Then he roughly pushed her from him.

His trembling fingers fumbled at the buttons on his britches as he hurried into the pitch-dark room where his wife waited.

Chapter Eleven

This morning after her visit to the outhouse that had been moved and made usable, Jenny stood outside the back door and brushed her hair. She loved this time of day. She had brought a fresh bucket of water to the kitchen as Colleen carried an armload of wood for the stove. Granny was cooking breakfast.

As Jenny ran the stiff bristles of the brush through her long thick hair, she scheduled her work. By evening the schoolroom should be ready. She would ask Whit, once again, to take her to the tribal elders. Should he refuse, she would ask Ike. Between now and the time her pupils arrived, she wanted to make a trip to Sweetwater.

A week had passed since Trell McCall had come to Stoney Creek. Every night she had added to the report she would send to the Bureau. Last night she had written about the visit from Havelshell. She had ended the report with the request that all her mail be sent to Forest City. She had also written to Uncle Noah asking him to inquire about a fund set up for Whit Whitaker's college education, and to speak to his influential friends about having Havelshell removed as Indian agent of the Shoshoni reservation.

She had not expected to like this wild beautiful land; but if something should happen that prevented her from fulfilling her contract and the land came up for auction, she would buy it. She had no idea what it would cost, but her inheritance was sizable; and if it was not enough, she was sure Uncle Noah would invest.

She heard the whinny of a horse before she saw the rider slowly emerge from the fog. Jenny was aware that he was leading something, but she had eyes only for the man on the horse. He sat tall in the saddle and wore a hat with the brim rolled at the sides.

Her heart began to flutter like a caged bird. She held the brush in both hands and pressed them tightly to her chest as Trell McCall rode into the yard leading a plodding white-faced cow.

"Morning." The dark gaze that fastened on Jenny's face became soft and searching.

"Morning," she murmured. Her gaze met and held his in a moment of sparkling sweetness.

"Found a cow along the way. Thought maybe she was yours."

"You know we don't have a cow, Trell McCall! Where did you *find* her?"

Trell dismounted. Winding the lead rope about his hand, he pulled the bawling cow forward.

"Rancher between my place and Forest City had her. He already had one milch cow and the calf of this one. He didn't need her so I took her off his hands." He didn't mention that he had traded a halter-broken mustang and a good iron-rimmed wagon wheel for her. The cow mooed again. "She needs milking."

"Whatever he charged I'll be happy to pay."

"No money changed hands. I traded a broomtail I was going to turn loose on the range anyway."

"Thank you. It will be wonderful having milk again."

Colleen and the girls came from the house. Beatrice ran straight for Trell. He handed the rope to Jenny and scooped the child up in his arms.

"My frog went to his mama and didn't come back."

"We'll have to find another one."

"It's about time you got here, Trell. We've been looking for you every day." Cassandra walked around the cow and jumped back when the cow began to let water. "Ugh! Who's she for?"

"She's for all of you." Trell greeted Colleen and then set Beatrice on her feet, all the while conscious of a pair of green eyes watching him. "But I got something for you and Beatrice."

Trell opened a cloth bag hanging on his saddlehorn and took out a brown-and-black bundle of fur. He held the puppy close to his chest. It whined and licked his face. He squatted down on his haunches. Cassandra came close and he shoved the little animal into her arms.

"Every kid should have a dog." He looked up at Jenny with a broad grin.

"Oh, my." For once Cassandra was too surprised to say more than, "Can . . . we keep him, Jenny?"

"Of course. Every kid should have a dog." Jenny echoed Trell's words and her sparkling eyes caught his.

"I . . . always wanted a dog. Margaret and Charles hated

them." The little girl hugged the puppy and rubbed her cheek against the soft, furry head.

"Can I hold her?" Beatrice stroked whatever part of the puppy she could reach.

"It's a *him*," Cassandra explained to her younger sister. "I noticed that right away."

The cow mooed. She was clearly in distress and needed milking.

"Where shall we put her, Colleen?" Jenny said, suddenly remembering that her hair was hanging down her back. She handed the cow's rope to Colleen, gathered her hair at the nape of her neck and tied it with a ribbon she took from her pocket.

"In the shed, for now. I'll get a pail and we'll milk her."

"I got the pail." Granny came out followed by Ike. "From the looks of that full bag, she's a good milker. Ain't she, Ike?"

"How in tarnation would I know? I'm a tellin' ya straight and pure-dee, Miz. Murphy. I ain't milkin' no dad-blasted cow."

"I ain't hearin' nobody askin' ya to, *Mister* Klein," Granny retorted, then to Colleen, "Get me a box to sit on, child."

Colleen brought the box. "Careful, Granny. Way she's fidgetin' around, she may be a kicker."

"She ain't no kicker." Granny patted the cow's sides. "She's hurtin' with that full bag. I allus was fond of a good milch cow." Her bright eyes settled on Ike. "Ya ain't too persnickety to clean out that cellar, air ye?"

"Yer goin' to put her in the cellar?"

"Don't be a clabberhead! We got to have a good cool place to store milk if I'm goin' to be makin' the milk gravy and buttermilk biscuits ya been hintin' for."

* * *

If Trell had thought about it, he would have been absolutely sure he had never been happier in his life. He sat with the *family* at the breakfast table and was the center of attention as he told about leaving his ranch during the early morning hours and leading the balky cow across the river.

"She's got a mind of her own. When she wanted to rest, she dug in her feet and stopped. I put her on a long rope. My horse didn't like her much. She made too much racket to suit him."

"Some males are not at all tolerant of female discomfort."

Cassandra made the statement, then looked around the table with raised brows expecting a comment, but none came forth. By now, all were able to hide the amusement they felt when the child offered "words of wisdom."

What to name the cow and the puppy was discussed at length. It was decided to call the cow Sweet Betsy, in honor of the song that gave Ike his nickname. Cassandra was determined to give the puppy a *dignified* name. "Blackie" and "Spot" were scornfully rejected when they were suggested.

"We should name him after a president. Ulysses S. Grant was our eighteenth president. We should name him Hiram."

"Why Hiram if you're naming him after President Grant?" Jenny asked.

"The president's original name was Hiram Ulysses Grant. He evidently didn't like Hiram. I prefer it to Ulysses. Everybody knows how to spell Hiram. Hardly anyone knows how to spell Ulysses. I don't like him. He may have been all right as a general of the army because he had a lot of help from experienced military men. But he was a sorry president."

"I never knew his real name was Hiram."

"He was born in Ohio and christened Hiram Ulysses Grant. Later he changed his name to Ulysses Simpson Grant. Why, I don't know."

The adults at the table were relieved to learn that there was something this child *didn't* know.

"If you don't like him, why honor him by giving the puppy his name?"

"The way I see it, Virginia, *he* should be honored that the puppy has his name after the mess he made of the government while he was in office. Besides he's a *Republican*."

"Oh, dear," Jenny said in mock horror.

Later in the morning, Trell fastened the pulley he had brought from his ranch to the crosspiece over the well, ran the rope through it and attached a bucket. Ike was working on the smokehouse. When Trell needed help holding the crosspiece, he called for Colleen. Jenny and Cassandra were at the schoolhouse. Beatrice sat on the doorstone holding Hiram.

"Are you and your granny gettin' along all right here?" Trell asked Colleen.

"We're doin' fine. We miss Papa—"

"I'm sure you do."

"I want to thank ya for bringin' us here. Jenny and the girls has made us welcome. Granny's in heaven havin' the girls to fuss over."

From the door of the school, Jenny saw Trell and Colleen talking and laughing as they worked. They looked good together—like a team. Colleen still wore her overalls.

Jenny had never imagined a woman could look feminine in men's attire, but Colleen did. Ike was right; she was the kind of woman Trell should have.

"Do you like him, Virginia?"

"Mr. McCall?" Jenny answered quickly and whirled away from the door.

"Who else?" Cassandra signed.

"Of course."

"Would you consider marrying him?"

"Flitter! I hardly know the man."

"You wouldn't say so if you did. I think he likes you more than he likes Colleen. He looks at you a lot. Poor Colleen. It's possible that she's in love with him. I can't tell . . . yet."

"Cassandra! Don't say anything like that to Colleen or Trell. Promise me."

"Virginia!" the child replied in the same shocked tone. "I've not completely lost my mind. But at times I think you have. If you like Trell, set your cap for him. You'll not find many men who would put up with me and Beatrice. I'll not do anything to scare him off."

Jenny looked at the ceiling. "Lord, help me."

Later when Cassandra had gone to the house, Whit slipped silently in the door and stood looking around.

"Whit, I was hoping you would come today."

"I not come till squawker go."

"Oh, my. I wish you and Cassandra got along better."

"Sneaking Weasel hides in the bushes and watches to see who comes here and if I cross over the line."

"Is he out there now?"

"Under the bushes with white flowers."

"I know the place. From there he can watch the door of

the school as well as the house and report to Mrs. Havelshell."

"She does not care who comes here. Havelshell cares."

"Does Linus have family around here?"

Whit shrugged. "He come about time Havelshell come. He tell everything to him."

"Granny gave me a bar of lye soap so I could scrub the floor." Jenny picked up a heavy bucket. "Excuse me, Whit. I must empty this water."

Jenny marched out the door, leaning to one side because the bucket she was carrying was so heavy. She went straight to where Whit said Linus was hiding and threw the dirty, soapy water into the bushes.

Linus came out of the bush as if he were shot from a cannon, rubbing his eyes and swearing. His head and face were wet and he was trying to wipe the water from his eyes with the sleeve of his shirt.

"Forevermore!" Jenny exclaimed. "What in the world were you doing under that bush?"

"Ya goddamn bitch! Ya tryin' to put my eyes out?"

"Call me that name again and I'll . . . smash your face with this bucket." The humor suddenly went out of the situation and Jenny shouted. "You lowlife, sneaking . . . little weasel! Don't you have anything better to do than crawl on your belly in the bushes and spy on people?"

"I'll wring yore neck—"

"No!"

Jenny heard Whit's voice behind her and held her arm out to prevent him from passing her.

"Don't dirty your hands with him, Whit. He's not worth it. He's a poor excuse for a human being."

Jenny's scorn lashed Linus like a slap across the face.

"I ain't no goddamn red-ass Indian lover!" he shouted.

"You're pitiful. I feel sorry for you."

Linus was fairly dancing with anger. Nothing had gone right since this prissy woman had come here. Alvin, in a sour mood, had left at dawn, and Arvella was like a bear with a sore tail. This morning Moonrock had disappeared. He had looked all over for her and wanted to go to her camp, but instead he had to come spy on the teacher.

"Ya ain't goin' to stay here. Alvin ain't goin' to let ya. Ya ain't nothin, but a town-bit—"

"Watch your mouth!" Trell's voice came from beside Jenny.

"What'er ya buttin' in? Air ya hopin' ter get ya—"

"Shut up! If you wasn't just a wet-eared kid, I'd give you the thrashing you deserve."

"Ya ain't got no say-so here." Linus was as defiant as a cornered wildcat.

"And you've got no manners. But I'll not argue with you, boy. Stay away from the school. Next time you may get something a little stronger than a pail of water."

"She's ain't goin' to be learnin' them heathens nothin'. They ain't comin' to no damn school." His hate-filled eyes settled on Whit.

"You're wrong," Jenny said kindly. "They'll come and I'll teach them to read. I would teach you, too, if you'd come to school."

It was as if Jenny had handed him the ultimate insult. He spit in the grass at her feet.

"I ain't hobnobbin' with no red-asses!"

"You'd better go before I brand your butt with the sole of my boot." It infuriated Trell that the stupid kid would throw Jenny's offer back in her face.

Linus found his hat under the bush and slammed it down on his head. He turned his angry eyes on Trell.

"Ya'd better watch out, is what ya'd better do. I ain't forgettin' this." It was his parting shot as he disappeared behind the thick screening of bushes.

"I get angry at him, but I can't help but feel sorry for him, too."

"Ahhh—" The sound came from Whit. "Offer him a hand and he bite you!"

"I know. Whit, this is Mr. McCall. He has a ranch across the river and is a friend of ours."

Trell smiled and offered his hand. "Hello, Whit."

The boy hesitated, then stuck out his hand.

"You helped bury Murphy. I watch . . . from reservation land."

"You've been a help to Miss Gray. It took guts to take out Havelshell's dam."

"Guts? Took strong back."

"That too."

They walked back to the schoolhouse. Whit hesitated until Jenny put her hand on his back and gave him a gentle nudge. The boy needed a friend like Trell.

"Did Linus have a horse? I didn't see one."

"He have one. I untie and set on trail to agency. Sneaking Weasel walk."

"You did good, boy." Trell put his hand on Whit's shoulder.

Jenny saw Whit flinch when Trell touched him. Trell appeared not to notice. He looked around the schoolroom. A map of the world and a picture of George Washington were on the wall. The room was clean . . . and bare except for a couple of broken benches.

"You need a table and a chair."

"I'll bring a chair from the house. Whit tells me my students won't mind sitting on the floor. It would be nice to have a table to put the slates and books on."

"I'll see what I can do . . . if you can wait a while for the extra bunk."

"Oh, I forgot to tell you. Colleen brought in a cot. Cassandra claimed it, leaving the bed for me and Beatrice."

"Then you'll have your table."

For the next couple of hours Jenny sorted pieces of the torn books and tried to salvage as much of them as possible. Trell and Whit worked on the table. Trell skillfully maneuvered Whit into sharpening a hatchet on a small grindstone from the Murphy wagon. Whit smoothed the uneven plank with the hatchet while Trell shaped others with the axe. When finished, the table was rough, but sturdy. They moved it to the front of the room.

"Oh, thank you. Thank *both of you*." Jenny looked from the tall man to the boy and her heart took off like a runaway train.

"We could have done a better job if we'd had the right tools, huh, Whit?"

"Good, strong table." A rare smile flickered across the boy's face.

"It sure is. I'll cover it with a colorful cloth and put the books on it. I want the room to be attractive so the children will want to come."

Jenny was surprised that her voice was so normal because she certainly didn't feel normal. For goodness sake! *Why did she feel so absurdly nervous in Trell's presence?* His physical nearness almost paralyzed her thought process, but she was foolishly happy when she was with him.

While working with Whit, Trell became aware of the boy's quick mind and his skill with the hatchet. The legs he shaped for the table were far better than he himself could have done. Trell wondered if someone had taught him to use the hatchet. Later, he had asked him.

"Whit, how come you're so handy with that blade?"

"Father taught me. He made things with a knife and a hatchet."

"What sort of things?"

The boy hesitated, then said, "I show you. Come."

They followed him out the door and into the woods. A dozen yards from the school, the boy stopped at a fir tree whose spiny branches swept the ground. He hesitated for a moment, then dropped to the ground, crawled underneath and came out with a large bundle tied with a thong. His eyes surveyed the area before he started back toward the school, staggering under the heavy load.

Trell and Jenny followed both knowing that this was something very important to the boy and that he was honoring them by sharing it with them.

Whit was breathing hard by the time he got to the school and placed the bundle on the table he and Trell had just made. He untied the thong and pulled back what appeared to be a bear skin. He lifted one of the individually wrapped items and carefully removed the rabbit skin to reveal a wood-carved bust of a woman. It was nearly life-size, and the detail was so fine you could see the arched brows over her eyes. Noticing the curve of the high cheekbones, the small straight nose and sensitive lips Jenny knew immediately who the subject was.

"Your mother! Oh, Whit, she was beautiful."

"Yes." The boy rubbed his finger lovingly over the dark wood that had been polished to a bright sheen. "Father made another one and one of me, but they are gone."

He unwrapped another skin and revealed a bird in flight, its wings extended, its long neck stretched. You could see the downy feathers on the bird's breast. One after the other Whit showed them a dozen of his father's carvings; bear, deer, buffalo and even a fish.

"Little ones were left. Big ones taken except this one." He touched the bust of his mother with a gentle finger.

"Who took them?" Jenny asked, but she knew.

"After Father die, agent and Havelshell come. Havelshell not agent then. They told me and Father's wife to go. When I come back, all gone but these."

"So you took them."

"They are mine!"

"I know. They're very good, aren't they, Trell?"

"They are. I don't know a lot about these things, but I've seen a few pieces in Denver that sold for a lot of money."

"I never take money." Whit began to rewrap the pieces in the rabbit pelts.

"Was your father teaching you how to carve?" Jenny asked.

"With the hatchet. We made bear head out of stump. Gone now."

"The injustice makes me furious!" Jenny's flashing green eyes caught and held Trell's. "How dare they run roughshod over the rights this boy has to his father's estate? He is as much white as he is Indian. Even if he were not, it would still be wrong, wrong, wrong!"

"They're holding all the cards, Jenny," Trell said. "In

order to get things changed, you'll have to go to the higher-ups."

"That's just what I'm doing. I've written a full report to the Bureau."

"When I leave here I'll go straight to Forest City and mail it."

"I've asked them to send my mail there."

"When I pick up mine, I'll get yours."

It was early evening when Trell saddled up to leave. He didn't want to go, but wanted to be across the river before dark. He stood by the corral fence talking to Colleen for what seemed to Jenny a long time. Not wanting to intrude in their conversation, Jenny remained indoors until he came to the house, Colleen walking beside him.

"I was telling Colleen that if you womenfolk decide to go to town, all of you should go. There's safety in numbers."

"Do you think we should? I'm afraid to leave the house and the school without someone here."

"I spoke to Ike. He'll stay while you're gone."

"Oh, but—"

Trell laughed. "Don't underestimate that old man. He's a ring-tailed tooter when he's riled up."

"What's that?" Cassandra asked. "You Westerners have some peculiar expressions."

With a look of real affection in his face, Trell looked down at the child.

"Cass, if I had half your brains, I'd be rich."

"I'm glad you're not. Being rich and being corrupt often go hand in hand. Besides, being happy is more important."

"You may be right."

"I *am* right. I was rich and miserable. Now I'm poor and happy."

Trell looked quickly at Jenny. She hugged her sister and then extended her hand to him.

"We thank you—all of us, for the cow and the puppy and all you did today."

"You're welcome." He squeezed her hand gently before he released it.

"Most of all, we thank you for bringing Colleen and Granny. They're our family now. The girls and I hope they stay with us forever and ever."

"Don't be silly, Virginia. Colleen will want to marry someday." Cassandra rolled her eyes in disgust.

"So will you, but you'll still be my family."

"That's true. I'm afraid you're stuck with me."

"I want a word with Whit before I go." Trell strode toward the school and Whit who was sitting on the door-stone.

"Do you know how to get to my ranch?" Trell asked. Whit nodded. "If Havelshell gets too rough here, and you need to leave, come to me. I'll get you to people who will know what to do."

"I not leave teacher now." He stood straight and proud, his arms folded over his chest.

"If she should need help, come to me."

Whit nodded.

Trell went back to the group waiting to say good-bye. He had hoped for some private time with Jenny, but that wasn't to be unless he asked for it. He looked at her face, storing away every feature to bring back and remember on the long ride home.

He said good-bye to Colleen and the girls, thanked Granny for the meals, then looked at Jenny.

"Walk with me a ways?"

Jenny glanced at the others. Cassandra rolled her eyes, winked and murmured, "I told you so."

Jenny was agonizingly aware of the man at her side. They walked alongside the pole corral, Trell leading his horse. When out of sight of the house he stopped and turned to Jenny. She wasn't sure how it happened, but her hand was held tightly in his.

"I'll be back, Jenny. If you should need me during the next few days, send Whit."

"I will. Are you sure you don't mind posting my letters?"

"Not at all. I've already sent a letter to my half brother, Pack Gallagher in Laramie. I told him what was going on here and asked him to get in touch with Marshal Clive Stark."

"How can I thank you?"

"Don't."

The evening light fell gently on her face, molding it. She had a wistfulness about her tonight. He liked the way she looked and talked. She was a woman, yet she was a girl, too. She was nice and tall and held herself proudly. He wanted more than anything in the world to pull her to him and hold her in his arms as he had done earlier. The moment crackled with tension.

As Trell's eyes roamed her face, strange feelings stirred in Jenny. Her heart fluttered, and she drew the tip of her tongue across dry lips. She wished that he would hold her and kiss her. The boldness of the thought, the sheer wonder of it happening, sent a thrill of excitement through her.

"Jen . . . ny, you're . . . awfully pretty."

"Like this?" She laughed nervously and moved her free hand up to smooth her hair.

The shimmer in her eyes and the smile on her soft mouth made him feel shaky inside. He dropped the reins, captured her other hand and pressed both palms to his chest.

"I wish I didn't have to go."

"I . . . wish it, too."

She looked at him with wide, clear eyes. As if vaporized, Jenny's thoughts fled, and emotion took over. Forces stronger than she compelled her to sway toward him. Feeling more daring than ever before in her life, she lifted her face to his. Their breaths mingled for an instant before he covered her mouth with his. Although his lips were soft and gentle, they entrapped hers with a fiery heat. There was such a sweet taste to his mouth!

With a leap of joy, Trell realized he had actually kissed this angel of a woman. He could not speak above the sound of his thundering heart. Silently, he held her close, his cheek pressed tightly to hers.

"I'll watch until you're back in the house." His voice came finally in a husky whisper.

"You . . . must go?" Her hands were still pressed to his chest.

"Yes, but I'll be back." He lifted her palm to his lips. "Jenny, I . . . I don't usually act so bold—"

"Neither do I. I wanted you to kiss me. It doesn't have to mean anything unless we want it to."

"I want it to." He kissed her again, hard and quick, then dropped her hands and picked up the reins. "I'll be back—"

He walked with her to the edge of the corral, then

mounted his horse. Jenny stood alone. She lifted her hand and waved. He put his heels to his horse.

He looked over his shoulder after he was halfway across the grassland, hoping to see her one last time. She was still standing there, the evening breeze pressing her skirt against her legs.

She lifted her hand again.

Chapter Twelve

"I should stay here with Ike." Colleen helped Granny up onto the seat of the wagon.

"Why's that? Ya think I'm too damned old to take care of thin's here?"

"I don't think that and you know it."

"McCall said it warn't a good idey fer Jenny to go to town by her lonesome. He said no man in his right mind was goin' to stand up to three armed womenfolk and fer ya to stay together."

Ike waited for Colleen to climb up the wheel. It was the first time any of them other than Granny had seen her in a dress. She was right pretty, he thought, even with her pa's gun belt strapped about her waist.

"Trell told me that, too," Jenny said.

"What he said was, 'There's safety in numbers.'" Cassandra chimed in.

"He was countin' on Colleen drawin' that six-gun if need be. Said she warn't no slouch with that rifle a'tall."

Colleen's face reddened a little on hearing the compliment and hurried to take the attention from herself.

"Jenny's pretty handy with that little peashooter she carries in her pocket."

"Somebody's going to have to teach *me* to fire a gun," Cassandra said from where she and Beatrice sat on a box behind the seat.

"Lordy mercy, Cassandra!" Jenny glanced over her shoulder at her sister. "You forget sometimes that you're a child."

"You don't have to be a certain size or age to pull a trigger, Virginia. Boys my age fought in the War. I'm going to ask Trell to give me some shooting lessons like you took at Uncle Noah's club."

"We could call ya Cassandra Jane, like that there Calamity Jane." Colleen took up the reins and slapped them against the back of the team.

"She's *ugly*! She drives a mule team and wears men's pants!"

"So do I." Colleen turned the team and headed down the wagon track toward town. "They're more comfortable than this darned old skirt."

"But you're pretty. Trell thinks you're pretty, too. I asked him, and he said you were as pretty as a covey of quail. He considered that a compliment. I'd rather be compared to a sunset or a flower than a stupid bird."

Jenny heard a small chuckle and click of the tongue come from Granny, who was sitting between her and Colleen. *Trell thought Colleen pretty.* Jenny couldn't fault him for that, but she felt a twinge of jealousy anyway. Today Colleen wore a white shirt with the sleeves rolled up to her elbows and a calico skirt slightly frayed around the bottom. The tight waistband showed off her small waist and generous bosom. Her freshly washed hair was tied back with a ribbon and her suntanned face contrasted becomingly with her light blue eyes.

Jenny was ashamed of the uncomfortable feeling in the region of her heart when she thought of Trell and Colleen. In the short time she had known the Murphys, they had become very dear to her. Colleen deserved a good man like Trellis McCall. *But it was me he kissed!* Jenny adjusted her small-brimmed straw hat and tried not to think of Colleen and Trell together.

She had not dressed to impress the population of Sweetwater as she had done when she went to the Agency store. The two-piece dress she wore today was called a wash suit back in Baltimore. It was made of tan-and-white-striped percale. It was not at all fancy, and she had rolled the sleeves up to her elbows to make it appear to be even less so.

It had not been easy to ride away from the ranch and the school knowing what *could* happen while she was gone. She had expressed these concerns to Whit the night before, and this morning he had appeared at the school with the man who had helped him take out the dam. She had gone to speak to him.

"Be careful, Whit. I'd rather have the schoolroom destroyed again than to have you hurt."

"I not alone. Others follow."

"What do you mean?"

"Father's second wife speak with elders. Others will come to watch school while teacher is away."

"That's wonderful. Then the elders are not opposed to the school?"

"They say school is foolish. They do it for Father. He give much meat when they were hungry. He give blankets when they were cold."

As he spoke a dozen horsemen came out of the woods and stopped at the edge of the clearing. They were fearless, primitive-looking men, some with bows and quivers of arrows on their backs, others with rifles. They stared at Jenny. She knew better than to wave and was uncertain how to acknowledge their presence.

"You do not have to speak to them." Whit seemed to have read her mind. "They do not expect it from a woman."

"Well, good! I didn't know what to say anyway."

Whit had smiled one of his rare smiles. "Teacher not like Girl-Who-Squawk-Like-Jaybird."

Thinking about it now, Jenny realized how much she had come to like and depend on Whit. Some way or the other she was going to see that he got the education his father wanted him to have and eventually share with him the homeplace that was his birthright.

To Jenny the landscape seemed even more beautiful than it had been the day they passed through it going to Stoney Creek. The trail ran alongside a stand of tall pines and cedars. The breeze carried their scent and the tweet-tweeting of the birds in their branches. On the other side, a meadow stretched to another stand of pines in the distance and from it came the song of a meadow lark and the cooing of mourning doves.

"I'm thirsty, Cassy."

"Don't call me Cassy, *Beatrice*. You just want to drink out of the fruit jar."

"Jenny—?"

"Give her a drink, Cassandra."

"Then she'll want to wet."

"If she does, we'll stop."

"I will never have children when I grow up. Never! Never! Never!"

"You'd make a wonderful mother," Jenny replied patiently.

"Of course, I would. But I'll *never* do what you have to do to become a mother. It's too revolting even to think about."

Jenny opened her mouth, then closed it. She glanced at Colleen and saw that her lips were pressed tightly together to hold back the laughter.

The town with its rutted streets and plank buildings, fronted with boardwalks, seemed even smaller to Jenny than it had the day they arrived. The street was bare except for a buckboard and a few horses tied at the rails in front of the stores. Oblivious to the stares of the men who occupied the slab benches and the gawkers who paused along the boardwalk, Colleen turned the team into the first side street and stopped. She climbed from the seat and then helped her grandmother.

"This is a town?" Cassandra's sarcastic remark required no answer as they moved in a group to the corner and stepped up onto the boardwalk. At the door to the mercantile Jenny took a paper from the drawstring purse that hung over her wrist and gave it to Granny.

"This is the list you and Cassandra made out. I need to

go to the bank and to the post office. Girls, stay with Colleen and Granny. I'll not be long."

Jenny walked purposefully down the walk past the saloon, the restaurant and the hotel, and crossed the street to the bank.

The door was set in the corner of the building, the glass pane decorated with a gold-leaf design. She went up three steps and into the building. A teller in a visor cap looked up from behind the bars that separated them. He pursed his lips as if to whistle, but no sound came out.

"Good morning. I would like to see the bank president."

"Mornin'." The clerk stood and leaned his forearms on the teller counter. His black eyes stared at her boldly. His waxed mustache twitched when he spoke. "You're the Indian teacher, aren't you?"

"Yes, I'm Virginia Gray."

"Figured you was."

"Now that you know who I am, please tell the bank president that I am here."

"Not many city women make it as far as Sweetwater." He ignored her request. "How'er you likin' it out there at Stoney Creek?"

"I like it just fine."

"Have you taught the little heathens how to cipher yet? Haw! Haw! Haw!"

Jenny's face turned icy cold. She lifted her brows and stared him in the eye for a full minute. Words were not necessary. His face slowly began to turn red.

"I can open an account if that's what you want," he said trying to recover his bravado.

"I want to see Mr. Norman Held, the president of this bank."

"Maybe he ain't here."

"And maybe he is." Before he could speak, she turned and walked quickly to the glass-paned door and opened it.

"You . . . can't—" the teller stammered.

Jenny ignored him, closed the door, and smiled at the man who rose from the rolltop desk.

"I'm Virginia Gray." She held out her hand.

"Norman Held, ma'am." The erect, impeccably dressed, gray-haired man of fifty took her hand, then motioned to a chair. "Please sit down."

"I'm sure you know who I am and why I am here in Sweetwater, so I will skip over that. I will be writing checks on a bank in Laramie and I'm here to find out if that bank has contacted you."

"Yes, I had a letter from Gerald Spelling of First Community Bank requesting that I honor your drafts. I understand that you have a substantial amount in your account."

"Yes, I have. Do I have your assurance that the information is confidential?"

"Absolutely."

"Would you be kind enough to answer a few questions about the area?"

"Anything, ma'am. I'm at your service."

"Does the territory have a law-enforcement officer?"

"Federal marshals come in from time to time."

"Has anything been done to notify the authorities about the murder of Mr. Murphy? He was killed by men who were sent to warn him off Stoney Creek land."

"It's my understanding the killing was not murder, but a matter of self-defense."

"And where did you get that information?"

"From reliable sources." The banker gritted his teeth.

"Mr. Murphy's daughter and mother were there. They say it was murder."

"It would be to their advantage to say whatever would create sympathy for their situation."

Jenny let her silence be her answer to what she considered a crude, unfeeling remark. She looked at him coolly, but went on to the next question.

"Who will benefit if the terms of Walt Whitaker's will are not met?"

"I am not privy to all the terms of the will, but again, it's my understanding the land will be put up for auction."

The banker searched his memory for every bit of information he had heard about this woman. A pampered city lady, Havelshell had said, who would not last out the summer. He would bet a box of his best cigars that Havelshell was wrong. Virginia Gray was not the weak-kneed woman Havelshell painted her to be. She was pretty, she had grit, money, and influential friends back East, a tough combination to beat.

"Mr. Held, if you are finished with your assessment of me, I have a few more questions."

The banker flushed. "I beg your pardon, ma'am. I . . . was thinking that I had seen you someplace before."

A small smile, not at all nice, curled the corners of her mouth. *She knew he lied.*

"Have you spent time in Baltimore, Mr. Held?"

"No, I have not."

"Well, then, I doubt we've met. I want to know whose herd is grazing on Stoney Creek ranch and if the owner of that herd is paying a grazing fee."

"Mr. Havelshell is head of the Sweetwater Cattle Company. You'll have to ask him."

"That is not the straightforward answer I would expect from the local banker, but never mind. Did you know that Mr. Whitaker had a son?"

"I'm not surprised. Many men take their comfort with squaws when *white* women are not available."

Jenny looked steadily at the man after the comment. Her clear green eyes were unwavering and filled with disgust.

"I had expected more of a man of your obvious education." Her voice was cool and crisp. She stood and with an obstinate tilt to her chin looked at him as he got to his feet. "Good day, Mr. Held." Without offering her hand, she opened the door to confront the teller who had obviously been listening. He scurried back to his stool in the teller's cage.

Jenny was so intent on her angry thoughts when she left the bank that she had walked the two blocks to the post office in the stage station before she realized it. She chided herself for believing that the banker would be a man of integrity. He was a small-minded . . . jackass! She had no doubt that he was hand in glove with Havelshell.

"Well . . . hel . . . lo." Harvey scrambled out from behind the counter when Jenny stepped inside the door of the building where the stage had stopped the day they arrived.

"This *is* the post office, isn't it?"

"Yes, ma'am. Two years come fall."

"Is there mail for Miss Virginia Gray?"

"Virginia Gray? Oh, yes, ma'am. There was. Mr. Havelshell picked it up for you." Harvey's grin disappeared when he saw her mouth snap shut, her eyes narrow and an angry flush cover her face.

"What? You gave my mail to someone without my authorization to do so?" Anger raised her voice to near shouting. "*That* is against the law! Mail is the private property of the addressee. I'll have you removed as postmaster." She didn't know if she could or not, but it sounded good when she said it.

"I . . . I . . . he said—" Harvey stammered.

"Do you take your orders from Mr. Havelshell or the Postmaster General? Get it back. Right now!" She pounded her fist on the counter. "If the seal is broken on one piece of my mail, you'll answer to the postal authorities."

"I . . . can't . . . leave now." His eyes pleaded for understanding.

"Why not? You broke the law by giving my mail to a person who is almost a total stranger to me. You can break it again by closing this office and getting it back." Jenny knew nothing about laws regarding the mail, and evidently the postmaster knew less because he didn't argue the point.

Attracted by the angry female voice, several men had come to stand in the doorway. Harvey spoke to one of them.

"Wesley, could ya . . . stay here while I to go . . . to Mr. Havelshell's?"

"Reckon so." A stoop-shouldered old man with a stained white mustache pushed his way through the door. He was plainly amused. "Get yore tail in a crack, Harvey?"

The man, whose gray head came only to Jenny's shoulder, looked up with twinkling eyes and winked in such a manner that she couldn't possibly be offended. If she hadn't been so angry, she would have smiled.

"Just stay here, Wesley, and don't mess with anythin'."

"What is your name?" Jenny demanded as Harvey moved by her to go to the door.

"Harvey Moore."

"Mr. Moore, I'll be in the mercantile. Bring my mail there. *All* of it. And never give my mail to anyone unless you have written permission from me."

"Yes, ma'am."

Head up, back straight, Jenny marched past the group of gawkers on the porch and headed up the street toward the mercantile. *Was everyone in this town a dimwit?*

Two women in calico dresses and sunbonnets came toward her as she stepped up onto the walk fronting the store. Each of them was carrying a basket on her arm. As they approached they moved over and stopped in front of Jenny.

"Yo're the Indian teacher, ain't ya?" The older of the two had a hard, weathered face.

"Yes. I'm Virginia Gray."

"Ain't ya got no shame a'tall?"

Before Jenny could gather her wits to answer, the other woman demanded:

"Are ya a Christian woman?"

"I try to be."

"If ya air, what'er ya doin' out there with them heathens with no menfolk about? I ain't knowin' what folks do in them big cities, but out here no *decent* woman is goin' to do such and have herself talked about."

Jenny stifled the retort that came to her mind. Instead, she smiled sweetly—too sweetly, if the women were at all observant.

"I'm a God-fearing woman, ma'am. I'm doing the Lord's work by helping to place the feet of those poor misguided *heathens* on the path of righteousness. They, too, are God's children."

"It ain't right that them Indian kids has a teacher and ours don't."

"You don't have a teacher here in Sweetwater? I'm surprised to hear it. This is such a lovely little town, I'd think any number of teachers would want to come and settle here." Jenny gave no indication of the contempt she felt for the attitude of these women.

"They want to come all right! They just ain't got the grit to stay. 'Sides all they send is sissy-pants know-it-alls that ain't got sense enough to pound sand down a rathole." The woman let out a snort of disgust.

"Humm . . ." Jenny put her finger to her cheek as if in deep study. "You do have a problem. Well. It's quite a distance to Stoney Creek, but your children are welcome to attend classes there." She smiled brightly, ignoring the horrified looks that came over their faces.

"Ah . . ." The older woman almost strangled. "Ya think we'd let our younguns go to school with savages? Nosiree bobtail!"

"I'd not let ya teach my younguns if ya come to town after ya been hobnobbin' like ya been doin' with them redskin devils. A woman what ain't got no shame ain't got no place 'round decent younguns."

"And a woman who doesn't have the brains of a . . . goose, shouldn't be allowed to produce, ah . . . younguns. Good day, ladies." Jenny stepped around them.

"Well, I never!"

"What'd she mean?"

"I ain't knowin', but she ain't better be gettin' so smarty with me."

Jenny heard the remarks of outrage as she strode down the walk and into the store. Her head was beginning to throb. She could hardly wait to load her family back in the wagon and go . . . home.

She made her way through the maze of barrels, crates and tables piled with goods. She had never seen such a jumbled assortment—dress goods and bonnets next to shovels and barrels of chains and dried apples.

"Here's Jenny." Cassandra and Beatrice each had a stick of candy "Compliments of—" Cassandra waved the stick toward the man behind the counter. "He wasn't going to fill our order until he saw the money, but I told him that you were one of the richest women in Baltimore."

"Cassandra! I declare!"

Jenny glanced at the clerk. "I'm far from being the richest woman in Baltimore. But if you need to be assured that we can pay before you load the goods in the wagon, check with Mr. Held at the bank. Just don't ever expect us to trade with you again."

"No, ma'am. I'd not do that. It was . . . just . . . well, the amount the lady asked for—" The clerk's Adam's apple was jumping up and down, and his worried eyes were swinging back and forth between Jenny, Granny and an amused Colleen, who leaned against the table holding the dress goods.

"Granny, may I speak with you and Colleen privately for a moment?" Jenny led the way to the other side of the store.

"Every place I've been I'm met with hostility. I don't want to come back here for a long, long time. Let's double up on all the basic supplies if we have to hire a dray wagon to take them to Stoney Creek."

"That ort to make the little runt happy," Colleen said dryly.

"Was he rude to you?"

"Not after Cass told him how rich ya were. He 'bout peed his drawers." Colleen grinned.

Jenny sighed. "That girl!"

"If'n it's what ya want," Granny said. "We'll make the little runt happy."

Back at the counter Granny issued orders like a drill sergeant.

"We want two hundred pounds of flour . . . in tins."

The clerk looked quickly at Jenny, then spoke to Granny.

"Ma'am, it comes in double canvas sacks, but I can sell you a large tin."

"With a order this big, ya can give us the tin." She waited until he nodded his head before she continued. "Hundred-pound sack a sugar, fifty pounds a coffee beans, fifty pounds salt, twenty pounds a black tea, tin a soda, three gallon jugs vinegar, fifty-pound bag cornmeal—"

Jenny moved away from the counter as the clerk scurried to fill the order. With Cassandra's help, she picked up every slate, reader, speller and any books she could use in the classroom and piled them on a separate table.

"Colleen, help me pick out some dress goods for the girls. Oh, I wonder if he has one of Mr. Singer's sewing machines."

Ten minutes later she was interrupted by Harvey Moore, the postmaster coming into the store.

"Miss . . . ? Ah, here's your mail."

Jenny took the three envelopes. "Are you sure this is all you gave to Mr. Havelshell?"

"Oh, yes, ma'am. Three letters."

Jenny took a paper and a pencil from her bag. She wrote her name on the paper and gave it to the postmaster.

"This is my signature. Don't give my mail to anyone unless they have a note from me. Understand?"

"Yes, ma'am." He hesitated and Jenny felt a little sorry for him, but not enough to tell him what he wanted to hear until he asked.

"Ya'll not . . . report me? I'd . . . lose my job."

"I'll not report you this time. I would hope that from now on you would take your responsibilities more seriously."

"I will. I certainly will." He scurried out the door.

Jenny examined the canned goods they were buying to make sure the lids on the cans were not sealed with lead. A chemist back in Baltimore had told her about the danger of lead poisoning.

"Do you have medicated paper?" she asked the flustered clerk and watched his face redden.

"Yes, ma'am. Comes in packets of five hundred sheets for a dollar." He avoided looking at her.

"Back East Gayetty's Medicated Paper sells for fifty cents for five hundred sheets."

"Well . . . ah . . . we don't have much call for it—"

"Really?" Jenny wrinkled her nose. "We'll take six packets."

"Margaret and Charles used that," Cassandra said aside to Colleen. "They made me and Beatrice use pages out of a catalog."

By the time the shopping was complete, Beatrice was tired and whining for something to eat. Granny was also tired and Colleen moved a stool out from behind the counter for her to sit on.

When Jenny asked Cassandra to check the addition on the bill, the clerk appeared to be insulted. His indignation turned to embarrassment when she found an error.

"If beans are seven cents a pound why did you charge us two dollars and fifteen cents for thirty pounds?"

"This," Jenny said indicating the pile of books, slates and strings of counting beads, "is to go on a separate bill. Mr. Havelshell does have an account here, doesn't he?"

"Yes, ma'am."

"Charge it to his account."

"But—"

"Charge it to his account," Jenny said firmly.

"Yes, ma'am."

"I'll get the wagon." Colleen left the store grinning broadly.

With the supplies loaded, the girls sitting in the back, each happily licking a candy stick, Jenny helped Granny up onto the wagon seat. She climbed up and Colleen took up the reins. Jenny had just settled herself on the seat beside Granny when she saw Trell coming toward them on horseback.

She felt a wild fluttering in the region of her heart, and a smile hovered about her lips. She opened her mouth to call a greeting when she noticed that he had eyes only for *Colleen!* He came alongside the wagon, tipped his hat, *winked* at . . . Colleen and rode on.

Jenny was stunned!

Being snubbed by the man, who just a few days before had held her in his arms and kissed her, cut her to the quick.

"Wasn't that Mr. McCall?" Granny asked.

Both Jenny and Colleen seemed incapable of speech.

"It looked like him, but it wasn't him," Cassandra declared.

"What do you mean?" Jenny's mind stumbled.

"That man wasn't Trell."

"I've got eyes. I can see perfectly clearly. It was *him.*"

"Sure as shootin' looked like him," Colleen said tersely.

"It . . . wasn't . . . him," the child insisted.

"I say it was. But suit yourself. There's no changing your mind once you've made it up." In her disappointment, Jenny spoke more sharply than she'd ever spoken to either of her sisters.

Colleen suddenly swung the team around in a wide arc to head back in the direction of the store. The white-aproned clerk stood on the porch looking after the departing wagon. He had finally sold that blasted sewing machine he'd bought at a foolishly high price from a peddler. The rest of the town might resent the Indian teacher, but he hoped she'd come back real soon—and bring her money.

Colleen pulled the team to a stop in front of the store.

"Who was the rider who rode out on the buckskin?"

"That was McCall. He has the Double T Ranch south of here."

"Thanks. Handsome horse," she murmured, and sailed the whip over the backs of the team.

"That settles that." Jenny's eyes were suddenly moist.

"You don't want me to say this, but I must. It wasn't Trell."

"For crying out loud, Cass," Colleen sputtered. "The store man knows him."

"I don't care," the child shouted angrily. "Trell wears his hat pulled down more."

Jenny was surprised to see that Cassandra was near tears. She hadn't even cried the night she had come out of the house, naked, with Beatrice on her back.

Her little sister was hurting. She didn't want to believe a man whom she'd grown fond of and trusted would ignore her. She was trying to justify it by denying that it was Trell.

Jenny was sorry that she'd been so sharp. She had displayed her own disappointment in the tone of her voice. Cassandra needed kindness. While Jenny searched her tangled thinking for words of apology, Beatrice leaned on her shoulder.

"Jenny," she whispered. "Why's ever'body mad?"

"Oh, honey. We're not mad. We're all tired, and we haven't had anything to eat. I'd planned for us to eat in the restaurant, but—" She didn't want to say that she felt uneasy and had wanted to get away from town, away from the watching eyes and the general disapproval.

"We can have a picnic," Colleen suggested. "There's a place up ahead where we can stop, eat, and water the horses."

"That's a good idea. We've got cheese, crackers, raisins and apples—" Jenny glanced at Cassandra's scowling face. Her arms were folded across her chest and she was looking at the sky.

"I'm sorry I was cross, Cassandra. This has not been a good day for me."

"I want to sit in Granny's lap," Beatrice whined.

"Honey, Granny's tired. When we stop for our picnic you can sit up here between Granny and Colleen. I'll sit back there with Cassandra."

As the wagon rolled along on the uneven track, each of the women was occupied with her own thoughts. Colleen was embarrassed that Trell had winked at *her*. She had believed that he was a decent man. And Jenny had become fond of him. Had the wink been a signal that Hartog was lying in wait along the trail? No, he was grinning when he winked. He was *flirting!* It certainly wasn't what she had come to expect from him.

Granny Murphy had lived a long time. She had seen good men, bad men, and stupid men come and go. She would have bet her last tin of snuff that Trell McCall was a good man. He had helped to bury her boy, had been concerned about her and Colleen and had brought them to Jenny's. He'd come back with a cow, knowing how badly they needed one, and spent the day working around the place.

He was exactly the kind of man she wanted for Colleen, but she'd seen his eyes going often to Jenny. She was a good woman, too, and deserved a good man. Could it be he had a woman in town and didn't want her to see him talking to Colleen and Jenny?

Jenny's thoughts were critical of herself. She had taken Trell at face value without knowing one thing about him except that he had a horse ranch, had appeared when she desperately needed help to put out the grass fire, and had brought Colleen and Granny to her. After he had kissed her so tenderly, she had allowed herself to fantasize that he was attracted to her even though Colleen was more suitable for his kind of life. And, come to think of it, she herself had initiated that kiss. *Darn! Damn!* She wished that she knew more cusswords. Now was the time to use them.

She tried to concentrate on the three letters the postmaster had brought to the store. One was from Uncle Noah, one from the Bureau and one from the banker in Laramie.

She would examine them closely to see if they had been steamed open. She was anxious to read the letter from Uncle Noah. He would know what had taken place when Charles and Margaret discovered the girls were gone.

By the time they drove into the yard at Stoney Creek, Jenny was exhausted in mind and body and longed for the cushioned surrey she had left back in Baltimore. But it was not a happy homecoming even though they had a wagonload of provisions that would allow Granny to cook decent meals. There was fabric to make dresses and nightclothes for the girls. Colleen had picked out dress material for herself and Granny, whispering to Jenny that she had money hidden away and would pay for them. She and Jenny carried the new sewing machine into the house and set it up in the kitchen.

The books and slates were taken to the school. Newly purchased blankets were put away in one of the trunks Jenny had emptied of clothing; boxes of ammunition for the rifles and handguns were stowed away. The slanting door on the root cellar was laid back and Colleen and Ike carried down sacks of potatoes, carrots and cabbage. Also stored in the cellar was a bushel of lemons and a bushel of apples. Bags of dried apples, peaches and raisins were hung from rafters in the cellar.

Colleen and Granny had never seen such a stock of foodstuffs outside of a store. The cost of it was staggering. Jenny explained that since she would be paid by the Indian Bureau and had money left to her by her mother's family, there was no reason why they should scrimp on food.

In the quiet of the room she shared with the girls, Jenny examined the letters and came to the conclusion that only the one from the Indian Bureau could have been opened. It was only a request that a list of students be included when she sent her first report. The letter from the banker assured her that he had made arrangements with the bank in Sweetwater to honor her drafts. She read the letter from Uncle Noah slowly, then went back and read parts of it again.

It was too funny, ducks. The bounder had to climb out a window onto the roof and shinny down a tree. He could not find the keys to let Maggie out. Our Cassy had taken care of that. The bloody fool had come out in his underdrawers and could not get into the house to get clothes on to go to town to get help. Tululla and Sandy had left early to market. (Dear Chas must have fresh fish for his noon meal.)

Jenny smiled as she read, knowing how much Uncle Noah had enjoyed Charles's discomfort.

Chas went to the magistrate and declared you a kidnapper. There was no proof, however, that you were anywhere near Allentown on that date. The magistrate did say that he would look into the matter. Your case went on the bottom of the list of matters he intended to look into. You've nothin' to worry about, ducks. I anxiously await hearing from you. I must warn you that I am seriously thinking of braving the frontier and coming for a visit.

She read the last part several times. Oh, if he only would! Uncle Noah was a man who could get things done. Mr. Havelshell would think he had run into a buzz saw if he came up against Uncle Noah.

Jenny tried hard not to think about what had happened in town. She could have endured the hostility of the townspeople, but to be snubbed by Trell McCall after he had wormed his way into their good graces, assured them that he was their friend and then—and then—

Well. She, Colleen and Granny were grown-up. They understood how fickle men could be, but Cassandra had become fond and trusting of him. She badly needed the assurance that not all men were as self-serving and unscrupulous as Charles Ransome.

Questions rattled around through the corridors of Jenny's mind. If, as he had planned, he had gone to Forest City the day before, then why would he make a trip to Sweetwater? Why would he look straight at Colleen and give her a flirtatious wink? It was completely out of character . . . or what she had thought was his character.

Why had he been so willing to make the long trip to Forest City with her mail? Oh, merciful heavens! Was he waiting to get his hands on it so that he could take it to Havelshell?

Jenny wanted to cry and promised herself she would . . . later on.

Chapter Thirteen

On the second morning after his visit to Stoney Creek, Trell woke at dawn, saddled up, and rode out after downing a cup of lukewarm coffee and eating a few cold biscuits. He had told Joe the night before that he was leaving for Forest City early and would be back home in the afternoon.

This was the busy season. For the next few weeks they would be selecting the mares for breeding in July and August and culling out the mustangs. Some they would halter-break and sell; others they would return to the range.

When he left the ranch, Trell struck straight south, following the river. Under him the buckskin's impatience was contagious. He let him out in full whenever the terrain was suitable. The big stallion had had several days rest and was eager to stretch his legs.

In his saddlebags Trell carried a thick packet to mail for Jenny. *Jenny.* Her name slipped unnoticed from his lips. There was something more than beauty in her face; there was breeding and a hint of fine steel. He still couldn't believe that he had kissed her and she had kissed him back!

Unlike his brother Travor, Trell was shy around women. If they went to a dance, he sat on the sidelines while Travor danced with every woman there, be she sixteen or sixty. Trell could never get up enough courage to ask one, although some flirted with him.

He was a fool, he decided, to have kissed Jenny. What could he offer such a woman? If he was looking for a woman, he asked himself, why not Colleen? The Irish girl would be a helpmate to a man. She and her granny would make a home for him. He'd have good hot meals and a woman in his bed to take comfort in during the long winter nights. Somehow the prospect didn't excite him.

Trell had not given serious thought to having a woman of his own. He had been reasonably sure that someday one would come along before he got too old to have a family. She had not had a face until now. And, he had to admit, when he had considered finding a wife he had thought she would be someone like Colleen, a woman who was well acquainted with ranch life and who would like it as much as he did.

The town of Forest City was a little larger than Sweetwater but had been laid out no better. The business section was on two sides of what was called the town square, which was no more than a half acre with a gigantic boulder in the middle of it. The founders had wanted to call the town Boulder, but there was already a town in Wyoming Territory named Boulder. So they named their town after the forest of lodgepole pines that surrounded it.

By the time Trell rode into town, the main street was already busy with wagons and horses. A freight wagon with a six-mule hitch clogged the street on one side of the town square. Trell turned down the side street that led to the livery and stepped from the saddle.

"Howdy, McCall. Never 'spected ya back so soon."

"Howdy. Never expected it myself." He tossed the man two bits. "Give my horse some grain. We've got to head back in an hour or so."

"Got ta be important fer ya to make that long ride so soon."

"Not really. Need to buy a thing or two."

Trell threw his saddlebags over his shoulder and headed uptown. He was hungry but decided to post Jenny's letters before eating.

Trell liked Forest City as well as he liked any town. The people were friendly, the stores well stocked. He came here about as often as he went to Sweetwater, even though it was ten miles farther from his ranch. Ten miles east was the timber town of Big Piney. He had been there a time or two. Joe Fiala had kinfolk there. Thinking of Joe caused him to remember that he'd not given the young couple a wedding present. *Guess he did need to buy something.*

The post office was in the mercantile store.

"Howdy, McCall. You thinkin' you got answers to your letters already?" The postmaster laughed, showing a gold tooth and a gap where another tooth was missing.

"Naw, I'm not thinking that. Got some more mail to post." Trell laid out the envelopes from his saddlebag.

"Christ on a horse! All this to the Bureau of Indian Affairs." He read the names on each envelope. "And to Mr. Noah Gray, Baltimore, Maryland. That's a long way from here."

"How much?"

"Four bits."

"Miss Virginia Gray will be getting mail here." Trell pulled a folded paper from his pocket. "Here is her request that I pick it up."

"She's the Indian teacher, ain't she? We've heard of her way over here."

"She is. I'd like to think that it won't be spread around that she's getting her *important* mail here. She was a little leery about it coming to the Sweetwater post office."

"She don't need to be worryin' her head none if it comes here."

"She'll like hearing that."

After posting Jenny's letters, Trell looked around for a gift for Joe and his bride. He decided on a small black-enameled music box decorated with white angels. When the lid was opened it played "Beautiful Dreamer." The tune was just the thing for a couple as much in love as Joe and Una May.

It surprised him that he also wanted to buy something for Jenny and for the girls. Colleen always wore her pa's overalls. She probably needed dress goods, and a good box of snuff would please Granny Murphy. Whit could use a really good carving knife—*Trell McCall, you're crazy as a drunk hoot owl. You act like you've been kicked in the head by a mule!*

With the music box in his saddlebag, Trell headed for the eatery.

"Nice seein' ya so soon, Mr. McCall. Sit ya down there and start helpin' yoreself."

"Thank you, Mrs. Fielding." Trell hung his hat on one of the hooks along the wall. "I couldn't come to town and not put my feet under your table."

"I'd shore be put out if you did. I'll brin' you coffee and a plate of hot biscuits."

When Trell had finished a satisfying meal and chatted over a second cup of coffee with Mrs. Fielding, it was time to head home. A cool breeze was blowing down from the north, and a few rain clouds hovered over the horizon when he left town. He pushed the horse as much as he dared. The animal had already covered a lot of miles and had had only a couple hours of rest.

After an hour of up-and-down riding, Trell reached the high-point of the trail as it followed the river to the place where it was safe to cross. The river was running fast and high owing to heavy rains in the mountains.

For some unknown reason, Trell felt uneasy. He had ridden this trail many times and had seldom met another rider. The rancher with whom he had bartered for the cow ran a few cattle along here. Trell had passed a few straggly steers a mile or so back, but had seen no one herding them. Still he had a prickly feeling at the nape of his neck as if someone was watching him, and he turned often to look behind him.

Here on the high trail, the wind was blowing at a pretty good clip. Trell pressed his hat down tighter on his head and resisted the urge to put his heels to the horse and get off this plateau.

He heard the bawling of a calf and pulled up to listen. When he heard it again, he walked his mount to the edge of the plateau and looked down. Not ten feet below, a calf that appeared to be not over a week or two old had its foot caught in a crevice.

Trell looked around for the mother and saw her standing at the edge of the woods. Something had scared her off;

otherwise, she would never have left her calf. It could have been a bobcat or a bear. If it had been a bobcat, Trell reasoned, it would have gone down after the calf. Whatever had scared her off was gone, but the animal's pitiful cries would soon attract another predator.

Trell stepped from the saddle and dropped his reins to ground-tie his horse. At the edge of the drop-off he turned to back down over the ledge. He had taken the first step when he felt something slam into the side of his head. Vaguely he saw his horse leap and run. Then he was falling toward the graveled slope and tumbling head over heels toward the rim of the fifty-foot drop-off.

It was the cold that awakened him.

He struggled back to something like consciousness. Wet as a drowned rat and shivering uncontrollably, he sensed only the cold—at first. Then he heard voices close by and clenched his jaws to keep his teeth from rattling.

"He's here some'r's."

"He washed on downriver."

"Ya ain't knowin' that."

"She . . . et. He was dead 'fore he fell. I ain't missin' no clear shot like that."

"So he's dead. Find the body."

"Hellfire! If he ain't here, he went in the river and down the rapids. That'd kill 'em if the bullet didn't."

"We'll go downriver and look till we find him."

The voices and the sound of a walking horse faded.

Trell lay in the river mud under the roots of a huge old sycamore. Had it been Hartog who had shot him and then followed up to make sure that he was dead? Well, if he didn't get warm soon he would surely die. One arm flopped helplessly. With the other he groped for a hold on something solid, grabbed a root and pulled himself up out of the mud and onto dry ground. He crawled along the dirt bank until he found a dark hole. It was small, but it was a shelter. He rolled into it and curled up like a babe in the womb.

Pain knifed through every muscle and bone in his body. The side of his face was on fire and he could see out of only one eye. His thoughts were fuzzy. He forced his mind away from his pain and tried to sort out what had happened. On the steep gravelly slope a calf had caught its foot in a crevice. He had turned to climb down and attempt to free it when something slammed into the side of his head.

The next thing he knew he was falling. He hit the slope and tumbled head over heels toward the rim of the fifty-foot drop-off. He remembered the wild, ugly yell that came from his throat as momentum propelled him over the edge into space. He must have bounced off an outcropping of crumbly rock ten feet below, for he continued to fall. This time he landed on brush growing out from the side of the cliff and ripped through it as he clawed for a grip. He landed on another slope of sharp shale and rolled a dozen feet more before plunging into a deep pool.

He came up gasping for air. The current caught him and swept him between the rocks and through the spillway of fast-moving water. It filled his mouth. He almost strangled as the swift current rushed him on and over another spillway and into the middle of the river. The rushing water carried him for what seemed like miles before swirling him into a pool where arching tree branches covered the river's edge. There he pulled himself from the river.

His head throbbed as if being pounded by a hammer. His shirt was torn to shreds, his heavy duck pants ripped. Somewhere along the way he had lost his boots. The wide gun belt was still buckled about his waist, but his gun and his bowie knife were gone.

In an agony of pain he drifted in and out of consciousness. One time during the night, he awakened to the sound of a voice—his own, calling Jenny's name. He didn't dare move. Movement meant pain. When awake, he fought to keep panic at bay.

Downriver some five miles, a rider pulled up to listen. He heard no sound except for the ripple of water and the occasional whisper of the wind in the pines. He could almost feel the silence pushing at him. Overhead the stars were disappearing behind a drifting cloud. Then saddle leather creaked as the tired horse began moving again. The roan needed rest as he did.

A few towns back he had run into an acquaintance who told him a sallow-faced man with lean cheeks and thin graying hair had come through there asking about him. When he was told the man wore a long white duster, the description had immediately rung a bell. It was Crocker, a hired gun who worked for whoever paid his price. He had heard that the killer was shrewd, tough and dangerous. And he played by no rules other than his own. He was reluctant to think Crocker was after him to kill him, but there was always the chance.

Could it be that old man Ashley was angered because he hadn't courted his feather-headed daughter and would want him dead for *that*? He'd given the rancher a full day's work for his pay. He'd even given him a month's notice when he left his employ.

That simpering little twit had been the subject of many bunkhouse remarks, especially on washday when she would hang a string of her underdrawers on the line facing the cookshack. He had not spent any more time than was absolutely necessary at the ranch that last month because Clara followed him like a shadow. A time or two she had burst into loud sobs. It had been as embarrassing as hell. The other hands had ribbed him unmercifully.

He rode cautiously into Sweetwater. He had to be careful. With a man like Crocker, there wasn't much leg room between the quick and those who hadn't been quite quick enough. Small clouds of dust swirled around his roan's feet as he went toward the saloon that boasted: DRINKS and EATS.

He crossed the porch and looked into the saloon over the pair of swinging doors. Seven or eight men lounged around, and a bartender wiped glasses. He scanned the faces carefully. Crocker wasn't among them.

As he flung back the doors and walked in, people turned to stare at the wide-shouldered man with blunt, bronzed features and sharp blue-black eyes. Taller than most men at six-foot-two in his stocking feet and more with his boots on, he was accustomed to folks giving him second looks.

"Howdy, McCall. What'll ya have?"

"Grub. What ya got?"

"How hungry are ya?"

"Hungry enough to eat the ass outta a skunk."

"I'll get ya a slab of meat and some eggs." The bartender went to the end of the bar and yelled into the back room. "Throw a steak in the pan for McCall and cook 'im a half dozen eggs." He slid a wet cloth along the bar on the way back. "Want somethin' to wet yore whistle while yo're waitin'?"

"Beer."

Gradually, McCall became aware of the lack of sound. The place had grown quiet as a tomb. He turned and stood with his back to the bar. Four men in range clothes sat at one table. The two at a second table appeared to be merchants. Two others had walked out while he was talking to the bartender. The four he had noticed first were giving him the once-over. One of them, a swarthy faced man, grinned at him, but not in a friendly way.

A big man with a flat round face and florid complexion murmured to the Mexican who responded with a snicker. Cold, ice-blue eyes fastened on McCall. Being able to read men like some folk read a newspaper, he knew this man was trouble even before he spoke.

"Ya been doin' a mite of night-ridin' ain't ya, McCall?"

"Is there a law against it?" He turned his back, downed his drink and waited for a refill.

"I'm talkin' to ya, mister."

McCall placed another coin on the counter and watched the man in the mirror over the bar.

"Talk if you're bound to. Some fellers just naturally got the runnin' off at the mouth."

"Don't turn yore back when I'm talkin' to ya!"

"You got it wrong, flap-jaw. You're not talkin' to me. You're yappin' 'cause ya don't know no better."

With the beer in his hand, McCall headed for a table at the end of the room. As he neared the table where the four men sat, the big man's foot shot out. McCall stumbled. After the frustration of the past few days, being harassed by this loudmouthed blowhard was too much. He flung his beer in the man's face.

"If you're itchin' for a fight, you got one."

The bully came up out of the chair with a roar.

"Ya . . . shit-eatin' sonofabitch!"

"Nobody calls me *that!*"

McCall dropped his glass and hit him. The man was almost his same height and somewhat heavier. McCall had been in enough barroom fights to know that the first punch counted for a lot. His right fist smashed the man in the nose, and the left fist came up under his chin, throwing his head back.

Blood spurted.

The man clawed for his gun. McCall grabbed his belt, pulled him forward, then threw him back over the table as people scrambled to get out of the way. The chair the bully landed on broke apart. He hit the floor with a thud and came up roaring like a bull, his face splotchy with rage.

McCall hit him in the mouth with one fist, and with the other came around and clobbered him on the ear. It was a blow meant to stun, and it did. The man stood swaying on spraddled legs like a pole-axed steer too stubborn to fall. McCall hammered his belly with both fists, then stretched him out on the plank flooring with a well-placed blow on the chin.

"Anybody takin' up this peckerneck's fight?"

"Wasn't our fight."

"My mother was *not* a bitch!" McCall said to the upturned bloody face on the floor. "Next time you see me call me *Mister* McCall."

He picked up the heavy glass he had dropped, set it on the bar and tossed out a couple of coins. "For the broken chair."

"Here's a refill on the house." The barkeep shoved a full glass of beer across the bar.

"Obliged."

McCall went to a table near the door and sat down. Soon he was joined by one of the men who had sat at the table with the bully.

"Take my advice, mister. Get on your horse and ride out of town. That's one mean sonofabitch you whipped."

"He might be mean, but he wasn't so tough. I could've whipped him with one hand tied behind my back."

"He ain't knowin' what *fair* is."

"Armstrong," the barkeep yelled. "Get that tub a guts outta my saloon. He's caused enough trouble."

"I've warned ya. It's all I can do," Armstrong continued in a low voice. "Hartog is mean—killer-mean. Brags that he's never lost a barroom fight."

"Well, ya can put a lie to that."

"He won't let it go. Reason he started in on ya was he thinks ya was with the Murphy girl when she shot him in the back."

"Is that right?"

"I was with Hartog when he killed her pa. I don't go along with shootin' a man down, and can't blame the girl none. He's the meanest with womenfolk I ever knowed. Crazy-mean. Ya'd better tell that girl to steer clear of him. He'll pleasure himself on 'er, then kill 'er."

"This Hartog sounds like a real nice fellow."

"*Señor*, give me a hand." The Mexican was trying to get Hartog off the floor.

The bartender stepped from behind the bar and threw a bucket of water on the unconscious man. Hartog sat up, dazed and confused.

"Get him outta here," the bartender ordered.

"Ya ain't better get hard-nosed 'bout it," the Mexican snarled. "Hartog'll take care a that feller, and come fer you."

"Let him come. I'll be waitin' with my old buffalo gun."

After the two men led Hartog out through the swinging doors, the barkeep spoke to the fourth man who had been sitting at the table when the fight started.

"Where do you fit in this, Pud?"

"I ain't fittin' in with them fellers a'tall, Oscar. They ain't friends of mine. Armstrong ain't a bad sort. Hartog's pure poison, and that speckled pup that's latched onto Hartog ain't got 'nuff brains to pour piss outta his boots."

Pud Harris had not been pleased when he had returned from the store to be told to keep an eye on Havelshell's men. He didn't like the agent and he didn't like the men he hired. But Pud's boss wanted to know what they were up to, and he was the man who paid Pud's wages.

Hartog had picked on the wrong man when he started pushing McCall. Pud had seen McCall around once or twice and he seemed to be a decent sort. But tonight he had a short fuse and wasn't to be messed with. Hartog got what he had coming.

The bartender rested elbows on the bar. "Somethin's fishy about Hartog killin' that nester. Don't make sense that a man with his girl and his ma beside him would draw down on three armed men. I'm thinkin' that Hartog is a low-down dirty skunk."

One of the two merchants spoke up. "We need a lawman if we're going to have a law-abiding town, or Sweetwater will be easy pickin's for bullies like that Hartog."

"That's what Reverend Longfellow told us Sunday at church meeting," the other merchant said.

"I ain't knowin' who we'd get." The bartender placed a double-barreled shotgun on the bar. "Meantime, I'm keepin' this handy."

McCall ate his steak and eggs, and listened to the conversation. Suddenly he was dead tired. The long ride and the short fight had been too much for a man who had had little sleep for the last three nights. He longed for a bed, but he still had to take his horse to the livery before he could find one at the hotel.

He slapped his hat on his head, stepped around the man mopping the floor and went to the bar. He fished in his pocket for money to pay for his meal.

"Sorry about the fracas."

"Hartog's been spoilin' for a fight for a couple of days. Glad you obliged him."

"Who's he work for?"

"Havelshell, I reckon." Oscar gave another swipe at the bar with his wet cloth. "Stayin' in town tonight, McCall?"

"If they've got a bed at the hotel."

"Melva'll have one. If she ain't, she'll let ya share hers."

"I'm too tired even for *that*." McCall grinned at the good-natured bartender.

"Hell! Ya must be plumb frazzled out!" Oscar scooped up the coins from the counter. "Keep an eye out for Hartog and that sneaky little Mexican. It ain't likely that they'll forget 'bout this little set-to."

Chapter Fourteen

Travor McCall chuckled as he rode out of town the next morning. The black-haired girl with the light blue eyes was something. He'd bet his bottom dollar that she'd not back down to anything or anybody. At first her mouth had dropped when he winked at her, then it snapped shut and her eyes shot daggers at him. Surely one with her looks had been winked at before.

It could be that they knew Trell, which was unlikely because when the liveryman told him the teacher was in town buying out the store, he'd said she'd only been in the territory for a short time. But if they had met, it was no wonder she was surprised. Winking at a woman was definitely something his brother would *not* do.

He made an attempt to banish the women from his mind and concentrated on being alert even though he was reasonably sure that Crocker had not reached Sweetwater. The saloon was the best source of information in any town. The bartender would have told him if a stranger had been there asking about a McCall.

Travor's thoughts kept returning to the black-haired girl. He realized suddenly and with greater clarity than ever before that he was a lonely man, a drifting man with no ties except to his brother and Mara Shannon and Pack, who had their own lives. He suddenly yearned to belong to a woman as Pack belonged, as his friend Sam Sparks belonged to his wife, Emily. Travor wanted to stop drifting, to settle down, break his own horses, brand his own cows. He wanted to look out over his own land and sleep in the same bed every night.

Thank God for Trell. While he'd been flitting from one place to the other, Trell had stayed tight and held their place together. He was back now to stay. And Trell no longer had to shoulder the whole load. As soon as he could get this business with Crocker settled, he just might visit that black-haired girl and see if she was as interesting as she looked.

When Travor rode into the yard of the Double T Ranch, Joe was coming out of the ranch house. He had met the cowboy one time a year ago. Trell seemed to like him, think he was trustworthy.

"Trell, for God's sake where've ya been. Yore horse come in a little bit ago. I already sent Curtis out lookin' fer ya and was just goin' myself."

Travor frowned and stepped from his horse. "I'm Travor. I met you about a year ago. What's this about Trell?"

"Godamighty! I'd a swore—"

"Yeah. Now what's this about Trell?"

"Well," Joe swiped his hand across his mouth. "Trell went to Forest City yesterday morning. Said for sure he'd be back in the afternoon to help sort the mares. He hasn't come back yet. Curtis found his horse, still saddled, 'bout a half mile from here. The horse was on his way back to the ranch."

"Any blood on the saddle?"

"I looked for some. It was clean. He had a package in his saddlebag so I figure whatever happened happened on the way back from Forest City."

"Any strangers been around? Have you seen a man in a white duster?"

"No. Curtis said a big man and a Mexican crossed the river yesterday afternoon."

"Headin' which way?"

"Toward Sweetwater."

A girl came out of the house with a big smile on her face.

"I told Joe not to worry none. Ya'd come home."

Joe held his hand out to her. "Honeybunch, it ain't Trell. 'Member I tol' ya Trell had a brother that looked just like him. This here is Travor. Him and Trell is look-alike twins. This is my wife, Una May."

"Howdy. Oh, I thought sure . . . ya was Trell."

"Howdy, ma'am." Travor's eyes traveled from one worried face to the other. "Did Trell say why he was going to Forest City?"

"I think it was to post some letters."

"Why not Sweetwater? It's closer."

"I not be knowin' that." Joe rubbed a hand over his worried face. "Una May's kept some vittles ready for Trell . . . when he came. I just had a bite."

"Then I'll eat, get a fresh horse and go down the river trail to Forest City." Travor began unsaddling his horse. "Stay here with your wife, Joe, and keep your eyes peeled for a man in a white duster or that big galoot and the Mexican. I had a set-to with him last night in town. He thought I was Trell."

"Now that I think about it, I come onto a feller camped out by the river 'bout a month ago. He had one of them long coats. Wasn't wearing it, but I saw it hangin' on a branch a dryin'. Feller was bald on top, but had a spot a hair just about his forehead and around his ears. Nice feller. We jawed a little. He said he was just passin' through."

Travor had stopped unsaddling and listened with interest.

"Did he ask about me?"

"No."

"Did you tell him that this was the McCall ranch?"

"Yeah. Seems like I did."

"His name is Crocker. He's a hired killer. I have reason to think he's looking for me. He may have found Trell, but I don't think so . . . yet. He was a few towns behind me. It's more likely that Trell ran into Hartog and the Mexican."

"That'd mean Trell spent the night in Forest City. He said he'd be back in the afternoon."

"Does he spend the night in town often?" Even as he asked Travor remembered the hotel woman saying something about he'd not spent the night there before.

"He's not stayed all night in town since I worked here. He did stay away all night a couple weeks ago. He helped bury a nester and put out a grass fire on Stoney Creek Ranch. A day or two ago he took a milch cow over to Stoney Creek."

"Would he have gone back over there?"

"Naw. If he'd been goin' there or stayin' in Forest City, he'd not a told me he'd be back in the afternoon to help with the mares. He knows we're behind with the work here." Joe was clearly distressed.

"If Crocker comes back, hole up in the bunkhouse or barn and don't come out. He'd think no more of shootin' you down than steppin' on an ant if he wanted to lie in wait for me."

By the time Travor had finished eating, Joe had saddled a horse, and had also strapped on a gun belt.

"He don't look like much. Fact is he's ugly as a mud pie," Joe said when he saw Travor eyeing the big gray horse with black-spotted hindquarters. "But he'll take ya to hell and back, that is, if he likes ya. He'll do anythin' fer Trell; thought he'd do the same for you."

Travor approached the horse head-on. The big animal rolled his eyes and jerked his head. Talking to him gently, Travor put out a hand. At first the gray bared his teeth, then gradually, Travor was allowed to rub his nose.

"Guess he's taken to ya. He'd bite my hand off if I tried that."

"What's the nearest town east of here?"

"Big Piney, but Trell's not said anythin' 'bout bein' there."

"When Curtis comes back, tell him to look around over at Orphan Butte. Trell might have gone there to check on his mustangs and somehow got thrown."

"That sorrel wouldn't'a left him if he was in sight or sound."

Travor mounted the horse and didn't speak again until after the animal stopped dancing in place and settled down.

"I don't know when I'll be back. I'll scout the trail from here to Forest City and try to find out when he left there. Joe, keep your wife out of sight if Hartog and that Mexican show up here. I hear he's crazy-mean where women are concerned."

"I'd blow that sucker clear to hell if he even looked at my wife!"

"Watch yourself. He's got away with it a few times. That's how a man builds a reputation like that."

Travor left the ranch filled with apprehension. If something had happened to Trell because of him, it sure as hell would be hard to live with. He couldn't imagine life without Trell. He'd always been there, sturdy as a rock. Hellfire! Without Trell he'd have probably gone off on the outlaw trail with their older half brother. He'd ended up shot in the back near a miner's shack up near Trinity.

Travor rode cautiously knowing that Hartog and the Mexican had left Sweetwater that morning. The trail was very still; there was no sound but the hoof falls of Mud Pie, a name Travor considered suitable for the gray-and-black horse. Dipping down, the path led into the aspens then up to the highest point. The horse walked, ears pricked, into the stillness on the high plateau.

This was a spooky place. A man could be picked off here in the open. Travor forced the horse to the edge of the bluff so he could look down. The river rushed by fifty or more feet below. Down on the slope were the remains of a calf that scavengers had feasted on. He backed Mud Pie off the ledge and continued on down the trail.

When Travor reached Forest City, he went directly to the post office and was greeted by the postmaster.

"Howdy, McCall. Got mail? Stage leaves in about half an hour."

"I take it you know Trell McCall."

The postmaster looked at him as if he'd been eating loco weed.

"'Course, I know him. You're him, ain't ya?"

"No, I'm his brother. We're often mistaken for each other. His horse came home without him and I'm looking for him."

"By golly, ya sure do look like him."

"So I've been told. When did you see him last?"

"A couple days ago. He was in and posted mail for the teacher at Stoney Creek Indian school." The worried postmaster rubbed a hand across his mouth. "I ain't suppose to be tellin' who posts mail."

"I'm obliged to you for letting me know he was here. He had a package in his saddlebag. Did he buy something here?"

"A music box. Said it was a wedding present. Said he was heading back after he got a bite to eat."

"Where would he go to eat?"

Travor went down the street to the restaurant after the postmaster pointed it out. Again he had to explain that he was Trell's brother and that they were often mistaken for each other. The proprietor told him Trell had eaten an early noon meal and had said that he'd like to give his horse a longer rest but that he needed to get back home.

Travor rode away from Forest City with two sure things in mind. Trell had planned to go straight back home and he had posted letters for the teacher at Stoney Creek. Why would he ride all the way to Forest City when she was going to Sweetwater, a couple of days later and could post them there?

Then a fresh thought hit him. If Trell knew the teacher at Stoney Creek well enough to tote her mail to Forest City, and if they had mistaken *him* for Trell, which most folks did, Trell was not only missing, he was in deep trouble with the woman at Stoney Creek for snubbing her. He hoped the black-haired girl wasn't the teacher.

It was dark when Trell approached the Double T. He proceeded cautiously. All was quiet. He whistled a signal he and Trell had used since they were boys. If Trell was there he would answer; if not, maybe he and Joe used the same signal. When the answering whistle came, Travor rode up to the house.

It was a worried Joe who met him.

"Find out anythin'?"

"Nothin'. I'll get a few hours' sleep and head out again in the morning."

Chapter Fifteen

The Grays and Murphys had just finished breakfast when Ike Klein spotted four men riding across the meadow toward the house.

"Havelshell's men," he said peering out the window. "I seen one of them afore. Name's Armstrong."

"I've seen one of 'em before, too. He was one of 'em who came to warn us off the place." Colleen took her father's gun belt off the hook beside the door and strapped it around her waist.

Granny stepped to the window, peered out, and then backed away, her eyes dark with worry, her gnarled hands pressed tightly together.

"He wasn't the murderer. Don't do anything foolish, child."

"He was part of it. I'll not be caught short-handed like Pa was."

"Let it go. I can't . . . lose ya—"

"Ya won't. Don't worry, Granny." Colleen put her arm around her grandmother's shoulders and hugged her.

Jenny was tired this morning, but she forgot her weariness the instant Ike said the men were headed their way. She went to the other room, took the little derringer off a top shelf and put it in her pocket.

Last night she had lain awake for hours, her mind refusing to shut off the unanswered questions that troubled her. Why had Trell McCall gone to Sweetwater? Why, if he was on a mission to betray her trust, had he made no effort to keep them from seeing him? Instead, he had flaunted his presence.

She returned to the kitchen to see the girls and Granny looking out the door. Colleen and Ike had gone outside.

"Girls, stay in the house with Granny until we find out what they want."

"It's foolish of you not to let someone teach me how to handle a gun, Virginia." Cassandra had not spoken a dozen words to any of them since the incident with Trell. "You know how to shoot, don't you, Granny?"

"If it should ever come to that, darlin', I'll load and you shoot. It's what I did when Colleen was yore age."

"What were you shooting at?"

"Wolves. It was dead a winter and they was hungry."

Jenny went out to stand beside Colleen and Ike as the men approached the house. Three of the riders stopped beside the corral. One took off his hat and approached Ike and the women.

"Mornin', ladies. Howdy, Ike."

"What'a ya wantin' here, Armstrong?"

"I figured it fair to tell ya that we come out to put the dam back in—it bein' agin the law and all fer water to come off Indian land for private use."

"That is not true! Mr. Havelshell is interpreting the law as he wants it to read." Jenny's temper was rising by leaps and bounds.

"I ain't knowin' nothin' 'bout the law, ma'am, 'cepts what Mr. Havelshell tells me. He says it's in the book; ya can't take water from the reservation."

"The water has been flowing into Stoney Creek for years. Mr. Havelshell is the one who interfered with nature when he had the source diverted toward the river. He did it, of course, to inconvenience us here at the homestead."

"I ain't knowin' none a that. He said put the dam back in. It's what we'll do."

"I would expect no less from his paid lackeys. It isn't what's right or wrong that matters, is it? It's the money he pays you. What a sad thing it is when a man will sacrifice a principle for the almighty dollar. As long as your principles are up for sale, Mr. Armstrong, I'll pay half again whatever Havelshell is paying you to go about your business and leave Stoney Creek alone."

"I can't do that, ma'am." Her scorn scorched him. He knew he was no match for her in an argument, so he tipped his hat to leave them.

Colleen's shrill, angry voice stopped him.

"Hold on, ya murderin' sonofabitch!" She slapped her hand on the gun that lay against her thigh. "Ya was one of 'em who shot down my pa in cold blood. He wasn't armed, but I am. Ya want to take yore chance with me, or do ya want it in the back?"

"Miss, I had nothin' to do with the killin' of yore pa." Armstrong held his hands up and away from the gun at his side.

"I was hopin' to God, I'd killed all of ya when ya come sneakin' back in the dark of night."

"We was sent to warn yore pa off and that's all. I got plenty a sins to answer for, but shootin' down a unarmed man ain't one of 'em."

"Ya did nothin' to stop it, ya slimy toad!"

"I never give a thought to what Hartog was goin' to do. And that's the God's truth. I broke with him over it. He's like a wild longhorn on loco weed. There ain't no knowin' what he'll do from one minute to the other."

"I'll shoot 'im when I see him. My pa was a good man who never did harm to anybody."

"Let Hartog be, ma'am. Ya got him in the back that night. Didn't do much damage to him, but ya or McCall— yeah I know it was him—damn near kilt the other feller."

"I was doin' my best to kill all of ya."

"And I ain't blamin' ya. It's what I'd a done. It might ease ya some to know that Hartog picked a fight with Mc-Call in the saloon the other night and McCall whipped him. Laid him out cold."

"I'm not askin' McCall or anybody else to fight my fights." Colleen shouted the words because Armstrong had motioned to the riders beside the corral and had turned his horse toward the reservation.

"Ike, they have no tools—"

"They ain't needin' any, Jenny. They'll blast."

"Blast? Use powder? Dynamite?"

"Probably packin' sticks in their saddlebags."

"Oh, my goodness! What'll we do?"

Ike scratched his head. "I ain't knowin' if we can do anythin'. I'm thinkin' it's not up to us now."

"No? Then who?"

"Shoshoni ain't wantin' 'em to put the dam back in. Whit couldn't a took it out 'less'n the elders said he could. The chief's up north in the Wind River leavin' the runnin' a thin's to the elders. They know what's goin' on even if they don't come this way hardly a'tall. They'd a took it out even if ya hadn't come here. Looky yonder."

Jenny looked toward the school. "Oh, my goodness!"

A group of Indian horsemen came galloping across the school yard, Whit among them, and passed out of sight into the woods.

"They're goin' to head Havelshell's men off. Do you think there'll be trouble?"

"Yeah, if the fools think they can stand off thirty warriors," Ike said dryly. "If ya want, I'll get on old Trouble and take a look-see."

"I don't want you hurt."

"I ain't gettin' twix' 'em." Ike threw a halter on his mule and climbed up onto the swayed back. "Ya'll keep yore eyes peeled. Hear?"

Ike reached the site where Whit and the Indian called Head-Gone-Bad had pried loose the piled rocks that had dammed the small, slow rivulet that formed Stoney Creek.

The shaman in full headdress was offering his thanks to the Great Spirit for the gift of the waters. Ike watched as the shaman said his words and each of the Indians drank from a common gourd filled with water from Stoney Creek. The ceremony took the good part of a half an hour.

Armstrong and his men stood well back from the creek as did Ike. When the shaman, Whit, and all the warriors had drunk, they mounted their ponies and in a group moved to where Armstrong and his men waited. The shaman motioned for Whit to move up beside him. He spoke to him for several minutes. Then Whit translated for him.

"The shaman say go from here. A place where water divides is a sacred place. Do not disturb Mother's land or Mother's water or Mother be very angry."

"What the hell's he talkin' 'bout?" one of the men growled.

Armstrong ignored him.

"Tell him we have blasting sticks and were told by the Indian agent to shut off the water because it belongs to the reservation."

Whit relayed the message to the shaman. The old man spoke at length in the language of the Shoshoni, and Whit summed up his words.

"He said that water belongs to no man. Many years ago, before the white man came, a brave warrior lay dying on the grassland. Mother caused the earth to rumble, and waters from this place were sent over a bed of stones to the warrior. He lived to lead his people for many years. It was not good that the agent sent men to disturb what Mother has made. Our chief, Washakie, will speak of it to the agent when he comes at the end of summer."

"Who's mother's he blabberin' 'bout? One stick'd scatter that ragtail bunch."

"Mother is the land, ya dumb ass," another said after Whit finished translating. "This is their land. If they want Stoney Creek to have some of their water, it ain't no skin off my butt. I had no likin' fer doin' this anyhow."

"Do ya think they'll fight us?"

"They ain't carryin' them weapons to hunt bear."

"We got the sticks—"

"No! This little old pissin' creek ain't worth a body dyin' for. Why Havelshell don't forget about it, I ain't knowin'.'"

"I'm thinkin' Havelshell's got his sights on this ranch. He's already got a thousand head a cattle on it."

"The cattle is for the reservation."

"Haw! Haw!"

"What'er we goin' to do, Armstrong? Air we backin' down?"

"It's the sensible thin', 'less yo're hell-bent on dyin'.'"

"Jeez! We got the sticks, ain't we? What'er they but a bunch a piss-poor Indians with a dozen rifles?"

"Goddammit! We ain't usin' no dynamite!"

"Boss ain't goin' to like it."

"Then to hell with 'im. He can do it hisself."

Armstrong kneed his horse, and the animal moved closer to where Whit waited beside the shaman.

"Tell him that we're leavin'. But more men may come. This will have to be settled with the agent."

"I will tell him. It is good that you go. The shaman know some English and know that one of your men want to use the blasting sticks. It would not do for that man to come this way alone."

"That bad, huh?"

Whit shrugged. "We have pride. We respect the Mother Earth and despise those who would destroy her."

Jenny, waiting for the sound of the blast or rifle fire, was relieved to see Armstrong and his men riding across the meadow toward the trail that led to town. Shortly after, the Indians pulled their ponies to a halt in front of the school. She hurried to meet them. Whit sat proudly on his pony beside a handsomely dressed man in a beaded tunic. He had weathered features and gray-streaked hair.

"The shaman wish to see where you will teach the young."

Jenny looked into the flat black eyes of the old man and smiled.

"Welcome." She waved her hand toward the door.

He slid from the back of the pony and followed her inside the school. Whit trailed after them. Jenny was grateful for his presence. She was unsure what to say to the dignified old man until he spoke.

"What this?" He indicated the map she had hung on the wall.

"This is a picture of the world." She spread her arms. "All the land, all the water. Our land is here." She put her forefinger on the place that was America. "I will tell the children about other lands and their own wonderful land."

He said nothing and she wondered if he understood. Desperate to make an impression, she picked up a slate and drew a letter W.

"I will teach them to read and write. I'll teach them the good ways of the white man and warn them about the bad ways. I am not a missionary. I will not try to convert them to Christianity. My job is to teach, not preach."

"That is good. We will send all the children." To Jenny's amazement, he spoke in perfect English.

Jenny looked quickly at Whit. His expression was stoic.

"*All* the children? I agree that all the children should learn, but it is difficult to teach many children at one time. It would be better if I start with this many." She held up ten fingers. "Then these could help me teach the others."

The shaman appeared to pay scant attention to what she said. He looked at everything in the room; from the table with the checked cloth to the glass jar filled with wild flowers she had picked along Stoney Creek. He paused at the picture of George Washington.

"Who this?"

"George Washington. The first president of our country."

"Where he live?"

"He has been dead for a long time."

"That is good."

Jenny didn't know what to say to that, so she said nothing. She also didn't know if she should tell him about ciphering or geography. She waited for a signal from Whit, but none was forthcoming. When the shaman took a last look around and walked out the door, the only thing that had been settled was that he would send *all* the children. She had visions of two hundred children appearing on the doorstep.

After speaking with Whit, the shaman mounted and the Indians rode away. Whit tied his pony to a bush and came to where Jenny stood beside the door.

"Did he like the school? How many children will he send?"

"So many questions. He say you good teacher. Yes and ten."

"What do you mean? Yes and ten?"

"Yes, he like school. He send ten children."

"Counting you?"

"I am not children. I will come help teacher."

"And learn, too. I want to start preparing you for college."

"My father talked of it."

"When will the children come?"

"He say soon. He say I watch school. Head-Gone-Bad watch to see if men with sticks come back."

"That's comforting to know." Jenny smiled with relief. "We'll bring you food from the house. I've sent a letter to the Bureau of Indian Affairs to complain about Mr. Havelshell and his strict orders that you or any other Shoshoni not leave the reservation land. I'm hoping that order will be modified or canceled altogether."

"Sneaking Weasel no longer spy on school. He look for Moonrock who went back to her father."

"The young girl who was at the store? Why did she leave?"

"She say Havelshell try to violate her chastity."

"Why . . . why . . . she was only a child," Jenny stammered.

The boy looked puzzled. "She'd had her bleeding time."

Jenny felt the heat that flooded her face.

"Without chastity," he explained, "she could never be first wife, only second or third wife."

"Will her father send her back?"

"He angry. Havelshell's woman angry."

"I invited her to come to school. Will she come?"

"No. Her father send her north to her mother's people."

"Will another girl go to work at the store?"

"No Shoshoni girl . . . now."

"The spy is not here. Come to the house for dinner." Jenny smiled fondly at the boy.

"No." He answered quickly. "My manners not good. It long since I sat at my father's table. Girl-Who-Squawk sure to notice."

"Cassandra would never mention your lack of table manners!"

"She would." He folded his arms over his chest. He had never looked so . . . Indian as he did now.

"When I'm preparing you for college, I will also teach you how to present yourself in public. It would be a pity for you to have the finest education and fear dining in a restaurant because of your table manners."

"Later I will come to your table," he said, as if it were his last word on the subject.

Chapter Sixteen

After Armstrong and his men left, Colleen and Ike had spent the rest of the morning scrubbing and delousing the bunkhouse. Ike had not said flatly that he would stay on and work at Stoney Creek, but allowed that if he did drop by now and then, he wouldn't mind having a *decent* place to stay. They had set up the bed from the Murphy wagon, a washstand and several chairs. Colleen seemed to be perfectly willing to use the furnishings from their burned-out cabin.

From the doorway of the bunkhouse, Jenny could view Stoney Creek homestead. A year's growth of grass and brush had been cleared from around the house. The afternoon sun shone on the clean windows. The woodpile was beginning to take on some semblance of order. The pole corral had been strengthened, and a new bucket hung by the well.

Most important to Jenny, little Beatrice romped happily in the yard with Hiram, the puppy.

This was home. Jenny decided that she had a lot to be thankful for. She had coped far better than she had thought she could when she arrived—thanks to Trell for helping her put out the fire and for bringing the Murphys to stay with her. She had him to thank for the cow . . . and for fixing the well, and for a dozen other things. Thinking about that caused a lump to form in her throat that was difficult to swallow.

She had made contact with one of the tribe's elders and the children would be coming to the school. Why was she not happy over this accomplishment? Why did she keep seeing a pair of blue-black eyes smiling into hers? She shook her head to banish the vision and turned back into the bunkhouse to help shake out the straw-packed mattress that went on the bunk built into the far wall.

It was Beatrice who saw the rider first and her childish voice rang with excitement.

"Jenny! Jenny! Trell comin'! Trell comin'!"

Jenny and Colleen stopped working and looked at each other. Jenny was speechless, but not Colleen.

"What's that rat's ass doin' coming here?"

"I . . . never thought he'd have the nerve."

Colleen stepped outside and Jenny followed as the rider rode into the yard. Cassandra came from the house and picked up the puppy. Travor pulled the big gray horse to a stop and sat looking at the two grim-faced women. The looks on their faces told him that he was in hostile territory, but he was too tired to care.

"Which one of you is the teacher?"

They stared at him with open mouths and said nothing. The long rides, sleepless nights, worry over Trell, and then this silent hostility caused his temper to erupt.

"Goddammit, answer me!" he shouted. "I'm Travor Mc-Call, Trell McCall's twin brother. He's been gone three days and I'm not going to sit here playin' niceity-nice with ya while waiting for an answer."

The harshness of his voice knocked all composure out of Jenny. She went deathly pale and pressed her hands against the wall of the bunkhouse to hold herself erect. He looked *exactly* like Trell even though dark whiskers covered his cheeks and his dark eyes blazed with anger.

"I'm . . . the teacher. It was you . . . we saw in town?" In this soundless void, her voice, when it finally came, sounded shallow and toneless.

"Yes, I saw you in town. I didn't know you were acquainted with my brother. He went to Forest City to post letters for you three days ago and hasn't come back."

"I told them you wasn't Trell." Cassandra looked up at Travor. "Trell pulls his hat lower and his boots aren't fancy."

"I'm Virginia Gray, this is Miss Colleen Murphy—" Despite the shock of seeing a man who *looked* like Trell, but wasn't Trell, Jenny remembered her manners.

Travor's eyes met and held Colleen's light blue ones. *Trell was with this girl when she shot Hartog in the back. Is he in love with her?*

"These are my sisters, Cassandra and Beatrice. Would you like a cool drink."

Travor brought his attention back to Jenny. He nodded at the girls and stepped down from his horse.

"I've not got much time. I need to get whackin'. I had hoped that Trell would be here."

He looks like Trell, his voice is the same . . . but he is not the gentle, sweet Trell who helped me put out the fire and brought the girls a puppy. These thoughts ran through Jenny's mind.

"He may have decided to go . . . on to another town." Jenny ventured the suggestion.

"No. He went to Forest City, posted the letters, ate in the restaurant and started back to the Double T. His saddled horse came in twenty-four hours later."

Jenny felt as if she were suffocating. Her hand went up to her mouth.

"Oh, my goodness! What . . . could have happened to him?"

"Any number of things, lady." Travor's face hardened. His dark eyes shifted from Jenny to Ike who had come from the bunkhouse.

"Ike, this is Trell's brother—"

"Figured it, if it wasn't Trell. Howdy."

"Howdy." Travor held out his hand. His eyes followed Colleen to the well. "I would like a drink, ma'am, then I'll be on my way."

Leading his horse, he approached the well and accepted the dipper of water from Colleen.

"Thanks."

"I'll water your horse." Colleen took the reins from his hands.

"Careful. He's . . . spooky."

"I can handle him."

Ike followed Travor to the well.

"I heared what ya said 'bout Trell. He and the girl yonder had a set-to with the men who shot down her pa. Feller named Hartog."

"I've met him. He took me for Trell in town the other night and picked a fight. I was told he shot down an unarmed man and that Trell took up the girl's fight. If he had ambushed Trell in the afternoon, he would have been surprised to see me in town that night. He wasn't."

"Ya say his horse come in?"

"The next day."

"Means the horse waited 'round fer him to come back. If'n that horse a had him in sight, he wouldn't'a left."

"Have ya seen any . . . buzzards circlin'?" Travor hated asking the question.

"Naw, boy, I ain't. It's what I'd'a looked for."

"I figured he might be lyin' hurt somewhere—"

"Have ya been to Pine City or Corbin?"

"I made a run to Corbin. Nothin' there."

"If'n ya want, I'll ask the Shoshoni. There's a stretch of the river from the Double T to Forest City that runs through the reservation. If'n he took the river trail, they might'a seen somethin'."

"I'd be obliged to you. Time is running out if he's been hurt. It's been more'n three days."

"I'll leave now." Ike stepped around Travor so that he could see if Whit's pony was at the school. "Where'll ya be?"

"Tell you the truth, I don't know what to do next."

"Ya look 'bout petered out. Why not stay here till I get back?"

"No. I got to keep goin'. I backtracked his horse to a bluff over the river. Thought I'd go back there and see if I missed something."

"Ya ain't goin' to help Trell none if ya get yoreself all tuckered out. I'll get me some Shoshonis to look along the river."

"They'll do that for you?"

"Hell, they be good folk."

"I'm about at the end of the . . . rope, old man." Travor's voice cracked.

"Yo're dead on yore feet is what ya are. The women here is mighty fond a yore brother and mighty cut up when they thought he'd turned his back on 'em. Stay here and rest up. I'll be back 'fore mornin' or send word."

Ike spoke to Jenny, then went to the corral for his mule.

"Mr. McCall—?"

"Yes, ma'am." Travor removed his hat and wiped his forehead with the sleeve of his shirt. The teacher's eyes met his and held, but he said nothing more, waiting for her.

"I imagine you're wondering why I didn't post my mail in Sweetwater. Your brother understood and offered to take it to Forest City. If something has happened to him because of me, I'll never forgive myself." Tears flooded her eyes making them look like shiny green pools.

"You're right, I was wondering why Trell made the trip to Forest City just to post your mail."

"I've reason to believe the Indian agent here is corrupt. He didn't want a teacher to come here and has made it as uncomfortable as he can for us. I don't know if he would go so far as to harm Trell—"

"Ma'am, I'm so tired I can hardly think straight. The old man said you'd not mind if I got a couple hours' sleep here."

"You're more than welcome. Have you eaten?"

"Sometime during the last few days, but I don't remember when or where."

"Use the bunkhouse. There's water there to wash in. We'll unsaddle your horse and feed him. I see Colleen is doing it already. Ike must have told her you will stay a while. I'll bring you a plate of food."

"I'm obliged."

"Whit is going with Ike." Cassandra had hung back—listening. Travor looked down at the little girl who had noticed that his boots were not like the ones Trell wore. She spoke with confidence. "Whit's part Shoshoni. His Indian name is *Woksois*. He's terribly irritating, and at times obnoxious, but he's very smart. And . . . he likes Trell a lot. If anyone can find Trell, Whit can."

Travor's tired mind absorbed only the fact that the child didn't speak like a child.

"What my sister says is true. I'm glad Whit is going with Ike. Whit seems to know . . . things."

"I hope to God you're right."

"I'll see about getting you something to eat."

Jenny went to the house on shaky legs. All this time she had been so angry at Trell, thinking that he had been ashamed to let the townspeople know that he knew her . . . and it hadn't been him at all. He had mentioned that he and his brother owned the Double T. But he hadn't said it was a *twin* brother who looked exactly like him.

Trell hasn't been seen in three days. He could be lying somewhere hurt or . . . dead. Oh, God, please don't let it be that.

Colleen had watched Travor McCall without appearing to do so. He looked like Trell, but he didn't *act* like Trell. They walked the same, moving long body and long legs, fluid and relaxed like a large cat ready to pounce on unsuspecting prey. They held their heads at the same angle, but inside they were different. This man's eyes held hers, searching there, prying where he didn't belong. Trell never would have looked at her like that, winked at her or any other woman he didn't know.

Colleen had never felt aware of Trell as she was aware of this *rogue*. Even with bloodshot eyes and whiskered cheeks, it was evident to her that Travor McCall attracted women like a lightning rod.

After unsaddling Travor's horse, Colleen threw his saddlebags over her shoulder and headed for the bunkhouse.

"Here's your saddlebags," she said, and flung them in the open door.

"Come in. Please—"

He was at the large tin washbowl she had placed on the washstand. He had wet his face and hair with his cupped hands.

"There's a towel in the drawer under the basin," She lingered in the doorway while he dried his face. "I'm sorry about Trell. He's a good man."

"Yes, he is. When they were handin' out *goodness* Trell got my part, too. I've never known a better man, even if he is my brother."

"What do you think happened to him?"

"I've got a couple notions roamin' around in my head. If I don't hear something from him in a day or two, I'm going to do some manhunting myself." He hung the towel on the bar at the end of the washstand.

"Ya think it was Hartog?"

"No. Someone else. Which one of you women was Trell interested in?" His eyes were holding hers again.

"You don't know yore brother very well, do ya? Ya think he had courtin' on his mind when he offered to help." Colleen straightened to her full height and put her fists on her hips. "Trell McCall was . . . is as decent a man as I ever knowed. He'd have helped us if Jenny and I both were bald and toothless. You're judgin' him by what *you'd* have done in his place."

"How do you know what I'd have done?"

"Decent men don't go 'round winkin' at strange women."

"You were insulted? I saw a pretty girl and I wanted her to know that I thought she was pretty. What's so bad about that?" He sat down on the bunk and started pulling off his boots.

"Granny fixed him a plate of food." Jenny came to the doorway and held out the plate. She made a brave attempt to conceal the fact that she had been crying.

Colleen took the plate, stomped across the room and plunked it down. The fork lying on the side of the plate fell to the floor. She ignored it and walked out the door. Jenny looked at the man sitting on the bunk. He was holding his boot in his hand, his eyes on the empty doorway.

"Would you like a drink of cool buttermilk, Mr. Mc-Call?"

"No, thank you, ma'am."

"Then I'll leave you to eat and get some rest." She backed out the door and closed it behind her.

Alvin Havelshell unlocked the door to his office, went inside and slammed the door shut. The glass rattled and for an instant he thought it would fall to the floor. He threw his hat on his desk and with his hands in his pants pockets, stood at the door and stared out the window at the side street below.

He was sick of taking orders from that hypocritical old fool! The unreasonable old bastard wanted the teacher off Stoney Creek Ranch and he didn't care how it was accomplished. Five thousand head of cattle were due in another six weeks.

Some idiot in Washington had come up with the idea that each of the Indians on the reservation be given one hundred and sixty acres of land to farm and a certain number of cattle. Shoshonis were not farmers even if the land was suitable to farm, which it was not. Give them cattle and they would kill one at a time, eat part of it and leave the rest to be food for the scavengers.

The herd, when it arrived, would be grazed on Stoney Creek land. Naturally they would mix with the herd owned by the Sweetwater Cattle Company. When the company cut out their cattle, at least half the Indian cattle would go with them. This meant a sizable chunk of money in the old man's pocket. There would be a lot of activity on Stoney Creek and it wouldn't do for a nosy teacher with connections to the Indian Bureau to be there.

He'd heard about McCall being out there. He was probably courting the Murphy girl. Get rid of the girl and you'd be rid of McCall, who would be sure to know what was taking place when they cut out their herd. With the teacher no longer in residence, the land would go up for auction at the end of the year. Hell, she could come to town and teach. *If only he wasn't tied to that lump of lard out at the Agency store!*

Alvin's mind filled with thoughts of Jenny. He had ceased to think of her as Miss Gray, or even Virginia Gray. Quite unexpectedly, Jenny now dominated his thoughts, vibrantly real and disturbing. She was the most fascinating woman he'd ever met. His feelings for her were different from the feverish desire he felt for other women.

The sound of boots on the steps leading to the office was

an unwelcome intrusion in his thoughts. He went quickly to his desk and sat down for fear that the evidence of his fantasy be noted.

Armstrong came in to stand just inside the door.

"That didn't take long," Alvin said curtly.

"We didn't use the sticks. We'd a had to fight 'bout forty Shoshoni and their medicine man. Old man said where water split off was a sacred place and something about the ground bein' upheaved years ago to take water to a warrior. It's sure they'd fight if we tried to block that stream."

Havelshell rocked back in his chair, and Armstrong stood nervously twirling his hat around and around in his hands. A minute or two passed while he waited for Havelshell to blow up and curse him for failing to do the job. Instead he asked a simple unexpected question.

"Did you see the teacher?"

"We saw her. She's feisty as a—"

"What did she say?" Alvin cut in sharply, not wanting to hear the rest of the remark.

"Said you was tryin' to run her off. That other'n—the Murphy girl, she's madder than a hornet 'bout Hartog shootin' her pa. Says she's goin' to kill him."

"That isn't likely. Maybe I should turn him loose out there."

Armstrong's lips set in a firm line, and he stared unblinkingly at the seated man.

"Hartog is pure-dee old mean with womenfolk, Mr. Havelshell. The teacher ain't deservin'—"

"Hell, I'm not talking about the teacher. If Hartog bothers her, I'll kill him myself. I'm talking about that black-haired bitch that walks around with a six-gun strapped on.

If she wears a gun, she's fair game. Get her out of there, and Jenny will be more likely to give it up."

"She'd still have McCall. He mopped the floor with Hartog the other night."

"I heard about it. He'll get his. We don't have to worry about him. Hartog will take care of him."

Alvin reached into a drawer and threw a tin star out onto the desk.

"Put it on, Armstrong. I'm appointing you sheriff of Sweetwater and the surrounding territory."

Armstrong stood rooted in his tracks. "Ain't ya put out that we didn't blow up the dam?"

"No. Let her have the water. There's more than one way to skin a cat."

Still not satisfied, Armstrong asked, "What do ya want me to do for the star?"

"Keep law and order. Occasionally take orders from me. Pays twenty dollars a month. You can't make that kind of money anyplace else."

Armstrong was tempted, but hesitated. "I'm not a killer, Mr. Havelshell. I don't shoot a man 'less he's shootin' at me."

"Good idea."

"Hartog'd not just kill that girl. He'd rape and torture her first."

"That happens in this country."

"Not to white women, it don't."

"If he does it, you'd have to bring him in and turn him over to a Territorial marshal . . . or kill him."

"He'd not let me take him in."

"Hell, Armstrong. Why worry about that now? Take the badge and keep order in the town."

"Folk'll think there ort to a been a election."

"When there is one, I'll be elected mayor of this town. I've got a right to appoint a sheriff. If you get lip from anyone, send them to me."

Armstrong reached for the star and pinned it on his shirt.

"Looks good there, Sheriff Armstrong. Sure does."

It was what Armstrong had always wanted. Being sheriff meant being respected. But there was a price attached to it. And he feared it would be more than he wanted to pay.

Arvella Havelshell sat in the parlor behind the store. She hated being isolated out here at the Agency store. She hated being alone. It had not been so bad with Moonrock here. The girl was company. She had liked teaching her things. *He* had even taken that small pleasure from her. When Linus had returned from the Indian camp to say that Moonrock would not come back because of the agent's near rape of her, she had known the girl was speaking truthfully.

Alvin had come to her room that night and, still fully dressed, had fallen on her and shoved his way into her. For his visit, she had prepared herself with petroleum jelly. Even so, he had hurt her dreadfully. She had cried out and, in his frenzy to satisfy himself, he had slapped her. When he had finished, he sat on the side of the bed, holding his face in his hands and cursing her.

Now tears rolled down Arvella's fat cheeks. She had endured Alvin's rutting because it was what she had to do to get a child. It was her father's fondest wish to have a grandchild; and if she gave him one, he might soften his attitude toward her and stop making her so miserable. All her life she had striven for his approval. All her life she had been told that she was a disappointment to him.

She wished that she were dead.

Arvella could not remember a time when she had not been plump. Even as a child she'd had little fat arms, legs, and a little round belly. She had never rolled a hoop or played tag with other children. Her mother had been educated in the best schools and took great pride in teaching her only child. It had not been necessary for Arvella to attend school. Her childhood had been spent sitting at her mother's knee doing algebra or reading the Greek classics. When her mother died, the world as she had known it came to an end.

The door opened at the back of the house. Arvella paid scant attention. It had to be Linus. At times she hated the boy. At other times she pitied him. He was detested by Alvin just as she was.

When Linus heard what Alvin had done to Moonrock, he had threatened to go to town and kill him. His hatred of the Indians had not included Moonrock. The girl had been kind to him, and Arvella suspected that the boy was a little in love with her.

Arvella was wise enough to know that Linus had to feel that he was better than *someone,* and the Indians were handy.

The sound of bootheels that were not Linus's came toward the parlor. Arvella turned and sucked in a deep breath.

"Why are you here? Did he . . . come back?"

"No. He's still in town."

"You're not suppose to be in here."

"I know." Pud Harris stood holding his hat in his hand. "Why're ya crying?"

"I'm not! Did you come to spy on me? What do you think I can do out here?"

"I'm not here to spy. Yore pa sent me to keep an eye on thin's."

"That's spying."

"Not on you, Miss Arvella. Alvin sent men to put the dam back in. Yore pa told me to keep an eye on them, too."

"But what are you doing in here?"

"I wanted to see how ya was doin'. I never see ya when I come with Havelshell."

Arvella raised her eyes to look at the man's homely face. Pud Harris had come to work for her father before she married Alvin and had spoken to her a time or two. *He was not looking at her as if she were a freak.* There was genuine concern in his soft brown eyes.

Her eyes flooded with tears. She covered her face with her handkerchief.

Pud squatted down beside her chair and placed his hat on the floor.

"Why'er ya cryin'? Did I say somethin'?"

Arvella answered with a shake of her head. When her hand dropped to her lap, a rough palm patted it gently. After a few minutes, Pud stood, and for an instant she felt his hand on the top of her head.

He left the room quickly. She heard his bootheels on the kitchen floor and then the closing of the back door.

Chapter Seventeen

Trell awoke to face the stark realization that if he didn't move soon, he would die here in a hole in a dirt bank. He was in bad shape. One arm and one leg were useless. His upper body was covered with cuts from the shale and his face bloody. He came close to panic when he closed one eye and could see nothing. His head was not working very well; his thoughts came slowly, but he knew enough to realize that he was without a horse or a gun and was being hunted by men who wanted him dead.

The first movement brought pain so severe that waves of blue-and-red lights flashed behind his closed lids. Using one arm and one leg, he sidled along the ground until he was out from under the branches of the tree and into the sunlight where he lay gasping.

If you find me, you bastards, I won't be hidin' in a dirt hole.

Inch by inch, he crawled up the incline. One bare foot sought purchase to push his body along. Hours passed—he had no way of knowing how many. His head felt as if it weighed a ton—he could hardly hold it off the ground, but he would not give up. His desire to see Jenny again and his stubbornness kept him going.

"Jenny, Jenny, Jenny—"

He murmured the name over and over, at times in a whisper and at other times aloud. His good hand searched for something to grip as he inched over the ground. Waves of sickness washed over him, but he doggedly persisted.

Finally he pulled himself over the rise to flat land and ruts that could only be a wagon track. He didn't know where he was and he didn't care. His strength was nearly gone, but he managed to roll to the foot of a pine. He lay on his back. A lark was singing nearby.

"I made it, Jenny." For a moment he thought he was lying in a sweet meadow grass near his old home. Then pain consumed him, numbness crept into his brain and he fell into a fitful sleep.

A sharp pain awakened him. He opened his eyes and looked into a face bending over him. A hand was searching his pockets.

"Don't . . . don't—"

"Ya ain't dead!"

"Not . . . yet."

"Thought ya was. I was lookin' fer a name ter put ter ya."

"Do what you come to do. I . . . can't stop you."

"I didn't come ter do nothin. I not be robbin' a helpless mon. I saw ye lyin' here and stopped. Ye're in bad shape, me laddie."

"You're not . . . one of *them?*"

"I be a peddler. Is it the law that's after ye?"

"No. I don't know who, or why. Shot me. I fell over the bluff . . . into the river."

"Well, mon, I can't be leavin' ye here ter die, but I not be knowin' how ter get ye in the wagon, big as ye are."

The peddler stood and walked away. Horror swept over Trell at the thought of being left alone. He tried to turn his head but it was too painful. Then he heard the tinkling sound of the peddler's wagon and the man's voice.

"Rosie, me darlin' girrl, I be needin' yer help. Yer a good girrl and the light of me life. Pay attention ter what I be sayin'. Most likely the laddie will die, but as mather says, while there's life there's hope. Once he was a strong, fine, Irish laddie. But now he be a poor, hurtin' soul. Back up, Rosie, and I'll be singin' ya a tune . . . later on."

The wagon stopped with the back of it just above Trell's head. He could hear the peddler arranging things inside the caravan, then the back gate dropped. He stepped out and knelt down.

"I be tellin' ye straight, mon. I can't get ye in the wagon 'less ye help. I ain't big, but I be strong. Can ye stand?"

"I'll try—"

"That be all I be askin', lad. Take a long swig a this good Irish whiskey ter get yer blood a goin'." He tipped a long-necked bottle and the fiery liquid went into Trell's open, bloody mouth. The peddler took a drink from the bottle and slapped the cork in place.

Trell rolled over and got on his knees, groans of pain rumbling from his throat. Holding to the wagon with one hand and with the help of the small man, he pulled himself up and stood swaying on one leg, not daring to put the other on the ground.

"There ye be, laddie. All ye need ter be doin' is ter put

yer backside on the tailgate while I be holdin' yer hurt leg. Scoot yerself back. I fixed ye a nice pallet. It be long way from a feather bed, but 'tis better than what ye was on. I be takin' ye home fer Mather to tend."

The drone of the peddler's voice filled his mind, driving him on. Trell concentrated on what the man was telling him to do. For the first time since he had been shot, he had hope. Then, agonizing pain took possession of him and he sank into a black void.

> *"I'll take ye home again, Kathleen,*
> *Across the ocean wild and wide—"*

Trell came out of the darkness aware that he was moving and that someone was singing. Then he sank back into the black pit where demons with pitchforks poked and prodded his body and burned his flesh with torches.

In early-morning light, Colleen came out of the house with a lantern and a milk pail and went into the shed that housed the cow. She hung the lantern on a post and pulled up an overturned bucket to sit on.

"Betsy, Betsy," she said tiredly and rested her head against the side of the cow. She liked the smell of the shed, the milch cow and the warm milk. She nudged the udder and squeezed the cow's teat with her long, slender fingers. Milk shot into the bucket she held between her feet.

A minute later she jumped to her feet and whirled. Her hand going to the gun on her thigh, her foot kicking over the bucket of milk. Travor McCall was lounging against the shed door.

"Ya tryin' to get yoreself shot?" she spit out angrily.

"How did you know I was here?"

"Easy. A mouse ran *toward* me and not to the door." One quick glance had told her that he had been in the pond. His hair was wet and his face clean-shaven. Her insides were shaking, but her features were composed.

"Sorry I scared you."

"What'a ya want?"

"I don't dare tell you." The tone more than the words gave meaning to his answer.

She was too stunned to answer, and her lips parted softly in surprise. The glitter in his eyes made her feel as though her heart might leap from her breast, and she stared at him in total panic while her mind searched frantically for something to say.

"Then get the hell out of here so I can finish milkin'."

"I want to talk to you. There's a few things you should know."

"I'm knowin' that. I ain't the smartest person in the world, but I know enough to keep clear of a slybooter who thinks he's the only billy goat on the mountain."

"Slybooter, huh? I've not been called that before."

She watched the firm line of his mouth curve in a smile that softened the hard contours of his face. His smile was wicked, teasing, and jarred her to say something she instantly regretted.

"How can ya smile when yore brother could be lyin' dead som'e'rs?"

Her words wiped the smile off his face. She looked into his dark blue eyes. Deep grooves marked the corners, worn there by years of squinting against the sun. There were other lines, too, that experience, tiredness, or hard winter weather had etched.

"You know how to cut to the quick, don't you?"

"If I have to. Now get out, I've got to milk."

"Go ahead. I'll not bother you."

"Yo're damn right, 'cause ya won't be here." She slapped the gun on her thigh with the palm of her hand.

"She wears pants, packs a gun and . . . she swears," he muttered, shaking his head. Then, "All right, all right." With hands lifted, palms out, he backed out the door.

Travor leaned against the wall of the bunkhouse and lit a cigarette. He was surprised to find himself angry. Why was he so riled up? No answer came readily to his mind. He didn't understand the little blue-eyed witch's attitude toward him, and his logical mind asked him why he should give a damn. Hell, he'd only winked at her.

Ten minutes later, the teacher went to the outhouse, and Colleen came out of the shed with the pail of milk. Without even a glance in his direction, she went to the house.

Jenny had risen and dressed just as the light of dawn streaked the eastern sky. She had spent a restless, sleepless night worrying about Trell. Being careful not to waken her sisters, she went quietly from the room. Granny was in the kitchen.

"Morning, Granny."

"Yore eyes look like two burnt holes in a blanket, child. Did ya get any sleep a'tall?"

"Some. Do you need anything?"

"Nothin' that won't wait. Go on out and do yore necessary. I been there. No need to fear snakes."

Jenny went to the outhouse. Snakes . . . the word brought back her near miss with one when Trell had saved her and held her in his arms. She blinked back the tears.

Where was Trell now? Ike had cut the grass and weeds from around the small building and cleared away any large pieces of bark or wood a rattler could crawl under. Oh, if all troubles could be as easily seen to!

When she came out she stood for a long moment listening to the birds chirping in the treetops and hoping that this day would bring news of Trell and that he would be all right. Dejectedly, she headed back toward the house.

"Ma'am—"

At the sound of the voice, so like Trell's, Jenny's heart jumped out of rhythm. First she saw the glow of a cigarette, then the man leaning against the wall of the bunkhouse.

"Mr. McCall?"

"Yes, ma'am. I didn't mean to scare you."

"I can't say you didn't. I'm not used to anyone being around—"

"Earlier a boy on a dun horse sat over there in the school yard and watched the house."

"That would be Linus. He sometimes watches who comes and goes from here and reports to the Indian agent. I thought he'd stopped his spying. Is he still there?"

"He left about an hour ago. The agent's got a poor spy. I got so close to him that I could've pulled him off the horse, and he didn't know I was there."

"He also watches to see if Whit Whitaker crosses the reservation line. Linus is harmless except for his tattling. I kind of feel sorry for him."

"Why should he care if Whit comes here?"

"According to the agent, the Indians must stay on the reservation. He enforces that law to the letter. The line runs between the house and the school. If Whit comes even this far, he can be punished," Jenny said bitterly.

"I hear a horse." Travor dropped his cigarette and stepped on it.

Jenny strained her eyes toward the school. Out of the early-morning gloom she saw the shape of Whit on his pony.

"It's Whit." She started out away from the house.

"Wait until we're sure he's alone." Travor moved protectively in front of her.

"Teacher—"

"Come on over, Whit," Jenny called. "No one's watching."

"He's the boy who went with the old man."

"Yes. He's very special. This was his father's ranch. He's not allowed on it because he's half-Shoshoni."

Whit came into the yard and slid from the back of his pony.

"I see you here, teacher."

"You must have eyes like a hawk. Whit, this is Mr. McCall's brother. Have you found any trace of Trell?"

"Crazy Swallow tell me about brother who look like Trell."

"Is Ike with you?"

"He go to Pine City. We find Head-Gone-Bad who went down river three days ago to hunt rabbit. He see a hurt man put in strange wagon full of pots and pans. He tell Crazy Swallow. Crazy Swallow know of peddler man in Pine City with such a wagon. He tell me to come tell Trell's brother."

"Did the Indian think the man was my brother?" Travor asked anxiously.

"He don't know who. He go to place when wagon is gone. He see signs that hurt man drag himself up from river."

"I backtracked Trell's horse to the high bluff above the river. If he went over the cliff he could have washed a mile or so down in that fast moving water. It could be Trell the peddler found." Travor's dark eyes scrutinized the boy. "Which way is Pine City?"

"South and west. I take you across reservation. Much faster."

"Have breakfast first," Jenny insisted. "Come in, Whit. Linus was here earlier. Mr. McCall said he left about an hour ago."

Whit hesitated and looked to where the light spilled out the kitchen door.

"Please, Whit. You both need a meal under your belt," Jenny added firmly.

Colleen came from the house with the water bucket. Travor went to meet her and took the bucket from her hand.

"I'll get it."

"Fine with me." She turned to go back into the house. He took her arm. She jerked it free of his grasp.

"I need to talk to you."

"Talk."

She stared up at him through thick, dark lashes, all her nerve ends tingling under the scrutiny of his dark eyes. She fervently hoped that he didn't notice how breathless she was.

"You took that wink serious, didn't you?"

"Yo're thinkin' yo're pretty special, if ya think that."

"If it wasn't the wink, why are you so hostile to me? You've been like a bear with a sore tail ever since I got here."

"Is that what ya wanted to talk about?"

"No."

"Then say it if ya've got somethin' fit to say."

Color tinged her cheeks as his gaze traveled over her face, taking in the freckles on her nose, the wisps of curly hair that had escaped her braid. She stared back at him, her blue eyes holding a definite shimmer of defiance against the effect he was having on her breathing. Her defenses were raised. She felt a desperate need to protect herself from the damage this man could do to her heart.

"The Indian boy—"

"He's got a name. It's Whit."

"All right. Whit said a peddler picked up an injured man down river. Ike thinks the peddler is from Pine City. I'm going there. First I want to know if a man in a white duster has been by here the last week or so." He let the well bucket fall to the waterline. It landed with a *PLOP*.

"No."

"If he shows up, look out for him. He's a hired gunman. I think he may have been looking for me and found Trell."

"Is he a bounty hunter? Are you an outlaw?"

Travor pulled up the bucket and poured the water in the pail before he answered.

"He's not a bounty hunter. I'm not an outlaw. I've known some pretty decent bounty hunters. This man is a hunter and he kills for money."

"Someone must want you dead pretty bad to pay for it."

"It's a long story. I doubt you'd be interested."

"Yo're right. I ain't." She tried to pick up the bucket. Travor beat her to it. His hand touched hers and she let go of the bail on the pail as if it were red-hot.

"Another one you'd better look out for is a man named Hartog. He went down river with a Mexican the morning after he and I had a set-to in town. He's crazy-mean."

"I know it. I'm not wearin' this gun 'cause I want to."

"Don't try to use it on him! If he didn't get you, the Mexican would."

"Don't ya be tellin' me what to do, ya slack-handed, flirtin' jackass!"

"Christ on a horse!"

"Ya'd better not let Granny hear ya takin' the Lord's name in vain, either. She's got old-timey religion, and she ain't puttin' up with no such talk."

"Thanks for the advice," he said dryly, then, "You women are like sittin' ducks out here. Crocker and Hartog or any number of bush-bottom trail-scum could come here, and you women wouldn't stand a chance against them."

"I'd not be sittin' on my hands. Jenny'd not roll over and play dead either. She looks ladylike but she's got sand in her craw. She's pulled that pistol she carries in her pocket more'n once. Me and Granny has been in a few tight spots, and we know a snake when we see one."

They reached the house far too soon to suit Travor. He followed Colleen inside and set the water pail on the washstand.

"Ya sure 'nuff look like Trell," Granny said. "Do ya eat like him?"

"I reckon I do, ma'am. Big eaters run in the McCall family."

"Yore mama must'a had her hands full."

"Yes, ma'am."

"I see I got me another youngun to feed," Granny said as Whit and Jenny came in.

Whit stood just inside the door, his back straight, his head up. Jenny looked quickly to see if it offended him to be called a youngun. She could read nothing in his stoic expression but saw that his eyes were darting hungrily around the room.

"What can I do to help, Granny? Whit and I washed out at the well."

"Nothin'. Sit. All of ya. Colleen, see if the biscuits is done."

"Whit, you and Mr. McCall sit on the other side of the table. Colleen and I will be on this side. Granny sits at the head."

"Good morning, everyone." Cassandra came from the other room, closing the door softly behind her. Her eyes went directly to Whit.

An uncharacteristic groan came from the boy. As soft as it was, Jenny heard and prayed that for once Cassandra would be tactful and not mention that Whit had removed the feather from his headband or offer her usual sarcastic remarks.

"Sit there on the other side of Mr. McCall, Cassandra. I'll get you a plate."

Jenny breathed a sigh of relief when the child sat down. With Travor seated between her and Whit, she would be unable to look at him; therefore, she might not address her conversation to him.

Travor ate heartily, Whit sparingly, but Jenny could see that his table manners were passable. Travor seemed preoccupied and spoke only when he was spoken to. When he emptied his plate and refused a refill, Jenny stood.

"Please don't stand on ceremony, Mr. McCall. We understand that you are anxious to be on your way to Pine

City. Granny and I will prepare a package of food for you and Whit to take with you."

"Thank you, ma'am. For the first time in several days, I've hope of finding my brother alive." After thanking Granny for breakfast, Travor took his hat off the rack beside the door. "Finish your meal, Whit. I'll saddle my horse and we'll get whackin'."

"I'm ready." Whit left the table and as he passed Granny he parroted Travor's words and murmured, "Thanks for the meal." Then he scurried out the door.

It was daylight when Jenny stood beside Colleen and Cassandra, and watched Whit lead the way into the dense forest on the reservation.

"I told you Whit would find Trell." Cassandra spoke when the riders were out of sight.

"He didn't find him, honey," Jenny said tiredly. "He found someone who thinks it may have been Trell the peddler picked up."

"Same difference." Cassandra took her sister's hand. "Don't worry, Jenny. Travor and Whit will find Trell. I think I like Travor almost as much as I like Trell. Do you like him, Colleen?"

"Who? Whit?"

"Travor, silly. Whit's too young for you."

"But just right for you, huh?"

"He's the first boy I've met that's almost as smart as I am."

"Then why are you always needling him?" Jenny asked.

"Because he needs to talk, to argue. How do you think he'll get along in college if he doesn't improve his speech and stays stone-faced all the time," Cassandra said with an impish grin. "And, Virginia, if you notice, I said nothing to him this morning. I knew that you were scared to death I would, and I knew that he was uncomfortable. He's been squatting before a fire to eat for the past few years and was unsure of himself at a table. I understand that."

"It's commendable of you." Jenny spoke dryly. "Now what in the world will we do to make this day go faster?"

"Wash." Colleen spun on her heels and went to the shed where she had put the iron washpot.

"Doesn't sound like much fun to me," Cassandra grumbled.

"Ma used to wash when she was worried about somethin'. I'll fill the pot and put a fire under it." Colleen started drawing water from the well. "Gather up yore dirty clothes, Cassy, and tell Granny to get our bed sheets."

Jenny welcomed the activity. Never in her life, until she had come to Stoney Creek, had she scrubbed clothes on a washboard. Today, she rolled up her sleeves and buried her arms in the soapy water and was grateful for the labor. Keeping thoughts of Trell at bay, she washed, rinsed and hung the bedding on the bushes that rimmed the yard.

Still the day dragged on. The grim-faced women didn't talk about the anxiety they were feeling. Only little Beatrice played happily with the puppy, completely unaware of the tension that gripped her sisters, Granny and Colleen.

Evening came. After a supper of apple cobbler and cream, Jenny got out the sadiron and set it on the cookstove to heat.

"Ya've worked all day, Jenny. Ain't ya tired?" Granny sat in her rocking chair with Beatrice cuddled in her lap.

"I don't know if I'm tired or not. I just know I've got to keep doing something." Jenny brought out the ironing board and set it on the backs of two chairs. "Where's Colleen?"

"Out prowlin' 'round. She's antsy, too."

"I've no idea how far it is to Pine City." Jenny placed the basket of dampened and rolled clothes on the chair seat.

"We come through it to get here. If I recollect right, it's a little bitty place. 'Course it could'a growed by now."

"I don't expect them back today." Jenny put her thoughts into words. "If they come back too soon, it'll mean they didn't find him."

It was a moonlit night. Colleen circled the house. Walking softly and staying in the shadows, she tried to remember all her father had taught her about being alert to night sounds. Listen for the *absence* of familiar sounds, he had told her. If the frogs down at the creek stop croaking, or the cicadas suddenly cease their racket, it's sure something unfamiliar is among them.

Tonight there were no cicada sounds because there were still more than six weeks until the first frost. Granny had told her that. She wasn't sure it was true, she'd never put it to a test. There *were* frogs at the pond and a while back they had suddenly stopped croaking.

Colleen, silent as a shadow, moved from tree to tree until she was behind the schoolhouse. She stopped, listened, and heard little muttering sounds. Going along the side of the building to the front, she stopped again and looked around the corner. Just as she suspected, Linus, sitting on the ground with his back to the building, was holding and talking to his pet raccoon. His horse was behind the school cropping grass. It was when he watered the animal at the pond that the frogs had stopped croaking.

"Hello, Linus," Colleen called softly. The boy jumped up, the raccoon left his lap and scurried into the woods. "Stay put while I decide if I'm goin' to shoot ya or not."

"Who? Where are . . . ya?"

"Here." Colleen came around the corner and faced him. "What'er ya doin' here?" She held the pistol up where he could see it.

"Nothin'."

"Ya got it in mind to tear up the school again?"

"No. I'm just . . . waitin'."

"Waitin' for what?"

"Daylight."

"Do ya stay out here ever' night?"

"Most nights."

"Does Whit know yo're here?"

"Ain't nothin' gets by that red peckerwood."

"Why do you hate him? What's he done to you?"

"Why ain't he here tonight?" Linus ignored her questions and asked one of his own.

Colleen shrugged. "Maybe he is. He moves around like a whiff of smoke."

"He ain't here. His pony's in the corral and the other'n is gone."

"Is that right? I hadn't noticed."

"Crazy Swallow's gone, too."

"Ya'd better pull foot and get that news to Havelshell."

"I ain't tellin' him everythin' . . . no more."

"Found out he's a snake, did ya? Well, it took ya long enough."

"I ain't tellin' you nothin' either."

"I doubt ya have anythin' I want to hear."

"Are ya goin' to shoot me or what?"

"I reckon not . . . tonight." She shoved the gun back into the holster. "Are you hungry?"

"What'd ya want to know that for?"

"Back when we lived in Timbertown I fed all the stray pups."

"I ain't no *dog!*"

"Didn't say ya was. There's a world of difference 'tween a dog and a pup."

"I ain't goin' over *there*."

"You don't have to. I'll brin' ya some biscuits and meat."

"Why'er ya doin' that for?"

"Let's say I'm butterin' ya up to get on yore good side. Might need yore help someday." She melted back into the darkness and Linus sank down next to the building again.

He was dumbfounded. She wasn't the crazy, mean bitch Alvin said she was. Why was she prowlin' 'round at night? What was she up to?

Chapter Eighteen

Morning came and with it Alvin Havelshell.

"Guess who's comin'?" Colleen stuck her head in the door and by the turned-down corners of her mouth, Jenny knew that as far as Colleen was concerned, the visitor wasn't welcome even before she announced, "The great Mr. Havelshell has come to call."

Colleen looked at her friend anxiously. Faint lines of strain had appeared this morning between Jenny's brows and at the corners of her eyes and mouth, and worry shadowed her eyes.

The agent was accompanied by Frank Wilson, the man who had brought Jenny and the girls out in the wagon the day they arrived in Sweetwater. The buggy stopped within a few yards of where Jenny and Colleen waited beside the door, Granny and the girls behind them.

"Morning," he said pleasantly to Jenny, ignoring everyone else. He climbed down out of the buggy and tossed the reins to the grinning Frank, who had moved up beside him. "Water the horse," he said curtly.

Jenny stared at him coolly and did not return his greeting.

"How are you?" He smiled into her eyes. When she remained silent, he said, "Don't worry about the dam being put back in. I've decided to let it go for now."

Jenny made no reply. She had learned that silence could be far more disconcerting than an angry tirade of: *YOU decided? The Shoshoni decided, you low-caliber, jerkwater crook!*

A long silent moment passed before Havelshell's patience snapped.

"This is an official visit. I came to inspect the school."

"You have no *official* obligation to inspect the school."

"That's where you're wrong. Everything and everybody on the reservation is my official *obligation*."

"I beg to differ. The school is my responsibility and mine alone." Jenny met his gaze squarely, contemptuously. His eyes became hard as stones as he looked back at her.

"You come with me to inspect the school, Virginia, or I'll send men out to board it up or . . . burn it down."

"You're . . . despicable!"

And you're the most exciting woman I've ever met. I'll have you, Virginia, and you'll love every minute of it.

"Despicable or not, I'm the agent in charge. Are you coming?"

Without a word, Jenny moved past him and headed for the school.

"And you stay here," Alvin snarled at Colleen, then to Frank, "See that she does."

Head up, shoulders straight, her body as stiff as a board, Jenny led the way. She threw back the door, entered the school and stepped aside for the agent to enter.

Alvin had followed closely behind her, watching her

skirt swirl about her ankles and her hips sway with each step she took. He had looked forward with breathless anticipation to being alone with this sensuous creature and had planned exactly what he would say to her.

He hadn't anticipated such hostility. He had given her time to think about their last meeting and assumed that she would have come to realize that he was the authority here. He had not expected her to bow to his wishes immediately but at least to be civil. But no matter. He would say what he had come to say; and if she refused, he would consider an alternative plan.

"Sit down, Virginia. I see no reason for us to be enemies."

"We are not on a first-name basis, Mr. Havelshell. I will thank you not to forget that. "

"I think of you as Virginia. I see no reason why I shouldn't call you that."

"I do. Only my friends call me by my first name. I do not consider you a friend."

"More than a friend, Virginia?" He leered at her.

"A mere acquaintance, Mr. Havelshell." Her lips curled in disdain.

"We'll not split hairs over that."

"Have you finished your *inspection?*"

"I want to talk to you about your position here and . . . how hopeless it is."

"Hopeless? I see it as far from hopeless."

"Have you not thought about the conversation we had when I was here before?"

"Not for one minute after you walked out the door."

"You'll get no help here, Virginia. Come winter, Crazy Ike will find a squaw and hole up till spring. Don't count on help from McCall or that female out there in men's pants. You and your sisters will be here alone. When the snow is on the ground and food is scarce, the Indians will come and take yours."

"As much as you wish it to be true, we will not be alone. The Murphys will be here, and I've made friends with the Shoshoni. They are sending their children to the school. And I've no doubt that they want the school to succeed."

"And you're counting on their word? Ha! You know little of these savages. They would cut your throat and that of your sisters if the notion struck."

"I don't believe that. Your scare tactics won't work."

"Mark my word." He was almost shouting now. "The Murphy girl is a slut. I'm sure that word is offensive to you, but it is true. Do you want your little sisters living in a house with a woman who'll spread her legs for anyone with a couple of dollars? Or has she set up business in the bunkhouse?"

"Get out!" Jenny stood beside the door and waved her arm. "You've got a nasty mind and a nasty mouth!"

"Calm down. I'm merely telling you what folks think is going on out here."

"I've met your *folks* in town, and what they think doesn't mean a brass farthing to me."

"Virginia, listen to me carefully. We have an empty school in town. It's equipped with everything you would need to teach grades one through six. You are needed there and would be a valuable addition to the Sweetwater community. For your own good and the good of your sisters, I urge you to consider coming to Sweetwater. A nice house will be provided . . . with a cook. You aren't the type of woman who should live in a log shack, use an outhouse and draw water from a well."

Jenny stared at him with disbelief in her eyes. He was either the most dense person she had ever met or the most devious. Did he take her for a complete fool?

"The Reverend Longfellow asked me to assure you that as a member of the schoolboard, he would see to it that you had free rein at the school. He also said to tell you that he looks forward to seeing you in church, and that he would provide a horse and buggy for your use," Alvin added confidently.

"You may be surprised to know that I'm not in the least flattered by your offer. In fact, I've never before had my intelligence so insulted. You're not only despicable, you're downright stupid if you think I'd even consider such an offer. How did you ever get a law degree, Mr. Havelshell? How on God's green earth did you ever land the job as agent for the southern part of this reservation?"

Her scorn, loftiness, and the curl of her lip, burst the dam of Alvin's carefully planned civility. He took two quick strides to reach her. His hand shot out and gripped her upper arm.

"Don't look down your aristocratic nose at me, you snooty bitch. No woman of your standing would leave her easy life and come out here to teach the *poor Indians* unless she had to get away. With your money, you didn't need a ranch you've no idea how to operate. You're running from something, *Virginia*, and I intend to find out what it is."

"Let go of my arm!"

Jenny was livid. If he had not grabbed her right arm, she would have pulled out her little pistol from her pocket and shot him. When he failed to release her, she swung her left arm and gave him a resounding slap across the face.

"Let go my arm!"

"You'll . . . regret that!" His angry eyes left hers and flicked to the doorway.

"Jenny . . ." Granny stood there, a brass-tipped walking stick in her hand. "I broke the thread on the sewin' machine."

"Get out of here, old woman," Alvin snarled.

"Don't . . . talk to her like that!" Jenny jerked loose from his grip. Her hand darted into her pocket and came up with the pistol. "Get out . . . and don't come back."

"You'll regret this, Virginia." Alvin adjusted his coat, leaving his hands fastened to the lapels and his dark eyes to her face.

"I think not."

"You'll be seeing me again. I'm in charge here, and the sooner you come to terms with that fact, the better off you'll be." He left the building and strode quickly down the path to his buggy.

Jenny assisted Granny down the path with her hand beneath her elbow. She held her head up and forced her trembling legs to carry her. Her chest hurt, her throat felt as if a hand were squeezing it, and her eyes burned. *What was this place doing to her?* She had never struck another human being in her life. Yet, without a second thought, she had slapped Alvin Havelshell. And she believed that had he made a move toward her or Granny, she would have shot him!

They reached the yard between the house and the outbuildings in time to see Alvin climb into the buggy and send the whip out over the back of the mare. The startled animal jumped and took off in a fast run. The buggy circled the house, bounced over the rough prairie grass and careened down the trail leading to town.

Frank, with a silly grin on his face, untied his horse and swung into the saddle. He paused and leered at Colleen.

"Ya gonna miss me, pretty gal?"

"Yeah, like a dog misses a batch a fleas."

"Don't worry, hon. I'll be back."

"Ya do and I'll meet ya with a load of buckshot, ya pig-ugly jackass!"

"I'm claimin' ya for my girl," he shouted and wheeled the horse to follow the buggy.

Suddenly the animal stiffened and stopped. With a cry of rage, the horse went up in the air and came down with a jolt. Frank went over the horse's head and landed on his back on the hard-packed trail. He rolled over on his knees and hung there shaking his head. When he got to his feet, a string of curses spewed from his mouth.

Jenny started laughing first; it was a high-pitched, nervous giggle. Cassandra joined in, and Colleen let loose with a rebel yell.

Frank came toward them menacingly. "What'd ya do?"

The women continued to laugh. He was unaware that the laughter was the result of two days of nervous tension and that tears were streaming from the eyes of both women.

"Ah . . . hell!" He yanked on the reins and the quivering horse stood still while he mounted. He rode away as Jenny's laughter turned to sobs.

"What did that horse's ass do to you, Virginia?" Cassandra's small freckled face was creased with worry. She had never seen her older sister cry except when their father died.

"Nothing, honey. And . . . what did you say?"

"I don't think I should repeat it. Little ears, you know." She indicated Beatrice, who was paying rapt attention to every word.

"What did ya do, Cass?" Colleen asked. "I saw ya hidin' that slingshot Ike gave ya."

"It pays to practice, doesn't it?"

"I reckon."

Cassandra preened and lifted her chin in a gesture of superiority. She brought several small, straight sticks from her pocket. Each had a sewing needle stuck in the end.

"I figured that if a stone would hurt, a dart would hurt more. Drat it! I wanted to try it on Havelshell's horse, but he got away before I could get it in place."

"Cassandra! Where did you get such an idea?"

"It's really your fault. You won't let anyone show me how to use a gun, so I have to use my own inventive skills. Pygmies in Africa use blowguns. I knew I didn't have enough wind for that, so I combined the dart and the slingshot."

"Cass hurt the horse." Beatrice tugged at Jenny's hand.

"Well, yes, I regret that," Cassandra said. "But it sure was fun to see old Frank bite the dust. Besides, it didn't really hurt the horse; it only startled him. I didn't dip the needle in poison or . . . anything."

Damn, damn her!

Unmindful that the horse was tiring, Alvin continued to run the animal. Jenny had practically spit on him—thrown his offer back in his face! There were at least a dozen women he could call to his bed in an hour's notice. And they were not whores, just women who appreciated the kind of man he was.

She needed to be taught a lesson. He was as good as she was. Hadn't he managed to get himself educated despite being one of eight kids of a tugboat pilot on the Mississippi River? Eight? Hell, there were probably dozens of bastards up and down the river. The old man wasn't known for keeping his britches buttoned.

Long ago Alvin had distanced himself from the Havelshells that the quality folk in St. Paul considered trash. He had shoved the memories of his family to the back of his mind. Now the snooty bitch had brought it all back. He wasn't even good enough to address her by her first name! *Damn her!*

Alvin was still fuming about the sacrifices he had made to get to where he was now: marriage to that fat cow, kow-towing to the old man, taking shit from the likes of Hartog, when Frank rode up and grabbed the halter on the horse pulling the buggy.

"You tryin' to kill this horse?" he said when he had stopped the running, lathered animal.

"It's my horse! Let go!" Alvin snarled.

"She'll drop in another mile runnin' full out pullin' this buggy. Then how'll ya get to town?"

"How come you let that old woman come over to the school? I'll have no man working for me that can't take orders."

"Ya didn't say nothin' 'bout the old woman. Ya said keep the girl there, and that's what I done." Frank released the halter on the horse and backed his own mount away.

Alvin walked the horse slowly down the trail, and Frank fell in behind the buggy. For sure, the teacher had gotten under the agent's skin. Frank had never seen him so riled. He was pretty well riled up himself after being dumped from his horse and laughed at.

But what the hell! He wanted to wring the neck of that blue-eyed witch in men's pants, but he'd never touch her. He wasn't so low-down he'd beat a woman. He wasn't too sure about Havelshell, and something told him that he'd better hit the trail and put some distance between himself and the agent before he found himself in more trouble than he could handle.

The remainder of the day passed in slow motion for Jenny. As the hours dragged by and evening approached she recalled the last words Trell said to her.

"I'll be back, Jenny. I'll be back."

When she closed her eyes, she could summon up his face, serious most of the time, but when he smiled . . . so endearing.

I've fallen in love with you. Please come back. If you don't love me . . . I'll understand—

Never in her life had Jenny felt such an overpowering feeling of dread. Never had she felt more like praying. Sweet, gentle Trell could be somewhere suffering . . . alone. She tried to close her mind to the possibility that he was dead, would never come back, and she'd never again know the joy of being held close in his arms, giving and receiving his kisses—

Cassandra dashed into the kitchen. "Whit's back! He went into the school."

Jenny dropped the towel she had been using to dry dishes and hurried out the door. By the time she reached the yard, Whit had come out of the school with a large bundle in his arms.

"Whit!" she called to him. "Whit! Whit—" He ignored her, jumped on his pony and rode into the woods.

"Forevermore!"

"What's he doing? What did he take out of the school?"

"I don't know what he's doing, but it looks like he took his wood carvings. I wonder why."

"He'll have a reason, and I'll probably not agree with it." A note of frustration echoed in Cassandra's voice.

"I'll look around." Colleen, wearing her six-gun and carrying her rifle, started up the path to the school. "One of us should stay here with Granny and the girls."

"I'll stay here." Jenny felt in her pocket for her little pistol.

"Be careful, child."

"I will, Granny."

To those watching, it seemed to take an unbearably long time for Colleen to circle the building, then look inside. She came out, stood for a moment, then went to the edge of the clearing. Loping along with the rifle cradled in her arms, she circled the area, then disappeared in the deep shadowy forest.

Night was coming on fast. Waiting with Granny and the girls, Jenny kept her eyes on the edge of the forest. Her heart thumped heavily, her breathing was shallow. No one spoke, not even Cassandra or little Beatrice, who clung to Granny's hand.

Then Ike, on his mule, came out of the woods with Colleen. They spoke for a brief moment, before he turned Trouble toward the pond and Colleen trotted toward the house. The women and the girls moved in a group to the edge of the yard to meet her.

"They've got Trell. He's been hurt. Whit came ahead to see if Linus was snoopin', and if he was, to lead him away so they could brin' Trell in. Ike's lookin' around the pond makin' sure nobody's there."

"Thank God! Oh, thank God!" Jenny's shoulders sagged with relief. "Is Trell hurt . . . bad?"

"I . . . think so. They're bringin' him in the peddler's wagon. Ike said get the bed in the bunkhouse ready."

"Oh, but . . . if he's hurt, he should be in the house where we can take care of him."

"Ike said bunkhouse. For some reason they don't want anyone to know he's here. Ike said he'd explain it later."

"I'll get the medical kit I brought from home. Oh, I'll wait. I don't know what we'll need. Oh, dear—" Jenny's hands were clasped tightly together.

"Now isn't the time to get all clabber-headed, Virginia." It upset Cassandra to see her sister so distraught.

"You're right, honey. Let's get the medical kit and some extra sheets and blankets."

"I'll light the lantern." Colleen disappeared inside the bunkhouse.

"Guess I ort to get a meal goin'. Them men'll be hungry. Come help me, sugarfoot." Granny and Beatrice hurried to the house.

Chapter Nineteen

Trell had awakened from a laudanum-induced sleep to see his brother bending over him. He thought he was dreaming.

"Trav—?" His voice was hoarse from disuse.

"Yeah, it's me. How ya feelin'?"

"Rougher'n a cob. How'd ya . . . find me?"

"Long story, bud. Who did this to you?"

"Don't know who or why. Feller shot me. Fell over the bluff into the river. When I crawled out, I heard 'em talkin'. Wanted to find . . . me. Make sure—"

"Messed ya up a bit. Yo're a sorry sight."

"Yeah. I don't have enough strength to spit."

"Don't fret about it. We're takin' ya home."

"I'd . . . not make it."

"Takin' ya in the wagon, bud. Take another dab a this laudanum and go back to sleep." Trell held a glass to his brother's lips.

"Trav, pay . . . these good folks."

"I will. Don't worry 'bout it."

Travor had been elated to find his brother alive, and shocked at his appearance. One side of his face was raw and covered with a heavy coat of salve; his lips were puffed and his cheeks sunken. In order to treat the cut made by the bullet that passed across his skull and knocked him into the river, the peddler or his mother had cut away a strip of hair.

Devin McGriff had told him about the broken leg and ribs, and about the fever. Travor thanked God the peddler had come along and had been decent enough to pick up his brother and hide him, or he'd surely have died either from his injuries or another bullet from Crocker.

Ike had suggested taking him to Stoney Creek when Travor mentioned that the man who had tried to kill him would be watching the ranch. Travor was pretty sure that Crocker had mistaken Trell for him, and would still be around looking for the body to make sure of the kill. He would have to take all or part of it back to Silas Ashley to collect the rest of his money.

Rage at what had been done to his brother boiled up in Travor. Trell was the most decent man he knew and didn't deserve to be cut down just because he was his twin. After he finished with Crocker, Travor vowed, he would pay a call on Ashley and that sniveling daughter of his. He had just flirted with that little feather-head, nothing more. It certainly wasn't a reason to kill a man. His own stupidity had almost cost his brother's life. It would be a long time, if ever, before he could forgive himself for that.

Trell awakened off and on during the long day in the slow-moving wagon. Frequently Travor or the peddler brought him some water. He hurt in places he didn't even know he had. His mind was foggy, and he couldn't keep his eyes open for very long at a time. He didn't even try to figure out how his brother had found him. He felt only a tremendous relief that he had.

After dark Ike led the wagon past the school and into the yard of the homestead. As soon as the wagon stopped, Travor dismounted and tied his horse to a corral pole. The other horses in the enclosure nickered a greeting. Jenny and Cassandra waited beside the bunkhouse door. But Travor saw only Colleen waiting with a lighted lantern.

"Ain't nobody 'round 'less'n it's that Indian, Head-Gone-Bad. He be the one that saw McGriff put Trell in the wagon. He ain't sayin' nothin' to nobody but Whit." Ike slid from the back of his mule. "Whit must'a led Linus off on a wild-goose chase."

"Ike, is Trell hurt . . . bad?" Jenny asked, her heart pounding so hard she was almost breathless.

"Bad enough, I reckon."

Travor opened the double doors at the back of the wagon and stepped inside. Colleen held up the lantern. Trell lay on his back his face turned away.

"He's still sleepin'. Let's get him out before he wakes up. He's goin' to hurt like hell when we move him."

Trell was lying on a canvas litter on a feather bed placed on the floor of the wagon. With Travor at his head and with help from Ike and the peddler, they pulled him from the wagon and carried him into the bunkhouse. Even in a deep sleep, Trell cried out once when the stretcher bumped against the doorframe.

The light from the lantern fell on Trell's sunken eyes and ravaged face. The blanket that covered him reached only to his knees and Jenny could see that one leg was encased in wooden splints, the other splotched with cuts and bruises.

Gently, as if they were handling a baby, Travor and the peddler lifted Trell off the stretcher and onto the bed. When Trellis moaned, Jenny's heart dropped like a rock. She tried to blink away the tears as she looked at Travor.

"Has . . . he been sleeping long?"

"Most all the day. He be havin' the laudanum to ease him." The peddler, McGriff, answered. "He better not be havin' more to my way a thinkin'. Doctor say he could be gettin' a cravin' for it."

"I've seen it happen," Travor said. "It got him through the day. But I agree, no more for several days."

"Ma'am, I be Devin McGriff." The peddler pulled the shabby cap from his head when he spoke to Jenny. She held out her hand.

"Virginia Gray. And . . . thank you for looking after Trell and bringing him back to us."

"'Twas but what any decent mon would be doin'."

"This is Miss Murphy, and my sister, Cassandra." Jenny made the introductions automatically.

"It be a pleasure, ladies. I got ter tend to my Rosie. 'Twas a hard day she be havin', pullin' the wagon."

"Mr. McGriff, I'd like to look at your goods and place an order before you go."

"Ya don't hafta be doin' it, ma'am."

"Oh, I'm not doing it to pay back for what you've done for Trell. I've no intention of going back to Sweetwater, and it's too far for me to travel to Forest City. I need supplies, sir, and if I can arrange for them to be delivered to me, it would take care of the problem."

"Well, in that case, I'd be happy ter be of service ter ye."

"Supper's bein' readied." Colleen looked at Travor for the first time and saw that he was watching her. She picked up the lantern and followed Ike and McGriff outside.

Jenny went closer to the bed and looked down at Trell, then up at his brother.

"I'm glad you brought him here. Ike said that whoever did this to him may try to finish the job and would be watching his ranch. He'll play hob getting to him here."

"I'll be here . . . off and on."

Jenny reached out and smoothed the hair off Trell's forehead. She let her palm linger there.

"Oh, Trell, I'll never forgive myself if this was done to you because of me." She looked up at his brother. "I'm not good at doctoring, but Granny is. I know she'll want to feed him. Honey," she said to Cassandra, "run to the house and tell Granny that Trell will need something to eat when he wakes up. She'll know what to fix."

"I told my sister that Whit would find Trell, but she's been in a terrible snit ever since we found out he was missing and didn't believe me." Cassandra looked up at Travor. "I'm beginning to suspect that she's in love with your brother."

"Cassandra!" Jenny gasped and put her hands to her flaming cheeks. "Oh, Lord!"

"I didn't mean to embarrass you, Virginia. I only said that I *suspect*. I never said that you were. Don't I have the right to suspect things about my own sister?"

After Cassandra walked calmly out the door, Jenny looked everywhere except at Travor. Finally his words and tone of voice brought her startled gaze to his face.

"Do you think my brother so far beneath you that you're ashamed your sister may think you're in love with him?"

"No! I don't think that at all! Cassandra is bright beyond her years but far too ready to make judgments and speak her mind. And so are you!"

"Is my brother in love with you?"

"No!" she said for the second time and just as emphatically. "He's . . . a very good friend."

"How about Colleen?"

"You'll have to ask him."

"Did Colleen tell you that the man who shot Trell may have been after me?"

"Yes, and she didn't know why. I had thought he might have been shot because he had been here helping me."

"Do you think Havelshell would go that far to run you off?"

"I don't know."

"More likely it was a man named Crocker, a hired gunman. I got on the wrong side of a feller, and he sent Crocker to kill me. He didn't know I had a twin brother. I'd just as soon folks didn't know that there are two of us. I'll go over to the Double T and tell Joe, our foreman, to keep quiet about me being here. I'd be obliged if you'd let Trell stay till he's on his feet."

Jenny nodded. "If you want to go in and eat, I'll stay with Trell."

"I'll hunt meat while Trell is here."

"We have enough for now."

When she was alone with Trell, she covered him with one of the new blankets she had bought in Sweetwater. His chest was bare except for the cloth wrapped around to support his broken ribs. A dark bruise extended from his collarbone to wrap about his shoulder. His legs were also bare. If he wore anything at all beneath the sheet it would be a pair of drawers. A cool breeze blew in through the open door. She partially closed it before she moved a chair over to the bed and sat down.

Jenny leaned close and studied the face turned toward her. The crease made from the bullet that passed across his head had scabbed over. The dark layer of salve kept her from seeing the deep cuts and scrapes he'd suffered on the one side of his face. The skin over the cheekbone on the other side of his face had been scraped raw.

She reached out and gently stroked the hair from his forehead, then removed her hand guiltily. She had no right to touch him, comfort him. He had kissed her, but she may have read more into the caress than he intended.

She sat for a long time, her eyes on his face. Suddenly the thick lashes parted and he was looking at her. His lips moved and he spoke.

"Jenny, is it . . . you?"

"Trell!" She sat up straighter and a smile brightened her face. "Oh, Trell, I've been so worried—" Her voice trailed and she swallowed the lump that came up in her throat.

"Jenny—" He moved his hand out from under the cover and reached for her. "I was afraid . . . I'd never see you again." His voice was painfully weak.

She held his hand between her palms and raised it to her cheek. Tears sparkled in her eyes. The days of worry had taken a toll on her self-control.

"I was afraid . . . too. I prayed you'd be all right."

"Where . . . am I?"

"Here at Stoney Creek. In the bunkhouse. Ike and

Colleen had just fixed it up. Your brother brought you here."

"You've so much to do. I'll be a bother."

"You'll not be a bother. I'm so glad you're here." A growling, gurgling noise came from his stomach. "Are you hungry?"

"As a wolf."

"Granny's fixing something. Can I get you some water?"

"I bet I'm a sorry sight . . . and probably stink like a wet goat."

"A sight for sore eyes is what you are, Trellis McCall."

"Come close so I can see you."

"Oh, Trell, hurry and get well." Jenny bent close to him and stroked his hair with her fingertips. An unchecked tear rolled down her cheek.

"Why are you cryin'? Did someone hurt you?"

"I'm crying because I'm so glad you're here. I was so worried about you."

"I don't want you to cry."

"I've so much to tell you. We saw your brother in town and thought it was you. Havelshell sent men out to put the dam back in and Whit brought the Shoshoni shaman and a group of warriors. They scared the men off. Havelshell came yesterday and said he decided to leave it for now. I spoke to the shaman and he's sending ten children to my school. Oh, I'm talking too much, and you're tired."

"No. Keep talkin'." He gripped her hand tighter. His eyes drifted shut, then opened wide. "I can't keep my eyes open, and I want to look at you."

"You'll not be left alone," she promised. "If I'm not here, your brother, Colleen or Granny will be."

"You, Jenny." His voice was the merest of whispers. "I kept tellin' myself that I had to get back to . . . Jenny—" The words drifted away and his eyes closed.

Jenny continued to watch him. His hand gripped hers with surprising strength. The tight hold she had kept on her emotions for days loosened. A flood of silent tears rolled down her cheeks. Trell wanted *her!* He was safe; her world had stopped tilting.

Whit slipped through the partially opened door like a shadow and stood waiting for Jenny to acknowledge him. When she looked up, he went to the bed and looked down at Trell. She hastily dried her eyes.

"He live?"

"We think so, unless complications develop."

"What's that?"

"Unless . . . his wounds poison, or he gets a fever, or any number of other things." Jenny saw the lines of fatigue in Whit's face. "You're tired, Whit. How long has it been since you slept?"

"I am not tired." He straightened his shoulders.

"How about hungry?"

"Hungry, yes. But I can wait for food."

"You will eat here. You led Linus away, didn't you?"

"I knew he would follow if I took something from the school."

"You took your wood carvings."

"No. I took sticks I put there to keep dry. I hide them in crevice far away and wait for Sneaking Weasel to leave his horse and climb the rocks to see what I hide. I take his horse. Sneaking Weasel will be long time getting back."

Jenny smiled. "That was clever of you. We saw you leave with the bundle. Thank you, Whit, for finding Trell."

"I no find him. Head-Gone-Bad see him put in wagon. Head-Gone-Bad very proud to help teacher."

"I must see him and thank him."

"He no understand thank you; he understand food."

"Then he shall have some. As much as he wants."

"He watch while I come here. But Sneaking Weasel not be back soon."

"Virginia, Granny said you needed this." Cassandra had pushed the door open and stood there holding Jenny's shawl.

"I do need it. Thank you, honey."

"Hello, Whit." Cassandra spoke after she went to her sister and draped the shawl about her shoulders.

Whit folded his arms across his chest and gave her a stoic stare.

"The least you could do is answer my greeting. You don't have to stand there like a . . . like a dumb—"

"Dumb Indian?"

"I wasn't going to say that."

"What then?"

"Like a dumb cluck! So there!"

Whit's dark eyes went to Jenny. "What's dumb cluck?"

Jenny lifted her shoulders. "I'm not . . . sure."

He turned on Cassandra. "Why you call me name teacher don't know?"

"You call me Girl-Who-Squawk, and I don't get all huffy about it. Dumb cluck is only a figure of speech. And if you must know, it means woodenhead, bumpkin, puddinghead, numbskull."

"I know woodenhead." He tapped his skull with his finger. "My head is not made of wood."

"No. It's made of . . . jelly!" Cassandra tilted her small face and stuck her tongue out at him.

The action was so childish that Jenny laughed. Her little sister was a child after all.

"Will you go to the house to eat, Whit?"

"I go back to schoolhouse."

"Cassandra, ask Granny to fix a packet of food for Whit and Head-Gone-Bad."

Cassandra flounced to the door. "I've a notion to douse it good with . . . croton oil," she announced and made a hasty retreat.

"Squawk, squawk, squawk," Whit said. "What she mean?"

"She says things to get you to argue with her. She's really a very bright little girl and thinks that you're bright, too."

"She need switch on her legs to close her mouth."

"There are times when I agree with you."

"I go now."

"Stay . . . until they bring the food."

"Will Squawker bring it?"

"I don't know. But if she does, why don't you surprise her and say 'thank you.' Then she'd have no reason to squawk."

Whit thought about it, then nodded. He sat on the floor beside the door. The room was quiet. Minutes passed, then Trell mumbled in his sleep and frowned. He gripped Jenny's hand hard. She stroked the hair back from his face and put her lips close to his ear.

"You're all right. You're here with Jenny," she murmured. "Rest, sweetheart. No one will hurt you . . . I promise—" The endearment came so easily from her lips that she wasn't even aware that she said it.

*   *   *

Colleen had unsaddled the big spotted horse and was rubbing him down with a gunnysack when Travor came out of the bunkhouse.

"What's his name?"

"I don't know. I've been callin' him Mud Pie, cause he's so ugly." Somehow Travor knew that would rile her and it did.

"He isn't ugly!"

"He sure ain't pretty."

"You'd not take any prizes either."

"You would."

"Ha!"

"Is the teacher in love with my brother?"

Colleen threw the sack over the rail and crawled through the bars.

"Why ask me? Ask her?"

"I did. She said he was a good friend."

"Well?"

"Is he in love with you?"

"Ain't ya ever heard a man and a woman bein' *friends*?" She gave a derisive snort. "I can see that yo're one a them that don't see no further than gettin' a woman in bed."

"There's a lot to be said for that, too." He was grinning broadly, and she caught the gleam of his white teeth in the dark.

"Yeah? Well, I ain't interested in hearin' 'bout it."

"What've I done to get your back up, besides winkin' at you?"

"I told ya I don't like flirty men who think a woman is only good for washin' his dirty clothes, cookin' his meals and warmin' his bed! Get the hell away from me before I put a hole in you with my knife."

"What kind of man do you want?" Travor asked calmly, ignoring her threat.

"Not a man like you! I ain't takin' just any man so me and Granny will have a roof over our heads. I'm goin' to walk *beside* my man, not behind him. I'm goin' to have a say in what we do or don't do. We'll be full partners . . . like my ma and pa was."

"And . . . you'll love him?"

"With all my heart!"

"My brother is the kind of man you want." It wasn't a question.

"He's a good man who came and helped us when no one else would. He *cared* about what happened to me and Granny. He *cared* about what happened to Jenny and the girls."

"Has he kissed you?"

"No!"

"Then I'm going to."

Before Colleen could grasp his meaning, his hands shot out, fastened onto her shoulders and pulled her up against him. His arms wrapped around her like a steel trap. His mouth came down, hard, on hers. He held her crushed against him, her hands pinned between them, while his mouth ravaged hers.

Suddenly his lips softened and he kissed her gently again and again; soft, gentle, incredibly sweet kisses. The sweetness of his kisses, the smell of his skin, the hardness of his body were intoxicating. In spite of herself she wanted this madness to go on and on. Her head felt light and her mind foggy. His heavy breathing brought her to her senses and she began to struggle.

His mouth moved to the side of her face.

"Ah . . . be still, little wildcat! That's the first of many kisses you're goin' to give me," he whispered. "I liked 'em and so did you."

"Give?" She tried to push away from him, but he held her clamped to him. "I didn't give ya a dang-blasted thin'! Ya took!"

"You kissed me! Admit it."

"Let go of me, or . . . or I'll cut ya with my knife," she threatened, her voice husky and trembling.

His face was a scant inch away from hers; his breath warm on her wet lips. He watched her soft red mouth spilling out the angry words and was more than ever convinced that this was the woman for him. He liked everything about her, her spunk, her courage, her frankness. She'd not made the slightest effort to pretty herself up, but then she didn't need to. It was a treat just to look at her.

"You won't cut me, my darlin' Colleen."

"Give me a chance, ya horny jackass, and I'll show ya."

He laughed, a husky laugh against her cheek.

"Lord! I'm glad I met you. I've looked for a woman like you ever since I knew the difference between a male and a female. No man is ever going to touch you . . . but me."

"Ya know nothin' 'bout me a'tall. I could be a whore for all you know."

He laughed again and she could feel against her breast the chuckles that came from deep in his chest.

"You're no whore, sweetheart. I'd bet my life on it."

"Ya've knowed plenty, so ya'd know."

"Jealous, already?"

"I don't wear dresses," she said desperately. "I wear men's pants . . . all the time."

"I saw you in town in a dress. Anyway, I've had a lot of experience takin' off pants. My own, of course."

"Of course!"

"Kiss me and I'll let you go."

"I'd as soon kiss a warthog!"

"Then I'll kiss you."

"I'll . . . scream—"

"No, you won't. You don't want your granny or Jenny to know that I'm kissin' you and . . . you're kissin' me."

"Ya wouldn't be doin' this if . . . if my pa was alive. He'd . . . horsewhip ya."

"Ah, sweetheart. I'm sorry about your pa."

"Why? Ya didn't even know him." She was doing her best not to cry despite the helpless tears that gathered in her eyes.

"I know you," he said in a strange, thickened voice.

He bent his head and kissed her gently on the lips. It was a minute before she realized that his arms had dropped from around her and she was free to move away from him. She stepped away and, instead of going to the house or the bunkhouse, she went to the well and stood there for a long moment. Ike came from the house and the two of them went to the bunkhouse.

After a few minutes Whit came out and loped up the path to the school. Travor watched him. He and Trell owed a debt of gratitude to the boy. Their brother, Pack Gallagher, would know how they could help him. If Stoney Creek had been his father's ranch, and he was Walt Whitaker's son, he was certainly entitled to it, half-Shoshoni or not.

Travor didn't know why he had acted as he had with Colleen. He had pushed his attraction for her to the back of his mind while he hunted for Trell. Travor knew his brother was interested in the teacher. The peddler said Trell had talked of a woman named Jenny, and Jenny had tried her best to hide the fact that she was in love with him; but the signs were there.

All he had to do now, Travor mused, was take care of Crocker if he was still around. Then he was going to court Colleen Murphy and marry her. He chuckled. Trell wouldn't believe it. He could hardly wait to see his face when he told him.

He leaned against the corral poles. He couldn't keep the smile off his face. She would make a dandy wife and mother. He'd always feared settling down with a woman who in time would grow heavy and dull. Not this woman. She would grow heavy—but with his child.

Chapter Twenty

Alvin swiveled around in his chair when the door of his office was thrown open. Wind swept papers from his desk. He muttered a curse and stooped to pick them up. A small shiny black shoe sat firmly on one of them. Alvin ignored the rude gesture, picked up the rest of the papers, stacked them on the desk and secured them with a glass paper weight. Then he greeted his visitor.

"What brings you here?"

"Thank you, I will." The small man in the carefully brushed derby seated himself in Alvin's chair. It was an action taken to put the agent firmly in his place for being discourteous. When Alvin began to pace the floor, he said, "Sit down, Alvin. It hurts my neck to look at you."

"I have work to do. I'm trying to maintain my law practice, you know." Alvin sat down in a high-backed chair next to his desk and drummed his blunt fingertips on the top.

"You went to Stoney Creek yesterday."

"Yes, I went there. I offered the teacher a job in town. She turned it down."

"You didn't think offering her a job was important enough to talk over with me beforehand?"

"I figured you'd find out if she took the job, which she didn't."

"You didn't go see Arvella."

"Did Frank beat a path to your door to tell you that?"

"I would have found out anyway. Pud Harris is out there."

"Looking after your interest, I presume."

"I don't appreciate your sarcasm, my friend."

Friend, my hind leg! You'd cut my throat in a minute if you didn't need me.

"I hear we have a new sheriff."

"Sid Armstrong."

"You're taking a lot on yourself, Alvin. I don't like for you to go over my head."

"Do you have a better man in mind?"

"That isn't the point. In a little more than six weeks the army will be bringing in five thousand head of cattle to divide among the tribes. We don't need a puffed-up, tinhorn sheriff nosing around."

"If we didn't have him, we'd have someone else. The merchants are making noise about law and order."

"I think it's time you went to visit your wife." It was the habit of the man to change the subject rapidly to catch Alvin off guard.

Alvin stood. "I was there two weeks ago."

"I'll go with you when you go again."

"I think not!" Alvin's voice bounced from wall to wall.

"No need to shout." The little man got to his feet. "Arvella's girl ran off. Did you know that?"

"I knew it. Linus came in and told me."

"I'm sending your wife another girl. The orphanage over in Rawlings was only too happy to provide one. She's too young for you to diddle with."

Alvin spun around to glare at the little man.

"What . . . what do you mean by that?"

"I think you know. You diddled with Moonrock, causing her to go back to her tribe. Don't do it with this girl. If you feel the urge to *diddle*, do it with your wife." His cold eyes boring into Alvin's. "One more thing, *friend*. Don't forget that I put you where you are, and I can put you six feet under. Get the job done and soon or Arvella will end up a widow, a rich widow with any number of opportunists eager to climb into her bed and give me a grandson."

After the little man left, Alvin sat down and pounded his fist on the desk. *Six feet under! My God! He means to have me killed!* That's the only way Arvella could become a *widow*. For a long while the agent sat at his desk staring at the wall in front of him. *The pious little bastard!*

His mind kept going back to the day about a month after he had come to Sweetwater with a brand-new certificate to practice law in his valise. He had worked hard, cheated a little, and was ready to make his fortune. As the only lawyer in the area, he had a clear field.

The Reverend Henry W. Longfellow, rancher and preacher, had come to the territory the year before and was firmly established when he built the church. The man could charm the skin off a snake. He could make you believe that black was white and cow shit was apple pie if he set his mind to it.

Soon Alvin was going to church on Sunday and like the rest of the congregation listening with rapt attention to the fire-and-brimstone sermons. He, however, had recognized

Longfellow immediately for what he was: a confidence man, a schemer who could wheedle a man-hating old maid out of her drawers and sucker a community into thinking he was Saint Peter reincarnated. Unlike the gullible towns-people, Alvin listened and admired the man only for his duplicity.

It seemed the Reverend Longfellow had larger game in mind than fleecing the congregation out of a few dollars. He wanted Stoney Creek Ranch and a large share of the cattle being sent by the government to feed the Indians on the reservation.

When he put his proposition to Alvin, he was careful to drop information he had received from the police of the town where Alvin had gone to school. Alvin had been angry and had sworn that he had not been with his fellow law student when he broke into the professor's office and stole papers that would prepare him for an examination.

"Your name is here in the report, Alvin. But don't fret about it. It can be taken care of, just as easily as new charges can be added." The chubby little man spoke kindly, but Alvin got the message.

From that time on, The Reverend Longfellow had Alvin firmly in his pocket. The preacher had dug into every cor-ner of Alvin's life. He had found out about his father's nu-merous offspring spread up and down the Mississippi River.

"The Havelshell family appears to be a horny lot." He made the comment one day in the middle of a discussion about getting Alvin appointed Indian agent. "Out of fifteen *known* offspring your father sired, including the bastards, eleven of them were males."

Alvin was too stunned to reply and Longfellow continued.

"Two out of three of yours are male."

"Goddammit! What the hell are you getting at?" Alvin found his voice.

The preacher's usually jovial face was suddenly frozen in lines of disapproval.

"Never take the Lord's name in vain in my presence. Do I make myself clear, Alvin?"

"No, you don't make yourself clear. What are you getting out?"

"I want you to marry my daughter and get her pregnant. There is a very good chance she would give me a grandson."

"Marry . . . Arvella?" Alvin felt the floor sink out from under him. The thought was so repulsive, he was almost sick.

"*Miss* Arvella. I'll thank you to have some respect for my daughter."

"Marry *her*?"

"Why of course. You don't think I'd let you fornicate with her without marrying her do you?"

"I . . . couldn't—"

"I think you can. I think you *will*."

The matter was closed. A month later the wedding was held in the church with the bride's beaming father officiating.

It was the beginning of a nightmare for Alvin, the only bright spots were his appointment as Indian agent to the southern section of the Wind River Reservation and meeting Virginia Gray. He managed to find out that Arvella's mother's family had left a sizable fortune to the first male born into the family. Arvella was the end of the line, and it was up to her to produce the heir or the fortune would go to charity. Henry Longfellow intended to have control of that comfortable fortune.

Alvin knew for certain that if Arvella had a son, it would not put one extra dime in *his* pocket; and after Longfellow had used him, he would get rid of him. There was a good chance that he'd not be able to give the preacher what he wanted. It was getting harder and harder to go to bed with the fat woman. Moonrock had helped to arouse him the last time. God only knew what it would take the next time to get him primed to perform his husbandly duties.

He had no trouble dredging up desire when he thought of Virginia Gray—it spread like fire in his loins. But when he was with Arvella he blocked her completely from his mind, not wanting to soil his daydreams. Virginia was a constant reminder of what he had always planned for himself and what his life could have been if he had not come to this backwater town of Sweetwater and met the Reverend Longfellow.

Alvin came to the decision then and there not to wait for Longfellow to kill him. Where in the hell was Hartog? The bastard was willing to take his money for killing Murphy. He'd pay him twice as much for doing in Longfellow.

After the deed was done, he would leave Sweetwater, change his name, and start up someplace else! What did he have to lose? *Virginia Gray!* He would not go without seeing her, at least once, and more if he could persuade her to go with him. He was pretty good at persuasion. Hadn't he talked the banker's wife into going to bed with him?

He recalled the guilty look on Virginia's face when he had thrown out the accusation that she had been running from something when she came to Sweetwater. It had been a straw in the wind. Nevertheless, he had already sent a wire to the Pinkerton Agency inquiring about her.

Regardless of the outcome of that inquiry, he would have her—bury himself in that aristocratic body. Before he finished with her, she would know what it meant to be loved by a real man. She'd follow him anywhere. Yearning had become delusion; desire had become obsession. Alvin Havelshell's mind had begun to slip out of reality and into fantasy.

Trell improved greatly during the days that followed. Granny tempted his appetite with strength-building meals, and Jenny saw to it that he ate them despite his sore jaws.

Blessing the invention of the sewing machine, Jenny cut out a nightshirt from material she had bought at the store to make gowns for the girls. Cassandra sewed it, pleased to be doing something for Trell. Travor helped his brother to bathe completely for the first time since the ambush, then slipped the garment over Trell's head.

"Cass made the nightshirt. She'll be in to see if it fits. Too bad it isn't Jenny visitin'. Want me to sprinkle some bay rum to kill the smell of that salve."

"You're funny, Trav. Real funny.

"Stop watching the door. Jenny's at the school."

"What's she doing there. Any kids showed up yet?"

"Not yet. She'll tell you when they do."

"I've got to get out of this bed and move around."

"Why? You've got two pretty girls waitin' on you."

"Don't forget Cass."

"It's impossible to forget Cass. She won't stand for it. I like the little twit. She tells me things."

"For instance—"

"She told me she thought her sister might be in love with you."

"Oh, Lord!" Trell tried to sit up. His ribs hurt so bad he sank back down. "When did she say that?"

"The night we brought you here. Jenny about croaked. But she didn't deny it. She denied it, though, when I asked if you were in love with *her*. She said you were a very good . . . *friend*."

"Godamighty, Trav! You've got a nerve."

"I wanted to know. I had to know if you'd staked a claim on her or Colleen. You may as well know, Trell, I've got my eye on Colleen. She's everythin' I want in a woman, and I'm goin' to do my damnedest to get her."

Trell studied his brother's face for a moment before he spoke.

"Don't trifle with Colleen's feelings, Trav. I know how you are with women. I don't want you to hurt her."

"I won't hurt her and I'll not let anyone else hurt her." Travor spoke so sincerely that Trell had to believe him. "I'll marry her if she'll have me."

"I never thought this day would come. I'm glad, Trav. Colleen is a fine girl, but . . . she'll not put up with any monkeyshines from you."

"She'll not have to. I've seen what's on the other side of the mountain, and it's no better than what's on this side. I want to sleep in the same bed every night and put my feet under the same table. I want to hear a little peckerwood callin' me 'Papa.'"

"I hope it works out for you, Trav."

"All I've got to do now is convince Colleen. A horny jackass and a hairy-chinned billy goat are only a couple of the things she's called me. She's threatened to shoot me and cut me with her knife." Travor grinned. His eyes shone with more light than Trell had seen in a long time.

"Looks like you've got your work cut out. Good luck."

"I've got to go over to the Double T and help Joe for a few days. I already made one fast trip to tell him we'd found you. But before I go again, I want to ride into Sweetwater and look around. The gunman I told you about might still be hanging around."

"Wait until I'm on my feet so I can go with you."

"I think it best if I go alone. If he's the one who shot you, he'll be caught off guard when he sees me. Besides, he may be long gone. I'll find out from the barkeep at the saloon."

Jenny was extremely happy. Trell was improving. Last night she had spent the evening at his bedside. They had talked of many things. She told him about her childhood, saving for another time the story of why she and the girls had come to Stoney Creek. Instead, she amused him with anecdotes about Uncle Noah. Trell told her about his mother and Mara Shannon, also saving some of the details for another time. Both Jenny and Trell knew how important it was that they learn more about each other, but every fleeting touch seemed to reveal more than words.

Jenny could not resist brushing back a lock that fell across his forehead. Trell felt the softness of her breast as she leaned over him, and his fingers ached to caress it. His thoughts brought heat to his face, and Jenny, responding to the warmth, pressed her hand against his forehead. Maybe he had a fever! When he caught her hand and drew it to his lips, she was suddenly as hot with desire as he. *Virginia Gray*, she cautioned herself, *you are encouraging this shy man to take liberties.* Slowly, regretfully, she had withdrawn her hand. She blushed now, as she remembered the incident. Tonight, when she went to see him, she must be less forward.

Tonight . . . she could hardly wait for tonight.

Travor had taken it upon himself to build up the wood supply. In two days' time he had dragged deadfalls to the homestead and cut a cord of firewood. Trell's twin might be a flirt, but he dearly loved his brother, and he was not lazy. He flirted with Colleen at every opportunity. She was not shy about telling him what she thought of his outrageous behavior. Granny looked on and occasionally smiled when her granddaughter wasn't looking.

Early one morning a group of Shoshoni arrived and set up poles for a lodge in the dense woods north of the school. When they finished, they left a pile of skins, jumped on their ponies and rode away.

"For the children who come to school," Whit explained. "They will have shelter from the rain and a cookfire."

"Why didn't they finish it?" Jenny asked.

"Rest is woman's work," Whit said with a frown.

"Won't the children go back to their families at night?"

"No family. They will live here."

"But . . . who will take care of them?"

"Woman who have no husband will come. Tribe bring food."

Whit answered her questions patiently even though he did not understand why she asked them.

Later that afternoon, the Reverend Longfellow paid a visit to the homestead. As soon as the buggy, accompanied by a rider, was spotted coming across the meadow toward the house, a flurry of activity ensued.

Trell was cautioned to make no sound before the bunk-house door was firmly closed. The tracks made by the peddler's wagon had already been swept away. Beatrice was Jenny's only worry. The child didn't understand the reason for keeping quiet about Trell. She liked sitting beside his bed and snuggling the puppy who was getting almost too big for her to hold.

Jenny suggested at first that the minister might be an ally. Ike shook his head.

"He be hand in glove with Havelshell. He even let him wed his girl. Some think he be a playin' the tune the agent's a dancin' to."

"That's got nothing to do with the men who tried to kill Trell," Jenny insisted.

"We ain't knowin' that yet, missy."

"I agree," Travor said. "Let's play the cards close to our chest for the time being."

Jenny came out the back door of the house as the buggy and rider came into the yard. The rider was Frank Wilson. He hung back, leaning on his saddlehorn, his eyes taking in the cut wood, the shed that had been made more secure for the cow and meadow grass that had been cut with a scythe and stacked outside the pole corral.

The preacher alighted from the buggy before Jenny spoke.

"Afternoon."

"Afternoon. It's a lovely day for a ride. How are you, my dear."

"Very well, and you?"

"Couldn't be better. I've looked for you every Sunday. I began to worry and thought I should ride out and see if you were all right. So many things could happen to a woman living alone."

"I'm not alone, as you can see. Can I get you a cold drink?"

"Why yes, I'd like a cool drink of water. Are the Murphys still here?"

"Of course." Jenny turned to see Travor approach. "Reverend Longfellow, have you met Mr. McCall?"

"I've not had the pleasure, but I've seen him in Sweetwater from time to time." The preacher stuck out his pudgy hand. "How do you do?"

"Very well, thank you." The two men shook hands. Travor towered over the pudgy little man.

"It's Christian of you to help out our teacher. God writes good deeds down in his book."

"That's what I thought. I wondered why the church in Sweetwater had not offered to send a crew to cut wood for the teacher. Where I come from, neighbors help neighbors."

"Where are you from, Mr. McCall?"

"A ranch west of Laramie. You may have heard of my half brother, Pack Gallager."

"No, I can't say that I have. Although I've been to Laramie a few times."

"Perhaps you know our friend, Charlie McCourtney, who helped to build the new Federal prison over there."

Jenny glanced quickly at Travor and saw that his face was grim and his dark eyes were fastened on the preacher's pleasantly smiling face. Longfellow, acting as though he was unaware of the scrutiny, turned to Jenny without answering.

"Thank you, my dear." He accepted a dipper of water. "I would like to see your school."

"The inside of the school and the supplies were destroyed when I got here. It's taken me all this time to get the schoolhouse ready, but the students will be arriving soon."

Anxious to get the preacher away from Travor and the bunkhouse where Trell lay, Jenny led the way up the path to the school. Before they reached it, Whit came out the door, mounted his pony and rode away.

"Do you let the Indians roam free in and out of the school?"

"Of course. It's their school. That was Whit Whitaker. His father donated the school and the money to supply a teacher. He has more right here than any of us."

"He's a breed, ma'am. Breeds are not recognized as legitimate heirs."

"Now isn't that strange." Jenny cocked her head to one side, and became the personification of puzzlement. "Offspring of Frenchmen are legitimate heirs, as are Mexican and German."

It clearly required all Jenny's self-restraint to keep the sneer out of her voice. She kept in mind Ike's warning that it was possible that the preacher was playing the tune Havelshell was dancing to. Something about him did not ring true to her either. She decided to be cautious.

Travor waited until Jenny and Longfellow disappeared into the school before he went back to chopping wood. The preacher's name had struck a chord in his memory. He had thrown out the information about Charlie's helping to build the Federal prison to test the man's reaction. He'd heard the name Longfellow mentioned somewhere and in a way unconnected to the poet. This Longfellow was smooth to a fault, hadn't batted an eyelash. Too nice, too glib. Travor didn't trust him.

He suddenly remembered the man who had ridden in with the preacher. He looked around and saw his horse tied to a corral pole and the saddle empty. Moving quickly, Travor sank the axe blade into a stump and went to look for him, fearing that he would discover Trell in the bunkhouse. He walked to the back of the shed where Colleen and Ike were sharpening the scythe and grass-cutting knives on a grindstone. Before he turned the corner, he heard Colleen's loud, angry voice. He eased to the corner and waited to see what was going on before he barged in.

"Ya heard me, unless yo're deaf as well as dumb as a doorknob."

"What'd ya say, honeybunch?"

"I said—get the hell away from here. Ya ain't welcome."

"Sure I am, pretty gal. Ya jist ain't knowin' it yet."

"Yo're about as welcome as a nest of hornets in an outhouse."

"Come on. 'Fess up. Ya've been wishin' I'd come back."

"Maybe I've been needin' another laugh. Last time I saw ya, ya was flat on yore back in the dirt and I was laughin' my head off."

"Yeah." Frank laughed, showing the wide space between his front teeth. "Ya bested me that time. Next time ya'll be lyin' flat on yore back . . . and I'll be doin' somethin' 'sides laughin'." He lifted his heavy eyebrows suggestively.

Travor stepped around the corner and hit him square in the mouth. Frank backtracked a few steps before he sprawled on the ground. His hat bounced off his head, rolled under the corral fence and stopped against a pile of cow droppings.

"You'll be the one stretched out if you as much as look at her crossways," Travor said, looking down at him as if he were something that smelled exceedingly bad. "When you wake up, you'll be lookin' for your teeth and trying to unscramble your brain."

"What'd you do that for," Colleen yelled. "I can fight my own battles, kill my own snakes."

"Yo're McCall—" Frank got to his feet, dabbing his split lips with the sleeve of his shirt.

"And you're a smart-mouthed sonofabitch. That's no way to talk to a lady."

"Lady?" Frank snorted.

Travor hit him again. Frank staggered back against the pole corral.

"Better call it quits, cowboy, and apologize to the lady. I can hurt you."

Travor stood calmly rewrapping the neckerchief around his knuckles. He had known as soon as he heard Colleen's voice that he was going to hit someone and had prepared. He had kept himself alive in many a tight situation by taking care of his gun hand. He trained his eyes on the man he'd just knocked off his feet, despite an angry hiss that came from Colleen.

"This . . . skirt yores?" Frank jerked his head toward Colleen.

"I don't like the way you put it, but, yes, the lady's mine."

"I ain't no such thin'," Colleen yelled.

"Hush up, honey. It's goin' to get out sooner or later. It might as well be this loudmouth that spreads the news."

"Don't . . . be callin' me that, you slack-jawed, pig-ugly bunghead!"

"Pretty when she gets her wind up, ain't she?" Travor smiled at her proudly.

"Don't sound to me like she's yore girl," Frank mumbled, his lips swelling and still bleeding.

"She is. After she's halter-broke, she'll do just fine."

Frank leaned between the rails, scooped his hat up off the ground and slammed it down on his head.

"Yo're welcome to 'er, mister. Tamin' her'll be 'bout as easy as stretching a skeeter's ass over a rain barrel." He turned to leave.

"Hold on. I didn't hear you apologize to the lady."

"Sorry," Frank mumbled and beat a hasty retreat.

"Hee, hee, hee—" Ike laughed as Frank walked away.

"What'er you laughin' for, ya old . . . buzzard?" Colleen's eyes glittered with the light of battle.

"You two remind me of a couple wildcats with one tree 'tween 'em."

"—And ya remind me of an . . . old goat!"

"Now, now, sweetheart." Travor put his hand on her arm. "Don't take your mad out on Ike. Take it out on me."

"Ya . . . shut up, ya . . . struttin' rooster!" She twisted under his clamped hand, jerked free and angrily stomped away.

Travor turned to see that Ike's weathered face was stiff.

"I ain't figgerin' ya to be a man who'd trifle with a sweet little gal like Colleen."

"You figgered right, old man."

"The little gal's pure hickory. Straight as a string. I ain't standin' by and seein' a good woman's name dragged in the mud 'cause a man's got it in mind t'pleasure hisself."

Ike paused and waited for some response from the still-faced man and finally it came.

"If you've got more to say, say it."

"The little gal is workin' her tail off to make a place for her and her granny. If yore intentions t'ords her ain't on the up 'n up, ya better hightail it outta here. The gal's been caught in a gully-washer. Her pa was killed and her home burned. She's come through it with a scar or two. I ain't standin' by and seein' her get more. I be killin' ya if I hafta." Ike finished with a wintry smile.

Travor had listened carefully to what the old man was saying. He cocked his head to one side, as if seeing him for the first time.

"You'd do it. Or at least, you'd try."

"There'd be no tryin', boy. I'll do it, and ya'd more'n likely never know what hit ya. I won't be givin' ya no chance at me. When somethin' needs killin', I kill it. It makes me no never mind how."

Travor leaned forward and tapped Ike's chest with a forefinger.

"It's no business of yours, old man, but I'll tell you so you don't get your bowels in an uproar. I'm going to marry that girl and take care of her, and her granny, too, for as long as the old lady's around."

"It don't 'pear she wants ya. And if she don't . . . back off."

"We got started off on the wrong foot, but she'll come around. Right now she's figgerin' on how to back down and save face."

"Ya better be right, boyo."

Ike picked up the scythe and began to sharpen it. Travor returned to the woodpile with a lot on his mind.

Chapter Twenty-one

"I've got to get out of this bed."

"What's the hurry?" Jenny had brought Trell his plate of food. Cassandra had wanted to bring it, but Jenny was too eager to wait until evening to see him. Now she sat quietly by as he ate.

"That's what Travor said. He told me how lucky I was to have two pretty women to wait on me."

"Travor is a blatant flirt and full of Irish blarney."

"But he's right about you being pretty."

"Thank you, Mr. McCall." Pleasure lighted Jenny's eyes and brought a slight blush to her cheeks. "You'd better stop talking and finish eating if you want to get out of that bed."

"I'm trying to eat slow because you'll leave when I finish."

"I won't leave."

"Thanks for the nightshirt. I've never had one before."

"Cass and I thought it would be comfortable."

There was an uneasy silence, during which time Trell ate the last bite of food on the plate, eating slowly not only because he wanted her to stay but also because of his sore jaws. Jenny placed the empty dish on the washstand and returned to the chair beside the bed.

"Do you have a mirror?" he asked quietly. "I'd like to see what I look like."

"I didn't realize you hadn't seen yourself since the . . . accident. I'll get one."

She returned from the house minutes later and handed him the mirror. He looked at his face for several minutes, then placed the mirror on the bed.

"Folks won't be confused now about which is me and which is Trav. I'll be the scar-faced McCall."

"Does that bother you?"

"No one wants their face tore up."

Jenny leaned forward and took his hand in both of hers.

"I wish the scar wasn't there, but only because of the pain you endured. I know the man behind the face. What is on the outside of him isn't all that important to me."

"Jenny, Jenny—you may think so now, but later—" His voice trailed as his eyes looked deeply into hers.

"I'm not put off by the scar on your face."

"It'll be there for as long as I live."

Jenny then did something that surprised her so completely that she was to wonder about it for months, years. Forgetting her resolve to be less forward, she leaned over him and kissed him gently on the lips.

When he caught his breath, he didn't even feel the pain from his broken ribs. It was over all too quickly. She moved her head back. He could still taste her lips, smell her warm breath.

"I've got nothing to offer a woman like you," he whispered brokenly. "You should live in a fine house and do all the things a refined lady does—"

"Such as?"

"You know what I mean," he said harshly. "All I have is half a ranch, a few horses and a few cows."

"I'm responsible for my two young sisters, I'm committed to the Indian school and helping Whit go to college. I'm also in deep conflict with the Indian agent . . . and there's more. I'm no prize, Trell."

"You are to me. The only education I've had is what I learned after I was fourteen years old."

"I've known educated men who were dumb as stumps. You're a good man, thoughtful and capable. I knew that the first day when you pitched right in to help me. And you were kind to a little girl who has suffered a terrible blow to her self-esteem this past year. With your kindness you won her over, which was not easy to do."

"Jenny, listen," he said urgently. "Trav and I had another brother, beside Pack, who turned outlaw and was killed by another outlaw. Our father drank and almost gambled away the inheritance of his niece. Thank God she came to Laramie before it was all gone. My background is that of poor Irish—"

"Is that all?"

"No. I'm not only poor as Job's turkey, now I've got a face that will scare children." His voice was so low that she could hardly hear. "I won't burden you with it. I want you to know that I'll stand by you and see to it that you're left alone here."

"Burden *me*? Don't make excuses, Trell. I realize that I'm not suitable for life on a ranch. Colleen would be a far better helpmate."

"Colleen is a fine girl and I'll welcome her to the family when Trav marries her."

"That isn't likely to happen. She doesn't even like him."

"Trav is in love with her. He'll win her over."

"Trell, I came to Wyoming because I *had* to come. I want to tell you why I left the security of family and friends to come here with my two sisters."

"I saw you and the girls get off the stage that day and I thought about you all the way home."

"Sweetwater, Stoney Creek, the school—none of it was up to my expectations. Things only started going right when you came and helped me put out the fire."

"I fell in love with you that day." His voice was so low that she could hardly hear. There was so much love and concern in his eyes that she would have known what he said if she hadn't heard.

"Trell! My heart's been aflutter over you for weeks."

"You're not just saying . . . that—?"

"No, no, my sweet man! But I want to tell you why the girls and I came here. There's something you need to know about me, Trell. If I should leave the territory, I would be arrested for kidnapping."

For the next half hour Jenny leaned close to the man on the bed and told him of her life in Allentown and all the events leading up to her taking the girls and fleeing to Wyoming Territory.

"That sonofabi—"

"It's all right. Say it. I've called Charles that many times in my thoughts. He will never get his hands on the girls again. I think . . . I really think I would kill him first."

"You wouldn't have to, honey. You've got me and Trav. We'll take care of it, if it comes to that. I wish I wasn't in this damn bed!"

"What would you do?"

"I'd hold you in my arms and kiss you."

"I was hoping you'd say that."

"Come closer," he whispered.

Trell put his free hand at the nape of her neck and pulled her face down to his. His lips were warm and firm. He kissed her deeply and sweetly, careful not to smear her with the salve on his cheek. Jenny closed her eyes and gave herself up to the sweetness of his kiss.

Dear and generous God, I thank you for bringing this wonderful man into my life. I will love him, respect him, and cherish him for as long as I live.

When she lifted her head, she looked down at Trell with eyes shining with love. Gentle fingers stroked the hair at his temple.

"It broke my heart to think of you lying out there alone and hurt. If you hadn't come . . . back—" Her voice broke.

"But I did, my love. I don't have much, Jenny, but it's yours."

"No one has ever offered me so much. I'm proud to accept it and you. Everything I have will be yours. We'll share the good and the bad. Oh, Trell. I wish I could kiss all the hurt places on your dear face and they would be well. I've never been in love before. I had a few schoolgirl crushes that lasted a week or two. It's a grand feeling to know that a wonderful man loves me and that I love him."

"Do you really love *me*? It's like reaching for a star and suddenly you have it in your hand. I'll spend my life taking care of you and the girls if you let me."

Trell already knew many of the things that had happened since she arrived. Jenny had told him about slapping the agent, and about today's visit from the Reverend Longfellow.

"Uncle Noah would say that the preacher talked out of both sides of his mouth. Whit said he talked with a forked tongue. I had the feeling he was here to see what he could find out. He said he just dropped by on his way to the Agency store. Wouldn't you think he would have mentioned that he was going to visit his daughter?"

"He didn't?"

"No. He told me a pitiful story about the children in Sweetwater who wanted to go to school, but had no teacher. Mr. Havelshell had already offered me the job. Longfellow didn't care whether or not the Indian children had a teacher. *My dear, they may learn a word or two, but what good will it do? They will never let go of their savage ways.*" She mimicked the preacher's soft voice.

"And, Trell, he thought Whit had no right to anything of his father's because he was a half-breed bastard. I told him that Mr. Whitaker and Whit's mother were married according to Shoshoni customs. He actually laughed and shook his head in such a patronizing way that I wanted to hit him."

"Don't get upset, sweetheart. Most of the people who came to settle the West feel like that about the Indians. It'll take years for them to realize that this was *their* land, and their customs are as old or older than some of ours."

"Another reason that I love you is that we think alike. Hurry and get well," she whispered close to his ear.

"I'd be up tomorrow if I had a crutch."

"I asked Mr. McGriff to bring a pair when he comes back next week. But you shouldn't get on your feet too soon."

"It was hard to stay in here today when the preacher came. I didn't know what was happening or if you needed me."

"Your brother represented you very well. I don't think you'll be able to count the preacher as a close friend."

"Trav has a way of rubbing folks the wrong way."

"Did Ike tell you that Trav knocked Frank Wilson off his feet?" Jenny chuckled softly.

"They don't come too big for Trav to take on. Wilson was lucky he didn't loose some teeth."

"Cassandra was put out because she didn't see Trav do it."

"She told me about the dart and the slingshot." Trell smiled with one side of his mouth. "She had intended it for Havelshell's horse."

"Cassandra is a strong-willed little girl. She doesn't hesitate to take matters into her own hands."

"I know. She's asked me several times if I wanted to marry you."

"Oh, no! Oh, my goodness. I'm glad I didn't know that. That isn't why—"

"Silly girl! I wanted you the first day I came here but didn't dare think I had a chance."

"Thank goodness Beatrice takes after her mother and Cassandra is one of a kind."

"Cass knew I wanted to be alone with you. She's giving me the chance to court you."

"I'm beginning to like *your* brother a lot, and I wish *my* sister was small enough to spank!"

"Our luck could run out any minute and . . . I want to kiss you again. I love you, Jenny. Are you afraid of it?"

"No, my love. I'm grateful that I'm the one you want."

"I want you . . . very much."

He stared gravely at her, then pulled her to him. He held the back of her head in his large hand, working his fingers through her hair while his lips made little caressing movements against her. His hand was firm, his lips soft. He gave her no chance to withdraw and she did not want to. At the soft touch of his tongue on her lower lip, emotion surged from deep inside her, and impulsively she pressed his hand close to her breast. He kept it there for a long moment.

They drew away together. She let her breath out slowly. When she looked in his eyes, she knew that he hadn't wanted the kiss to end.

"We'll have other times together," she whispered, then laughed softly, her breath feathering his wet lips. "I don't think I'll sleep a wink tonight. I'll want to remember each and every word we said to each other. Oh, dear! I'm acting as if I were sixteen."

"I'll not sleep either. I'll be wishing you were here with me. Instead I'll have to listen to Trav snore."

"He said at supper that he was going over to the Double T for a few days, that is, if Ike was going to be here."

"First he's stopping in Sweetwater to see if he can find out anything about the fellers that shot me. I wish he'd wait because I sent a letter to our brother Pack and told him what was going on here and asked him to get in touch with a friend of ours who is a Federal marshal. The last I heard Cleve was in Big Timber, Montana Territory, and I'm sure he'll come down soon, if he isn't tied up with another investigation."

"I hope he does. There's something wrong here. Terribly wrong."

"Be extra careful while Trav is away."

"I will. Now, I should go and let you get some sleep. Travor will be wanting to go to bed. He's probably sitting outside waiting for me to leave."

"Kiss me again and tell me—"

"That I love you? I do. Believe me, I do."

"You've given me the world." His hand stroked up and down her arm, then moved to smooth the hair back from her cheek.

The lamplight slanted onto his face and his thick lashes made fans of darkness in the hollows beneath his eyes. A new feeling grew in Jenny, a wish to take away his hurt, absorb his pain, and to give herself to him wholly and completely.

They gazed at each other for a moment that was so still that it seemed time had stopped moving. Then, slowly, tenderly, she lowered her mouth to his again.

Jenny and Colleen, with help from Cassandra, usually washed the supper dishes. Granny cooked the meal, and they insisted that she sit in her chair while they did the cleaning. Tonight Cassandra took the drying towel and instructed Beatrice to reset the table with the clean dishes, placing the plates facedown and covering with a cloth the *necessaries* Granny left on the table.

Ike, who never stayed indoors any longer than was necessary, went out as soon as he finished his meal.

"Meal was . . . fair. Thanky."

"Ya didn't hafta eat it," Granny retorted.

"'Twas eat or starve."

"Ya can starve, fer all I care."

"Ya'd miss me somethin' awful, if'n I did." Ike laughed his dry chuckle and hurried out the door.

Granny rocked in her chair and Travor, while pretending to read a newspaper that had been left by McGriff, watched Colleen. She had braided her hair Indian-fashion and wore baggy old overalls, but she was the most desirable, fascinating woman he'd ever met. He recorded in his mind every movement, every gesture, to bring out and mull over when he was away from her.

When the cleaning was almost completed, he went out, returned with an armload of firewood for the woodbox and went out again. He lit a cigarette and waited beside the well for Colleen. He knew that she would not go to bed with an empty water bucket on the washstand.

The door finally opened, but it was Cassandra who came toward him, the glow of his cigarette serving as a beacon for her.

"I'm making sure you don't go to the bunkhouse for a while," she said, coming right to the reason for her being there. "Give Trell some time to be alone with Jenny."

"Well, if you aren't the little matchmaker."

"I try to be. They are right for each other, and Trell is in love with her."

"How do you know that?"

"I asked him. How else would I find out what I want to know?"

"And what did he say?"

"He didn't say anything. He hemmed and hawed around. But he didn't have to say anything. I knew he was smitten with her the first day he came here. Just as I know that you're smitten with Colleen and are waiting for her to come out to fill the water bucket."

"You're a regular little miss know-it-all. A man wouldn't stand a chance if you wanted him."

"The man I choose will be extra smart. I can't abide stupidity."

"Is that the reason you like me so much?" he teased.

"You're not dumb, Travor, but not overly smart either. You've backed Colleen into a corner with your flirty ways, which, by the way, she hates. She's put up so much resistance to you now that it will be hard for her to admit that she likes you without looking and feeling like a fool."

"You think she likes me?"

"I'd have to be deaf, blind and dumb not to know that. And if you're as smart as I think you are, you know it, too."

"What does Granny think?"

"Why not ask her?"

"I'm afraid to, that's why, little miss wise-owl."

"Granny is very smart. Oh, not in book learning, but in experience and horse sense, which at times is more valuable to a person than a college education."

"You've figured this all out, have you?"

"Of course. Granny realizes that she'll not be around for many more years. She loves her granddaughter and wants to see her settled with a good man who will take care of her. I think she wanted Trell for Colleen, but it was clear from the start that he wanted Jenny."

"Godamighty!" Travor dropped his cigarette and stepped on it. "Are you sure you're not a thirty-year-old midget?"

"I'm nine years old, Travor, as you well know." Cassandra spoke in a resigned tone of voice, as if she were bored with having to repeatedly tell her age. "I'll be ten in two months. Age has little to do with intelligence. You either have it or you don't."

"And you have it."

"It was not my doing. My parents were responsible. Now, it's not hard to figure out what's going on here.

You're waiting like a little boy hoping for a glimpse of the princess."

"What do you suggest I do?"

"A man with serious intentions would go to Granny and ask her permission to walk out with her granddaughter."

"What if she turned me down?"

"It would be up to you to persuade her that your intentions are honorable."

"Hmmm—You may have a point." He stuck out his hand and Cassandra put hers into it. "Let's give it a try. If this works, I'll get your advice on a few other problems I have."

"Anytime. Glad to help. Go on in. If we go in together, Colleen will think we've been plotting."

Travor went determinedly to the door and flung it open. Colleen stood there with the water bucket in hand. He took it from her, then with his hand on her back prodded her to where Granny sat in her chair.

"Mrs. Murphy, I'd like your permission to walk out with your granddaughter. My intentions are honorable, and I will bring her back to you within an hour."

"Why, you puffed-up jackass!" Colleen turned on him. "What game are you playin' now?"

Travor ignored her and looked at Granny.

"I'll see that no harm comes to her, ma'am. I'll guard her with my life."

"Young man, 'pears to me yore life is what needs guardin' if you go out in the dark with my granddaughter."

"I'll handle her without hurtin' her. I promise."

"Then go on. Take her for an hour."

"Gran . . . ny!" Colleen sputtered. "Are ya tellin' me to go out in the dark with this . . . this horny toad?"

"Ya got yore gun, ain't ya? And yore knife. If he gets outta line, cut him a little. Ain't nothin' like a show a blood to cool a feller off, 'specially if it's his."

"Thank you, Granny." Travor grabbed Colleen's arm and steered her toward the door.

"Turn loose a me, ya smooth-talkin' warthog!" Colleen tried to shake loose from his hand.

"Now, now, honey. Don't make a show of yourself in front of your granny, or she might not let you come with me again." By this time they were out the door and Colleen was gasping with rage.

"That was . . . low! To fool Granny like that."

"I wasn't foolin' her."

"Ya fooled her into thinkin' ya wasn't goin' to get me out here to try and paw me."

"Now don't go puttin' ideas in my head. If that's what you're wantin' me to do, honey, I'll be glad to oblige."

Colleen dug in her heels. "Ya think every woman ya flirt with wants ya. Well, I *don't*!"

"Maybe not now, sweetheart. But you'll change your mind."

They reached the well. Travor loosened the rope. It slid through his hand until the bucket hit the water. He pulled it up quickly and poured the water into the bucket they had brought from the kitchen.

"Let's take this in. I told Granny I'd bring you back in an hour, and I don't want to waste any of my time with you."

"Back from where?"

"From a stroll. Haven't you ever walked out with a feller?"

"Yeah, and it was anythin' but a picnic. Most of 'em had as many hands as a spider has legs."

They had reached the door. "Stay right here, sweetheart. I'll take the water bucket in."

Travor went into the kitchen and set the bucket on the shelf. When he turned, he caught Granny's eye and winked.

A chuckle died in his throat when he saw that Colleen was not where he left her. He peered into the darkness between the house and the bunkhouse. Unleashing a string of cusswords, he went to the side of the house, then back to look toward the school.

"Shit, shit, shitfire!" he murmured. "Dad-blasted woman!"

"She's in the shed." Cassandra's voice came from the dark shadow beside the house.

"Thanks, Cass. Go in and keep Granny company. If I catch you spyin' on us, I'll whop your bottom."

"Horseshit!"

"That's no way for a child to talk," Travor scolded.

"I'm not a child. I'm a thirty-year-old midget. Remember?"

Travor waited until Cassandra went into the house, then headed for the shed. He had exceptionally good night vision and saw Colleen at the end of the shed where they had piled the fresh green grass they had cut for the cow.

"If you'd rather lie in the grass than take a walk, sweetheart, it's all right with me."

Colleen shot past him before he could catch hold of her. She was off and running around the house. Travor knew he'd never be able to catch her, so he darted around the house in the opposite direction. They came together on the corner and both fell to the ground, with Travor rolling so that he wouldn't fall on her.

The breath was knocked out of him, but he held on to the struggling girl. Her elbow caught him in the ribs and he grunted.

"Dammit! Be still."

"Let go of me, you . . . pisspot!"

"I don't like nasty words coming out of your pretty mouth," he gritted angrily, turned, and pinned her beneath him.

"It's no business of yores what I say!"

"Yes it is. Now be still and I'll let you up."

Suddenly she stopped struggling. "Let me up."

"I want to kiss you."

"Wantin' and gettin' is two different thin's."

"I won't take it. I want you to give it to me."

"Horse-hockey!" she sputtered. "It'll rain silver dollars first!"

"Ouch! One just dropped on my head."

Colleen laughed, then broke it off as she realized what she was doing.

"Too bad it wasn't a rock the size of yore big head."

"I'll turn your hands loose if you put your arms around my neck."

"I'll put 'em at yore throat," she snarled.

"Colleen, sweetheart. Be nice. I've got to leave in the morning."

"Be nice? Ya get my back up. Why can't ya be like Trell?"

"'Cause Trell is Trell and I'm me. Trell has always been the nice one, I've been the hellraiser. But I'm tired of ramming around. I want to settle down . . . with you."

The weight of his body on hers was not unpleasant. She felt none of the panic she had felt when other men had grabbed her. She searched the face so close to hers. He was quietly staring down at her.

"If I kiss ya, will ya let me up?"

"I said I would and I will. But it's nice holding you like this. You're a soft, sweet woman, Colleen McCall."

"Murphy."

"Someday you'll be Colleen McCall and I'll hold you in my arms all night long, touch you all over, kiss you—"

"Ya think yo're the only rooster in the henhouse, don't ya?"

"Can you feel my heart pounding against your bosom? It's racing like a runaway horse . . . because of you."

"I thought it was the silver dollars fallin' on yore back."

When he laughed she could feel the movement against her breasts and the small puffs of his breath on her face.

"Thank God, I found you. Until now I've not been living; just existing. Now I have something to live and work for."

"I've . . . kissed lots a fellers," she lied. "But didn't marry 'em."

"Maybe. But you'll kiss only me from now on."

As Travor lowered his head, she lifted her lips to meet his. It was like no kiss he'd ever had before. After the first touch, her lips were as eager as his. For an endless time he held her clamped to him, desperate in his hunger to feel every inch of her.

When he realized that her arms were wrapped about his neck, joyous laughter bubbled in his throat.

"You're more than I ever dreamed of, my darlin' Irish Colleen," he murmured between frantic kisses. "Sweetheart, I've never said these words before . . . not even to my blessed mother, but I'll say them to you. I love you, darlin' girl. I love you." The words trailed off as his mouth traced the pattern of love on hers.

"Travor." His name came shivering from her throat. "Please don't say somethin' you don't mean. I don't know ya and ya don't know me. I always swore I'd never get mixed up with a triflin' man."

"I know you. And someday soon . . . I'll know you better." His lips moved over her face. "I want to be with you forever, live with you. Be your mate. I'll take care of you and Granny. But I've got to know if you love me." He waited in an agony of suspense for her answer.

"I . . . think I do. I've never felt like this about . . . anyone. I must love ya or ya wouldn't make me so . . . mad."

Their lips caught and clung and smiled against each other. They laughed intimately, and their fingers moved over each other's faces.

"I shaved. I was determined to kiss you and I didn't want to scratch your pretty face."

"How'd ya know I'd let ya?"

"I didn't," he whispered against her cheek. "But I hoped."

"Why me, Travor?"

"Because I like everything about you; the way you look, your independent spirit, the way you are with me."

"Why'd ya wink at me that day and not Jenny? We thought ya was Trell. Her feelin's was hurt, and I was madder than a steer with its tail caught in the fence."

"I was in the hotel across from the store and watched you load the supplies in the wagon. I couldn't keep from lookin' at ya. Yo're pretty in a dress, but just as pretty in overalls."

"Don't . . . trifle with me." Her voice quivered.

"I won't . . . I'm not. I swear it on my mother's grave." His whispered vow brushed past her ear.

"I want to believe ya."

"Do ya want lots of younguns? I do. Trell and I were all our folks had together. Pa had a boy before he married Ma. She had Pack before she married Pa. We'll make beautiful babies together, sweetheart. I hope they have your eyes."

"There won't be a blond-headed one in the bunch." Colleen laughed happily and stroked the inky black hair from his forehead.

Travor kissed her with hunger. Her ragged breath was trapped in her mouth by his plundering kiss. Her mouth was warm, sweet beyond imagination. His hand roamed over her, caressing every inch of her back and sides. The long fingers on one hand cupped her rounded breast while the other shaped itself over her lean buttocks and held her tightly to his aroused body.

He moved his mouth from hers and took great gulps of air.

"Colleen, sweetheart, I'd better stop while I can."

He pulled her up. They sat with their backs to the house, his arms around her, her head on his shoulder. They talked of their hopes and dreams, shared secrets, and intimate kisses.

It was more than three hours before Travor took her to the house. They opened the door and found Granny's chair empty.

Chapter Twenty-two

Arvella's nerves were stretched to the breaking point by the time her father's buggy came into the yard behind the store. The past couple of weeks she had tried to keep thoughts of her father and Alvin in the back of her mind during the time she spent with the kindest man she had encountered since she became an adult.

The friendship with Pud Harris began the day he had come to the house and found her crying. A few mornings after that, he had called to her from the back door.

"Miss Arvella, come out to the barn. I got somethin' to show ya."

"Can't you bring it here?"

"No. Ya gotta come out."

"I don't ever go . . . out—"

"Then it's time ya did. Come on. It'll not take but a minute."

Grateful for the kind attention he had shown to her and not wanting it to end, she stepped out into the bright sunlight. It felt strange walking on the uneven ground and being outside the safe walls of the house. Without the solid figure of Pud beside her, she would have been terrified. She was sure a hundred eyes were watching her. She wanted to flee back into the house, but she didn't dare for fear that he would ridicule her for being afraid.

She followed him into the dim, cool, smelly barn. At the far end Pud stopped at a stall and rubbed the nose of a blaze-faced sorrel that nickered a greeting.

"How'er ya doin', Lady?"

Arvella hung back. She was not fond of horses. They scared her.

"Come look," Pud urged.

Arvella looked into the stall to see a newborn foal standing on shaky legs next to its mother.

"She was born about an hour ago." Pud continued to stroke the mother's nose.

"And she can stand already?"

"She was on her feet in a matter of minutes." Pud's broad face creased with a grin. "That's nature's way of lettin' her protect herself against somethin' that'd want to brin' her down. She'll be runnin' by tomorrow."

"Is she yours?"

"I brought her out here when the old man told me to come stay. I knew she was about ready to foal. Ain't she a beauty?"

"She sure is. It's been a long time since I've seen a foal this young."

"I thought you'd like to see her."

"What's her name?"

"Her mama's name is Lady. I haven't put a name to the baby. Ya got one in mind?"

"I'm not good . . . at—"

"Think about it. We don't have to name her right off."

After that Arvella went to the barn sometimes twice a day to visit the foal. Pud's words stuck in her mind. *"We* don't have to name her right away." When they spoke of a name for the foal again, she suggested that they name her Rosemary.

Pud was pleased with Arvella's interest in things outside the house. Within a week she was going to the chicken house, the barn, or to the garden. She didn't seem to be quite so breathless now when she walked beside him.

Arvella knew that Pud would be sent back to Sweetwater if her father suspected she took any pleasure from his company. She also knew that it was wicked to detest her papa and to wish him and Alvin dead. She'd never kill them. She didn't even have the nerve to talk back to him or refuse to do his bidding. In his presence she was completely spineless.

Until she was fourteen years old, Arvella had seen her father only once or twice a year. Then he had come to her grandparents' house and taken her away after her mother died. She had not known then why she had been taken from her beloved grandparents. She understood now that it was the money he had expected her to inherit when they died.

The grandparents had lived another five years. During that time Arvella and her father had made frequent visits to the old folks in order to ensure that she would inherit the bulk of their enormous estate. But it had not been left to her. It was put in a trust for her firstborn son with the boy's legitimate father as executor.

The terms of the will had infuriated Longfellow but had not deterred him from his purpose. He had set out to find Arvella a husband, one that he could control. He had chosen Alvin Havelshell and demanded that they produce a son,

Arvella had been a shy plump girl but a talented cook and housekeeper. Her father's constant harping on her looks and inability to socialize had so eroded her self-esteem that she turned to cooking and eating for comfort. Her weight had ballooned as had her father's contempt and criticism. With a look or a word he was able to make her feel as lowly as a worm and as insignificant as a fly on the wall.

This morning Linus had come to tell her that her father was on his way and that he had Frank Wilson with him.

"Oh, dear! I'm a mess . . . the kitchen isn't clean and . . . he'll want dinner—"

"Arvella," Linus said sternly. "Ya ain't got time to stand there moanin' and wringin' yore hands. Clean yoreself up. I'll wash the dishes."

"Is Pud here?"

"He'll be here in a bit. He told me to come help ya."

Now waiting in a fresh dress, her hair combed and the quarters behind the store in immaculate order, she tried to still the shaking of her hands and the quiver in her voice as she stood beside Pud on the porch.

"I put the pheasants in the oven. He likes pheasant."

"Miss Arvella, don't act scared of him."

"I can't help it. But I'll try."

"He'll not like it if he knows I've been eatin' in here."

"Linus washed up the dishes. I told him to stay out of sight. Maybe you should, too."

"I'm prepared for him, Miss Arvella. He sent me out here 'cause he didn't trust Alvin. I'll tell him what he wants to hear."

"Thank God Alvin isn't with him."

Pud stepped out to hold the horse while the preacher got out of the buggy.

"Howdy, Reverend."

"This place is looking shoddier and shoddier. I need a cool drink, Arvella." Longfellow walked up onto the porch and, without greeting his daughter, passed her and went into the house. "I swear to God! You've put on more fat since the last time I was here," he murmured loudly enough for Pud to hear.

With head bent, Arvella followed him into the house.

Pud gritted his teeth and cursed under his breath.

"There's a cool breeze in the sitting room, Papa. Sit down and I'll bring you a glass of lemonade." She returned a minute later with a glass wrapped in a napkin to keep the drink cool. "I've got pheasant in the oven. I should see to it—"

"Are you still cooking for that bastard?"

"He eats in here . . . sometimes."

"Jesus! I don't know why Alvin doesn't get rid of him."

"He works."

"Doing what? Plowing the Indian gals?" When she looked puzzled, he snorted in disgust, and said, "Sit down. You stand there like a swaying elephant about to topple over on me."

Arvella eased her bulk down in the chair opposite him, glad that Pud was not near to hear his disparaging remarks. She opened a folding fan she took from the table beside the chair and began to fan her flushed face. It was something to do.

"A girl from the orphans' home over in Rawlings will be coming out. I want you to train her to keep house and to cook. Old Bertha won't last forever; and by the time she's gone, this new girl should be ready to take her place."

Arvella couldn't think of anything to say, so she nodded.

"She's eleven years old. Irish girls grow up fast so she may look older. I don't want Linus getting into her. Understand? He rapes her, and I'll nail his balls to a stump."

"Linus didn't . . . with Moonrock—"

"How do you know? Were you watching every minute. That kid was like a dog after a bitch in heat all the time she was here. I could see it, so could Alvin."

"Linus is mouthy, but he isn't bad . . . like that—"

"All men, if they're any kind of man, are bad like that. Which reminds me . . . have you caught yet?"

Arvella shook her head.

"When did you bleed last?"

Arvella felt as if her face was on fire. She hated these frank conversations with her father. There was nothing too personal for him to discuss openly.

"After . . . Alvin was here—"

"Hmmm . . . Maybe I should have him do it *while* you're bleeding. There should be some way for his seed to get through all that fat."

"Papa! No. I . . . couldn't—"

"What do you mean, you couldn't?"

"Sometimes I get cramps in my stomach."

"Don't say no to me again, or I'll slap those fat jaws. You'll do whatever it takes to get pregnant. I'll talk to the doctor. I may even go to Forest City and talk to one there. I'll tell him how anxious you are to give your husband an heir and see what he says."

"Please . . . don't—"

"If he says there's a chance you could catch if you did it during your bleeding time, you send Linus to me the minute you see a spot of blood. You'll birth a son one way or the other, Arvella. I've waited long enough."

"I can't help it—"

"If this doesn't work, I'm seriously thinking of having Alvin impregnate another woman and send her out here for you to keep out of sight until she gives birth. Then, if it's a boy you can claim the child as your own."

"A woman wouldn't just give me her baby."

"Don't be a fool. She'd have nothing to say about it. Now get up off your fat ass and fix dinner. I've got to be getting back to town and prepare my sermon for tomorrow."

After the preacher left, Pud waited a good half hour before he went to the house. He knew Arvella would be upset and would need time to settle down. He was surprised to see her usually immaculate kitchen had not been cleaned. The remainder of the pheasant and sage dressing was still in the roasting pan. The soiled dishes were still on the dining-room table.

The door to Arvella's room was closed.

Pud knocked gently on the door. "Miss Arvella. It's me. Pud."

"I've . . . gone to bed." Her voice was broken and he knew that she was crying. "You and Linus eat what's left of the dinner. I'll clean up tomorrow."

"Are ya all right?"

"I got a headache, is all."

Pud knew what had given her a headache. At times, he'd like to bust the cocky little bastard right in the nose. Longfellow was a con man hiding behind the cloak of a preacher. Pud knew it the first week he worked for him, but the pay was good and he'd not been asked to do anything that he considered wrong. He wished there was a way he could get Miss Arvella to stand up to her father.

Pud didn't understand the constant remarks made by Longfellow and Havelshell about Arvella's size. Pud's mother had been a large woman and so had his two sisters. Arvella had put on considerable weight since he had first seen her, but her face was still pretty. He remembered one of his sisters had almost doubled her weight after her husband was killed. In her grief, she had eaten everything she could get her hands on. Time passed, she'd met another man, busied herself making a home and had slimmed down quite a bit.

Pud left the house in search of Linus and found him sitting in the semidarkened barn with his raccoon on his lap. The little animal scampered away and Linus got to his feet.

"Miss Arvella's gone to bed. She said for us to eat."

"Why's the preacher so mean to her? I allus thought preachers was nice to ever'body, till I met him."

"'Cause ya call yoreself a preacher don't make ya better'n anybody else. Look at Chivington, the Methodist preacher who killed all them old Indians, women and kids at Sand Creek. The old bastard ort to a been strung up and left there to dry out."

"I ain't knowin' 'bout that. What I do know is that I ain't sure which I want dead the most, Alvin or that old fart."

They reached the house and, moving quietly so as not to disturb Arvella, filled plates from the food on the stove.

"How come yo're not watchin' the schoolhouse?" Pud asked.

"I ain't tellin' Alvin nothin' no more."

"Why not?"

"I ain't sure what he's doin' now is right. The teacher ain't so bad even if she is a snooty bitch."

"The Murphy girl is a purty little piece even in her pa's overalls."

"She's all right. She brought me somethin' to eat a time or two. Wasn't right for Hartog to shoot down her pa."

"He's a gunman. Alvin hired him to get rid of the nesters."

"Alvin tried to get in Moonrock's drawers, then said I did it. I never did anythin' like that with Moonrock. Moonrock told the tribe elders it was Alvin."

"Longfellow told me before he left that he's bringin' another girl to keep Arvella company. He said that I'm to watch and see that you don't rape her."

"Hell! That randy old goat or Alvin is the one who'd do it," Linus exclaimed angrily. "I ain't never done nothin' like that. I only been with two whores. Alvin gave me the money the first time. I think he watched through a peephole. They got 'em there in the whorehouse and charge two bits to look through 'em. I looked a time or two."

"Ya best not spread around what ya saw through that peephole."

"I ain't. I got sense enough to know that."

Pud had changed his mind about Linus. At first he'd detested him for a sneak with no more loyalty than a rat. Now he felt sorry for the boy who hadn't had a soul to care about him since he was a tad. The kid had a spark of good in him. Guess he hadn't turned out too bad . . . considering.

With the family gathered around Trell's bed, he announced that he and Jenny would be married as soon as he was on his feet and able to make the trip to Forest City.

Early that morning Jenny had whispered the news to her sisters, and they were delighted. Travor and then Ike shook Trell's hand; Granny and Colleen kissed Jenny on the cheeks.

"My turn." Travor grabbed Jenny and kissed her soundly on the mouth. "Welcome to the McCall family, Sis."

"Thank you." Jenny's cheeks were slightly flushed and her sparkling eyes seemed all the brighter, clearer. Looking on, Trell's smile was beautiful and his eyes flashed continually to the woman standing beside the bed.

"That's the one and only time you'll be kissing my girl." Trell grabbed Jenny's hand and pulled her closer.

Beatrice was not sure what was going on. Cassandra was quiet.

"What do you think about it, Cass?" Trell asked.

"Well. I'm not surprised. You're aware that Virginia can't cook and you're willing to take her anyway. You must love her."

"I do. And I'm depending on Granny to teach her to cook." Trell's grin was lopsided. His dark eyes shone.

"Will we live here or move to your place?"

Jenny remained quiet and let Trell answer.

"We'll stay here so Jenny can carry on with the school. And I'll run some cattle on Stoney Creek land."

"Will Granny stay with us or move to the Double T with Travor and Colleen?"

"That's up to Gr—" His words were cut off by a loud snort from Colleen.

"If yo're wantin' to get rid of me and Granny, Cass, why don't ya just come right out and say so." She was angry, and angry words spewed from her mouth. She turned on

Cassandra with a red face, flashing eyes and her fists on her hips. "I might be a dumb cluck to yore notion, but I'll take care of me and Granny without any help from you or . . . anybody else."

"I didn't—mean—" Cassandra was taken aback by Colleen's anger and was unable to respond. "I thought you were going to marry—"

"Yo're wrong, Miss Know-it-all. I wouldn't marry that struttin' rooster if my life depended on it!" Colleen headed for the door. Before she reached it Travor was there and barred her way.

"Cass didn't mean anythin', honey. It's my fault. I told her I was goin' to marry ya."

"Well, ya can just tell her ya lied. Now get outta my way, ya slick-talkin' lyin' . . . mule's ass!"

When Travor dropped his arm, she darted past him. He paused, looked at the others, then followed her out into the yard.

Cassandra burst into tears and ran to Granny.

Ike scurried out the door.

The only sound in the room was the sobbing of the child.

"Pay no never mind, darlin'. Colleen's got a lot on her mind. She ain't knowin' what's what. When she thinks on it, she'll be sorry." Granny folded Cassandra in her arms.

"I'm sorry, I'm sorry—"

Beatrice began to cry and pull on Jenny's skirt.

"What's the matter with Cass? Is . . . Charles comin' to get us?"

"No, honey—"

"Come here, little pretty." Trell reached for the child. She leaned over the bed and placed her head on his shoulder. He patted her back. "Nobody will take you away from us. When Jenny and I are married, you'll be my little girl. You don't have to worry about anyone taking you or Cass away."

Jenny's heart swelled with pride. She loved this man with the blue-black eyes. She loved the sound of his calm voice, the line of his jaw, the curve of his mouth and even the scar that would be forever slashed across his cheek. She left him to console Beatrice and went to Cassandra, who was crying as if her heart would break. The child's tear-wet face was pressed against the old lady's bosom.

Her little sister was hurting. She had come to love Colleen, and the sharp words had cut her to the quick.

Travor found Colleen under the big elm tree at the front of the house. She was leaning against the massive trunk, her face buried in the bend of her arm. She was perfectly still, but he knew that she was crying. He placed his hand on her shoulder.

"Honey, don't cry."

"Get away from me!" She turned to push him away. Her face was streaked with tears. "It's yore fault! Ya caused me to lash out at Cass. I hate yore guts, Travor McCall."

"No, you don't."

"Ya think I don't know my own mind? Nothin's been right since ya come here. Me'n Granny'll have to go . . . 'cause a you!"

"And why is that?" Travor demanded crisply. His dark brows drew together in a frown. "All I did was fall in love with ya, ya thickheaded Irish lass. Ya owe Cass an apology. Ya had no cause to hurt her feelin's."

"Don't ya think I know that, ya . . . dolt?"

"What made ya so damn mad all of a sudden? Are you jealous 'cause Trell loves Jenny?"

"No!" Her foot lashed out and connected with his shin. She swung at him with a balled fist.

Travor winced and grabbed her arms to hold her away from him.

"Stop that! Behave yoreself. What the hell's the matter with you? After last night I thought we had an understandin'."

"Well, we didn't. I hadn't ort to a let ya kiss me. I should've poked ya with my knife."

"You liked it," he snarled. "Deny it if ya can."

"I've had better."

"Careful, Colleen," he cautioned through teeth clenched tight with suppressed anger.

"Or ya'll hit me?"

"I'm tempted." Travor's fingers bit into her shoulders and he jerked her to him. As he towered over her, she felt his rage. "I offered ya what I've offered no other woman. I wanted to share my life with ya. But I'll be no whippin' boy for every time ya lose yore temper."

His words caused her to tremble. She tried to move away from him, but his hands on her shoulders gripped her tightly. She had never seen his eyes so dark, so savage. Her own eyes were stricken and blurred with tears.

"And, Colleen, I'll not stand for ya hurtin' little Cass. She thinks the world of ya and just wanted to see ya happy. Understand me?"

"I'm sorry . . . I hurt Cass." Tears rolled down Colleen's cheeks. "But she had no right to . . . tell ever'body I'd be livin' at the Double T when . . . when ya ain't even asked me."

"Ask ya what?" His frown deepened as he shook her gently. "Ask ya to marry me? Hell! Didn't I tell that ya a dozen times how much I love ya."

"Ya never asked me to marry ya . . . or live with ya at the Double T. First I heard 'bout livin' there was from Cass." Her words were strong, not at all a reflection of what she was feeling. She was ashamed of the tears on her cheeks.

A growl came from Travor's throat. His face was tilted down toward hers and she could see the frustration that narrowed his eyes.

"Do you think I'm the kind of man who would tell a woman he loves her and talk about makin' babies with her without intendin' to marry her?"

"Ya never said nothin' 'bout marryin' me," she said stubbornly.

"Did ya think we'd live in sin?"

"I . . . thought ya was spinnin' a . . . windy."

"Ya thought no such thing!"

"Ya *never* said the words!"

"I'll say 'em if it'll make ya happy!" he yelled.

"Don't strain yoreself, Travor McCall."

"Colleen Murphy, will you marry me?"

"Yo're just askin' cause of what I said to Cass."

"Dammit! Yes or no?" he yelled. "Damn you, it better be yes."

"Yes." The whispered word came haltingly. She drew a quivering breath and began to smile.

Looking down into her wide tear-washed eyes, he laughed joyously and lifted her off her feet and kissed her. Their lips caught and clung. Their kisses spoke of newly discovered love.

"Tell me, sweetheart—"

"I love ya."

"Say it again."

"I love ya, ya flop-eared mule!"

He laughed and hugged her tightly.

"I'm goin' to town but I'll be back tomorrow, then I've got to spend a few days at the Double T helping Joe. Do ya want to be married here at Stoney Creek with yore granny lookin' on? Or do ya want to go to Forest City?"

"Here. And . . . I'll have to have time to make a new dress—"

"We'll talk to Trell and Jenny. We might be able to get the preacher to come here. Kiss me again, honey. Before I go we've got to talk to Cass."

They exchanged tender, sweet kisses, then walked, arms around each other, back to the bunkhouse so that Colleen could make peace with Cassandra.

Chapter Twenty-three

"I wish you'd wait until I could sit a horse, Trav. It shouldn't be more than a couple weeks."

"We'll both be married in a couple weeks. I need to know if that killer is still around or if he's gone back north. I can't see startin' married life lookin' over my shoulder."

"Colleen's got a stake in this, too."

"It's somethin' I've got to do. She understands that."

"Might be he's given up finding me . . . you, and left the country."

"He won't leave without proof that I'm dead. Killin' is his business. He's been at it for years, hirin' out for pay, traveling wherever a man would meet his price. He's got a reputation to hold up. I'm bettin' he's still around."

"There were two of them, Trav. I don't like you going up against them by yourself."

"If he thinks he killed me when he shot you, think of his shock when he sees me. I'll have an edge. It isn't Crocker's style to face a man, and he isn't known for his speed."

"If you find him, will you call him out?"

"I don't know yet. I'll have to play it by ear."

"It's going to be hard lying here waiting for you to come back."

"I know. It would be same for me."

"I still wish you wouldn't go."

"Stop worryin'. Ya got a whole family to think about now. I'll send a card to Mara Shannon and Pack tellin' them the news."

"You hadn't better send it from Sweetwater. The postmaster there gave Jenny's mail to Havelshell."

"He's more'n likely in the pocket of that slick-talkin' preacher that was here than Havelshell. There's a smell about that Longfellow. He reminds me of a snake-oil salesman. I've heard about him from someplace, but can't put my finger on it. When Marshal Stark gets here, he'll find out."

"Take Ike with you. He'd be an extra pair of eyes."

"I'd rather he stay here until you get on your feet. Besides, I'm used to workin' alone and not havin' to look out for anyone but myself." Travor got up and moved his chair back.

"There's a few good folks in Sweetwater, Trav. Oscar at the saloon is an all-right fellow."

"I met him. He's rougher than a cob. I've got to get goin'. I want to ride into Sweetwater around suppertime."

When Travor left the bunkhouse, Colleen was waiting beside his saddled horse. His steps quickened. He had eyes only for her.

Sunlight glinted in her blue-black hair. Her eyes held the beginning of a smile, a soft glow that gave the irises the clear color of a sun-filled sky. He knew her face, he could see it with his eyes closed, yet as he approached she seemed even more beautiful than the image he kept in his mind. Then she smiled at him, an open smile of such startling warmth that an answering flame ignited within him.

"Don't move, sweetheart. I just want to look at you."

The tip of his finger moved across her lips. He closed his eyes for a fleeting moment as his palms molded themselves to the contours of her face. His thumbs stroked her eyebrows, her eyelids, then moved down to outline the shape of her mouth. His hand curled around her throat gently lifting her chin.

He kissed her tenderly, sweetly.

"Please come back," she whispered.

"A railroad engine couldn't keep me away from you now."

He held her tightly, not caring if the whole world was watching. She turned her head so that their lips met. His mouth closed over hers with supplicant pressure until her lips parted, yielded, accepted the wanderings of his, then became urgent in their own seeking. Her mouth was warm, sweet beyond imagination.

He lifted his head and looked down at her, his lips just inches from her lips, her breath in his mouth. Each sensed a mystery and loneliness and aching beauty that was precious beyond their comprehension. Their lips met again and again, clung and then parted reluctantly.

"'Bye, sweetheart."

"Be careful."

"You too."

"I love you."

"I love you, too."

He mounted his horse. It pleased him that she didn't beg him not to go; she knew what he had to do. He looked back once. She was still standing beside the corral. He waved. She lifted her hand. The picture of her stayed with him as he rode away.

"Jenny come quick. Whit has brought your students."

In midafternoon Cassandra came to the bunkhouse with the news that two Shoshoni women and ten children were in the woods north of the school where the warriors had set up the lodge poles.

With Cassandra beside her, Jenny hurried up the path to the school then beyond to the woods to watch the women unload the travoises that had been pulled by the ponies. They began immediately to lace the skins on the pole structure that had been standing bare for several days. Two of the girls were big enough to help. The others moved out of the way and sat down on the ground.

Jenny almost despaired when she looked at them. Several of them could not have been more than four years old. There were only two boys in the group. One of them had a lame leg. The two girls helping the squaws were Cassandra's size. It was difficult to estimate their age.

Whit, squatting beside the school building, got up when Jenny and Cassandra approached.

"Why are you just sitting here?" Cassandra demanded. "A *man* would help the women with the hard work."

Whit glared at her and crossed his arms over his chest.

"A *warrior* does not do women's work."

"You're not a warrior, Whit Whitaker. You're just a kid."

"Squawk! Squawk!"

"You make me so mad." Cassandra put her fist on her hips and glared up at the stony-faced Indian boy.

"Whit, should I try to talk to the women?" Jenny asked.

"No. They not understand you. Wait until they finish work."

"I fear some of the children are too young for school."

"Why too young? Young learn fast. No learning to undo."

"Maybe you're right. Tell them school starts tomorrow."

"Why tomorrow. Why not now?"

"Well. All right. Tell them to come in."

Oh, dear. I don't know if I'm ready for this. Jenny opened the door to the schoolhouse and stood waiting while Whit talked to the children. When she applied for the job she'd had visions of standing at the door of the school greeting brown-faced, eager-to-learn children. What she was confronting now were eight little Indians staring at her with impassive expressions.

It was difficult to tell which were the girls and which were the boys. All had long, greasy black hair. Two of the little girls wore leggings and loose cotton shirts. Others wore colorless sack dresses. The boys wore an assortment of doeskin and calico. They were all dirty. Jenny wondered if they ever bathed or washed their clothes. Their mothers could have at least cleaned them up for the first day of school.

They stood obediently when Whit spoke to them and followed him into the school. The older girls, helping the women, ignored Whit's call and continued working.

"Hello. I'm your teacher, Miss Gray." Jenny spoke in her most cheerful manner. They looked at her curiously. No one uttered a sound. "I am probably strange to you as you are to me. But we'll get to know each other. I'd like for you to meet my sister. Her name is Cassandra. Ca . . . sand

. . . ra." Jenny pushed Cassandra forward. "She will help some of the younger children."

Whit snorted. "She no teacher. She just kid." It was an echo of what she had said to him earlier.

"We won't argue. The children will be confused."

"They don't understand a word you say."

"I knew they didn't speak fluent English, but I thought they'd get some of it."

"No."

"Will you tell them my name and that I'm glad they're here?"

The children's eyes fastened on Whit when he spoke in rapid Shoshoni. Jenny caught the words, "Miss Gray." He talked more, then pointed at Cassandra and said, "Squawk, squawk." The expressions on the faces of the children changed; some of them smiled. It was encouraging to know they had a sense of humor, even if it was at Cassandra's expense.

"What are their names, Whit?"

"Wasveke." He placed his hand on the head of a small boy then went down the line. "Scocequa, Mokespe—"

"Whit! I'll never remember the names."

Whit shrugged.

"Oh, hello," Jenny said to the two older girls who slipped into the room and squatted on the floor.

"Posiqua know some English." Whit pointed at the older girl.

"I'm so glad. May I call you Posy?" After a long pause, the girl nodded. She was quite pretty and reminded Jenny of the girl Moonrock. The girls were looking at Cassandra. Jenny pushed her forward. "My sister, Ca . . . sand . . . ra."

"Oh, just call me Cass."

"Squawk," Whit said. A titter came from one of the small ones.

Jenny looked quickly at her sister. She was glaring at Whit. Suddenly Cassandra picked up a long white feather and poked it into her hair. Then put her thumbs in the corners of her mouth, her forefingers at the corners of her eyes. Stretching open her mouth and pulling down her eyes, she wiggled her tongue at Whit. The children burst out laughing and pointed at Whit. Whit smiled one of his rare, beautiful smiles.

Jenny's heart lifted. It was going to be all right.

As suppertime approached and she dismissed the class for the day, she wasn't so sure of her prediction. She had given each of the students a small slate and a piece of chalk. With Whit translating, she tried to explain how they were to be used: how to make a mark and how to rub it out. One child bit off a piece of chalk and chewed it. Another used up half a stick rubbing it on the floor. When she tried to take what was left of the stick, the child hung on to it and snarled at her.

"He fight for what he has. He won't give it up."

"What on earth do you mean?"

"All of them throwaways. Not belong to anyone and eat at the fire of anyone who let them. They hold what they have or they be hungry."

"All of the children are orphans?"

"The shaman sent those to you who not needed to care for parents or younger children."

"That was good of him," she said sarcastically. "He may have done these children the favor of their lives. I will teach them English first . . . with your help and . . . Cassandra's. Whit, how can I tell them to take a bath and wash their clothes?"

Whit shook his head. "Teacher must crawl before she walk, walk before she run. They not understand."

"You are clean—"

"My mother teach me. They have no one to care if they are clean."

"They have me now. I will teach them . . . later."

"Sneaking Weasel no longer comes to school to watch."

"What does it mean?"

"Because of Moonrock. Weasel liked her. He mad at Havelshell 'cause she not at the store."

"You can come over to your father's house if no one is watching."

"I will come."

"Come tonight for supper."

"Tonight I eat at the fire with little ones. This a strange place. I will tell them it is good place, and it is good they chosen to learn."

"Whit, I'm so proud of you. Your father would be proud of you if he were here. You're more of a man than many I have met. You'll let me know if they have enough food?"

"It is so."

"I'm going to marry Trell. We'll live here on Stoney Creek and hold on to this homestead . . . for you. When the time comes that you can take over, we'll move out and build a home someplace else."

"The land is yours if you stay and teach. It was my father's wish."

"There is enough land for both of us. Trell and I may be able to buy more."

"We will not talk of it now."

Later, Jenny sat beside Trell's bed and repeated the conversation.

"I wish you could have seen him, Trell. He was so good with the children. I think he really cares about them. After I hear from the Bureau and get permission for him to leave the reservation, I want him to spend time with us so he can get accustomed to the white man's way. It will make things easier for him when he goes to college."

"In a week or two we can ask Ike to pick up our mail in Forest City. They would give it to him if he had a letter from us. I'm anxious to know if my brother, Pack, got in touch with the Federal marshal."

"You're worried about Travor, aren't you?"

"Yes. I wanted him to wait. He's bullheaded. He wants Crocker out of the way when he marries Colleen."

"She's worried about him, too. She's been cutting meadow grass with the scythe all afternoon."

"She's good for Travor and he's crazy about her."

"I'm crazy about you."

"You talking about me?" Trell's eyes lovingly searched her face.

"Yes, sir. You are Trellis McCall, aren't you?"

"I've never been so glad to be Trellis McCall. Damn this bed! I can't wait to be on my feet and hold you in my arms."

Jenny laughed happily. "You don't have to be on your feet to kiss me, you silly man. Let me demonstrate."

The moment Jenny's lips touched his, her demonstration of love was overtaken by the power of his. All the strength he had been slowly regaining seemed concentrated in the muscles of his good arm as he drew her tightly against him. All the longing that had been building up in him was released in the passion of his eager mouth claiming hers.

When they paused to draw breath, Jenny was trembling. Beneath the gentleness she had so cherished in Trell lay an intensity that startled and delighted her.

She left the bunkhouse, her heart beating loudly and her imagination stimulated by the prospect of what new things she was yet to learn about her "shy" lover.

The fire was small and built with dry sticks. It gave off almost no smoke; and with the direction of the wind, whatever smoke there was would be drawn down the canyon of the Sweetwater River.

Sitting with his back to a boulder, Hartog sipped his coffee and gazed off down the river valley. He had come out of the fight with McCall worse off than he let on. When he hit the floor he had injured his lower back. He had ridden to Forest City in a fog of pain. Now, the wound from the gunshot was almost healed, but because of the chronic pain in his lower back and his suddenly loose bowels, he was as grumpy as a cow with her tail tied in a knot.

Hartog heard a whistle and lifted his head. He returned the signal and waited for the Mexican to ride into camp. Jesus Mendosa was a follower, a hanger-on, who was happy to take orders and bask in the attention a man like Hartog generated. He was small and wiry in dirty buckskin-fringed britches.

Mendosa slid from his horse and headed for the coffeepot.

"Take care of yore horse. Ya want him shittin' where we eat?"

The Mexican turned on his heel and led his horse behind

a screen of scrub and brush. When he returned he filled a tin cup with coffee. He sat back on his heels and waited for Hartog to speak.

"Well, are ya goin' to sit there like a dumb-ass, or are ya tellin' me what ya found out at Stoney Creek."

"*Si, Señor.* McCall headed for Sweetwater this afternoon."

"Yeah? We got plenty a time to get him."

"Only womenfolk and old Ike at Stoney Creek."

"That nosey kid from the agency still hangin' around?"

"Not at Stoney Creek, *Señor.*"

"Not at Stoney Creek, *Señor,*" Hartog mocked. "Where is he hangin' 'round?"

"At Agency store."

"I told ya to watch Stoney Creek and not be seen," Hartog said angrily. "What in hell were ya doin' at the Agency store?"

"Gettin' tobacco." Mendosa lowered his head. More than anything, he feared Hartog's anger. "Linus was there . . . and the fat woman. Pud was there, too."

"I don't give a shit who was at the store. What'd ya see at Stoney Creek, dumb-ass?"

"Saw black-haired girl cuttin' grass. Saw the teacher at the school. Shoshoni set up lodge in woods for brats goin' to teacher's school. Old Ike dressin' out a deer—"

"Can ya get in close without bein' seen?"

"Not close, *Señor.*"

"It makes no never mind. Ya'll ride in there tomorrow and give 'er a sad tale 'bout yore woman havin' a brat and needin' a woman's help. She'll follow ya to the edge of the woods and we'll get 'er. If she don't come, we'll ride in there shootin' and get her anyway. One way or the other she'll pay for shootin' me in the back."

"*Si, Señor.*" The Mexican's grin was wolfish.

Hartog watched the man with narrowed eyes. He knew what he was thinking. Stupid fool was thinkin' 'bout his promise to let him plow the gal. When a man's pecker got hard, his brain got soft. The Mexican was dumb enough to think that he'd live after he saw what Hartog was goin' to do to the Murphy bitch.

Hartog shook his head wearily and closed his eyes. He'd not rest until he had his revenge on the girl and on McCall.

Chapter Twenty-four

Mud Pie was a good horse and took to the rough country as if he were born to it. Travor had followed the trail across the meadow, then turned off it and headed toward Sweetwater through the scrub oak, avoiding the regularly traveled road to town.

From time to time he drew up to study the country. He would stop his horse among the brush and look back across at the fine sweep of land that comprised Stoney Creek Ranch. It was not only beautiful country, but good grazing land where several thousand head of extra cattle would go unnoticed. No wonder Havelshell wanted it.

In the brief half-light between day and night Travor rode into Sweetwater. He had chosen the time when most folks had had their supper, and the eateries would be nearly empty.

He was being cautious. He had a lot more to live for than when he was here last.

Walking his horse slowly up the street, he took special notice of the horses tied to the rails in front of the saloons.

He looked the town over carefully. There wasn't enough of it to take more than a minute or two.

He stopped at the eatery across from the blacksmith. An unshaved man in shirtsleeves was washing dishes back of the counter. The two long tables, flanked by backless benches, were empty.

"Am I too late for grub?"

"Howdy, McCall. Ain't seen ya in a while. Have a seat. I've always got somethin' in the pot. Can ya go for venison stew?" He winked. "Leastways that's what I call it. Some folks get mighty touchy when they lose a cow or two, and I aim to keep my hide and bones together."

"I never heard of anybody recognizin' their cow from stew meat."

"Yo're right 'bout that." He chuckled as he dished up a bowl of the bubbly stew and brought it to the table. "Yo're in kinda late. Spendin' the night?"

"Thinkin' of it."

"Need to get yore rocks knocked off? Huh?"

"Thinkin' on it," Travor said again and forced a grin. "This really is fine stew. Ya musta cooked in a cow camp. I remember eatin' beef ever' day for three months. Would've give a month's pay for a hunk of somethin' else."

"Yeah, I done it. Went with the big herds to Dodge and Ogallala," he said proudly. "What runs did ya make?"

"Wrangled horses one time. Another time I was with a bunch that brought longhorns up from Texas. That was enough for me. Them cockeyed steers is crazy as a bunch a drunk hoot owls. They don't get too old or too weak to try to kill ya."

The cook felt that because Travor had ridden the cow

trails he was an old friend. Travor turned sideways on the bench, watched the street and listened to the man talk.

"This is a dead, flea-bitten town." Travor had to wait for the man to take a breath to make the remark. "Someday it'll dry up and blow away."

"We have a little excitement once in a while."

"Somebody drop dead in the middle of the street at high noon?" Travor asked with a blank face.

"Nothin' that excitin'. Couple a fellers come in sayin' they saw a body floatin' downriver. Wondered if anybody'd found it."

"Yeah. Anybody round here missin'?"

"Not that I'm knowin' about."

"Heard a feller over at Forest City hadn't been seen for a spell. Could've been him. The fellers still around?"

"Come to think on it, I saw 'em this mornin'. They et here a few times. They were in the saloon the other night. Don't say much. Sit around listenin' to talk." The cook threw the dishwater out the door. "I ain't worryin' 'bout this town none. It'll be a big cattle town what with the big herd comin' in. Longfellow's bringin' in pert nigh three thousand head when the army brin's in the herd for the reservation. He's hirin' men to cut out his. He's somethin', that preacher is. Straight as a string. He don't put up with any cussin' and carousin'. He can stir a crowd with his preachin'—" The man's voice droned on.

Yeah, Longfellow is somethin', all right. He's a damn crook! Three thousand head, my hind leg. Five thousand are comin' for the reservation. The old sonofabitch is goin' to take more than half.

"Better get movin'." Travor got to his feet and placed a coin on the counter.

"If yo're goin' to the Pleasure Place, McCall, try Flossie." He winked again. "It'll cost ya a dollar and four bits, but ya'll get yore money's worth."

"Thanks." Travor forced another grin and left the eatery.

It was dark. There were few people and only a team and wagon and four or five horses on the streets. Lamps were lighted in the stores. Travor led his horse to the watering tank, then walked him behind the buildings to the livery. When he pounded on the door, an old man came out of the shed attached to the barn.

"Howdy, McCall. Yo're in kinda late."

"Not so late. My belly button was dancing up and down my backbone. Stopped to eat a bite." Travor unsaddled his horse. "Where you want him?"

"Take him on down to that end stall. I ain't wantin' him to be kickin' the guts out of a horse he don't take a likin' to."

"Anybody ride outta here today. Heard some shots comin' in. Sounded like a forty-five."

"Some rowdies been hangin' 'round. Ain't here now. Nobody what left their horses here rode south today."

Travor stood in the dark after he left the livery and checked the gun in his holster. The only information he got from the liveryman was that Crocker and his man hadn't ridden south. They could be here or gone north to report to Ashley.

He thought of checking at the hotel. Crocker would stay at the best place in town. Then he remembered Trell telling him it was rumored that the woman who ran the hotel was Havelshell's. He didn't think Crocker had had time to tie up with the agent. If he had, Havelshell, mistaking him for

Trell, might decide to have him ambushed and blame it on Crocker.

Travor headed for the Pleasure Palace. A man waiting around would get bored and might pass the time with the *ladies*. A bell jingled when he opened the door, stepped into the parlor and removed his hat.

A woman came out of a back room. She was stout, not fat, with broad shoulders. Her enormous breasts were pushed up by a stiff corset and bulged above her heavy satin dress. A green feather was stuck in her high-piled henna-colored hair. She was almost as tall as Travor and old enough to be his mother.

"Hi, honey. I've seen you around town. You've not been here before. You're name is—" She snapped her fingers as if it would help her remember, and gave him a gap-toothed smile.

"—McCall."

"Oh, sure. You got a horse ranch south of here."

"Yo're right as rain, sweetie." Travor gave her his best smile. "Flossie busy?"

"She is right now, honey. Would one of the other girls do?"

"How about you, sugar?" He winked, letting her know that he knew she was not available.

"Come on, now." She reached out and pinched his cheek so hard he was almost sure she had broken a blood vessel. "I'd a showed you a high old time in my younger days, you handsome devil."

"I'm not doubtin' that." He stroked the top of her breast with a forefinger and smiled into her eyes even though his cheek was numb. "I was to meet a friend here. I think I'll look him up and we'll be back."

"A feller was in here last night. When he left, he asked if ya ever come in."

"Quiet feller? Thin hair?"

"Older'n you? Flossie said he didn't waste words. He was all business."

"That's him. He told me about Flossie. I'm early and was trying to beat his time with her. I'll find him and we'll be back." Travor pinched her gently on the cheek, then touched the end of her nose with his forefinger.

Outside, he stepped off the porch and moved into the shadows. He was reasonably sure now that Crocker was here waiting to see whether Trell's body had washed up on the riverbank, or if someone would find him caught in a snag. *Sonofabitchin' cold-blooded bastard!*

Travor walked up onto the porch fronting the first of the two saloons in town. He stood in the doorway and scanned the dimly lit room. A few men stood at the bar. Crocker was not at the one table of card players in the center of the room. Travor decided not to waste any more time there and backed out the door.

The saloon where he had fought Hartog was larger and well lighted. Travor stepped up to the double swinging doors and peered over the top. There were no men at the bar and, as far as he could see, four tables were occupied, two of them with card players. He was unable to see the faces of any of them.

As soon as he shoved open the door and stepped inside, the bellowing voice of the bartender greeted him.

"Howdy, McCall."

In the quiet that followed, a hoarse voice said, "It's him!"

A chair scraped on the floor drawing Travor's eyes to the

corner of the room. There, staring as if transfixed, was Crocker. Beside him was a younger man with blond facial hair. Travor's eyes homed in on Crocker.

"Hello, Crocker. I hear ya've been lookin' for me."

Crocker's mouth opened then closed, his eyes remained on Travor. He was slow in responding, but his companion sprang to his feet.

"Draw, ya sonofabitch!"

The boy was fast, but not as fast as Travor. He put a bullet in the boy's heart as he was bringing his gun up. A surprised look came over the young face before he backed up and sat down hard on the floor. Travor had dropped into a crouch when he drew his gun. When Crocker fired, the bullet went over the top of his shoulder and into the backbar behind the counter.

Travor fired one shot at Crocker. The hired killer backtracked to the wall and hung there. Then his legs refused to hold him and he crumpled to the floor, his hand still holding the gun, but without the strength to lift it.

The three shots fired had come in rapid succession. Most of the men in the room had not had time to do more than fall out of their chairs to the floor, not knowing what would come next. One of the men kicked the gun out of Crocker's hand. Travor holstered his and went to where Crocker lay against the wall. The bartender, with his buffalo gun in his hand, was beside him.

Crocker was still alive.

"Here's one scalp ya'll not collect on, you back-shootin' bastard!"

"Thought we'd . . . got ya, McCall, when . . . ya went in the river." A froth of blood came from his mouth. "Was . . .

waitin' 'round to find your ... stinkin' hide ... to take back to Ashley."

"Yeah, I figured he sent ya. Ya shot my brother, Trell, you son of a bitch, and knocked *him* in the river! He came out of it alive, or I'd take ya out now and string ya up for the buzzards to pick your bones clean."

"Brother? Hell—I'd a swore it was you. I'd a got him, but let the kid—" His eyes began to glaze over. "He'd a not made a ... hunter ... nohow—"

"Ya got the kid killed, Crocker. You'll meet him in hell."

"He's dead, McCall. Yo're talkin' to a dead man." The bartender spoke from beside him.

Travor stood and looked at the men crowding around the dead men. There was no sympathy on their faces.

A commotion at the door drew Travor's attention. Two men had entered. One was the man who had warned him about Hartog the last time he was here. The other was dressed in a dark suit, white shirt and a black string tie.

"What happened here, Oscar?" The man who spoke had a tin star pinned to his chest.

"What'a ya think?" Oscar went back to place his gun on the bar. "I got me a mess to clean up."

"Who shot first." The sheriff knelt and looked into the faces of the men on the floor.

"One drew first and didn't get off a shot. The other'n missed. McCall nailed both of them."

"This one is a hired killer named Crocker." Travor nudged Crocker with the toe of his boot. "The other was in trainin' to be a hired killer."

"Arrest him." The man in the suit spoke for the first time. All eyes turned to him. The sheriff frowned.

"Why, Mr. Havelshell? 'Pears to me it was a fair fight."

"Arrest him. A judge will decide."

"Now see here, Alvin." The booming voice of the bartender filled the room. "Ever' man jack in this room saw what happened. The kid drew first—"

"Ain't so, Mr. Havelshell." Travor noticed Frank Wilson for the first time. "He drew and shot 'em down."

"Godamighty, Frank!" Oscar exclaimed. "Ya know that ain't what happened."

"I was closer than you, Oscar."

Frank's mouth was still swollen from the brutal meeting with Travor's fist. He leaned against the bar and glowered at him.

"We have a witness." Havelshell spoke in a tone of authority. "Arrest him, Armstrong, and hold him for trial."

The sheriff frowned at Havelshell, then turned to the more than a dozen men who stood beside the tables.

"How many of you saw McCall draw first and shoot these men down?" No one moved. "Show of hands if you saw what Frank said he saw," he urged, then waited, looking into the face of each man. Still no one moved.

"All right. Who saw what Oscar saw?"

All hands went up.

"Oscar saw it right, Sheriff." The merchant, a gunsmith, spoke up.

"You got a stake in this?" Alvin asked curtly.

"No. But what's right is right. The boy drew on McCall. The other man drew, shot and missed. McCall's got a right to defend himself."

"We've got a witness that says otherwise. Do your duty, Sheriff. Arrest him and hold him for the circuit judge."

"I'm not goin' to arrest a man for defendin' himself."

"Goddamn you!" Alvin's face turned ugly. "I gave you that star and I can take it away."

"No, you can't, Alvin." The gunsmith spoke again. "Armstrong has done a good job keeping drunks off the street and controlling fights. We've formed a town council. It will take two-thirds of a vote from the council to fire him."

"Town council? Why wasn't I told of it?"

"We sent word to your office three times. You chose to ignore it. We proceeded without you. Armstrong stays on. We plan to elect a sheriff and a mayor in the fall. I hope he runs for the job."

"You been going behind my back." Alvin turned on Armstrong. "I should have listened to Hartog. You got no guts!"

"I've no taste for arrestin' a man for defendin' hisself, if that's what ya mean." Armstrong unpinned the star from his vest and shoved it into Havelshell's hand. "Here's yore star. If the council wants me to stay on, I'll take one from them."

"I'll call a meeting in the morning," the gunsmith said. "Meanwhile, I'd be obliged if you'd finish out the night."

"Be glad to." Armstrong looked steadily at Havelshell. "I ain't nobody's bought man. I thought I made that straight when I took the badge and told ya that Hartog wasn't fit to shoot."

"You two-bit, gutless piece of horseshit. Hartog's got ten times the guts you got. You took my money quick enough."

"I thought the money came from the city, or I'd not a touched one dirty dime of your money," Armstrong said quietly.

Smoldering in rage, Alvin stomped out the door.

Frank, feeling the sudden hostility of the other men in the saloon, followed.

"Thanks for speakin' up." Travor stuck his hand out to the merchant. "Travor McCall. You may know my brother, Trell."

"It needed to be done," he said after shaking Travor's hand. "I'm puzzled some. Aren't *you* Trell McCall?"

"I'm Travor McCall, Trell's brother. Only our maw could tell us apart. At times it's more trouble trying to explain that there are two of us than to let it go. Crocker was sent to kill me. He ambushed my brother instead."

"Well, horse-hockey!" Oscar exclaimed. "Was it you who come in here last week and twisted Hartog's tail?"

"It was me." Travor grinned.

"If that don't beat all! Trell's been in here off and on for several years. Yo're as alike as two peas in a pod."

"Yeah. Trell and I got used to that a long time ago."

"About Hartog. He's a bad'n."

"The sheriff, here, told me that last week." Travor turned to Armstrong and stuck out his hand. "Thanks."

"No thanks necessary. I was just doin' what I thought a sheriff ort to do."

"Gettin' us a town council and a law-and-order sheriff calls for a drink on the house. That is—"

"Gawdamighty, Oscar! You sick or somethin'?"

"—That is, if I get help washin' the glasses."

"He ain't sick. Haw! Haw! Haw!"

Chapter Twenty-five

"Mr. Havelshell," Frank called, as Alvin stepped off the porch and into the street. "Mr. Havelshell—"

Alvin turned on him like a snarling dog.

"Get the hell away from me, you stupid son of a bitch."

"I was tryin' to help, Mr. Havelshell—"

"Help? You dumb ass! You're like the others . . . trying to drag me down to your level. I won't be dragged down. Understand? I've got a law degree from the best law school west of the Mississippi. I was appointed Indian agent because I'm the most qualified man for the job. I'm not an ignorant clod like the rest of you." Alvin's voice rose to a screech. "Get away from me! Get away! Get away!"

Frank stopped in shock and backed away. Alvin hurried down the dark street toward his house, the blood pounding in his head so intensely he could hardly walk without stumbling. The humiliation he had endured at the saloon ate into him like a canker sore. He'd never be able to hold his head up in this town again. They'd had a council meeting without him. He'd received the messages but figured they'd not hold a meeting without him. *He* was the most important man in this town.

Alvin shoved his shaking hands into his pockets, then brought them out and hit the rough bark of a tree with his closed fist.

"Bastards! Bastards!" he croaked in a cracked off-key whisper, not even feeling the pain of the broken skin across his knuckles.

Alvin had been a total wreck, hardly able to concentrate on business at hand since he had realized that Longfellow was going to have him killed. Since that time he had not had an hour of uninterrupted sleep; fear haunted his dreams, food had stuck in his throat and when it did go down, it settled like a rock in his stomach. The only time he felt reasonably safe was when he was behind the locked doors of his house.

For four days Alvin had waited anxiously for Hartog to return. Aware that he was a marked man, he had kept himself in near seclusion, not even venturing out when he got the messages about the merchants forming a town council. Tonight he had gone to speak to the one man whom he had believed loyal. Then the shooting had occurred.

Alvin had planned to tell Armstrong about Longfellow's threat. Because if Hartog didn't come back, and the opportunity presented itself, he could kill the preacher himself and have an alibi of self-defense. Now that plan was shot to hell. Armstrong had gone over to the enemy. The whole damn town was against him after all he'd done for them. He hadn't had to come here. He would have been welcome in a hundred, no, a thousand towns in the West. He'd chosen the stinking town of Sweetwater, and they hadn't appreciated him; instead they'd been taken in and looked up to a two-bit phony preacher.

Alvin's mind whirled out of control and into a frenzy of self-pity.

Thinking it possible that Jenny had slept with McCall, he shook with rage and frustration. He stumbled, then stopped and leaned against an oak tree. Jenny was not for a *cowboy*; a piss-poor horse rancher who could hardly read and write. She deserved an educated man, like himself. He could give her the kind of life she deserved. As soon as she understood him and what they could accomplish together, she would be grateful that he had saved her from a life of drudgery at that blasted Indian school.

They would leave this one-horse town that didn't appreciate a man of his caliber and a woman of her breeding. He and Jenny would go to San Francisco, where he would set up a law practice and build her a fine home. They would be the toast of the town, he for his business sense and Jenny for her grace and beauty.

He began to smile, and then his high-pitched laughter rang in the stillness of the dark night. He headed home again with a jaunty spring to his step.

Havelshell reached home unaware that his thinking process had gone awry, that his mind was no longer functioning normally. The logical part of it had shut down. In an almost joyous mood, he pulled out a leather satchel and began to pack the things he wanted to take with him: money that he hadn't wanted the banker and Longfellow to know he had, his certificate from law school, a set of clean clothes.

He made a quick trip to his law office and brought back to the house the contents of his file cabinet and his safe, took out what papers he wanted and strewed the rest over the dining-room table. He didn't want Longfellow to get his hands on a single piece of his correspondence that might tie *him* to the theft of the reservation cattle.

In the stable at the back of the house, he saddled the thoroughbred mare he had planned to ride in a parade down through the center of town when he was officially made mayor of Sweetwater. He brought the horse to the front of the house and tied the leather satchel on behind the saddle.

Back in the house he went through it and methodically opened all the windows. When he was satisfied that he had created a sufficient draft, he splashed lamp oil onto the papers on the table, the floors and walls.

At the front door he looked back at the disarray that had once been his tidy home, and without a pang of regret, tossed a lighted match to the floor. He waited until the ribbon of fire had traveled to a large pool of oil and begun creeping up the dining-room table legs before he calmly walked off the porch, down the path and mounted his horse.

At the edge of town, he turned the horse to look back. All the downstairs windows of his house were alight with the fire growing within. He felt strong, relaxed, content, and almost unbearably pleased with himself. There was a special exhilaration in seeing the results of his actions.

He licked his lips and rode recklessly through the night toward Stoney Creek.

This was to be washday.

The dark clouds that rolled in from the southwest held a strong promise of rain. Colleen, her blue eyes dark-circled from worry about Travor and lack of sleep, went about preparing to wash regardless, saying the clothes could be dried later. Knowing that Colleen needed the work to help her through the day, Granny agreed.

Ike set up the iron washpot beneath the shelter of the shed overhang and built a fire under it. When finished, he announced that he was going to the river to catch a mess of fish for supper.

At daylight Jenny took breakfast to Trell. She found him sitting on the edge of the bed, his splint-encased leg stuck out in front of him. He was rubbing his knee.

"Morning," she said softly. "Are you hurting?"

"Morning, sweetheart. Set that coffeepot down before you burn yourself."

She placed the pot and the plate of food on the extra chair.

"Are you hurting?" she asked again.

"No more than usual. I could get up and hop around if it wasn't for these damn ribs."

"McGriff said he'd be back as soon as possible with the crutches. Maybe he'll come today." She pulled the chair with the plate of fried meat, biscuits and gravy closer to the bed. "Granny said this would give you strength."

"I've not got much of an appetite, honey."

"I know. You're worried about Travor. We all are. Colleen looks like she's been dragged through a knothole. You said that he was capable of taking care of himself. We've got to hold on to that until he comes back."

"Travor takes chances . . . sometimes."

"He'll be all right, Trell." She knelt beside him, leaned over and kissed him on his good cheek. "Do you need more salve on your cheek? Granny said that if it started feeling tight we should keep the skin soft with the salve."

"I'll put some on later. You're so pretty, honey. How can you stand to look at me?"

"I stand it very well because I love you. I didn't fall in love with just your face, Trellis McCall. I fell in love with all of you. You make me angry, Trell, when you think I would be put off by a little scar."

"It isn't little, sweetheart. But I'll say no more about it." He put his arms around her and placed his good cheek next to hers.

"I wish I could stay here with you."

"So do I. Kiss me. It'll have to do until you come back." They kissed, gently, sweetly.

She sighed and leaned against him. He pulled her hair aside and kissed her neck, made a chain of kisses along the smooth, sweet skin. Against his lips he felt one of her arteries throb, a strong pulse, a rapid pulse, faster now and faster still.

She seemed to melt back against him. Nothing had ever felt this soft, this warm, this achingly wonderful to him.

She murmured wordlessly, a feline sound.

He slid a palm up and over her breasts, cupping and squeezing.

She drew back only inches. Their eyes met; hers were a fiercely bright shade of green and his were dark with longing.

Another kiss. This one was harder and hungrier than the first.

She moved out of his arms and stood. Both knew there would be other times when they would come together, when there would be no obligation to put a curb on their passions.

"Go to your students. I'll be all right."

At the door, she glanced back at him, smiled and lifted her hand.

The picture books Jenny carried to the school were meant to stir the curiosity of the children and inspire them to want to know what the pictures were about. She also carried the alphabet cards. If she taught them a letter each day it would take more than a month for them to learn the alphabet. It seemed an overwhelming task.

She wished that she'd been able to talk to someone who had been through this before. Cassandra was a great help. Her further education and Whit's would have to be put off a while.

Jenny was thinking these thoughts as she opened the door, entered the school and walked across the plank floor to the table that served as a desk. She had set the books down and stooped to pick up a cylinder of chalk when she saw him. She made no sound, but her heart almost stopped, and her skin tingled with fear.

"I'm sorry if I frightened you, Virginia." Alvin Havelshell moved out of the corner and came toward her.

"You just surprised me," she said calmly, despite her splintered nerves. "What are you doing here? Why didn't you come to the house?"

"Because I didn't want anyone to see me. I'm leaving the country. I came here at considerable risk to myself to tell you that you and your sisters are in great danger."

"Danger? From whom?" Jenny was baffled by his statement.

"From a source you would never suspect. It's important that I talk to you . . . privately." His anxious eyes shifted about the room, then looked into hers.

"It's private here."

"Someone could come in."

"It would only be my sister or one of my students."

"No one must know that I'm here! It would mean . . . my life!" He paused, then said, "You went to the bunkhouse this morning . . . carrying the coffeepot."

"Ike is sick." Jenny was grateful the lie came so fast.

"We can go out back, Miss Gray. Just out of sight . . . in case—"

It was the respectful way he had said *Miss Gray* that chipped away at her suspicion and began to make her think that he was sincere. That . . . and the way he constantly kept watch out the window toward the homestead to see if anyone was coming.

"I would like to be on my way. I'd hoped to be away from the reservation by now."

"Why are you leaving? Who will be the agent?"

"I'm leaving because I'll be killed if I stay." He went to the small door in the back of the building, opened it and peered out, then retraced his steps to the window. "Your sister is coming!" He hurried back to the small door. "Please. Let me help you. It's the least I can do to make up for the inconvenience I've caused you."

Jenny went to the door and stepped out into a light drizzle. Alvin closed the door behind them and took her elbow to urge her into the wooded area behind the school building. She shrugged loose from his hand and would have stopped as soon as they were behind a screen of dense brush, but his pressure on her back urged her on.

"I've got some papers in my saddlebag you should have. My horse is just a little way from here."

"I don't understand any of this—"

"You will. We're almost there."

Jenny had no idea how far they were from the school. They had been walking rapidly for several minutes and had gone so deep into the woods that only small patches of sky were visible. She had begun to feel a twinge of doubt when she saw a saddled horse behind a screen of scrub and brush.

"Here we are."

Alvin opened a leather bag tied behind the saddle and took out a handful of papers. He looked at them intently, then shoved them back into the bag.

"What do you have to tell me? I must be getting back to the school."

"Before I give you the papers, I've got to explain a few things."

Jenny waited for him to say more. He took his hat off and hung it over the saddlehorn. It was a cool morning, yet there was a sheen of perspiration on his forehead. He wiped a hand over his face and took several deep breaths. He went on, then, trying to keep his voice calm, but only half-succeeding.

"Longfellow will send men to kill you if you don't give up the ranch and go back East. I came to warn you."

"The preach . . . er?" Jenny exclaimed. So Ike's suspicions were warranted!

"I'll take you away from here and keep you safe. We can send for your sisters . . . later."

She became aware of an evil glitter when she looked into the man's eyes. She had been wrong to come out here with him.

"I don't believe a word of this." She turned to leave.

"Wait! Here's proof!" He put his hand in the satchel

again. "Of the five thousand head of cattle coming in to feed the Indians, he will take three thousand. I wouldn't go along with it, and now he's planning to have me killed. That's why I'm leaving behind everything I've worked for. He's going to kill you and the girls so that you can't fulfill your contract. He'll buy up Stoney Creek land for a song. He's an evil, greedy man."

"But . . . aren't you married to his daughter?"

"He forced me to marry that fat cow!" His voice rose angrily. "She has nothing to do with us."

"There is no . . . *us*! Give me the papers and you can be on your way."

"I know why you came to the territory, Jenny. I can help you." Alvin felt terribly clever bringing that up. He had not heard from the Pinkerton Agency, but he could tell by the quick way she turned her head that his words had struck home. "I've not told anyone, and I won't. You can trust me. I'll help you through this."

"I don't know what you're talking about. I must go. The children will be at the school."

"They won't come until you go for them. The heathens have no sense of time." He pretended to scan the papers he held in his hand.

"That may be. I thank you for your concern, but I must get back. If you give me the papers, I'll get in touch with the proper authorities."

Jenny took a step toward him and held out her hand for the documents. Suddenly his hand shot out and gripped her wrist, pulling her up so close that she could feel his hot breath on her face.

"I'm . . . trying to . . . help you," he snarled. Then his voice softened into a whine. "I love you, Jenny. Can't you see that? Come away with me. We'll build a house in San Francisco. You'll be the belle of Nob Hill society. Together we'll make the snobs sit up and take notice. I've got plans—we'll be rich. Folks will look up to Mr. and Mrs. Alvin Havelshell. They'll compete for an invitation to our home." His eyes had taken on a fevered light.

He's crazy! Fear traveled down Jenny's spine like a writhing serpent.

"Let go of me, you stupid fool. I'll not go anywhere with you!"

He shoved the papers down in the bag and, quick as a wink, he twisted her arm behind her back, clamped a hand over her mouth and pulled her back against him.

"You'll go where I tell you to go and be damned glad of it." His lips were against her ear, his voice loud, his words came so fast that they ran together. She humped her back in an effort to move her hips away from his sex, which nestled against her buttocks. He let go of her wrist and wrapped an arm about her waist, holding her tightly to him.

One part of Jenny responded in anger, one part in panic and the rest of her in utter terror. The anger was chiefly at herself for not tucking the derringer in her pocket that morning when she dressed. *Keep calm. Don't give him a reason to hurt you.* She couldn't speak with his hand over her mouth, so she made little grunting noises in her throat.

"You lying bitch!" he snarled, as if he understood what she had said. "You're just trying to get away. You won't! You won't!"

Jenny shook her head and made more sounds in her throat.

"Yes, you would!" he said in answer to the sounds. "You

prissy-assed, arrogant old maid! Think you're better than me, don't you?"

He's crazy. Insane! Why hadn't she seen it? Jenny made more sounds and tried to butt him with her head.

"Be still!"

Suddenly his hand was gone from her mouth. When she opened it, to take a deep breath to scream, a cloth was shoved inside so deep she gagged. Rendering her helpless with choking and gagging, he was able to tie a silk scarf over her mouth so she couldn't spit out the gag.

He dragged her backwards toward the horse. She dug in her heels, but her strength was no match for his. He tried to throw her across the saddle. The horse shied. The eyes that looked down into hers were so bright they appeared to be tear-wet. His mouth was loose, his laugh was high-pitched, almost hysterical.

"I'm taking you with me, Jenny, Jenny, Jenny." He repeated her name in a childish taunting tone. "High-toned Miss Virginia Gray will be Mrs. Alvin Havelshell. You'll not stop me with your haughty stare this time, *Your Prissyness.*"

Jenny's heart was whamming, but it didn't seem to be pumping enough air into her lungs. Her eyes moved wildly about. There was no doubt in her mind what he intended to do. If she didn't go with him, he would kill her. *I love you, Trell. I wanted us to grow together—*

"You've ruined everything!" Holding her hands with one of his, he used the other to slap her hard across the face. "Bitch! Whore! Slut!" The next blow landed on her ear and her head rang as if a bell were inside.

He grabbed Jenny's dress at the neck and jerked. Buttons popped off. The bodice opened to expose her camisole. In his frenzy to bind her hands, he ripped at the delicate voile, and Jenny felt the cold air sweep across her naked breasts. Panic consumed her. She screamed inside, kicked and tried to buck him off as they fell to the ground. He laughed as if he enjoyed her struggles, and tied her wrists together.

"I should show you what you're going to get when we get away from here. You ought to be proud that you can get it this hard. Hell! I had to feel up that little Indian brat to get it hard enough to get on the fat cow. But we got no time for that now. He flopped her over and sat on her back facing her feet.

"You bitch! There was a stuck-up bitch like you back in Winona. She looked down her nose at me like you did that day at the school; like you were a queen and I was a dog. I took the starch out of her. I rammed her good. When her belly begin to swell, she jumped into the river." He snickered.

He continued to talk as he tried to bind her thrashing legs. His weight kept her pinned to the ground. Her skirt was up around her thighs.

"Be still, damn you!" He reared back to look at them, then lowered his head and sank his teeth into the skin above her knee. Severe pain caused her to rear up in spite of his weight and grunts came from her throat. "I'll not hurt you anymore if you'll be still. Once we're away from here, you'll be glad—"

Dear God, I can't bear this. What have I done that you'd let this insane man do this to me? Please help me.

Jenny looked up at the trees wavering, swaying and tipping dizzily. She tried to close her mind and think of something dear to her.

Dear, sweet, gentle Trell, so worried about the scar on his face—

She almost strangled on the gag jammed in her mouth and tears welled when she realized how helpless she was, bound hand and foot. Her eyes moved to her tormentor now kneeling beside her, and saw the maniacal smile on his face and the glitter of madness in his eyes. She feared that she would lose her sanity and prayed with a grim, terrible strength of will.

Please God. Help me. Don't let him do this!

Somewhere from the darkness that began to float down around her came a piercing cry. A crushing weight dropped on her chest. The image that danced before her eyes before she sank into a black pit was of a snarling face, long black hair, a red headband, and the glimmer of a knife.

Whit had noted the disappointed look on the teacher's face when she saw the children the shaman had sent for her to teach. They were ragged and dirty. This morning, knowing that the Indian women were required only to cook for them, and cared not how unkempt they were, he had taken them to the pond to wash. He carried with him a jug containing a liquid made from larkspur to rid them of lice.

The children protested long and loud when forced into the water. The two older girls, the one called Posy and the other, whose Shoshoni name meant Small Owl, helped Whit with the younger children. Both girls had eyes for Whit and wanted to please him. They wrapped the children in blankets, then combed and braided their hair. Back at the lodge they hung their wet clothes on sticks near the fire and waited for the teacher to come for them.

Whit stood beneath the thick sheltering branches of a spruce tree, wanting to go to the school, but also wanting to wait and go with the children and hear them greet their teacher. When the Indian known as Head-Gone-Bad loped into the camp, he went to meet him with a worried frown. The man was large and old and not very bright. He never ran. He was so out of breath when he reached Whit that he could hardly speak. The few words he managed to say caused Whit to fire a question at him. The Indian nodded his head vigorously and turned back into the woods.

Whit followed, snapping more questions.

Rain came down in earnest, but only a drizzle came through the thick canopy of tree branches. Running swiftly through the woods, Whit dodged trees and jumped dead-falls, putting distance between himself and his Indian friend. *Agent was hurting teacher!* How could it be that the teacher was in the woods with the agent?

He first saw the horse standing patiently, head lowered. Then he saw the couple on the ground. The teacher's hands and feet were bound, her stockings were down around her ankles, her white thighs exposed. The man was slapping her hard across the face.

With a warrior's scream of battle, Whit freed his knife from the sash at his waist and ran toward the pair. He sprang onto the agent's back and grabbed a handful of hair. Alvin collapsed on Jenny, his arms reaching for the boy on his back. With a cry of rage, he bucked, trying to throw the boy off. They rolled. Whit's back hit the ground, his legs wrapped around the agent's waist, one hand locked in his hair, the other gripping the knife.

The opportunity came when Alvin lowered his arms to unlock the boy's legs. The sharp, steel knife slashed a path across his throat so deep it grated against bone. A gush of blood followed and Alvin's lifeless body became dead-weight. Whit rolled out from under it and sprang to his feet. He looked down. The agent's head was almost severed from his body. Still feeling rage, Whit kicked him viciously in the side and then spit in his face.

He went to Jenny, pulled her skirt down over her legs and untied the scarf that held the gag in her mouth. She lay limp and unmoving. At first he feared that she was dead. He placed an ear over her heart and heard its steady beat. She had swooned. Knowing that white women were embarrassed by their nakedness, he covered her breasts with her torn bodice and quickly cut the bonds on her hands and feet.

Whit felt helpless. He couldn't leave her to go get the women. Head-Gone-Bad was concerned only for the horse; he stood beside it patting its face. Not knowing what else to do, Whit got behind the teacher, gripped her under the arms and dragged her out from under the tree branches. The cold rain pelted down soaking her hair, her dress, and mixed with the agent's blood running down Whit's arms and diluting the blood on his shirt.

Jenny came out of her swoon and was instantly alert. She looked up into the boy's anxious face.

"Whit? Am . . . I all right?" Her voice was ragged, her throat dry.

"Yes, teacher."

"He didn't . . . he didn't—"

"No."

"Thank God!" She looked fearfully around. "Did he go away?"

"He is dead. I killed him." The boy spoke as calmly as if telling her he had killed a rattlesnake.

Chapter Twenty-six

"You *killed* him! Oh, Whit!"

Jenny pushed herself to a sitting position and realized her bodice was open. She held it together as she gazed at the boy's expressionless face.

"How did you know I was here."

"Head-Gone-Bad come to tell me."

"What will we do?" She rose, with Whit's help, avoiding looking at the body on the ground. "You must go!" Her voice rose to a near-hysterical pitch when she realized what this would mean for Whit when it was learned that he had killed the agent. "Give me the knife. I will say that I did it."

"No! I no hide behind teacher."

"Please, Whit. They won't do anything to me when I tell them he was trying to kidnap me." She grasped the boy's hand. "You have become very dear to me. I can't let them . . . hang you for saving me."

"You owe nothing. I do same for Moonrock or Posy."

"I know."

Jenny began to cry. Tears mingled with rain on her face. Hair was plastered to her cheeks; her wet dress clung to her body. She was so miserable that she didn't even feel the cold.

Head-Gone-Bad came to talk to Whit. They spoke rapidly in their native tongue. After a minute or two, Whit nodded, and the Indian went to untie Alvin's horse.

"We know place where agent won't be found. It is far from here. We put saddle in hole with him. Head-Gone-Bad will take horse to our people in the north. I would go, but if I do that, Sweetwater people think they not find agent because of me."

Jenny took his hand and held it in both of hers.

"I don't know how to properly thank you. Havelshell wanted me to go away with him. He wouldn't have let me live after I refused him."

"It is done. We will not speak of it." His set face was beautiful. It showed his proud Indian heritage and maturity beyond his years.

"All right. I want you to come with me to tell Trell what happened. We will tell no one else."

"I come, but first I go with Head-Gone-Bad."

Whit stood in the rain and removed his calico shirt. He spread it on the ground while he rubbed his arms and shoulders and chest to rid them of the agent's blood. He picked up his shirt, wrung it out, and slipped it back over his head.

Head-Gone-Bad brought the horse to within a few feet of Alvin's body. The animal, smelling blood, danced nervously.

"I want the satchel, Whit. He told me he had papers that would prove Reverend Longfellow was stealing cattle from the reservation."

"It is true."

"You knew?"

"Of course. Elders knew but could do nothing because of agent." He untied the leather bag.

"Something will be done now," Jenny said firmly and took the satchel from his hand.

Head-Gone-Bad was strong. While Whit held the nervous horse, he lifted the dead body and flung it facedown over the saddle. Whit spoke to his friend, and Head-Gone-Bad led the horse into the dark, rain-soaked forest.

"I show you way back to school, then I get pony and go with Head-Gone-Bad."

"I can't go there. The children—"

"They at lodge. No go to school till teacher come for them."

"I didn't know . . . I had to go get them." Jenny looked at the young boy helplessly, while holding the two halves of her bodice together to cover her breasts. The teacher was suddenly waiting for him to take the lead.

"Take papers to McCall." Whit pulled his shirt off over his head, took the satchel from her hand and handed her the shirt. "Put this on."

Without hesitation Jenny slipped the shirt on over her head.

"Come." Whit picked up the leather bag and trotted through the woods toward the school.

Jenny had difficulty keeping him in sight. She was breathless by the time she reached him at the back of the school.

"Wait," he said, and darted around the corner of the building. He was back a minute later. "I see no one. Go."

"Whit. You may not like it, but I've got to do this—" She put her arms around him and kissed his cheek. "Thank you," she whispered. "I'll always love you."

He stepped away, but not as quickly as she expected. His hand lingered for an instant on her arm.

"Take bag and go. I not be back today."

He waited as she ran down the path to the homestead and disappeared through the door of the bunkhouse. There was something he didn't want her to know and worry about . . . yet.

Sneaking Weasel had been watching while the body of the agent was put on the horse.

Trell appeared to be sleeping when Jenny came into the bunkhouse and closed the door behind her. She thanked God for the rain that kept the girls in the house with Granny. Trell sat up, and alarmed at her appearance, swung legs over the side of the bed.

"What's wrong? Jenny, honey—"

Jenny dropped the bag at the end of the bed and hurried around to drop on her knees and wrap her arms around Trell's waist.

"Trell! Oh, Trell!"

"Honey, you're wet to the bone!"

She sprang back. "I forgot I'm wet!"

"I don't care!" He pulled her back into his arms. "What's happened, sweetheart." He lifted her face with gentle fingers and looked into her eyes. He touched her bruised cheek and the swelling beneath her eye. "What the hell happened? Did someone hit you?"

"I thought I'd never see you again." She burrowed her face in the curve of his neck.

"Who hurt you?" He grasped her shoulders and held her away from him. "Who hurt you, Jenny? Isn't that Whit's shirt?"

Jenny's teeth began to chatter so badly, either from cold or from nervous reaction, that she couldn't talk. With her squatting between his knees, Trell pulled Whit's shirt off over her head. When he saw her torn bodice, he took a deep breath and muttered a string of curses. He pulled the blanket from the bed.

"You're shaking like a leaf. Get out of those wet clothes. I'll hold the blanket up, then wrap it around you. Hurry now."

"It was so awful, Trell. I just wanted to get back here to you." Her teeth clicked as she spoke from behind the blanket. She first untied and pulled off her shoes, then her wet stockings. Her dress and camisole came next.

"Sweetheart, are you all right? Who hurt you? Tell me!"

"I'm not . . . hurt, but . . . I'm not . . . all right. I never thought . . . anything like this would . . . happen to me."

"Get the other blanket off the cot, honey. Wrap yourself in it and come here."

Later, wrapped in the blankets and nestled in his arms, Jenny told him everything.

"Oh, God! Honey—" He held her tightly. "This was happening to you while I was lying here in this damn bed! The rotten . . . son of a bitch! If Whit hadn't killed him, I would have!"

"I was sure he was going to kill me! Suddenly someone was there. I remember seeing a face, hair and a knife. I didn't know it was Whit until I came out of my faint. He had taken the gag out of my mouth . . . and covered me. There was blood on his shirt and arms. He's just a boy, Trell. He's just a boy and he's killed a man, cut his throat to save me."

"Whit's more of a man than most I've met. Reasonable men would not want him punished for what he did. The trouble is I'm not sure who the reasonable men are here in Sweetwater. And Whit is an Indian. That clouds men's judgment. It was good that he had someone to help him hide the body."

"I almost forgot the bag. Mr. Havelshell said he had papers that would prove the preacher was stealing reservation cattle."

"We'll get to all of that later. Are you warm, honey?" He spread kisses over her face and smoothed the damp hair back from her forehead. "I don't want you getting sick."

The rain continued all day.

At the Agency compound, Linus sat in the far corner of the barn stroking the soft fur of his pet racoon. He had a lot to think about. What he'd seen that morning had turned his world upside down. He was glad in a way that it had happened, but he was confused as to what to do about it.

Living for the past few weeks with Arvella and Pud had been almost like belonging to a family. She had called him in for meals, washed his clothes, and nagged him to let her cut his hair. He had fixed fence and cleaned out the horse barn with Pud. The man had not told him, not even one time, how stupid and worthless he was, even when running the hand-plow down between the rows of beans, he had dug up half a row.

Kindness from a man was something new to Linus. Arvella had never been mean to him; but lately she had seemed happier, and it showed in the way she treated him, as if she maybe kind of liked him.

Linus was thinking about what he had witnessed that morning. He was trying to decide if he should tell Pud and Arvella. She should know that she wouldn't have to put up with Alvin's visits anymore. Linus hadn't understood why Alvin had married her because it was so obvious that he despised her.

The boy was deep in thought and hadn't noticed that someone was coming down the middle aisle of the barn. The raccoon, however, noticed and scurried off his lap and into the upended barrel that was his home.

"You here, Linus?" Pud called.

"Yeah."

"You sick or somethin'?" Pud came around the corner and saw Linus sitting in one of the stalls.

"Naw. Jist sittin' here."

"Arvella's worried. Ya didn't eat hardly any of the bread puddin'. She made it for ya, 'cause she knows yo're fond of it."

"I wasn't hungry." His knees were pulled up, his arms folded across them. Now he lowered his head and rested his forehead on his arms.

"Is somethin' wrong? If yo're bilious, boy, I've got a tonic. It'll give ya the shits but ya'll feel better."

"I feel a'right. I jist got stuff to decide."

"If there's anythin' I can help ya with, let me know." Pud put his hand on the boy's shoulder then turned to leave.

"Pud—" Linus's voice came quickly. "Stay a minute. I got to tell ya somethin'. I ain't knowin' what to do."

Pud hunkered down on his heels and picked up a straw.

"I might not know what to tell ya, son, but the two of us could hash it over."

Son. The words brought a mist to Linus's eyes. He'd never been called son by . . . anyone.

"I stopped watchin' at Stoney Creek."

"Ya told me."

"I went there this mornin'." For a minute the old defiance was back in his words and voice. "I really wanted to see . . . Miss Murphy," he amended with a guilty grin.

"Nothin' wrong with that. She ain't hard to look at."

"I stopped when I saw Alvin's mare in the woods 'tween here and the school—the one he bought from that man in Rawlins. Ain't no mistakin' that horse. Ain't one like it in the country."

"Horse set him back a dollar or two. Ain't no doubt about that. Alvin comin' here, boy?"

Linus shook his head and looked down at his clasped hands.

"Pud, Alvin had the teacher down on the ground and tied up." The words came out in a rush. "She was fightin' him. He'd stuffed a rag in her mouth and was laughin'. I ain't never heard him laugh much a'tall, and never like that. It was like he was . . . well, like he was somebody else."

Pud whistled through his teeth. "It ain't like Havelshell to do somethin' so . . . so harebrained. A man'd get hung quicker than scat for somethin' like that."

"I wasn't goin' to let him hurt her, Pud. Honest to God. I wasn't. It jist wasn't right. I didn't know what I was goin' to do, but I was goin' to do somethin'. I was gettin' off my horse when that Indian kid, old Whitaker's brat, come runnin' out of the woods. He yelled like the savage he is, and jumped on Alvin's back. Pud, that little sucker cut Alvin's throat from ear to ear!"

"Jesus, my God! He . . . killed him? Yo're sure?"

"Damn near cut his head off."

"Did he . . . had he raped her?"

"Don't think so. She'd swooned. Didn't scream or cry or nothin' when she come to. Pud—I ain't carin' none a'tall that the kid killed him." He paused, then said, "I suppose ya think I ort to."

"I ain't supposin' what ya ort to think, son. Havelshell, for all his schoolin', was a schemin' sonofabitch. I been expectin' one of the toughs in town to blow his head off when he was lordin' it over 'em."

"I ort to feel bad 'cause he was my pa."

"I knew that, son. Arvella told me. The way I look at it a pa is the man who takes care of his younguns if'n they be of his seed or not. He keeps their bellies full and teaches 'em right from wrong. Alvin was like one a them dandelion puffballs. The wind comes along and scatters the seed. I'm thinkin' that he scattered seeds jist like that, not carin' if they took root or not. That's not a pa to my notion."

"He knowed about me all my life and hated me and my ma. When she died, I come here. He was madder than a pissed-on snake when I showed up. Said he'd kill me if I ever told anybody he was my pa. Later, when he married Arvella, and she come out here, he sent me out to keep a eye on Stoney Creek.

"Ya know what, Pud? I'd busted my ass gettin' to town to tell him somethin'. He never oncet said a thanky, or asked me to stay to supper, or anythin' like that. He'd tell me to get the hell outta the house, even if it was midnight. A time or two he paid for me to go to the whorehouse. Now I think it was 'cause the horny old goat wanted to watch."

"The town'll be stirred up when they find out what happened. They'll hang the kid if they get their hands on him."

"Another Indian was with him. They put Alvin on the back of his horse and headed into the woods. There's places on that reservation where you could hide a herd of buffalo."

"They'll hide the body, but Indians won't destroy a horse. It'll vanish in the herds and be driven north."

"Besides the teacher and the Indians, Pud, I'm the only one that knows that little bastard killed him."

"'Pears that way, boy. What ya got against the kid? Seems he's in the same boat ya are."

"I jist don't like him!" Linus said firmly. "What'll I do, Pud?"

"Ya've got two choices. Ya tell or ya don't tell."

"Arvella ort to know she ain't got to put up with him no more."

Pud was quiet for a moment while he took out his pipe and filled it with tobacco.

"Her pa'll be lookin' for another man for her."

"Couldn't it be you, Pud. Yo're not mean to her like Alvin was."

"He'd not consider me, son. I'm just a rough cowboy."

"Arvella'll have to leave here. Where'll she go?"

"Home to her pa, I reckon."

"He ain't goin' to be wantin' me hangin' 'round."

"We'll have to wait and see how the wind blows."

"How long'll it be before that Bible-spoutin' old sonof-abitch knows Alvin is gone?"

"Guess it'll depend on who knew he was comin' out here. He had to a left Sweetwater last night or early this mornin'."

"I ain't tellin' nobody but you and Arvella. If the old man asks me, I'll say I ain't seen him. What'll you say, Pud?"

"I ain't seen him neither. And that's the God's truth." He grinned around the pipe stem in his mouth. "Come on.

Let's go tell Arvella. Don't figure she's goin' to be tore up about it a'tall."

Travor looked from the window in his hotel room onto the rain-soaked street of Sweetwater. Rain was still coming down. At times the wind drove it in sheets against the windowpane. He had been up half the night, as had most of the folks in town after the dreaded cry of "FIRE" was heard. The fire in Havelshell's house was off to a good start by the time the water brigade arrived, and there was no chance of saving it. The effort was concentrated on keeping the fire from traveling on the dry grass and wood fence to other houses nearby.

Alvin Havelshell had not been seen since he left the saloon, and it was assumed that he was in the house when it was reduced to a pile of smoldering ashes. The fire had traveled to the small barn and the hay inside had fueled the blaze. Havelshell's blooded mare had escaped and, according to hoofprints, had taken off across the grassland. Had the rain arrived several hours earlier, something of Havelshell's might have been saved.

Townspeople gathered under store-porch awnings to talk about the killings in the saloon and the death of Mr. Havelshell. Last night a dozen men had seen Sheriff Armstrong give him back the star; and early this morning it had been found among the wet ashes, giving some evidence that Havelshell had been in the house when it burned.

Travor stayed in his hotel room until hunger drove him to leave it for the eatery where he'd had supper the night before. He was in a hurry to get back to Stoney Creek and to the girl who waited there. The rain would be no bother, but he was not eager to ride with lightning forking down.

On the hotel porch, Travor hesitated about darting out into the heavy downpour. While he waited, two men came from around the corner of the hotel and leaped up onto the porch. They wore poncho rain gear and carried saddlebags.

"Come on, ole man. I was thinkin' I'd have to get behind ya and push." Both men were tall, but the younger was taller and broader.

"You think yo're so smart. Look at yore boots and look at mine. There ain't hardly no mud a'tall."

"It wouldn't a mattered on those old boots anyhow."

Travor nodded at the men and started to step off the porch.

"Trell? Trell McCall?"

Travor turned to see the older of the two men looking at him.

"Travor McCall. Trell's brother."

"I've heard about Trell's look-alike. Cleve Stark." He held out his hand. "This laughin' jackass is my most-of-the-time pain-in-the-butt sidekick, Dillon Tallman."

"Howdy." Travor's pleasure was genuine. "And I've heard about Marshal Stark and"—he grinned at Dillon—"his pain-in-the-butt sidekick, Dillon Tallman." He shook the hands of both men, then said, "Trell told me that he'd sent a wire to Pack to try and find you."

"Trell here?"

"No. A lot has happened since he sent the wire."

"Pack caught up with me; and knowin' Trell ain't one to get all rattled over nothin', I come on down. I spent a week with him out on the ranch a couple years ago. You were drivin' a herd of longhorns up from the Texas panhandle at the time. We didn't envy ya none a'tall."

"It's not somethin' I'll ever do again."

"We need to get us a decent meal in our bellies," Dillon said. "I've et nothin' but Cleve's trail cookin' for a week."

"It ain't been but two days," Cleve corrected, then to Travor, "Nothin' gets this kid's dander up like missin' a meal." Cleve hit his friend a playful blow on the shoulder.

"Just goin' to grab a bite myself. I'll pay my hotel bill and pick up my saddlebags."

"We were camped about five miles out last night and smelled smoke. Not wantin' to get caught in a forest fire, we saddled up and come on in. It'd started rainin' time we got here."

By this time they were standing in front of the hotel desk and Melva was looking them over.

"You stayin'?" She gave Cleve her brightest smile.

"Not knowin' yet."

"We'd be happy to have ya and will do everything we can to make ya comfortable."

"That's mighty nice of ya, ma'am."

"Where you from, stranger?"

"Any place west of the Mississippi."

Travor fetched his saddlebags and met Cleve and Dillon on the porch.

"The liveryman was full of talk 'bout the shootin'," Cleve remarked. "When he said McCall, I figured he meant Trell."

"Well, I'm not proud about killin' one of 'em. He was just a stupid kid. Killin' the other'n was like killin' a mad dog. He'd a gone on killin' for hire till he was stopped."

They went down the boardwalk to the eatery, hurrying from one porch to the next because rain was still coming down in a steady drizzle. The cook greeted Travor as if he were the town hero. Travor introduced Cleve and Dillon as friends passing through and led them to a table at the far end of the room. When plates of flapjacks and eggs were placed before them, Travor explained what had happened to his brother and how it led to his killing Crocker and his sidekick.

"Got witnesses," Travor concluded. "The kid drew first, Crocker missed his shot and I hit dead center."

"Looks cut-and-dried to me."

"I was reasonably sure it was Crocker who ambushed Trell, but it could have been a feller I had a run-in with the night I stopped here on my way to the ranch. He got under my skin and I mopped the floor with him. He's as ornery as a longhorn with a thorn in his pecker and he ain't a for-gettin' man. We'll go head to head again afore long."

"Are ya sure ya ain't a brother to this here hard-nosed clabberhead?" Cleve grinned and jerked his head toward Dillon. "He can get into trouble faster than I can tell ya about it."

"Now, Cleve. I'm just full of beans and vinegar. Pa warned ya."

"Yeah, and it was the first time in my life I failed to heed John Tallman's warnin'."

It was easy for Travor to see that these men had great affection for each other.

"We need to make sure Havelshell is dead." Cleve had turned serious again. "Then I'll send a wire to the Indian Bureau. I sent one already tellin' 'em I was coming to investigate some rustlin' of reservation cattle. They'll have to appoint another agent."

"I ain't envyin' ya goin' through them wet ashes."

"He could'a been on that horse that's missin'." Dillon poured syrup on another stack of flapjacks. "Good way to lose yourself—lettin' folks think ya burned up."

Later they stood in front of the eatery. The rain had eased up. The road between the two rows of buildings was a sea of mud.

"Here comes that preacher I was tellin' ya about," Travor said, as a buggy rattled into town. "Some folks say that he played the tune Havelshell, his son-in-law, danced to. His name is Longfellow. He came out to Stoney Creek once while I was there. Slimy, smooth-talkin' little toad to my notion."

"*Reverend* Longfellow. So this is where he landed."

"You've heard of him?"

"Oh, yes. He's got enough wind for a dozen preachers."

The horse was struggling to pull the preacher's buggy through the mire. The pudgy man looked neither left or right. He flayed the horse unmercifully with the buggy whip.

"Stupid sonofabitch!" Dillon gritted his teeth.

"Nothin' riles Dillon more than somebody beatin' a horse."

Another blow caused the horse to swerve and the buggy wheels sank to the hubs in a mud hole. Infuriated, the preacher stood and rained blow after blow on the helpless animal.

Dillon sprang off the porch as if propelled by a slingshot, and although he sank into mud to his ankles, quick strides carried him to the buggy. He reached in and jerked the whip from the preacher's hand just as he lifted it to lash the horse again.

"Ain't ya got no brains? You'll kill that horse!"

With surprising speed, Longfellow turned on Dillon, a small pistol in his hand.

"It's my horse, damn you." Gone was the pious look he affected in church. "Give me that whip."

"Mister, if a man draws on me he'd better shoot quick."

In an unthreatening manner, Dillon held out the whip, handle first. When Longfellow reached for it, Dillon's free hand lashed out like a striking snake. The pistol flew out of the preacher's hand and landed in the mud. The strong young hand that fastened on Longfellow's coat pulled him until he teetered on the edge of the buggy.

"If ya wasn't so damned old and so damned soft, I'd give ya a little of what ya was givin' that horse."

"Let go of me, you ruffian! I'll have you arrested."

"Ya'll have to pick yoreself up outta the mud first."

Dillon gave a little tug and then let go of the man's coat. The preacher teetered for a second or two, tried to get his balance, then fell. He landed, sprawled, in a foot of mud.

"Phew! You landed in a pile of wet horseshit."

"Get . . . away from me!" Longfellow tried to get to his feet, slipped and fell back down in the mud.

Dillon glanced down at him, then waded back to the porch of the eatery with a satisfied grin on his face.

"See what I mean?" Cleve said to Travor. "I figure it's time we got over to the livery, saddled our horses, and rode outta town."

Chapter Twenty-seven

Hartog awakened at daylight and moved out from under the shelter of the overhang where he and the Mexican had stayed the night before, when it seemed likely to rain before morning. He squatted in the bushes, his britches around his ankles. Between the pain in his back and his loose bowels, he had spent a miserable night. This was his fourth trip out from under the overhang. After he finished he went back to his bedroll and eased himself down.

The thought of riding five miles in a pouring rain didn't appeal to him at all.

"*Señor*, will we not go to Stoney Creek this mornin'?"

"Not in this rain, ya dumb-ass," Hartog growled.

"Yi, yi, yi—" Mendosa sighed.

"What's that mean?" Hartog demanded.

"Nothin', *señor*. Nothin'."

"Ain't no hurry. She ain't goin' no place. We'll go tomorrow, if it clears up."

Hartog stretched out on his back. *That sonofabitchin' McCall had damn near ruined his back, but he'd pay. I'll screw that black-haired bitch into the ground then go after him. There are plenty of places along the trail to get a clear shot.*

Meanwhile, Hartog didn't dare let Mendosa know how weak he was. The Mexican would cut his own mother's throat for a dollar, and he knew Hartog was carrying the money Havelshell had paid him for killing Murphy.

It was the longest, most miserable day of Colleen's life. Her mind was never far from Travor and what she imagined to be happening in Sweetwater.

Damn!

She hadn't wanted to care about that two-bit flirt. And more than likely that's what he was. But he'd crept into her heart, and nothing short of a miracle was going to get him out of it.

Is this the first of a million times I'll be waiting to see if he comes home full of holes—if he comes home at all?

After Colleen had washed two tubs of clothes, the rain was pelting down so hard that she had to quit or get soaking wet taking the clothes to the pond to rinse them. She was sitting in the shed looking out when Jenny came running down the path from the school and went into the bunkhouse . . . to Trell. *Lucky Jenny!*

Colleen had been reconsidering the advisability of marrying Travor McCall. She was wildly happy when she was with him and wildly miserable when away from him. Travor was vastly different from Trell, who had not felt a need to see what was over the mountain and around the bend.

Travor had wandered over the West like a drifting tumbleweed. How many women had he known? How many had he loved and left behind when he pulled foot? Would he get itchy feet and leave her with a houseful of little ones?

A south wind came up about noon and pushed the rain clouds to the north. The result was a misty, gloomy day. Colleen ventured out of the shed and knocked on the door of the bunkhouse before she opened it. Jenny was wrapped in a blanket and in Trell's arms.

"Come in, Colleen," Trell said. "Jenny's had a shock. She'll need some dry clothes."

"What happened?" Colleen came to the edge of the bed.

Trell looked down into Jenny's face. She nodded, and Trell gave Colleen a sketchy account of Havelshell's attack on Jenny and his attempt to carry her off. When he came to the part about Whit killing Havelshell as he was beating her, Colleen put her hand over her mouth.

"Oh, Jenny—"

"Havelshell would have killed her. He wouldn't have let her live to tell that he had tried to carry her off." Trell's voice was harsh. He was clearly frustrated at his inability to protect her.

"Whit killed him! Good for Whit!" Colleen gathered up Jenny's wet clothing.

"He's just a boy, but he didn't hesitate a minute," Jenny said. "I heard this . . . savage cry, then he was on the agent's back. I still can't believe it happened."

Trell told Colleen that Whit and Head-Gone-Bad were taking the body deep into the reservation with the hope that no one would know what had happened to Havelshell.

"We've got to protect Whit," Jenny added when Trell had finished.

"Old bastard got what was comin' to him," Colleen said

heatedly. "Pays him back, too, for havin' my pa killed. Ya don't want the girls knowin' about this?"

"Not Beatrice. But knowing Cass, she's doubtless already wondering why I haven't come to the house."

"You won't be able to hide it from her." Trell reluctantly loosened his arms so Jenny could move away.

"If you'll bring me some dry clothes, I'll explain to Granny and Cass what happened."

"I'll bring Beatrice out here. She's been wanting to come see Trell. I think she's sweet on him." Colleen raised her brows.

"She's not the only one," Jenny said, and brazenly placed a kiss on Trell's smooth cheek.

In the afternoon Ike returned with a string of catfish and went down to the pond to clean them. Jenny and Cassandra went to the Indian camp to lead the children to the schoolhouse.

Colleen finished the wash and hung it on the bushes to dry. Her heart was so filled with dread that she could hardly eat the noon meal. Trell was worried too but tried to comfort her by saying that the man Travor was looking for might not even be in Sweetwater.

To keep herself busy, Colleen cut kindling at the woodpile. Her eyes strayed often across the meadow to where the trail to town disappeared into the woods.

"If this sick feelin' is love, I'm not sure I want any of it," she muttered and brought the hatchet down to chop a sliver from a chunk of wood.

Ike returned from the pond, took the cleaned fish to the kitchen, then went to the bunkhouse to visit with Trell.

When Colleen glanced again at the edge of the woods, three riders had emerged. She stared. They came closer. When she recognized Mud Pie, she felt an incredible spurt of joy. Paying scant attention to the men riding with him, she only saw Travor. She sank the hatchet in the stump, wiped her hands on the legs of her overalls, and batted the tears of relief from her eyes.

As the men neared she could hear Travor talking to one of the men. He slapped his thigh with his hand as his laughter, his joking, teasing, beautiful laughter rang out. Colleen stood where she was by the woodpile.

He didn't have a care in the world. He'd been having a high old time while I've waited here as wrung out as a wet dish rag!

Sudden and unreasonable anger knifed through her. She looked for someplace to go, but they were already coming into the yard. *I'll not let that slack-jawed, flitter-headed, tally-whacker see me run or see me cry!* She stood, her feet planted on the ground, her arms folded over her chest, her face set in lines of resentment.

"Colleen!"

Travor had his charming, devilish smile on his face when he swung from the saddle. With his eyes still on her, he looped the reins over the rails. She was intensely aware of him from the top of her head to the tip of her tingling toes.

"That's my girl," he announced to the men who were dismounting. Then, "Trell's in the bunkhouse. Go on in." He went toward the woodpile where Colleen waited. "Sweetheart—" He stopped speaking when he saw the mutinous look on her face.

"Don't you sweetheart me, ya . . . egg-suckin', slick-talking, mule's ass!"

Her resolve not to cry crumbled. Tears filled her eyes and flowed down her cheeks. She was so angry at him, so angry at herself, that she sprang at him, the heels of her hands hit his shoulders and shoved. Travor caught her wrists.

"Stay away from me or . . . I'll strangle ya."

"Why'er ya mad? What the hell did I do?"

"I ain't marryin' ya. I ain't waitin' around half my life not knowin' if yo're dead or alive. Get yore hands off me or I'll . . . I'll—"

"Stop actin' up or I'll shake ya till yore teeth rattle." Travor's voice was rough. His hands moved from her wrists to her upper arms. "And you *are* goin' to marry me just as soon as I can get ya to a preacher. Then I'll teach ya to behave."

"Ha! Ya got about as much chance of *that* as ya got pissin' from here to Sweetwater!"

"Hush up that talk!" Travor gave her a couple of shakes. "I'll not have my wife usin' them words."

"Then get ya a namby-pamby wife. I'll talk any way I want to."

"What's the matter with ya?" Travor's brows were drawn together in a puzzled frown. "Don't ya want to know if I found Crocker? Don't ya want to know why I brought the marshal back with me?"

"Ya brought a . . . *marshal*? Mercy! What've ya done? We don't need no marshal here . . . *now*!"

Seeing the anguish on her face, Travor's frown deepened.

"What do you mean . . . now?"

"Oh, ya've just . . . got to go and put yore foot in it, don't ya?"

"Trell sent for the marshal to come because Havelshell was trying to run Jenny off and because he was stealing from the Indians. It's over now. Havelshell's dead."

"I know . . . *that*!"

"You know? How did you find out? Who's been here?"

"I'll not tell *you* nothin'."

"Colleen, I have the feelin' yo're goin' to make my life hell." He gazed into her rebellious face and shook his head. "But I can't live it without ya." Travor jerked her close and wrapped his arms around her. "I looked forward to bein' with ya every minute since I left ya. More than anythin' I wanted to hold you in my arms and see love shinin' in your eyes for me . . . only for me. Yore pigheadedness ain't goin' to keep me from gettin' my hello kiss."

His mouth, firm yet gentle, fastened on her trembling lips, stealing her breath away. The kiss was filled with sweetness . . . at first. When her lips remained firm, unyielding, he deepened the kiss until they softened. He lifted his head to look at her.

"Colleen, my sweet—"

Their breaths mingled for an instant before he covered her mouth again with his. He kissed her lingeringly, hungrily, but gently, as though she were infinitely fragile and precious. He held her tightly against him, drinking in her sweetness until his senses reeled.

She tried to wiggle out of his arms. "Somebody'll see us.

"Let 'em look, love." There was deep huskiness in his voice. "Wasn't ya just a little glad . . . to see me?" He watched her face with dark and anxious eyes.

"Ya know I was. I was dyin' . . . inside."

"Crocker's dead. It wasn't even close. I told ya he'd be surprised and I'd have the drop on him."

"It's . . . over?"

"Yes, sweetheart. I'm not sayin' I'll not have to do somethin' like that again."

"Did ya . . . see Hartog?"

"He's not been back to Sweetwater."

"I was . . . so worried." Colleen leaned her forehead against his shoulder for an instant then looked up at him. "I'm sorry I hit ya. It made me mad to see ya actin' like ya'd been on a picnic."

"Ya still love me?" he asked anxiously.

"If ya ain't knowin' that, yo're crazy as a coot." She reached up and kissed him on the chin.

He laughed happily. "I'm the luckiest man alive. Come, meet Cleve and Dillon. I want them to see my girl."

"No. Go on." She gave him a gentle push. "A lot has happened since ya left. Trell will tell ya about it. I'll go get Jenny, then clean up and help Granny with supper."

Three tall men got to their feet when Jenny appeared in the doorway of the bunkhouse. Her heart had almost stopped when Colleen told her Travor had returned with a marshal. The image of Whit jumping on the back of the man who was going to kill her popped into her mind and she vowed to do whatever it took to protect him.

Her eyes went first to Trell who was sitting on the side of the bed. Then to his brother.

"Travor!" She went quickly to him and placed her hand on his arm. "We were so worried about you."

"It's mighty comfortin' to be worried about by two pretty ladies."

Travor threw his arm across her shoulders in a casual, intimate way that endeared him to females young and old. Looking at his handsome brother, Trell was reminded of his own scarred face. He had brooded some about it but now a new thought struck him. For the first time in his life he would not be mistaken for his brother. He had an identity of his own.

"Get your hands off my woman, brother." Trell held out his hand to Jenny and she went to him. "Honey, I want you to meet Marshal Cleve Stark and Dillon Tallman."

"How do you do, gentlemen?" She extended her hand. "Welcome to Stoney Creek."

Trell held her hand tightly and gave it a little squeeze because he knew what he was going to say would be a shock.

"The marshal tells me that Havelshell's house burned down last night. They believe that he died in the fire."

Jenny's eyes widened. She looked searchingly into his eyes for a long moment. Her face was a mask of uncertainty. Finally she spoke in raspy whisper.

"Oh . . . Trell, how can they think that—"

"Sit down." He tugged on her hand and she sat down beside him. "They found a couple things in the ashes that make Cleve think he died in the fire."

"Have you—?"

"No."

"I couldn't bear it if something happened to—"

"We can let it ride if you want."

"What should we do?"

"You must decide."

"We'd be taking a chance."

"Not as much as you think, sweetheart."

It was deathly quiet in the room. The three men watched the two seated on the bed and listened to their whispered conversation. Something serious was being discussed by the two who seemed to be thinking with one mind.

"I thought we'd decided—" Jenny said and leaned her forehead against his upper arm.

"Things are changed now. Cleve is a reasonable man."

"Shouldn't I ask Whit first?"

"He's proud and will deny nothing."

"I know. I wanted to say I did it," Jenny whispered, then looked up at the marshal, her eyes swimming in tears.

"Mr. Havelshell didn't die in the fire. He died here, this morning. He had me on the ground, tied up, and was attempting to carry me off. A young Indian boy killed him." Now that the words were out she wished that she could take them back.

"Well, now—" Cleve sat down in a chair. Travor and Dillon squatted on their heels. Holding tightly to Trell's hand, Jenny batted the tears from her eyes, lifted her chin and began to talk.

"When I reached the school, it had just started to rain—"

She spoke quietly, blaming herself for being so gullible as to allow the agent to entice her into the woods where he said that he would give her papers proving the Reverend Longfellow was stealing from the Indians. She told of his asking her to go away with him and how, at her refusal, he had thrown her to the ground, tied her up, and begun to beat her.

"I was beginning to black out when Whit ran out of the woods and jumped on his back. Mr. Havelshell would have killed me. He would have killed Whit if he could. Whit is just a boy. A proud, intelligent Indian boy. He risked his life to save mine." Jenny's eyes were free of tears now; and when she looked at the marshal, they were bright with resolve. "I will use every dollar I have. I will call on every person of influence I know. I will go the Supreme Court if necessary to keep that boy from being punished for what he did."

"Well now," Cleve said again. He looked out the door and rubbed his chin. "There's no need a that. But the boy bein' a Indian—"

"—His father was Mr. Walt Whitaker who owned this ranch. Mr. Havelshell would not let him off the reservation even to come here to the home where he was born. I have reported that to the Indian Bureau in Washington."

"Some folks would think that reason enough to kill the agent."

"Some folks have such a low opinion of themselves they have to have someone to step on in order to elevate themselves," Jenny said heatedly, and waited for the marshal to say what he intended to do.

"Without a body, there's not much use in draggin' this out in the open. I'm thinkin' the boy knows where to put it so it won't be found."

"Ike—?" Jenny turned to speak to the old man squatting with his back to the wall.

Ike snorted. "It'd be like lookin' for a flea on a buffalo."

"Well, now—" Cleve said for the third time. "Folks think Havelshell burned up in the fire. I've not seen anything to make me think different."

It was quiet for half a minute, then Jenny let out a little cry.

"Thank you. Oh, thank you!"

"Don't need to be thankin' me, ma'am. At times ya have to call 'em as ya see 'em. I can't see draggin' the boy before a judge."

"It's called frontier justice, honey," Trell said. "Folks out here in the West use what we call horse sense in handling things. Cleve is going to look over the papers in Havelshell's satchel—and see how Longfellow fits into all this."

Hopping on one foot and with the help of Travor and Dillon, Trell came to the supper table. Jenny met him at the door with smiles of welcome. She had planned to change into something soft and pretty but decided not to when she saw that Colleen had put on the rather shabby, faded dress she had worn the day they went to town.

Travor's face lit up like a full moon when he saw her. Her suntanned face reddened when he continued to look at her.

"Did ya ever see a prettier gal, Dillon?"

"Can't say as I have. Ma'am, ya got this fish caught hook, line and sinker." Dillon's boyish good looks and his cheerful disposition had not been lost on Cassandra. She watched him with interest.

Thanks to Walt Whitaker who had purchased the large table long ago, they were all able to sit down at once. Granny fried the catfish and even bragged about Ike by saying that he could fish even if he wasn't good for anything else.

In the general conversation, Marshal Stark said he planned to ride over to the Agency headquarters the next morning. Now that the agent was gone, he was the only government official in the area. He would have to find someone to take charge until the Indian Bureau sent another agent.

"You go on out there, boss. I'll stay here." Dillon's teasing eyes went from Jenny to Colleen.

"Take him with you, Cleve," Trell said laughingly. "I might have to crack his head with my walkin' stick."

"You fellers have all the luck," Dillon exclaimed. "Cleve, how's it that we never can find us two sightly-lookin' women with a granny that cooks vittles better'n any we've had at Delmonico's?"

"What's that, Granny?" Beatrice's clear, childish voice filled the silence while Cleve was trying to think of something to say.

"A fancy restaurant," Cassandra whispered, then turned her eyes to Dillon. "How come you're not married, Dillon? You're not bad-lookin' and you're old enough."

Jenny looked at the ceiling. How would these men view her sister—calling them by their first names, asking personal questions? She needn't have worried. Dillon was not in the least offended.

"Well, now, Miss Pretty Little Puss, I do thank ya for the 'not bad-looking' part. You see if I'd a picked just one gal outta the bunch I had to choose from, the rest of them would have jumped in the river. I couldn't have that on my conscience."

Cleve snorted and murmured. "The kid's windy as a cyclone. Don't get it from his pa or his ma, that's sure."

"Tell her, Cleve. Tell her about how ya got to carry that big old club to keep the girls off me when we go into a town."

"Dillon! You're as full of hockey as a young robin."

"Cassandra!" Jenny was mortified.

Trell smiled broadly despite the soreness. Cleve's weathered face broke into a grin. All around the table there were smiles.

"Don't get in a snit, Virginia. Ike says that all the time, only he doesn't say . . . hockey!"

Jenny glared at Ike. His nose was about three inches from his plate, and his shoulders were shaking with silent laughter.

"Ike is going to get his mouth washed out with soap . . . along with yours," Jenny said sternly.

"Makes sense to me," Travor said, hoping to ease Jenny's embarrassment. "Not about the soap. About the pretty girls. I had the same problem once when—Ouch! Who kicked me?"

The only thing that would have made Jenny happier would have been to have Whit with them. He had said that he wouldn't be back today. As soon as he returned, she would bring him to meet the marshal. It was time Whit learned that there were many more good white men than there were bad.

Travor waited impatiently for Colleen, Jenny and Cassandra to clear the table and wash the dishes. The men moved to the end of the table and Colleen filled their coffee cups. He listened with only half an ear to the conversation, his eyes following Colleen's every move.

As soon as the last dish was put away and the wet towels hung to dry, Travor went to Colleen. He looked over her head to Granny and lifted his brows. The old woman nodded, her eyes twinkling. He took Colleen's arm and propelled her out the door.

"I ain't knowin' much about manners, Trav McCall, but I know ya ain't usin' any," Colleen sputtered as soon as the door closed behind them. "Hmm—"

Travor's mouth covered hers with a hunger that silenced her, forcing her lips to open beneath his. One hand moved up to hold her neck in a viselike grip, tilting her head so that she could not escape his passionate kiss.

"I . . . asked Granny."

"Did not." It was all she had time to say.

"I used every ounce of patience I had while I waited for this," he murmured huskily when he moved his mouth a fraction from hers.

They strained together, hearts beating wildly, and kissed as lovers long separated. His hands roamed from her shoulders to her hips and up and under her hair to the nape of her neck.

"Darlin', darlin'—" His lips moved over her cheeks. "I swear I don't know what's happenin' to me."

Colleen laughed, a sound that came out throaty and shaky.

"It can't be that yo're hungry. Ya packed away a heap of supper."

"I *am* hungry, sweetheart. I'm so damned hungry for ya—I can't hide it." He moved her hand down briefly over his hardened sex.

"Trav, I know what yo're hungry for. I know what goes on 'tween a man and a woman." She tilted her head to look at him. "Papa used to say, 'Run along, darlin', and stay with Granny. Me and yore mama are goin' to love each other.' " Her hand bracketed his jaws. "I don't remember when it come to me what they were doin'. A youngun that likes animals . . . just knows."

Travor's eyes roved over her upturned face. He inhaled a deep, shaky breath.

"Are ya shocked? Granny says *nice* girls don't know about such, and if they do they don't talk about it." She bit her bottom lip, her eyes anxious on his face.

"Thank God!" he said softly.

"Travor—" Her voice came shaky. "What'a ya mean?"

"Sweetheart, I was thankin' God, I found ya. I've been around a lot of women. Some were brazen, some pretended to be so nasty nice, some so . . . dumb that they think they'll get a baby if ya kiss 'em. None of them were as honest and sweet as you."

"I've not ever . . . ever—Don't think that!"

"I don't think that, honey. I'm just so proud ya can talk to me about it. I want us to tell each other ever'thing."

He lifted her arms up and over his shoulders so that she could wrap them around his neck. He devoured her mouth while his hands slid down to her buttocks, pressing their shifting muscles as he held her firmly against him until neither of them seemed able to strain close enough to the other.

The back door opened. Ike's voice, thankin' Granny for the supper, came to them. They moved as one around the corner of the house. Travor leaned against the wall, holding her firmly between his spread legs. His hand moved up to stroke her breast, his lips nuzzled her neck.

"There's a preacher in Forest City. Trell asked Ike to go ask him to come here."

"We don't have to wait." Her words were nearly unrecognizable, spoken as they were when he pressed his mouth again to hers.

His hands on her buttocks moved her hips in circles, pulling her tightly against his arousal and rocking her back and forth.

"I can . . . wait." An almost pained sound came raspily from his throat as his mouth left hers and fastened on the soft skin on the side of her neck. "I *want* to wait until I can have you all night long, love you all night long, make it somethin' for us to remember . . . when we're old."

He moved her away from him.

"Let's walk, sweetheart. I want ya to tell me ever'thin' ya've done ever' day of yore life."

Chapter Twenty-eight

The morning was bright and clear, but it went unnoticed by Pud and Linus as they stood on the porch of the store and watched the Reverend Longfellow's buggy approach.

"What's he back so soon for?" Linus growled.

"Arvella said he was bringin' out a girl, but there ain't nobody with him."

"He's got no rider with him, either. I'll wait and take the buggy so ya can stay by Arvella. He'll tear her up."

"Bein' loose from Alvin just this little while has give Arvella a little backbone. When I told her that her pa was coming, she just sat there. She didn't even jump up and start cookin' like she usually does."

As the buggy approached, Pud could see that the horse pulling it was lathered. The misuse of a good horse riled him as much as cruelty to a man. A few yards from the porch, the tired animal was jerked to a stop so suddenly that the buggy rocked. The horse stood with bowed head, its sides heaving. The preacher bounced down.

"That horse isn't worth the bullet it would take to blow its brains out. Get another horse and hitch it up. I won't be here long." He turned to walk up the steps to the porch.

"The horses here are hardly halter-broke," Pud said. "We don't have none that are broke to hitch."

"Didn't you bring that sorrel mare of yours out here? Hitch her up and be quick about it."

"I ain't doin' that."

"What did you say?"

"I said I won't hitch my mare to your buggy."

"Hitch her to my buggy or get the hell out of here." Longfellow glowered at the defiant man, who looked steadily back at him, then stomped across the porch to the door.

Before he followed Longfellow into the store, Pud told Linus to walk the horse to cool it, then rub it down and water it sparingly. He had promised Arvella he would stay nearby while her father was there, and he intended to keep the promise.

"Get up, you fat cow," Longfellow bellowed as soon as he entered the living quarters. "Get some things together. You're goin' back to town."

"Back to town? Why?" Arvella's voice quivered.

"'Cause I said so. You've got no right here now. Alvin's dead."

There was silence. It seemed to go on and on. Pud's heart thumped as he waited to hear what Arvella would say. The man had dominated her for so long that she was a different person in his presence. *God help her to keep her wits about her.*

"Alvin's dead?"

"You heard me. His house burned down last night with him in it. You're a widow now, and back under my roof."

Silence again.

"His house burned with him in it," she echoed his words when she finally spoke.

How could he have died in a fire? He was killed trying to carry off the teacher.

"It's what I said. The bastard burned to a crisp."

"I'm sorry to hear it."

"You don't sound sorry."

"I'm not . . . really. I hated him."

Longfellow paced the room. Since he'd discovered Alvin's safe empty, he'd had a gut feeling that Havelshell had been storing away documents to save his own hide and put the blame for their rustling activities on him. During the night he had decided the best thing to do was to take what money he had on hand and his other *asset* and head for the coast of California. There he was sure to find a man who would marry Arvella and get her with child.

"Why are you standing there? Get some things together—"

"I'm not leaving. I'm Alvin's widow, and I've got a right to stay until another agent arrives."

The preacher exploded in a spate of angry curses. Pud wished that folks in town who believed him to be so *Christian* could hear him.

"You damned bitch! You've no right to do anything, say anything or think anything unless I tell you. Get your fat ass in there and get a bag packed or you'll go without one."

"I'm not going."

"Don't you dare say no to me!" The preacher's voice had risen to screech.

"I'm not leaving. As Alvin's widow, I'm entitled to whatever he had."

"You're *entitled*? You're entitled to whatever I give you."

Pud heard the sound of the slap and the small cry that came from Arvella. He opened the door and went into the room. Longfellow's hand was raised.

"Don't hit her again."

Longfellow spun around in surprise, came up against Pud's solid frame and backed away. Pud's interference was totally unexpected.

"I told you to get the hell out!"

"I quit workin' for ya the day I rode out here."

Longfellow's eyes went from his daughter to Pud.

"Are you horny for this fat cow? I've heard about men that liked fat meat. There's even a whorehouse in Denver that keeps one or two. I've been thinking of taking this tub of grease—"

"Hush up your mouth!"

"Ho! Ho! So that's the way the wind blows."

"Pud—" Linus stood in the doorway. "McCall's here with two other fellers."

Longfellow looked alarmed, then issued the orders crisply.

"Get out there. See what they want."

Pud looked at Arvella. Her eyes begged him not to leave.

"See what they want, Linus."

"I didn't tell Linus. I told you," Longfellow said irritably. "And close the door."

Pud didn't move. And then heavy bootheels sounded on the plank floor of the store. The screen door slammed.

"Golly-damn! This is 'bout the sorriest Agency store I ever did see." The voice had a Texas drawl.

A tall man in a Texas-style hat came to the door and Linus moved out of the way.

"Who's in charge here?"

"I'm Mrs. Havelshell." Arvella crossed the room.

"Marshal Cleve Stark, ma'am." Cleve removed his hat. "Have you heard the news about your husband?"

"My father, Reverend Longfellow, just told me."

Until now, Cleve had not looked at Longfellow although he had recognized the buggy and knew he was there. The man came forward and held out his pudgy hand.

"Reverend Henry W. Longfellow, Marshal." He had the same pious look on his face that he wore in church. "I can see that you recognize my name and are wondering about my connection to my famous relative. We were cousins and close friends." He chuckled. "Folks are always expecting me to render verse after verse of Henry's poems. He's been gone for a couple of years now. God rest his soul."

"Golly-bill, Cleve! The little dude talks like a snake-oil salesman, and he cleans up pretty good, too." Dillon lounged in the doorway with a crooked grin on his face. He lifted his nose and sniffed. "I do believe he got that horse-hockey washed off."

Longfellow's eyes hardened. He shot Dillon a look laced with enough venom to drop an elephant; but when he turned to the marshal, he wore an expression of regret.

"No need to apologize, Marshal. I understand brash young folk. I'm sorry you had to witness my loss of patience yesterday morning. I was out of my mind with worry over my son-in-law, Mr. Havelshell."

Arvella backed up into a corner. The marshal, like everyone else, would be taken in by her father's smooth talk. Her eyes sought Pud for reassurance. She didn't understand why they were saying Alvin died in a fire. He was killed by the Indian boy. Linus had seen it, and Linus wouldn't lie about it.

"Come outside." Cleve beckoned to Longfellow.

"Of course." Longfellow headed for the door, then turned to speak kindly to Arvella. "Get your things together, dear. I'll take you home."

Pud lingered after the men left the room.

"Are ya goin' with him?"

"I don't want to."

"Then ya won't. Just sit tight. I'll see what's goin' on." Pud went through the store to the porch. He stopped so abruptly Linus bumped into him.

Longfellow stood with his arms around a porch post and his wrists shackled. A flood of foul language was spewing from his mouth.

"Goddamn you! What the hell are you doing? You sonofabitchin' bastard! Folks won't stand for you treating me like this."

"Now, now, preacher. You ain't never goin' to get to heaven a-cussin' like that." The young Texan patted Longfellow on the head as he would a child. "Settle down, little feller. Ya just might pull this porch top down on ya if ya keep yankin' on that post."

"Get your hands off me, you ignorant, two-bit bastard!"

"That's the second time ya called me that. Do it again and ya'll go to that brand-new Federal pen in Laramie with yore chin between yore eyes and yore eyes tied on top a yore head."

Pud and Linus gaped at Longfellow. He was livid with anger, but not so angry that he didn't realize the tall blond deputy was dangerous when pushed.

"Stay with Arvella, Linus, so she'll know what's goin' on." Pud prodded the boy back into the store, then stepped off the porch.

"Howdy, McCall," Pud said. "What this about?"

"You'll have to ask the marshal. He's the man in charge. His deputy is takin' care of the prisoner."

"Prisoner?"

"Marshal Stark, this is Pud," Travor said. "Sorry, I can't remember your other name."

"Harris," Pud said, and stuck out his hand.

"Are you and the boy the only men who work here?" Cleve asked as he shook Pud's hand.

"There's a couple of Indians that come in from time to time. Not much goin' on until the cattle come in."

"Were you here when the last allotment arrived?"

"No. I just hired on a couple months ago."

"Do you know if anyone made a count?"

"Mrs. Havelshell keeps tab on what comes *here*," Pud said.

"Glad to hear it. I'll have a look at the books."

"Will she have to leave right away?"

"I see no reason for it. It will take a month or so to get another agent here. McCall vouched for you—said he didn't know ya, but folks in town said ya was pretty straight. I'd like ya to stay on and keep thin's goin' till then."

Pud nodded. "Do ya mind tellin' me what Longfellow's done. Mrs. Havelshell'll want to know."

"I don't mind tellin' ya, and I'll tell her before we go—

that is, if she don't already know it. Federal agents have been looking for him for a long time. Longfellow isn't even his real name. It's Morris. Clarence Morris. But he's gone by half a dozen names. He killed a miner and stole the gold the man had worked for so he could bring his family out from Missouri. He's a rustler and a swindler. He's slicked more folks outta money than a dog's got fleas. He and Havelshell have been helpin' themselves to the Indians' cattle. When I get him to the Territorial capital, he'll be put away for a long while—if they don't hang him."

"Mrs. Havelshell had nothin' to do with any of that."

"I figured as much. Longfellow's ranch will be sold to pay for what he has stolen. Havelshell was fixin' to hightail it out of the country. I have a bag with papers and quite a bit of cash money. I'll see to it that Mrs. Havelshell gets some of it."

"Talk to her, Marshal. She's a smart lady. I think ya'll find out a bunch ya don't know."

"I'll do that, Harris. Thanks for yore help. My deputy and I will take Longfellow to the Territorial prison. If ya can take care of things till I get back I'll see yo're paid by the Indian Agency."

"Will ya be back before the herd gets here?"

"I ain't knowin'. I understand they graze 'em on Stoney Creek land. If they come, get a tally from the army."

"The army will bring 'em and go. It was Longfellow's men who drove the cattle onto Indian land." Pud's homely face showed his contempt for the action. "I'm thinkin' he figured I'd go along with the thievin', is why he sent me out here. Indians is folks like us. Some good, some bad."

"You acquainted with the tribe elders?"

"I've met up with a few of 'em. The Shoshoni are good

drovers, but Havelshell wouldn't let 'em off the reservation to drive their own cattle."

"I don't hold with that. There's no reason a peaceful Indian can't leave reservation land. Speak to the elders and tell them that there'll be changes made here. I'd tell 'em myself if I didn't have to take my prisoner to Laramie." Cleve looked toward the porch where Longfellow was shackled. "Does Mrs. Havelshell have relatives nearby?"

"She ain't got nobody, Marshal, but that little flimflammer. He married her to Havelshell, and they moved her out here to get her outta sight. Havelshell come out here once or twice a month is all. The boy in there is Havelshell's kid. He's taken a likin' to Mrs. Havelshell and her to him. 'Tween the two of us, we'll see to her."

"Glad to hear it, Harris. I don't like to see a woman left to fend for herself. Now, I'll go have a talk with her."

As soon as breakfast was over, Ike left to go to Forest City. Travor had offered him a five-dollar gold piece if he could get the preacher back here in two days' time. Colleen considered that with help from Granny and Cassandra it would take that long to cut down and fit the dress that Jenny insisted she wear for her wedding.

"Please, please take it," Jenny begged. "The clothes I brought from Baltimore belong to my former life. I'll never wear them again."

Marshal Stark and Dillon made ready to ride over to the Agency headquarters. They asked Travor to go along. Beatrice was delighted that Trell was settled in one of the comfortable chairs by the fireplace. She brought him her hairbrush and insisted that he be the one to brush and braid her hair.

"I think Cassandra's sweet on Dillon," Jenny whispered to Trell.

"At nine? You Gray girls start lovin' early."

"We're just smart enough to know when we've found the right man," Jenny said, giving Trell's arm a secret squeeze, "and I'm going to hang on to mine."

Jenny wanted to go to the Indian camp and see Whit. She left Cassandra at the school and went to fetch the children. They were waiting and all stood as she approached. Whit was nowhere to be seen. Feeling anxious about him, but hesitating to convey her worry to Posy, Jenny led the children back to the school.

For the next few months the children would be taught English. They were more comfortable with Cassandra and watched her with large dark eyes. Whit had taught them to say "teacher." Cassandra taught them one word at a time, then went back over the words she had taught them the day before. Yesterday they had learned two words—water and food. Today she was aiming for three—eat, sleep, drink.

The children were happily chanting, "Eat, sleep, drink," when Whit came silently into the schoolroom and squatted on the floor, his back to the wall. Relief swept over Jenny. She went to talk with him, but she could tell that it was an effort to keep his head up and his eyes open.

"Whit? Are you all right?"

"I am here."

"I can see that you are," Jenny retorted, irritated at his logic.

"Did you and Head-Gone-Bad . . . do what you—" She knelt on the floor beside him.

"It is done."

"I must talk to you."

"Talk."

"A marshal came yesterday."

"White lawman no friend of the Indian."

"He's a good man—a friend of Trell's." Jenny eased down onto the floor beside the boy. "Whit, he said the agent's house in Sweetwater burned to the ground. Folks think Havelshell died in the fire."

"Folks are wrong." The boy's expression never changed.

"I told the marshall how Havelshell died. I hope you don't mind. The marshal said as far as he was concerned the agent died in the fire."

"He say so now. But later—"

"He has no proof that anything else happened. Just because I told him does not make it so. He *thinks* he has proof that Havelshell died in the fire."

"How is that?"

"He has a tin star that Havelshell put in his pocket just before the fire. We don't have to worry, Whit. The marshal said you can leave the reservation anytime you want to. I want you to come live with us at Stoney Creek. Trell says we will build another cabin just for you. You can decide where you want it. The house your father built is yours, but we'll have to use it while I fulfill the contract so that the land can't be auctioned off. Whit—Whit?"

She looked at the boy, waiting for his response. His head was up, his hands clasped atop his upraised knees, his eyes half-closed.

He was sound asleep.

Shortly before noon the peddler, McGriff, arrived with crutches for Trell, an order he had filled at the store in Forest City for Jenny, and mail for both Jenny and Trell. Mc-

Griff declined the invitation to stay for the noon meal, saying that he had goods to deliver in Sweetwater and would stop again on his way back.

Trell's letter was from his sister-in-law, Mara Shannon. Jenny's letters were from her uncle Noah and one from the Indian Bureau. Jenny placed hers on the mantel to read later and helped Granny set the table for the noon meal.

"Mara Shannon and Pack are coming out in a few weeks." Trell announced when he finished reading his letter.

His smile was lopsided because of the injured muscles in his cheek; however, the salve Granny applied daily had kept the scar from being as disfiguring as expected.

"Mara Shannon says they sent a wire off to Cleve Stark and hoped he would be here by now. She also said she hadn't heard from Travor; and when she got her hands on him, he'd wish he'd taken time to write." Trell's eyes smiled into Jenny's. "Mara Shannon thinks we're still fourteen years old. I hope you like her, Jenny. She's been like a second mother to me and Trav."

"I've no doubt that I'll like her. What will she say about one of her twins taking on an old-maid schoolteacher and two young girls?"

"She'll say that if I don't treat you right, she'll take me to the woodshed! Jenny?" The grin slid from Trell's face as if a thought had pulled it off. "When things are straightened out back East, you might regret that you married me and feel that you are . . . stuck here. I'd not fit in your life . . . back there."

Jenny went to him, knelt down beside the chair and took his head in both of hers. She spoke in a low murmur for his ears only.

"Even if I had not met you . . . and I thank God every day that I did, I'd not go back there to stay. I might take the girls, but I'd come back. Life here is fuller, richer, more challenging. When I was younger I had rosy dreams of the man I would someday marry, how many babies we would have, and what we would name them. I'd about given up on finding the man of my dreams, Trell. Then I met you—"

His dark eyes were so clouded with concern that she wanted to hug his head to her breast. That being inappropriate with Granny nearby, she combed her fingers through his dark hair, moving it back from his forehead.

"My life is here, now. With you."

At that moment, Beatrice stuck her head in the door and yelled:

"Travor's back! And . . . and—"

The marshal and Travor rode into the yard. Travor's eyes were searching the yard for Colleen. Behind him Dillon was leading a horse with the Reverend Longfellow astride.

"Land sakes!" Jenny hurried back to Trell and handed him the crutches. "Come look. The marshal's back and he's got the preacher—handcuffed."

"Godamighty! That's McCall with two other fellers and they got . . . holy shit! They got Longfellow . . . and he's hog-tied to the saddle."

"How can that be, *Señor*?"

"Be quiet!"

Hartog lowered the glasses and squatted down in the bushes where they had been since midmorning. The only activity until now had been the peddler's arrival and departure. The Mexican had been on watch for two days while Hartog was sick. The Murphy woman had come out to move the cow to graze farther along the edge of the pond about noon each day. He had planned to be there today. There was good cover, and she'd not know what happened until she was bound and gagged.

He had considered riding in and taking her, but the Mexican had said Ike was there. That old buzzard carried a buffalo gun and didn't back down from anything. Mendosa had also reported that the day before a couple of riders had come in with McCall. Hartog knew now the riders were lawmen and figured that they must have left early this morning because there had been no sign of them until now.

Hartog surveyed the area. He and the Mexican were well concealed and would wait a while to see what was going on. The preacher had slipped up someplace along the line. He wasn't sorry they'd caught the tightfisted old bastard. He was so stingy he'd skin a flea for the hide. The men had done the work, taken the risk, and the old skinflint had sopped up all the gravy.

Chapter Twenty-nine

Colleen's world was suddenly bright and shining. She felt laughter bubbling up at the most unexpected times. She even pushed to the back of her mind the fact that Travor was leaving and she wouldn't see him for a day or two. There was no room inside her now for anything but the anticipation of a few minutes alone with him.

The marshal had said good-bye and was walking his horse across the grassland to the trail that led to the road going east and west. Dillon was taking Longfellow to the outhouse.

"If it was up to me, ya fat, slimy little toad, ya could piss yore pants," he muttered. "Yo're lucky Marshal Stark's in charge of ya."

Travor's horse was saddled. He would ride a short distance with the marshal and Dillon, then swing off and go to the Double T. It had been a week since he had been there. He explained to Colleen, when he told her that he was going, that he and that Trell owed it to Joe Fiala to let him know what was going on: that Travor and his bride would be there in a few days and that Trell would stay at Stoney Creek with his new wife.

When Colleen approached, Travor took her hand, drew her into the shelter of the cow shed and wrapped her in his arms.

"I don't want to leave—but I'd rather do it now than later. In a couple of days I'm goin' to tie ya to me and not make a move without ya by my side." His voice was husky, teasing, tender, and his lips nuzzled her ear.

Her arms tightened around him. "I'm as much yores now as I'll be in a few days."

The feeling of her warm body against his and the scent of her filled his head. Travor swallowed hard. He hadn't believed that a man could love a woman so much that the thought of losing her churned his guts. He didn't want to be away from her for even a day. His hand moved up and down her back and over her rounded hips, pulling her close.

"It's goin' to take a while for me to get my fill of lovin' my woman," he whispered passionately and kissed her long and hard.

"How long?" she gasped when she could catch her breath.

"Forty years . . . or more—"

She returned his kiss hungrily, feeling the pain of longing in her own loins, pressing against him, her breasts tingling as they had done last night when he caressed them.

"Darlin' girl." He raised his head so that he could look into her eyes. "Stick close to the house. I'm not thinkin' anythin' will happen, or I'd not leave ya. But to be on the safe side, stay close and let Trell know if ya see a rider, even if he don't come in."

"Hurry back!"

"I'll be back as soon as I can, you can bet on that."

"I'll be waitin'." She gazed at him, her eyes soft with love.

"Kiss me, sweet. It's got to last a long time."

His mouth parted her lips seeking fulfillment there. She clung to him, melting into his hard body. The kiss went on and on, both reluctant to end it.

"Trav!" Dillon yelled. "If it's takin' ya all this time to kiss that woman, ya better let me do it."

Colleen tried to pull away. Travor held her to him.

"Trav! They're waitin'." She laughed happily after he kissed her again.

"Let 'em wait. Kiss me again or I'll tell them ya won't let me go," he threatened teasingly.

After the kiss, he put his arm around her and they went out of the shed to where the others waited.

"Took ya long enough." Dillon sat on his horse, a wicked grin on his face. "I could've kissed her in half the time."

He put his heels to his horse to follow the marshal across the grassland. Longfellow on the tethered horse, his bound hands holding on to the pommel, bounced up and down as the horse trotted away from the homestead.

Travor moved his horse near to where Trell leaned on his crutches. Jenny, the girls, and Granny were beside him.

"'Bye, Granny." He leaned from the saddle and kissed the old lady on the cheek.

"Go on with ya!"

"Make my girl behave. Take care of our women, Trell. I'll be back late tomorrow sometime if all is well at the Double T. 'Bye, punkin." He saluted Beatrice and she giggled. "Thanks for the advice, Cass." He gigged Mud Pie. The frisky horse turned and took off on the run.

"Make sure you heed it, Trav," Cassandra called.

"What advice is that, Cassandra?" Jenny asked.

"Oh, this and that. I'm going back to the school. I wonder why Indians don't eat at noon like we do. Whit said they eat in the morning and again in the evening, or whenever they're hungry. He's watching them now to see that they don't eat the chalk."

"Do you like teaching, Cass?" Trell asked.

"I do, and it surprises me. I'm seeing them more and more as people and not dirty little urchins. I'm thinking seriously about teaching as a profession, not in a fancy academy, but in a school or perhaps a university for Indians."

"You're a good teacher," Jenny declared, then to Trell. "They pay more attention to her than to me. Honey, I want to read my mail, then I'll be over," she told Cassandra.

"Take your time. Whit and I can handle it. They have to learn English before you can teach them to read."

Trell and Jenny watched Cassandra walk sedately up the path to the school.

"I've never seen the like of that little girl."

"I don't think anyone else has either. She's strong or she wouldn't have been able to endure Charles's abuse and take care of Beatrice as she did."

"I hope he comes here," Trell said tightly. "I hope he tries to take the girls. He'll get his hide nailed to a tree. If I didn't do it, Trav would. He's taken a shine to the girls. I don't think I've ever seen him so happy and content."

Jenny laughed and hugged his arm.

"Rest a while. I'll read my letters then go back to the school."

Colleen came out of the shed. She carried the forked stick Ike insisted she use to poke around for snakes in the high grass that grew around the pond. She walked along the corral fence looking off in the direction Trav had taken.

"Colleen and Travor are completely suited to one another. She's crazy about him," Jenny said, watching Colleen.

"Mara Shannon always said that when Trav found the right woman, he'd give her his heart and soul. He's found her. And I've found mine."

"I love it here, Trell. I realize I've a lot to learn about living in this country. I'll do my best to be a good wife to you."

"Sweetheart! I just don't want you to regret—"

"Shh . . ." She placed a finger over his lips. "Never, never, never!" Jenny looked quickly around, then placed a quick kiss on his lips.

"You can do better than that," Trell teased.

"That's another thing I've got to get used to." Jenny laughed happily. "I'd not dare do such a thing out in the open if we were in Baltimore. But we're not, thank goodness."

She kissed him long and lingeringly. He groaned in frustration. He wanted to hold this sweet woman to him but he had to use his hands on the crutches to remain on his one foot.

"In a few days I'm going to touch you all over." He looked down into her face lovingly. "I'm going to take you to the bunkhouse, lock the door, and not let you out of bed for a week."

"Mr. McCall!" she exclaimed in mock horror. "You've been a very sick man. You shouldn't engage in . . . strenuous activities."

"I'll take it slow and easy," he promised, his eyes twinkling.

Jenny moved away from him. "Then rest and get your strength back. You'll need it!"

Her eyes danced and she couldn't keep the smile from tilting her lips as she went back to the house. Jenny was so happy that she was scared. She and Trell would live here. Colleen and Trav would be nearby. If she could have chosen another sister from all the women she had known, Colleen would have been her first pick. She and the girls would have a family now to gather around on Thanksgiving, Christmas and other special times.

Granny sat in her rocker sewing on Colleen's wedding dress. Beatrice played on the floor with Hiram, who was growing out of the puppy stage and would soon be banished to the outdoors.

"Why can't I go to school?" Beatrice had asked that question a dozen times since the Indian children arrived.

"I've told you, honey," Jenny said patiently. "As soon as the children can speak enough English to start learning the alphabet, you can come to the school."

"I already know A,B,C,D,E—"

Jenny listened until she finished. "Very good."

"Cass said I got to learn them backwards."

"Really? I don't think that is as important as learning the multiplication tables."

"Cass learned me the two's. Want to hear?"

"Taught you the two's. Not right now, honey. I want to read my letters."

Trell stretched out on the bed in the bunkhouse. He was tired, but less so than he had been the day before. He was gaining strength, but not fast enough to suit him.

He and Trav were getting married! It was hard to believe.

He wanted to be standing on his two feet when he married Jenny, but that was impossible unless he wanted to wait a month or two to make her his bride. He would settle for one foot and one crutch.

His thoughts went back to the days on the ranch near Laramie. He and Trav, only fourteen years old, were trying to sober up their father the morning after their mother died. He remembered standing in the kitchen and Pack telling them that he and Mara Shannon were married and they were to live there with them, and Mara Shannon saying it was time they had some schooling if they were going to fulfill their dream of having a horse ranch.

Trell could almost see how Mara Shannon would beam when she met Jenny and Colleen. She would have tears in her eyes and tell them how happy she was that her *boys* would be starting families of their own.

He was dozing and daydreaming when Jenny came into the room excitedly waving the letters McGriff had brought from Forest City. Instantly alert, he sat up in the bed.

"Trell!" She came to sit on the side of the bed and push him back down on the pillow. "I got custody of the girls! Dear blessed Uncle Noah took my case to state court. That's not all. Oh, you'll have to hear it for yourself. Let me read you the best part.

"After Tululla put out the word about how cruelly they had treated the girls, Margaret was snubbed by the ladies, and Charles's church lost most of its membership. The bloody bastard couldn't stand the heat. He and Margaret left for New York to board a ship for CHINA. They're going to carry the gospel to the heathens there.

"Come home, love! Send me a wire. I'll come as far as Chicago, meet you and the girls and we'll see the town.

"Tululla and Sandy are staying at the house. They will take care of things until you get here. You'll have to decide if you'll stay in Allentown or bring the girls and come back to Baltimore.

"That's the good news. The bad news is that Charles has stolen several thousand dollars of the girls' inheritance. Charges can be filed against him. I don't advise it at this time. He is leaving the country and fear of the charges will keep him from returning. You are rid of them, love. Come home."

Jenny folded the letter and put it back in the envelope. She failed to see the look of concern on Trell's face.

"I can't wait to tell Cassandra and Beatrice. Isn't it wonderful? Never in my wildest dreams did I think it would end like this. I'll put the two thousand dollars in the girls' inheritance to make up for their loss. It's worth it to be rid of Charles. I wanted to keep the girls away until they grew up. I explained to Cass that their money might all be gone. She didn't care ... and Beatrice didn't understand. It turned out far better than I hoped.

"Oh, I want to tell you about my other letter, then get a letter ready to send to Forest City when Mr. McGriff returns. I'll send a wire, too, but also a more detailed letter."

Jenny leaned over and kissed Trell on the lips.

"Isn't it grand?" she whispered, then straightened and looked down into his still, troubled face. "Trell?"

"Yes, honey. It's grand." His hand reached for hers and held it in a tight grip. "I'm glad for you and the girls."

"You ... don't act like you're glad." A frown wrinkled her brow.

"I'm a selfish man! I'm thinking only of myself."

"What are you thinking?" Then, as if a light had been turned on in her head, "You think that I'll go! That I'll not stay here now that I'm free to take the girls and go back East. Oh, Trell. How could you think that?"

"Whoa, now. You have a responsibility to the girls. I'll not stand in the way of you taking them home, and I'll not blame you—"

"Home? This is *my* home. I have a responsibility to myself and to you. I deserve to be happy. I can take care of the girls *here* as well as in Allentown now that I have you to help me. When they're older they can choose where they want to live."

"Then . . . you're not . . . going?"

"Of course, I'm not going. Not even if you don't want . . . me." Her voice broke, tears sparkled in her green eyes and her lips trembled.

"Want you? Lord, honey. I thought my heart was going to stop when I saw how happy you were that you could go back. All I could see was the long, lonely years ahead without you."

A tear rolled down her cheek. He reached to wipe it away with his thumb.

"You don't have much faith in me," she said slowly. "Or in my love for you."

He pulled her down and held her close.

"Forgive me, sweetheart," he whispered close to her ear. "Having you, loving you like I do, is so new to me. I keep waiting for something to happen to take it all away."

"Didn't you hear me when I told you I would never go back East to live? I'll stay here because I want to stay here. If . . . you don't want me . . . I'll still stay right here on

Stoney Creek and . . . it won't be because of Mr. Whitaker's will. I've . . . got enough money to buy this . . . ranch two or three times, and . . ."

"Don't say that I don't want you!" he said gruffly and buried his face in her hair. "And, honey, that's another thing—I couldn't scrape up a hundred dollars cash if my life depended on it."

She reared up and looked at him.

"And that's another thing," she repeated his words. "I thought you were a big enough man, secure in who you are and who I am, that it would make no difference who had the money. When we marry what I have will be yours, and what you have will be mine."

"Sweetheart, you have my heart . . . my life is yours. I want to work and take care of my woman, my family."

"I need you—"

"I need you, too, love."

He pulled her back down on the bed beside him and wrapped his arms around her. They were content for a while to lie there holding each other. He tilted her chin and kissed the tears from her face.

"It tears me up to see you cry. Don't worry. Together we'll take care of the girls and our own little ones when they get here."

"You'll be a wonderful papa."

He laughed happily. "We may have twins. Ma said twins run in her side of the family."

"Did you mind being a twin? You had to share the attention with Trav."

"Trav and I never knew anything else but sharing the attention. And we always had someone to play with."

"I used to long for a brother or sister near my age. Margaret was ten years older and couldn't stand the sight of me. Colleen is more of sister to me than Margaret ever was."

"I'm glad Trav fell in love with her. He was as hungry as I for a woman of his own."

"Trell." She pulled back so she could look at him. "I haven't told you about my letter from the Indian Bureau. They had already started investigating Alvin Havelshell and reconsidering the wisdom of appointing him as agent here. They were sending a man out to relieve him of his duties. Oh, poor Mrs. Havelshell. What will she do, Trell? Her husband is dead and her father taken away to prison."

"Cleve said she didn't even know her father's real name was Morris and not Longfellow. Cleve took part of the money out of Havelshell's bag and left it here for Trav to take over to her. She'll be all right."

"I hope so. The poor woman must be terribly unhappy trapped in that obese body."

Linus saddled his horse and rode slowly away from the Agency store. Pud was with Arvella. She was not sad or afraid of what was going to happen to her now that she was a widow and her father was either going to be hanged or spend his life in prison.

She had smiled as if a load had been lifted from her shoulders when Linus and Pud had assured her that she wouldn't be left to fend for herself. She had held one hand out to Linus and the other to Pud.

"We'll look out for each other, won't we? You'll be my family."

She had actually said the words, Linus thought now, as he guided the horse down the trail that led to the school.

With Pud's help, they could find a little place and he'd get a job . . . maybe they could open a restaurant. Arvella was a good cook—

Linus daydreamed as he rode amid the tall trees. Suddenly he realized he was about to ride within sight of the Indian camp. He turned into the woods and circled it and the school, coming out on the high ground above the pond. He rode to a bluff, dismounted and tied his horse so that he could crop the fresh green grass.

He took his raccoon out of the sling he carried her in and set her on the ground.

"Go nose around, Hot Twat." He remembered that Arvella was not pleased when she heard what he'd named his pet. "I reckon I'd better start callin' ya somethin' else. Think I'll call ya Miss M after Miss Murphy. She's a nice lady. Didn't look down her nose at me or nothin'."

He sat with his back to a boulder and looked down on Stoney Creek homestead. The marshal, his deputy and Longfellow rode out across the grassland. McCall followed shortly after. Linus could see the trail where they grouped and shook hands before they parted. McCall heading toward the river and others going east.

It was cool in the shelter of the boulder. Linus took off his battered hat, drew up his knees and folded his arms across them. He had a lot to think about. All his life he'd been known as a bastard. Even his mother had called him that. Arvella had liked him in spite of it. Pud knew and didn't seem to mind—

Linus suddenly straightened and stared at a spot where he'd seen a flash of light. He saw it again. It was either the sun reflecting on a mirror or a glass. He stood to study the spot and realized that someone other than he was watching the homestead, someone with a spyglass.

He moved cautiously down the slope toward the area above the pond. Across it he saw the bushes move and the swish of a horse's tail as the animal fought the pesky flies.

From his concealed position amid the thick elderberry bushes, he could see that the spotted cow staked at the edge of the pond had eaten all the long grass and was stretching its neck to reach more. Cows, he knew, needed grass long enough for them to wrap their tongues around, unlike horses who cropped the grass with their teeth.

As Linus watched, Colleen came from around the end of the corral, moved behind the barn, walked to the pond and along the edge of it toward the cow.

Chapter Thirty

Swishing her stick through the grass to scare away snakes, Colleen went along the edge of the pond. Her mind was on her wedding dress. Made of peach-colored silk, it was the most beautiful dress she'd ever seen. She wanted to be beautiful for Travor, who had seen her only in her pa's old duck pants and her one faded calico dress. When Jenny gave her the frothy silk dress, she had hesitated.

"It's a wedding gift from one sister to another. I'll be so proud to see you in it and proud, too, having you for my sister even if it is by marriage."

"I've nothing to give ya back."

"You've given me your friendship. It's worth far more to me than a dress." She spoke so sincerely, Colleen had to believe her.

Pa, I wish ya was here to see me get married. Ya'd like Trav, Pa. He reminds me of ya, in a way. Granny said ya was frisky as a colt when ya was young. Then ya met Ma. Ya loved her so much ya wanted to wrap her up and put her in yore pocket. Pa, I—

"I knew I'd get ya."

Colleen spun around. Her startled eyes glared full into the face of Hartog, the man who had killed her father. She swung the stick. The blow landed on his upper arm. She was fumbling for the gun strapped to her waist when a heavy weight on her back took her to the ground.

They were on her. Smothering her. She tried to scream, but a sweaty paw closed over her mouth.

"Ya want to fight; that is good! I can hurt ya more."

Colleen felt despair surround her. She knew that he would not only rape her, but kill her. Hatred was as strong as lust in the face of the man who straddled her.

"Ya shot me in the back, ya bitch!" he spat.

Colleen looked up and saw the man who held her arms on the ground above her head. He had a mass of black hair and a black mustache that curled down from his upper lips. His inky black eyes glittered with excitement.

Hartog ripped her shirt to expose the swelling mounds of her breasts, which he began to fondle roughly, kneading and pinching the tender flesh.

"Bah! I like big titties. These ain't no bigger'n a horse turd."

He twisted one nipple between thumb and forefinger until she writhed and sobbed in pain behind the hand clamped to her mouth. She clenched her jaws and endured his brutal attention. Then suddenly he stopped and raised himself up to get off her. Her chance came and she took it. Her knee came up and struck him a glancing blow in the groin. A howl of rage more than pain erupted from his twisted mouth.

She raised her head as he removed his palm from her mouth, but before she could open it to scream, his fist slammed into her face. The blow popped her head back against the ground and she dropped into unconsciousness.

"She . . . et!" Hartog stared down at her.

"We screw her now, *Señor*?" Mendosa asked hopefully and released her arms. He stood looking down at her exposed breasts and rubbed the bulge in his britches.

"Hell, no! She's gonna feel ever' inch I shove in 'er." He picked up the pistol that had fallen from the holster when they brought her to the ground. "Pick 'er up. We'll get 'er back to camp 'fore she comes to."

After Travor parted with Cleve and Dillon, he turned his horse toward the trail that led upward over the bluffs then down to the river crossing. This was beautiful country, and he wondered why he'd not noticed it before. He was acutely attuned to his surroundings, turning his head constantly, sending his sharp gaze skittering over the terrain in suspicious searching.

He felt at home and at peace amid the upthrust ridges, the crisscrossing canyons filled with pines and streams. He and Colleen would plant their roots here and raise a family that would grow and bloom. The thought brought a smile to his face.

Since they had left Stoney Creek there had been an urgency in Mud Pie, as if he sensed they were headed home. Travor allowed the animal to set his own pace. On the downward trail he traveled faster, as the summons to reach home grew stronger within him. Travor let him go, but slowed him cautiously when the trail on which they rode became steep and rocky before entering the thick grove of ponderosa pines and their dense undergrowth.

On his right the river water moved swiftly over boulders

and small waterfalls on its way to the sea. On his left was the forest that was the Indian reservation. He was turning to find the crossing when he heard a shout. He stopped and backed Mud Pie into the deep shadows and waited. He heard it again.

"Mc . . . Ca . . . ll—"

Alarmed when he realized the urgency in the voice, he moved out of the shadows, his eyes searching the hillside to the east. A horse shot out of the woods and raced toward him. Travor squinted his eyes to better see the rider. He recognized the long-haired, skinny kid from the Indian Agency store. He was bareheaded, his arms and legs flopping as he rode recklessly downhill.

"Mc . . . Call," he gasped as he pulled the horse to a skidding halt. "They got . . . they got . . . Miss Murphy."

"Colleen? Who's . . . got . . . Colleen?" Travor yelled hoarsely because suddenly his heart had stopped pumping air to his lungs. When Linus, who was having difficulty controlling his excited horse, couldn't answer, Travor shouted, "Who, damn you!"

"Hartog!"

"Hartog's got Colleen? Where?"

"Come." Linus turned his horse back into the hills.

Travor followed until they came to a clearing, then pulled up beside the boy.

"Did he ride on the homestead?"

"No. They took her from . . . the pond."

"They? How many?"

"Hartog and a Mexican. The Mexican carried her to the horses. They went south toward the red bluffs."

"I'll go on. Go after the marshal. I'm goin' to kill a man and he ought to know it. The marshal, his deputy and prisoner are headed east. I owe ya, boy. I won't forget it."

"Head for there." Travor's eyes followed Linus's pointed finger. "Ya'll cut their trail."

"Thanks. It's all I can say . . . for now." He gigged his horse and took off in a run.

Colleen awakened to find herself lying on the ground. She was on her stomach, her face in the grass. She opened her eyes a crack and peered through strands of tangled hair. As memory returned, so did reason. She swallowed the groan of pain that rose in her throat. She didn't move even though her head throbbed and her jaw ached.

"She waked up yet?" The voice reached Colleen from somewhere above her head.

"She ain't moved, *Señor*."

"If she moves a finger wake me. I'm goin' to catch a wink or two."

"I ain't seein' why we wait," the Mexican grumbled. "I ain't carin'—"

"Ya ain't got no say. We ain't humpin' 'er till she comes to. If ya ain't wantin' to take orders, light a shuck."

"*Yi, yi, yi.*" The Mexican sighed.

Colleen's face was turned and she couldn't see him, but she knew the Mexican was closer than Hartog, possibly only a few feet away. It was quiet. A bird chirped in the trees overhead, and from a distance came the call of a mourning dove. *How could things appear to be so normal when she was living a nightmare?*

Colleen's mind worked rapidly. *Thank God, her britches were still in place.* She knew that, unarmed, she was no match for two of them. She also knew that she wasn't going to lie like a sheep and let them have their way with her.

Travor, I'm sorry. We should have loved each other the way we both wanted and not waited for the preacher. Now these animals will try and take what I wanted with all my heart to give to you.

Colleen felt something sliding up and down over her bottom. She did her best not to stiffen. Instead she groaned softly and turned her head slightly to see two down-at-the-heel boots there on the ground beside her.

"Ya wakin' up, *Señorita*?" The whispered words of the man squatting over her barely reached her ears. "Wake up. I be good to you. Hartog asleep. He been sick. He shit for three days."

The hand slid up under her shirt. She stood it for as long as she could, but when the hand moved around under her arm to her breast, she straightened her legs and turned. Her hands were tied, she lifted them and brushed the hair from her face. He was grinning at her.

"Shh—" He placed a finger over his lips and jerked his head toward Hartog on the bedroll.

Colleen scooted back away from him. She was tethered to a tree with a rope around her ankle. Her ankles were not bound.

The animals wanted to get her legs apart!

"I will be good to you, *Señorita*. Mendosa know how to make love." He whispered the words and pointed to where Hartog lay on his bedroll. "He want to hurt you. He know how to make the hurt last a long time. I watch him screw Bannock squaw. He screw her front, then her behind. She scream long time. Scream more when he bring pup to suckle—"

Colleen closed her eyes tightly and shook her head. The horror of what he was telling her made her weak. The way he grinned while telling her indicated that he had no trace of compassion.

"Let me go."

"Pull off the britches," he whispered. "We make love. I let you go before Hartog wake up."

She shook her head again. Her eyes scanned the area for a weapon. Knowing she could do nothing sitting on the ground, she got quickly to her feet and found herself pinned against the tree with a long sharply pointed stick pressed firmly against her naked breast.

"Do not make noise, *Señorita*. Better me than Hartog."

He stood in front of her. They were of equal height, but to her he looked like a large, hungry rat. His black eyes glittered. His red mouth beneath the mustache hung open and his tongue lay on his lower lip.

"Yo're as much of a animal as he is." She put all the scorn she could muster in the sneering remark.

"It is not so. I advise you not to say that to Mendosa." He backed up a step, moving his hand along the stick to keep the point in place. "You like snake, *Señorita*? Mendosa very good at catchin' snake. See snakeskin on hat?" He wore a round-brimmed hat with a glistening snakeskin wrapped around the crown. "I catch him on the Rio Grande. He nine feet long. Snake meat better than rabbit."

Colleen watched with large almost unbelieving eyes as the Mexican stooped, his eyes still on her, and picked up a heavy leather bag. The hissing that came from within caused a cold clammy sweat to break out on her face. There was nothing in the world she was more afraid of than a snake. Any snake.

"Want to see my supper, *Señorita*? Maybe I let him bite ya. No? Maybe I let him bite Hartog."

One quick movement and he had jerked the thong from the top of the bag. Grinning, his bright eyes on Colleen, he swung the bag back and forth. Colleen heard a faint whirring sound. Suddenly he dropped the sack not more than two yards from where she stood. A long, thick snake came out of the bag. It was a rattler and as big around as her arm. Its mouth was open wide with fury. Mendosa danced around it waving the stick.

Almost paralyzed with fear, she looked frantically for something within reach to use to protect herself. She scooped up a broken tree branch and held it in both hands. The snake would have slithered away, but Mendosa urged it closer to her with the stick.

"Shoot it," she screamed, beating the ground with the club. "Shoot it!"

"What . . . the hell?" Hartog lunged up off the bedroll as if he'd been bitten by a scorpion. "Ya goddamn fool!" he yelled. "I told ya to leave them goddamn snakes alone. I'll kill ya—"

Mendosa danced around the other side of the snake, and as Hartog came up, gun in hand, he flipped the snake. The rattler fell across Hartog's shoulders and, with writhing fury, wrapped itself around his neck and sank its fangs into the flesh beneath his jaw.

Hartog screamed and dropped his gun. He tore the snake loose and flung it away.

"It bit me!" he cried in terror, and clamped his hand to his neck. "Do somethin', damn you!"

"Ain't nothin' to do, *Señor*," Mendosa said calmly. "You die soon. No way to stop poison in vein. Want I put tourniquet on neck?" A near-hysterical giggle came from him.

"Oh, my God! Oh, my God!" Crazed with fear, Hartog ran in an erratic circle around the camp, then in full panic took off into the woods in a dead run, screaming, "Oh, my God! I'll die! I'll die!"

"Don't run, *Señor!*" Mendosa yelled. "You die sooner." He watched the fleeing Hartog until he was out of sight. When he turned, he ran his lust-crazed eyes over Colleen. "It was foolish to run. He maybe live two, three hours if he lays still."

Colleen saw the fever of excitement in the Mexican's face and gripped the club.

"You say nothin', *Señorita.* You no say thank you to Mendosa for saving you from Hartog?"

"That's right. I say nothin', ya slimy little worm."

"Mendosa don't like worm." He frowned bringing his heavy brows together. "Call me snake. Snake a fighter."

"Ya call yoreself a fighter," she sneered. "Yo're just a little man tryin' to act big."

"*Señorita*, you foolish woman." With the stick he had used to toss the snake he pushed back her shirt, exposing her naked breasts. "You no make Mendosa angry. It you and me now."

"You're wrong! It's *you* and *me* now!"

Travor came into the clearing, his gun in his hand. He crouched. The wolfish look on his face made him hardly recognizable to Colleen. Startled, the Mexican turned. Blood blossomed on his chest as Travor's bullet hit its mark. The force of the bullet flung him backward. He was dead when he hit the ground. Travor scarcely looked at him. A few quick steps and he was in front of Colleen, shielding her with his body, his eyes searching the area.

"Hartog—" he gritted. "I heard yellin'."

"Ran off. Snake bit him."

Travor shoved the gun back into his holster and turned to her. He gently pulled her shirt over her naked breasts before he put his arms around her and held her tightly to him. After a moment, when he could speak, he gazed into her face.

"Did they . . . ?"

"No."

"Thank God!" He lifted her chin with a gentle finger. "The sonofabitches . . . hit ya!" He touched her swollen jaw with his fingertips, then pulled his knife and cut the thong that bound her hands.

"I'm all right." Tears of relief rolled from her eyes and down her cheeks. "How did ya find me."

"The kid from the store headed me off before I crossed the river. He saw 'em take ya."

"They sneaked up on me at the pond."

"When I heard the yell, I got off my horse and ran. I knew I was close." He knelt down and cut the rope from her ankle, freeing her from the tether.

"The Mexican was as mean as Hartog. He had a rattlesnake in a bag." Her trembling hands refused to let go of him.

Travor put his arms around her again and pressed her head to his shoulder. His eyes continued to search the edge of the woods as he stroked her hair.

"I never want to go through that again," he breathed. "I died a thousand times. I kept thinkin', what if I don't find her? How can I live the rest of my life without her? Sweetheart, darlin' girl, I'll not leave ya ever again."

"Can we leave here?" she whispered, her lips against his cheek.

"I got to see about Hartog."

"He dropped his gun when the snake bit him on the neck."

"Into a blood vessel, I hope. He won't last long, but I've got to make sure."

"I want Pa's gun. They took it."

"I'll get it for you. The boy went to get Cleve. This is Indian land and he's the man in charge. We'll stay till he gets here, then we'll go home to the Double T. Which way did Hartog go?"

Colleen pointed the way. He took her hand. Travor followed the trail of broken brush and staggering footprints and found Hartog lying on the ground. His neck and the side of his face were hideously swollen, his breathing labored and faint. He was still conscious, but seriously close to death.

He opened his eyes. When they focused on the two standing over him, he lifted a hand and let it fall back to the ground.

"McCall. Ya was next—ya sonofabitch—" The grunted words came from swollen lips.

"Yeah? What were ya gonna do? Backshoot me? Ya ain't man enough to meet me head-on, ya stinkin', low-down, dirty coward!"

"I'd . . . a had the gal but for that . . . goddamn Mex. Should'a cut his throat—"

"Ya'll be meetin' him soon. Tell him about it."

"Shoot me." His eyes pleaded. "Shoot . . . me—"

"Hell no!" Travor gritted out angrily. "I'll not waste a bullet. Ya shot Miles Murphy down with his ma and girl lookin' on. Ya stole her away to rape and kill her. Yo're on your way to hell. Lay there and think about it." Travor put his arm around Colleen. "Come on, honey. He's never goin' to move from that spot." They turned to retrace their steps.

"Ya ain't got . . . the guts to . . . shoot me," Hartog called in a raspy whisper, taunting, his last words filled with the hate that had marked his life.

Back in the clearing Colleen avoided looking at the body of the Mexican as Travor went through the saddle-bags. He found Miles Murphy's pistol, took it and the holster and strapped them around Colleen's waist. With his arm around her, he led her from the scene. Mud Pie was happily cropping grass in the place where Travor had left him. He nickered a greeting.

Travor leaned against the trunk of a large cottonwood. Colleen rested against him and placed her head on his shoulder. She could feel the steady beat of his heart against her breast.

I'm alive. I'll come to him unsoiled. God has been good to me.

Linus rode toward Stoney Creek on a mission for the marshal. He felt good about himself for the first time in a long time. McCall and the marshal had praised him for his quick thinking, and his reward would be the horses that had belonged to Hartog and the Mexican. Marshal Stark would use them to pack the bodies to town, then leave them at the livery in Sweetwater with papers declaring them his property for service to the Territory.

The boy could hardly wait to tell Arvella and Pud what McCall and the marshal had said to Longfellow when the preacher sneered at him and called him a no-good, lyin' bastard.

"Shut yore mouth, ya little pissant, or I'll jerk ya off that horse and stomp yore guts out!" McCall had been so angry that Miss Murphy had to hold his arm.

"One more bad word about that boy," the marshal had said, "and ya'll walk behind that horse all the way to Laramie Prison. He's more of a man than you are."

The most surprising thing Linus had learned was that there were two McCalls.

"Go tell my brother and Miss Gray that Colleen is all right. I'll bring her back to Stoney Creek in the morning."

Linus never felt so important in all his life as he did when he rode into the yard at Stoney Creek and saw the teacher, the old lady, a man on crutches and Whit, old Whitaker's Indian bastard, waiting. The kids from the school were there as well as the teacher's sisters.

"She's all right," he called when they all turned to face him.

"How you know that?" Whit demanded.

"I saw Hartog and a Mexican take her, and I went for McCall, that's why," Linus said belligerently. "What was *you* doin'? Learnin' yore ABC's?"

"Hold it." The man on the crutches said firmly. "We just discovered her missing a bit ago. Granny thought she was at the school. Jenny thought she was in the house."

"Yo're . . . the other . . . McCall?" Linus stepped down from his horse. "Miss Murphy's with yore brother. He said he'd bring her back in the mornin'. She's wore out."

"Did they . . . hurt her?" Jenny asked fearfully.

"McCall said not. Hartog got snakebit. McCall killed the Mexican."

"She's all right, Granny." The teacher had her arm around the old woman. "If she's with Travor, she's all right."

Chapter Thirty-one

Travor took Colleen to her new home, helped her to wash, dressed her in one of his shirts and put her to bed. Joe Fiala's wife, Una May, left their supper on the stove and went with Joe to their rooms in the bunkhouse. Travor brought Colleen a plate of food and insisted she sit up to eat it.

"You've not had much of a chance to look at the place, but do ya like what ya've seen?" Travor sat on the side of the bed when she finished eating. One arm stretched across her, the other hand cupped her bruised and swollen cheek.

"Very much. But I'd be happy in a dugout if you were there." She held out her arms and he bent over her. "Ya know what I was thinkin' when I was sure I didn't have a chance of gettin' back to ya? I wished that we'd loved each other like we wanted to that night when we was lyin' on the grass in the shed and ya said we'd wait till the preacher said the words."

"I wanted ya to marry me 'cause ya wanted me, not 'cause ya might think ya could be expectin'."

"Ya still don't want to . . . be with me . . . like that till we marry?"

"Ah . . . honey. I want ya so bad it's almost killin' me not to get in that bed with ya. Yo're the sweetest woman—" There was a deep huskiness in his voice. He nuzzled his face into the soft skin of her neck. She stroked his dark hair lovingly. "When I saw ya standin' there and that . . . sorry piece of dung lookin' at yore sweet bosom, I wanted to cut his heart out!"

"It's over. We won't think about it. Travor . . . get in bed with me. Hold me."

"Darlin' girl." He lifted his head to look at her. "Ya sure . . . ya want me to? I love ya so much. It'll be hard not to—do more than hold ya." His eyes were bright, raw with feeling. He brushed her lips with another kiss.

"I want ya to, Trav. I want ya to . . . do more than hold me."

He searched her eyes for confirmation of her words, and when she smiled at him, he could see her love in them.

"Kiss me, honey. I won't come to my woman smellin' like horse dung."

They whispered to each other, mouth to mouth, sharing breath and soft, sweet kisses. His fingers smoothed the hair back from her ears.

"Ya don't—smell like that."

"I'll be back in two shakes of a dog's tail."

"Don't leave me!"

"Darlin' girl, I'll be just outside the door at the washbench."

"Hurry." She kissed him with fiery sweetness.

Colleen lay waiting. Her heart hammered in anticipation of what was to come. Today she had thought she would never know the joy of being with her man. *Thank God for Linus.* She hadn't thanked him properly for going for Travor, but she would.

She heard Travor come back into the house and turned her eyes to the doorway. He appeared there shirtless, his broad chest covered with a light sprinkling of dark hair. With his eyes on her, he came soundlessly across the floor.

"I'll blow out the lamp, if ya want."

"Ya don't have to."

Travor got carefully into bed, and reached out to Colleen lying on the far side. He pulled her to him gently, as if she would break. He didn't speak until she lay fully against him.

"Come to me, darlin' girl. Ya feel so warm, so soft. I'm holdin' the whole world in my arms." His lips snuggled in her hair. She could feel the excitement begin to build in him.

"Ya feel good, too."

His lips moved down her cheek until they found her lips and kissed her until he began to tremble. Her mouth was eager against his as his hand traveled down her back to the fullness of her hips and pressed her to him. The silky down between her thighs teased his hardened flesh. When she moved her thigh between his, an inarticulate sound escaped him.

Travor gently turned her onto her back and raised himself on quivering arms to hover over her. His thumb caressed her lips before he kissed her, gently, wonderingly, the touch filled with love and promise.

"I'll love ya forever, darlin'." The words were wrung from him in an agonized whisper.

"I'll love ya, too, my sweet—" The rest of her murmured reply was lost in his kiss.

Borne beyond constraint, he lifted himself above her.

Scarcely believing that this was happening, Colleen opened her legs to welcome him when she felt the first firm touch of his hardened flesh probing the moist opening in her body and instinctively lifted her hips to the indriving shaft of pleasure.

In a haze of ethereal delight she was conscious of only a slight, swift tinge of pain. Then she was rocking, rocking, borne on a floating rhythm of a mighty wave. She writhed in her search for gratification; and when it came, she found she was no longer herself and whole, but a body of many fragments, alive with vibrant sensations.

Travor's mind and body came gradually back together with hers. He raised himself on his elbows and looked down into her face. Her magnificent blue eyes shone like a million stars.

"Thank you, sweetheart," he said when he was able to speak. "You've given me the greatest gift I've ever had or will have." The words were whispered against her lips before he kissed them as if he had never kissed them before.

She pressed her hands against his back when he would have moved from her.

"Not yet. Please stay."

"I may never leave." His chuckle was a low loving sound.

"Ya can't stay forever!"

"No, but I could stay all night." His chuckle was low and loving as he turned on his side taking her with him.

"Trav," she whispered several kisses later. "Do you think Trell and Jenny are as happy as we are?"

"I hope so, sweetheart. But I doubt it. No one in the whole world could be as happy as we are."

In the bunkhouse at Stoney Creek Jenny lay beside Trell. Colleen's capture by Hartog, her narrow escape, had made them realize how fragile life was. Tomorrow they would be married, but they still had tonight.

Her brilliant green eyes laughed up at him. She and Trell had come together as man and wife, as woman and man, as male and female, and their hearts were still pulsing with the joy of it. Her face was damp and flushed and lighted with a happy smile.

"You're not sorry we didn't wait?" he whispered, moving his hands down to her buttocks and kneading gently while being careful the splints on his broken leg didn't scrape her soft skin.

"No, no, no." She stroked his hair. Love for him filled her heart. "And I'm not ashamed of what we just did."

"This is a part of married life that some women don't like."

"Then they don't love their husbands as I love mine! I read somewhere that this is one of God's great gifts to mankind. I understand now what that means."

He caressed her mouth gently but firmly. A little sound of happiness came from his throat. He held her tightly to him and pressed her head to his shoulder.

"When I saw you at the stage station, and you flashed those green eyes at me, I was lost. You've not been out of my mind since. I never dreamed that I'd hold you like this."

Jenny laughed happily, her mouth against his smooth skin. Her fingers gently stroked his chest.

"I never thought I'd be so brazen as to lie naked in the arms of a man. I thought only whores did that."

"Well . . . do you like it?"

"I love it. And we can do it every night for the rest of our lives! Trell," she lifted her head as if a sudden thought had pulled it from his shoulder, "do you think Travor and Colleen are as happy as we are."

"I hope so, my love. But I doubt it. No one in the whole world could be as happy as we are."

In loving memory of my husband,

HERBERT L. GARLOCK, SR.
—forever in my heart.

*We are all visitors
to this time, this place.
We are just passing through.
Our purpose here is to observe,
to learn, to grow, to love . . .
and then we return Home.*

—Aborigine Philosophy

JOURNEY TO SWEETWATER

Sweetwater!
We'll soon be there.
We'll brush the dust out of our hair,
Drink God's nectar, cold and clear,
Quench our thirst, forget our fear.

Sweetwater!
Filthy town. Insulting leers.
Pay no heed. Hide your ears.
We'll ride tomorrow toward our goal.
Three sisters one—a family whole.

Our wagon jolts; the road is brutal.
I wonder if our scheme is futile:
To teach, to farm, to own our land,
To live in peace. That's all we planned.

The driver passes 'round a flask
To serve us water when we ask.
His mouth is foul—and he drinks first.
We can't refuse; we've such a thirst.

At last, our house. We look inside.
A wreck! We'd weep, but we have pride.
We'll clean, we'll scrub; we'll have our
dream.
See, yonder, there's a sparkling stream.

Stoney Creek
Its rocky ledges rush the flow.
So pure and clean. And now we know
A surge of joy, the rise of hope.
We run to drink, sure we can cope.

Sweetwater!
Home!
                    —F.S.I.